Better Days Ahead

*To: Susan
Enjoy
Charlie Valentine*

Charlie Valentine

This is a work of fiction. All names, places, characters, and incidents are entirely imaginary, and any resemblance to actual events, or to persons living or dead, is coincidental.

Copyright © 2006 Charlie Valentine

All rights reserved. No part of this book may be reproduced in any form or by any means electronic or mechanical, including photocopying, recording or by any information storage and retrieval systems, without written permission of the publisher or author except where permitted by law.

Published By
English Mill Press
P.O. Box 881
Woodinville, WA 98072 USA
EnglishMillPress.com
CharlieValentineBooks.com

Valentine, Charlie.

Better days ahead / Charlie Valentine. -- 1st ed. -- Woodinville, WA : English Mill Press, 2006.

p. ; cm.

ISBN-13: 978-0-9772187-0-7
ISBN-10: 0-9772187-0-8
First novel of a trilogy.

1. Hope--Fiction. 2. Family--Fiction. 3. Interpersonal relations--Fiction. 4. United States--Social life and customs--1945-1970--Fiction.
    I. Title.

PS3622.A446 B48 2006
813.6--dc22   0603

10 9 8 7 6 5 4 3 2 1

Cover Design and Internal layout by Tami Taylor
Original water color by Doina Cociuba

*This book is dedicated to my
wonderful husband Roger.
His support and ongoing
encouragement made it possible for me
to graduate from writer
to author.*

Acknowledgments

There are two critical things that I've learned this past year. First, a writer is only as good as the people with whom she surrounds herself, and second, writing a book is a collaborative effort.

I have had the good fortune of working with professionals who have guided me through the process of bringing *Better Days Ahead* to fruition. My greatest strength came from Jan Wright, of the Wright Word, whose deft line editing was a benefit to the manuscript. She is a brilliant editor and I'm eternally indebted to her for her insight into making this book an enjoyable read. Jennifer McCord of Jennifer McCord Associates, my well-respected project manager, was a godsend. She offered excellent suggestions to the content of the novel as well as the end product. Her knowledge of the book industry proved to me that experience makes all the difference in the world. My graphic artist, Tami Taylor, took the original watercolor by Doina Cociuba of Bothell, Washington, and designed this extraordinary cover. Tami is one of the most creative women I have ever known. Rounding out the team is Christine Grabowski, a diligent proofreader. Her efforts in polishing the manuscript are deeply appreciated. I am grateful that these women never ceased to believe in me and *Better Days Ahead*.

Other thank-yous go to my dear friends who read the original draft: Allan Weydahl, Sue Carroll, Tammi Morton Taranto, and Mary Tarabochia. To my friends and family who read early chapters and encouraged me to keep on writing: daughters Karri Anne

Davidson and Kristi Lynn Vairin; step-daughters Natalie Nino and Courtnee Valentine; my sister Shirley Tomlin; friends Jeani Dodd, Nanci Glogauer, Gayle Mead, Debi Owens, Cynthia Membrila, and Diana Lowe. Thank-you all for supporting me and bearing with the typos and dangling participles.

    I also want to say thank-you to three very special women: Cheryl Weydahl, Judy Metzger, and Dottie Lane. I sincerely appreciate their "eagle eyes" as well as their positive feedback. Their assistance in reviewing the book just prior to going to print was invaluable.

Main Characters

Drake Family in Alabama
        Thomas Drake
        Dolores Drake
        Sonya Drake, oldest daughter
        Brenda Drake, youngest daughter
        Ethan Drake, youngest child
        Ruthie Jackson
        Sheriff Pete Cornell
        Jesse Brown
        Leroy Pentz, the barber

Dvorak Family in Michigan
        Neil Dvorak
        Anne Dvorak
        Victoria Dvorak, Neil's youngest daughter
        Amy Dvorak, Neil's oldest daughter
        Janet Dvorak, Amy's mother
        Bernie Stocker, Neil's employer
        Joe and Catherine Moore, Neil's neighbors

Robbins Family in Ohio
        Sarah Robbins
        Billy Robbins, Sarah's son
        Judge Henry Kinslow
        Sam Donahue
        Fran Taylor, Sarah's friend
        Manny, the bartender

Stratton Family in California
        David Stratton
        Karen Stratton
        Jenni Lynn Stratton, David and Karen's daughter
        Delilah Stratton, David's mother
        Alfred Stratton, David's father
        Lieutenant John Allen, Karen's father
        Agnes Allen, Karen's mother
        Jessica Heisen
        Theo Bachman

one

SARAH AND SAM

Cleveland, 1949

No one, including Sarah Robbins herself, imagined that she was within hours of delivering a child. Of course, a keen eye may have noticed a discernible puffiness to her face, limbs, and stomach; but a bloated condition could easily be attributed to the increase in her nightly consumption of rum and colas. Her five foot four medium-built frame had never boasted an enviable hourglass figure. However, the twenty-three-year-old had unusually long, shapely legs that offset her drab brown hair and unremarkable brown eyes.

To compensate for her mediocre appearance, Sarah opted to wear the finest clothing available. Day wear consisted of either wool or linen suits accented with a single strand of natural pearls. The image she presented was conservative, appropriate, and highly respectable. But the same could not be said of her evening wear. As a nightclub singer, Sarah's "after eight" attire revealed a far more exotic flair. The wardrobe comprised floor-length evening gowns and multicolored sequined tops with matching palazzo pants. Her favorite pants were those enhanced with daring side slits, long enough to bare a thigh now and then.

Perhaps had it not been for a recent preference for free-flowing gowns, the small swelling of her abdomen might have been more prominent. But even if it had been noticeable, Sarah would have reasoned that a slightly swollen tummy was a small price to pay for unlimited drinks at the club.

Sarah placed the microphone on the piano at Donahue's and thanked the audience for their applause. As she stepped off stage, she gave Manny the bartender the usual sign. Without hesitation Manny poured a double shot of rum into a tall glass stacked with three ice cubes. To complete the elixir, he added a splash of cola that scarcely diluted its alcoholic content.

Relieved that set one was over, Sarah positioned herself onto her favorite barstool at the far end of the bar. Concealed in the shadows, it was the ideal hideaway for Sarah's often too-short intermissions. But as brief as they were, thanks to Manny's expeditious service she never waited long for her complimentary Cuba libres.

Sarah reached over to the garnish tray and removed a freshly cut segment of lime to complement the cocktail. She squeezed the wedge until its juice supplied the piquant flavor to her liking. Tart, but not too bitter. Tipping the glass to her mouth, she allowed a single rum-flavored ice cube to momentarily rest upon her tongue. When it disappeared, she swallowed promptly the last of the nectar. Manny, noting the empty glass, made her another drink.

"Thanks, Manny. You must have read my mind," she said as she confiscated another slice of lime.

Sarah closed her eyes and leaned her head up against the wood paneling. Feeling a bit woozy, she savored the sensation of the alcohol surging through her bloodstream. It was a good, yet all too familiar, feeling; one that derived from her habitual use of the free drinks at Donahue's. Alcohol had become Sarah's accidental addiction.

"Manny, do I look like I've put on a few pounds since the holidays? Usually, I drop off the weight by mid-January, but it's the end of the month and I still haven't lost a pound. Maybe I need a tighter girdle. What do you think?"

Manny extended her a friendly smile and refreshed her drink. After countless years of serving the inebriated, the old man had earned a wealth of wisdom. He knew that bartenders were there for the listening, and because advice, which was rarely welcomed, was generally disregarded anyway. No matter, Manny knew there was no point in responding to a lady who was well on her way...

Sarah's hands fell to her lap and onto the layers of smooth black satin. Moving the material from side to side, she cooled her swollen fingers. And there it was again. That damn stomach. Just one more thing that made her less attractive. She glanced down at the black-lace bodice and was relieved that she had chosen to wear a comfortable A-line gown rather than one that hugged every curve.

Perhaps it was the old adage in vino veritas (there is truth in wine), but after her first drink she had to admit that her stomach had significantly enlarged over the last month. *No girdle is going to hide this atrocity,* she thought. Handing her glass to Manny she reaffirmed, "I guess I should start a diet tomorrow, huh, Manny?"

This was another opportunity for Manny to display his good judgment. The seventy-year-old, who was a friend to everybody, knew that this was one question no bartender, or man for that matter, should answer. He handed her another drink instead.

Sarah nursed the beverage and unconsciously massaged her stomach. Even after the numbing effects of one-hundred-proof rum, her abdomen continued its incessant, dull throbbing. She concluded that the pain was from a bout of indigestion she encountered earlier in the day. Nothing too serious. Just a few cramps now and then, which she remedied with her personal concoction of bromine and antacids. It was the cure-all that kept her attendance at the club, so far, a perfect one. No, for Sarah to forego Manny's lime and cola cocktails, her head would have to be buried deep in a commode. Nothing less would keep her at home.

Sarah closed her eyes and remembered back to the days when she took ill as a child. Aunt Gertrude, her sole guardian, would tend to her every need with comforting luxuries like a hot-water bottle and homemade chicken-noodle soup. As for enriching Sarah's soul, Aunt Gertrude took full advantage on those days when Sarah was bedridden. Sitting just a few feet away in the corner rocking chair, she would read the Scriptures to Sarah from a German Bible. In other words, she cared for her niece body and soul.

Sarah longed for her aunt who had raised her since she was two years old. That was Sarah's age when her parents and four siblings perished in a household fire started by a smoldering ember gone awry. Aunt Gertrude, who had just come to America from Germany, pulled Sarah from her burning bed and carried her outside to safety. It was a mere ten seconds later when the entire house was engulfed in flames, leaving Sarah in the care of her aunt, who didn't understand one word of English. But now Aunt Gertrude was also dead, leaving Sarah nothing but memories.

"We go to church now, child," Aunt Gertrude would shout in German. She was a staunch and overpowering Lutheran and put the God-fearing way into Sarah. That was the way she remained until nineteen thirty-six when Sarah was ten years old. Overnight her aunt had softened her tone almost to a whisper. Talk of Hitler's conquests in Europe was running rampant in the States, and Aunt Gertrude did not want to draw attention to herself. So she kept a low profile, even among her fellow Lutheran churchgoers, who had known for some time that she was a foreigner. However, there was one parishioner with whom she had formed a strong bond. The newly appointed Judge Henry Kinslow had taken a special liking to Gertrude and her niece. Every week after church he would leave his own family to spend the afternoon with Gertrude and chat with her in their native tongue. The judge, although born and raised in America was also of pure German descent, yet he never divulged his heritage to anyone else, fearing that his personal convictions could interfere with his public ambitions. So he shared his ideals and opinions with the only person he could trust—Gertrude Weiss.

"I got a letter from my brother back home," the judge boasted in German. "He says this Adolf Hitler is going to take over the world."

"And what do you, my friend, think of that?" Gertrude asked inquisitively.

The judge paused, as if his answer was to be an intellectual one. "I don't believe he would cross the ocean, but you never know. He's

Better Days Ahead

come a long way since he was named chancellor. And now he is dictator. You can't help but respect the man who rules with an iron fist."

Chastising her friend, she scolded, "I have no admiration for him. If I had not come to America in '27 to visit my sister, I swear I would have fled Düsseldorf in '33 with only the clothes on my back to avoid Hitler's Germany."

"The clothes on your back? You make me laugh, Gerty. You've had it made since you came to America, thanks to your late brother-in-law. He was a smart man, insuring his family and his house. When times were tight you inherited a windfall, courtesy of the child you are rearing. And with that money you built a house." He looked around the small one-bedroom home and added, "Personally, I would have built a bigger one. But I suspect you hoarded the mother lode of cash and have it stashed underneath your mattress, guaranteeing that you won't have to work a day in your life on American soil. It was a good move on your part, Gerty. You slipped right past the Depression. Not too many true-blue English-speaking Americans can say that," he snickered.

Gertrude glanced toward her bedroom door and wondered how Henry had known where she had kept the money. She wondered if anyone else was as clever as he. Unnerved, she decided to open a bank account first thing the next morning.

"If I've told you once, Gertrude, then I have told you one-hundred times. My brother and I are proud of our home country. You should be, too, my fellow countrywoman," he said with arrogance.

"I may not speak the language of my neighbors, but I am an American lady now," she said, trying to downplay her German accent.

"Your roots say otherwise, Gerty."

The two of them would jokingly bicker while Sarah, who was just a few feet away, remained silent. It wasn't that she didn't understand the language, quite the contrary, since Sarah's second language was German. But she knew that if she didn't interrupt her aunt's conversation, Judge Henry would eventually speak directly to her in English. Sarah found that it was worth the wait because he had a way of making her feel special.

"Sarah, your rendition of 'Ave Maria' this morning was heavenly. The pastor seemed pleased with you, too. I was just telling him the other day that his choir would be nothing without you. I told him that you are the sole reason that his congregation has suddenly grown," the judge praised Sarah, while her aunt began to work on an afghan. Gertrude thought it was good for her niece to be articulate in the English language, so she didn't mind when Henry spent time with Sarah.

Modestly, Sarah replied, "Our choir teacher says that Jillian, the soprano, is the one who is gifted. That is why she gets to sing most of the solos."

"Hogwash, Sarah. You can reach the high notes just as easily as the low notes. It's a wide vocal range that's important. Sing me a song, Sarah—a popular one like 'Pennies from Heaven' or 'I've Got a Pocketful of Dreams,' any one of Bing Crosby's hits."

As much as Sarah would have liked to accommodate the judge, she only knew religious songs. She bowed her head and said, "I don't know how to sing that kind of music."

"With a voice like yours, it's about time you learned. Next week when I come to visit, I'll bring my harmonica along with some sheet music. The words and the notes are printed on them. I'll teach you how to read music, Sarah. Between the two of us, you'll be belting out the top tunes in no time at all."

Sarah remembered those years as her happiest. Protected and nurtured by her loving aunt, Sarah felt safe and secure. It was a wonderful life until shortly after she turned sixteen, when Aunt Gertrude suddenly passed away. Sarah, sadly, never learned if the malady was cancer, a stroke, or a heart attack. One morning Aunt Gertrude just didn't wake up.

Keenly aware that there were no other family members to care for Sarah, Judge Henry took it upon himself to oversee her needs. Through his political contacts, he made arrangements for Sarah to remain in her aunt's home under his personal supervision. She was told she would not be sent to an orphanage—as long as she followed his rules. "You are not to associate with young boys. Come home immediately after school and don't open the door for anyone, except me."

In the beginning it was merely requests. Soon after, those requests turned into promises of a future. "I will take care of you, Sarah. You'll never need anyone but me. I will file for divorce when you are eighteen, I promise."

The judge was in complete control over Sarah's life. He became power of attorney over Gertrude's assets, which turned out to be more substantial than he had anticipated. It was money that should have been put entirely into the trust fund for Sarah; however, the judge used a considerable amount of the funds for leverage within the community. With his buying power and the protection of the judge's office, he rapidly gained control of the city and found that he could make or break any company with the simple rap of his gavel.

✧ ✧ ✧

Sarah sat upright on the leather stool and pointed to an invisible watch on her arm. Manny was assisting a paying customer, but compliantly lifted the cuff of his shirt and checked the time. Without saying a word, he held up two fingers. Sarah mumbled, "Damn, break's over. And I was just starting to feel no pain." For that split second in time the pain had indeed diminished. But as quickly as it receded, it returned with a deviling vengeance.

God, what is this? Maybe I should have eased up on the antacids this afternoon. I probably mixed too many in my bromo, she thought.

Sarah slid off the stool and smoothed the creases of her gown. When she was satisfied with the last-minute grooming, she leaned across the bar and placed her glass into the aluminum washbasin. As she slowly stood upright, a swarm of piercing cramps targeted her lower intestines. The intensity and duration were almost unbearable. She couldn't move. She couldn't breathe. And she couldn't understand why Donahue's finest rum had yet to anesthetize her.

"Hey, Sarah, are you all right?" Sam Donahue asked while peeling her fingers off the edge of the bar.

"I'm all right, Sam. It's just that I had a stomachache this afternoon, and I think I might have overdone it on the antacids."

"Why didn't you call me? I would have told you to stay home."

"That's exactly why I didn't. You know me. I'm not about to pass up a free drink coming my way," she admitted. Candid and straightforward, that was Sarah's relationship with Sam, the owner of Donahue's. She could say anything to her best friend, confidant, and employer. He never judged her.

"Why don't you go home for the night? We'll make do with background music. Besides, I get the impression the piano player would jump at a solo op," Sam coaxed.

"No, I'll do one more set. If I don't feel better, I'll call it a night."

"I'm going to hold you to that!" He kissed the tips of her fingers and wished her good luck. "Knock 'em dead, lady."

Sam Donahue, whose flaming hair earned him the nickname Red, was one of Cleveland's most recognizable businessmen. At five foot seven, he carried a stocky build—not overweight—just big-boned for his size. As for the color of his skin, it should have been milky-white, but after forty-two years the sun's rays had tinted his face, chest, and arms with hundreds of brownish-orange freckles. From all appearances Sam was the typical Irishman, and yet, amid a family tree of purebred Irish, a single limb confessed to a vein of Polish ancestry. It was that bloodline that softened the Irish temper just enough to make Sam the benevolent businessman he was.

With a knack for food preparation, Sam was almost a shoo-in for success. From carved-to-order Angus steaks to table-side tossed salads, he consistently exceeded his customers' expectations. As well as the delectable cuisine, Sam had another ace in the hole. He had the bewitching voice of Sarah Robbins. She gave Donahue's the edge over his competitors. The other club owners said they couldn't justify the additional overhead for live entertainment; however, if Sarah Robbins had been available, any one of them would have found the funds to hire her on the spot. To them she was the pied piper of Donahue's, as she lured their patrons to Sam's establishment. But no one held that against Sam. They knew how Donahue's really came to be and how its success had been predetermined. And they knew it was not by Sam's hand.

❖ ❖ ❖

It was three years earlier when a rookie realtor escorted Sam to an old abandoned warehouse. Located just outside the city in an overgrown field, the lone structure could be seen for miles. Sam learned that geography was the property's only plus.

"Before we go inside, Mr. Donahue, I want to tell you that you shouldn't expect too much. The building has its shortcomings, but with a little work ... who knows. Heck, even my wife says it has potential. And it's well within your price range." The youth pointed to a ten-foot jagged opening and added, "We can enter over there. Just watch where you step and avoid the wood planks. They're covered with rusty nails."

As Sam stepped over the mountain of debris, he could see that the structure was in the worst condition imaginable. The roof was checkered with gaping holes and the floor was crisscrossed with fallen beams. There was scarcely any value to its remains, except to the birds and rodents who claimed it as their sanctuary.

"Keep in mind, Mr. Donahue, that it's a real bargain," he said enthusiastically. "All it needs is someone with imagination—that and a little elbow grease."

Sam moved deeper into the warehouse and away from the realtor. He needed to size up the project without any further interruptions from the overanxious youth. From the opposite side of the decrepit building the realtor yelled at the top of his lungs, "One more thing, Mr. Donahue. I know this guy who will haul all this junk away. Did you hear me, Mr. Donahue?" When Sam didn't respond, the young realtor trudged back to his car and added Sam Donahue to his list of "No Sales."

But unlike other potential buyers, Sam saw beyond the dilapidated flooring, broken windows, and half-plastered walls. Through all its flaws he was able to envision a bustling family-style smorgasbord. A restaurant where children were welcomed and the disorder that often accompanied young diners would be cheerfully overlooked.

After fifteen minutes Sam yanked off a silvered piece of wood and made himself another exit. He circled the building one last time and then headed back to the car where he found the young realtor slumped over the steering wheel.

"Hey, kid. I'm not sure there's enough wood in Ohio to fix this dump."

Wiping his eyes, the young man struggled to keep his wits about him. He had convinced himself that he wasn't cut out to be in real estate. When Sam approached him, he prepared himself for another blow to his ego. "I guess showing you this property was a mistake. I'm sorry I wasted your time, Mr. Donahue," he said as he opened the car door for him.

"Why look so glum, kid? I want to make you an offer of four grand with a twenty-one day escrow," Sam said with a broad smile.

"You want this dump?" A slip of the rookie's tongue caused him to make a quick retraction: "I mean, you *really* want to purchase this property?"

"I can't think of a better location. Let's do it, kid."

With an offer just shy of the asking price, the seller readily accepted the deal, even agreeing to the shortened time frame. As soon as the mortgage papers were signed, Sam hired a crew of workers to gut the building, or what was left of it. Working around the clock, seven days a week, the building's infrastructure began to take shape in less than two months. The roof had been reinforced with hardwood beams, and cedar shingles replaced the broken slates. The walls were reconstructed with sturdy four-by-eights. The floor was resurfaced and covered with wooden planks. Finally, a false ceiling was installed just twenty-five feet from the ground to offset its true height of three stories.

Everything was right on track until halfway through the renovation process when Judge Henry Kinslow paid Sam a surprise visit. "Hey, Red. Haven't seen you in a while. Come over here," the judge shouted from the far corner of the room. While the judge impatiently waited for Sam, he noticed adjacent walls with a dozen stained-glass windows on each. He wouldn't mention it to Sam, but he did admire the quality. "Red, get a move on. I haven't got all day. I need to be back in court in an hour."

Sam thought nothing of pitching in with the hired help. When the judge arrived, he had been assisting the delivery men unload a truck load of stainless steel kitchen fixtures. "You're on your own boys. I've got to see what Judge Kinslow wants."

Sam made his way toward the judge, whose arms were folded across his chest. The judge had been tapping his foot restlessly on the newly varnished floor. Judge Henry Kinslow did not like to be kept waiting.

"What can I do for you, Judge?"

"I see your building is coming along. Looks like your restaurant will be done in no time."

"Yes. I'm pleased that we are beating the deadlines. Hell, I'm even on track with the budget," Sam boasted.

"Are you still planning on making this a smorgasbord?" Before Sam had a chance to answer, the judge interrupted him and continued, "We already have three buffets in Cleveland. You'll be in direct competition with them."

"Yeah, I know. But I've got some great recipes from the old country," he said.

"Shit, Red. A smorgasbord is a smorgasbord. What we need is a place for the white collars. Somewhere we can conduct business during the day and take our wives or lady friends at night. You know, a first-class supper club. I can see it all now. Dimmed lights, small intimate booths, a few tables scattered throughout. Get the picture? None of that goulash crap."

Sam was momentarily speechless. He had already put a non-refundable deposit on a fifty-five-foot buffet table. "I don't know, Judge. Owning a smorgasbord has always been a dream of mine."

"So your dream went slightly off course. It's not like I expect you to give up your restaurant. I'm only asking that you change the style. I don't see that as much of a problem."

Sam argued, "Even if I did consider the change, I couldn't afford it. I've made deposits all over the place. And on most of them, I wouldn't get a dime back."

"Okay, Red. Exactly how much are we talking about? I'm an investor and I've got some extra cash that I wouldn't mind loaning you at, say, three percent interest. That's one percent less than the going rate. I'll give you two years to pay me back."

Sam was overcome with dismay. He wanted to flat-out refuse the offer, but no one ever challenged Judge Henry Kinslow. A business could be opened and closed the same day if Kinslow wanted it that way. All he had to do was find a technicality, legitimate or not, and he could terminate the business license.

"It's a good offer, Judge," he pretended. "But please understand that I really want to make this a family…"

The judge interrupted Sam again. "Red, you do this for me and I assure you that you will have a full house from day one. I will personally see to your success. Should you decide otherwise, I would hate to speculate on the outcome. A restaurant with no patrons wouldn't last a week in this town," he said chuckling, but his threat came through loud and clear.

"Sounds like a challenge, Judge. I guess I'm going to open a supper club," he conceded.

"Fine. It's a done deal. I'll have the papers drawn up tomorrow. Be at the courthouse at noon. You can sign then."

It took Sam's entire savings and a rather substantial loan from Judge Kinslow to complete the revised plans. It seemed risky at first, but just as Kinslow predicted, Donahue's became a roaring success. Six months after the opening night, Sam had the funds to repay the judge eighteen months ahead of schedule. He was about to settle the score when Judge Henry Kinslow surprised him with yet another proposition.

"Red, have you considered the option of expanding?"

"What do you mean, Judge? I just added Chateaubriand to the menu. It seems to be a hit."

"I had something else in mind. Have you considered live entertainment?"

"Well, no. For the first time I'm in the black." Sam hoped that would put an end to it. But the middle-aged man, who used his few strands of grey hair to comb over his balding head, was not finished with his quest. Ignoring Sam's response, he pointed to the center back wall.

"That area over there would make a good place for a stage. Put a piano on it, and I don't mean an upright. Buy a grand piano, even if it's a used one." The judge seized Sam's check and ripped it to shreds. "We'll keep the same terms and same interest. You've got two years to pay me back."

Blindsided by Judge Henry Kinslow again, Sam ran his fingers through his coarse red hair. He hadn't even considered entertainment, but as far as the judge was concerned, the conversation was over. There was no point in arguing.

As Kinslow stood up to leave he added, "One last thing, Red. I have a recommendation for you. She's a great little singer. I'll send her over for an audition. Of course, I assume you'll hold open tryouts for the public's sake and all. But as part financier of Donahue's, I'd like her on the payroll as soon as possible." As he walked out the door he yelled back, "By the way, her name is Sarah Robbins."

For the second time in less than a year Sam had been ambushed by the manipulative Judge Henry Kinslow. It was hopeless to go against a man who had become so powerful. So according to Kinslow's instructions, Sam purchased a black lacquer baby grand and positioned it on the left side of his newly built stage. This small addition magically transformed his intimate restaurant into a sophisticated supper club. The only thing missing was the entertainment.

Upon placing an ad that aired on the local radio station, Sam found that the pool of talent in the Cleveland area was extensive. In fact, any one of the applicants could have fit the bill, perhaps even added to Donahue's bottom-line profit. Sam was tempted but he knew better than to gamble on incurring the wrath of Judge Kinslow. To hire anyone other than the judge's protégée would be a grave mistake. So for appearances only, Sam spent two days auditioning singers, magicians, and comedy acts, none of whom stood a chance of procuring the spotlight at Donahue's.

"Hello, I'm Sarah Robbins. Judge Kinslow told me to be here at five o'clock for an audition. He said that you are looking for a singer."

Sam gave the woman with the sultry voice a polite once-over and said, "You're right on time, Sarah. Can you sing 'I'll Be Seeing You'?"

"Sure. E, please. It won't be as good as Bing Crosby, but here goes."

Filled with apprehension, Sam hit the requested piano key. This was the lady who was going to be his opening act, whether he liked it or not. He almost dreaded the outcome.

Sarah only sang the first four lines of the song when Sam lifted his hand up to stop her. "Thank you, Sarah. That will be all."

"I can sing something else. How about 'Over the Rainbow,' or something patriotic like 'Boogie Woogie Bugle Boy'?"

"No, that won't be necessary. I've been holding auditions for two days and there's some great talent out there, but I must admit something to you. The judge asked that I give you the job, as a favor to him. Under the circumstances, financial and all, I probably would have done just that. But I am about to do something on my own."

Sarah's shoulders drooped as she accepted what she thought was a rejection. She retrieved a nickel hidden beneath a pouch full of pennies in her wallet. "Mind if I use the pay phone? I need to call a taxi. Thanks for the audition."

"But you didn't let me finish, Sarah. I am the owner of this club and even though Judge Kinslow asked that I give you special consideration, I make my decisions on what is best for Donahue's."

Sarah didn't feel he owed her an explanation and repeated, "Where did you say the pay phone is?"

"What I'm trying to say, Sarah, is that I'd like it if you came to work for me. You've got a voice that's out of this world."

"Are you serious? I'm not that good."

"Quite the contrary, you have real star quality. Welcome to Donahue's," he said, formalizing the offer with a handshake.

"I can't thank you enough," she beamed.

"Now that you're an employee, Sarah, you can use the phone in my office to call a cab."

"No, I've changed my mind. I think I'll walk. The leaves are changing to brilliant oranges and reds. Soon the nights will be longer. Today is a good day for reflection. Thank you again, Mr. Donahue."

Sarah waltzed out of the club. Her elation made her body feel weightless. She couldn't wait to telephone Henry from the nearest pay phone, outside of Donahue's.

"Henry, it's me. It's in the bag. He hired me, just like you said he would."

The judge responded with only one syllable words—"yes, good, fine." His abruptness alerted her that he was not in a position to talk. Perhaps he was in the presence of his wife or a daughter, but Sarah never questioned him. It was not her place. It never was.

Knowing that their tête-à-tête would soon be concluded, Sarah referred to a clandestine rendezvous which was to take place later in the day. Indirectly she reminded him, "Six."

Just as he answered, "Fine," he heard a muffled sound on the line. He clicked the cradle button several times and shouted into the receiver, "Hang up your phone. My conversation is none of your business." Upon hearing the disconnect he mumbled, "Damn party line."

"I'll talk to you later," she whispered.

"Good, Mr. Smith," he said with added emphasis on Mr. Smith.

Sarah walked away from the phone booth happy just to have heard his voice. She had become accustomed to Henry's curt mannerisms whenever she crossed over into his private world. Taking a backseat to his family and career had become second nature. It was one of the consequences of falling in love with a prominent judge who was also a married man.

At the onset of their relationship Sarah fought off Judge Henry's subtle advances because he had been Aunt Gertrude's closest friend. As she grew older, she kept her distance because she knew that he was a married man. Then on the day she turned eighteen the judge presented Sarah with a legal document stating that he was divorcing his wife. Alone and anxious and without the insight of her aunt, Sarah believed the captivating judge on whom she had become totally dependent. Unfortunately, Judge Kinslow, who never loved Sarah the way she loved him, had no intention of serving his wife with the divorce papers.

A month after Sarah Robbins opened at the club she was enjoying rave reviews from critics throughout the state. She had become Donahue's main draw, although Sam's slow-roasted prime rib came in a close second. Between the two, the club was filled to capacity with a multitude of professionals and their special women friends. The infamous Judge Henry Kinslow could be found at his table every weeknight until closing—but on the weekends he played the roles of faithful husband and devoted father.

On the night Sarah celebrated her two-year anniversary at Donahue's, a special tribute was made on her behalf. Sam gave a toast in her honor, but an intoxicated Judge Kinslow rudely upstaged him.

"You're a great little gem, Sarah. I'm glad that Red took my advice and hired you. While I'm tooting my own horn, if it weren't for me, this place would have been another hole-in-the-wall smorgasbord, and Sarah, you'd still be nothing but a bean counter at the lumber mill. Come to think of it, Red," he hiccuped, "You'd probably been clean out of business. So here's to Sarah and to Sam. And here's to me. The one with the bucks and the brains."

The audience cheered and whistled. The judge, assuming the roars were for him, turned and bowed. But they couldn't care less about the arrogant "better than thou" judge. Their applause was intended for Donahue's dynamic duo: Sarah and Sam.

The following night the judge failed to show up at the club. No one, except Sarah, thought much of his absence until two weeks passed and his table was still unoccupied. People, anxious to procure his front and center table, speculated on his whereabouts. No one came close to the real reason why Judge Kinslow stayed clear of Donahue's, not even Sarah.

The day after the anniversary party the court clerk handed the judge a special-delivery letter in his chambers.

"What's this?" The judge asked, seeing the word "confidential" scribbled on the front and back.

"I don't know, Your Honor. It was on my desk when I arrived this morning."

The judge waved his hand in dismissal and said, "That will be all."

Opening the envelope the judge found a hand-printed letter. He quickly perused the page, just like he did with most court documents, and then paused to reread it word-for-word.

> Judge Kinslow:
>
> I know about your sex life with Sarah Robbins. Is she worth your career and marriage? I wonder. I demand that you stop seeing her immediately. Should you fail to comply, I will tell the newspapers every detail of your sordid affair. I'm holding your life in my hand. It's your call, Kinslow.
>
> J.

The coward in him prevented him from telling Sarah about the letter that was signed with only the initial J. Instead, he abruptly terminated their relationship. It was a devastating breakup for Sarah. Although the judge's absence from the club helped her move on with her life, it would be years before she loved again. As for Sam, he didn't miss the judge one iota. Having paid back the loans, there were no legal ties between them. So when the judge stopped coming around, Sam was elated to gain another table for four.

Sarah reached into her purse and extracted the last of her antacids. "Manny, can you pour me a bromo? I need a quick fix before I go on."

"Why don't you take Sam's advice and call it a night? You really don't look so good, Sarah. Besides, the snow is coming down pretty hard. You should be in bed."

"That's what my Aunt Gertrude would have said. But she's not here, so I'll do one more set," she said. "If I don't feel better after set two, I'll go home. God, I hate Cleveland winters."

It was shortly after ten and Sarah was halfway into her second set. As she inhaled a deep breath, a sudden spasm forced her to expel a note that was quite noticeably off-key. Clearing her throat, she tried to recapture the melody, but the escalating pain started to blur her senses. She shook her head, trying to overcome it, but a razor-sharp pain, more intense than all the others combined, caused her to double over. She was dumbfounded as she found herself staring at the floor and the large puddle of water she was standing in. *What is happening to me? What is going on?* In what seemed like a plea for mercy, Sarah let out an ungodly shriek and collapsed to the floor.

"Call an ambulance," Sam yelled, as he forced his way through the crowd and up the stage steps. He knelt down beside her and lifted her head. She was dazed and barely coherent. "Hang on, Sarah. The ambulance should be here shortly."

Although it was a mere three miles to Monrovia General Hospital, for Sarah the journey seemed endless. The straps that prevented her from falling off the stretcher made her even more uncomfortable. *If only I could pull my legs up to my chest, I know that I would feel better,* she reasoned.

As the medics wheeled her through the emergency corridor, all Sarah could hear were the sounds of the needy and suffering: a nine-car pileup on US 422 had injured twenty people. Victims waited for treatment based on the severity of their injuries. But the medics who drove Sarah to MGH bypassed each one and moved her to the front of the line.

"Admitting, where should we put her? She needs to be looked at STAT. She has severe cramping and her BP is 195 over 130."

The nurse pointed to the last vacant room and retorted sharply, "Just what I need. Put her in B-10."

It was clear that the victims of the multiple car accident had completely stripped the nurse of her patience. In her opinion there were just too many contusions and lacerations that required immediate attention. She believed that those injuries were far more critical than the woman with high blood pressure who was complaining of a stomachache.

With the help of two medics, Sarah rolled off the stretcher and onto the examination table. She was shivering, not from a chill, but because the pain had completely enveloped her. The older medic, recognizing her distress, unfolded a white woolen blanket and covered her. He would have consoled her too, except that he was interrupted by the overweight and overpowering nurse who traipsed into the room.

"I'll take over from here. You two just got another call. See you later, boys."

The abrasive nurse offered no sympathy as she questioned Sarah. "Your name is Sarah Robbins. I understand that you had a few cramps and then fainted. Is that accurate?"

"Sort of." She could barely breathe, let alone answer a page full of questions. "Please. I need a sedative."

Ignoring Sarah's request the nurse said, "Hmmmm. Your blood pressure is on the high side. Have you always had high blood pressure?"

"No, I don't think so. Please, will you at least give me a bromo?"

"You'll have to wait for the doctor. After all," she said as if two years in nursing earned her a degree in medicine, "it may be your appendix."

Sarah lay on her side and pulled her legs up to her chest. No longer able to control her tears, she sobbed as she waited for the doctor. The pain was just too much to bear.

Outside the examination room, the rigid nurse called out. "Dr. Clark, before you leave could you please take a look at Miss Sarah Robbins in B-10. She seems to be suffering from acute appendicitis!"

The slender dark-haired doctor scowled back at her in contempt for the unsolicited diagnosis. He was tired, having performed four surgeries in the last twelve hours. Ordinarily, he would have been at home, but today he had offered to help out in ER with the pileup victims. He was about to take a ten-minute break when the caustic nurse summoned him.

"I'm Dr. Clark, Sarah. I need you to roll onto your back and tell me where it hurts." The doctor placed the stethoscope into his ears and listened to her chest.

"Everywhere. Oh, God, everywhere."

"Okay, let's hear what's going on in there. He slowly moved the instrument from her chest to her abdomen. And then he knew. There was another distinct heartbeat rapidly beating in her uterus.

"My God, this woman is in labor. Help, NOW please, nurse, room B-10!" The tone of the doctor's voice galvanized the staff into action.

"I need a gurney in B-10 and transport to the operating room," the pudgy nurse called out into the hallway.

"Doctor, what did you say? Did you say 'labor'? That can't be. I'm not pregnant. I'm not having a baby," Sarah wailed.

The doctor didn't have time to reason with her. There was something wrong.

"Sarah, I need to take a look inside. Try to relax. But if you feel the urge to push, don't. Not yet. Sarah, when was the last time you had a period?"

Sarah could feel a rubber-gloved hand invading her. Hurriedly, she answered, "My menstrual cycles have always been irregular. I can't remember the last time." The probing became more than Sarah could take. No longer able to conceal her agony, she cried in vain.

"Okay, I'm finished with the examination. You're going to be moved into the operating room right away. We don't have much time. Your baby is breech—your baby is coming feet first."

"What baby? There's no baby," she insisted. She was delirious. Still refusing to accept the diagnosis she added, "You've made a terrible mistake. I'm not pregnant. I'm not even married."

"Be that as it may, but you are going to have a baby. And it's critical that we get it out now, before it's too late."

After a short ride to the OR, Sarah was lifted onto the operating table. The room was chaotic. So many people were speaking at the same time that Sarah couldn't understand anyone. The swinging door of the OR flew open to admit Dr. Clark.

"Okay, Sarah. Everything is going to be all right if you just listen to me. But don't push. Not until I tell you."

Sarah held her breath as best she could. But the moment Dr. Clark had his back to her, she bore down and a foreign object suddenly protruded between her legs.

"What's that? There's something between my legs."

The doctor pulled the sheet off Sarah. "There's no time for a C-section. The left leg is out. Get her under. And hand me the forceps. NOW," he shouted.

The nurse rolled a canister of gas next to the operating table. But it was too late. With every contraction, the baby's head was getting forced backward. Its neck was only a fraction of an inch from snapping.

Dr. Clark couldn't wait another second, not even for Sarah to inhale the gas. Without giving Sarah the benefit of anesthesia, he grasped the surgical knife and performed an emergency episiotomy. Having her female organs sliced was the last straw. As blood spurted out from the radical incision, Sarah expelled one last gut-wrenching scream that was silenced when her face was covered with the mask.

"Take deep breaths, Sarah. Take long deep bre…" That's all she heard. Her mind, surrendering to the tranquilizing gasses, floated into unconsciousness.

When Sarah came to, the events of the hour had escaped her. Her surroundings, including the blinding light that caused her to squint, were unfamiliar.

She heard a woman's voice, but had difficulty comprehending what was being said. "You have a baby boy, Sarah, a very tiny baby boy. Is there someone you'd like us to call? A family member or friend?"

Still disoriented, Sarah still did not understand. She asked, "Where am I? Why am I here? And what is *he* doing to me down there?"

"You're in Monrovia General and that's our intern, Dr. Schaeffer. He is suturing you."

"Was I in an accident?"

"No accident. You just gave birth to a baby boy."

This time she heard and remembered. "Oh, my God. Oh, my God." Sarah focused on the curved filaments of the light. She was slowly regaining her faculties. There was only one man with whom she had ever shared her bed, and she hadn't seen or heard from him in seven months. Even if she had, the last thing Henry Kinslow would want to know is that she had given birth to his baby. Then Sarah heard her son whimpering.

"What are they doing to him? He's so small and he looks so cold."

"Just rest, Sarah. Dr. Clark is tending to your baby. I'm sure everything is fine."

While the intern repaired her torn flesh, Sarah watched the doctor. As he held the infant, she noticed Dr. Clark was disturbed. Clearly, something was very wrong.

Dr. Clark checked the infant's heartbeat. Again, he looked discouraged when he wrote his findings on a medical chart. Unable to see what he had written, Sarah had to rely on her newfound maternal instincts. She wondered if her late-night lifestyle was somehow to blame for her baby's distress. She had heard that pregnant women were supposed to eat for two, whereas she, ignorant of her condition, had been eating less in an attempt to lose weight. If only she had known that she was pregnant.

"Okay, Sarah, you're good as new," the intern announced in the direction of Dr. Clark. Usually when an intern was finished, the senior doctor would critique the quality of his work. But not today. Dr. Clark never heard him. His focus was entirely on a frail three-pound infant whose respiratory system, irregular heartbeat, and vital signs were all less than desirable.

Dr. Clark carefully turned the infant onto his stomach and softly touched the back of his abnormally shaped head. The doctor moved his hand from the point at the top of the baby's head down to what should have been the back of a rounded skull, but was, instead, pancake flat. The doctor was certain that these malformations were created by the mother's serious weight deficiency. He continued his examination, but determined that chances for survival were slim to none. And if by some miracle the infant did live, the doctor believed there would be some form of mental retardation.

Dr. Clark rolled a stool next to Sarah to make eye contact as he spoke to her. He knew what he wanted to say, but finding just the right words was exhausting. He whispered so that only she could hear him. "Medical equipment will only prolong the inevitable, Sarah. You should just let him go. The best thing for your boy is to let him die peacefully. It's the most humane thing you can do. His head is grotesquely deformed and it's likely that he'll be retarded. You wouldn't want that, would you?"

Sarah forced her eyes from the doctor to the unresponsive baby who made no movement whatsoever. It was surreal. Only hours before she hadn't known that she was carrying Henry's child. Henry, the man who had held her heart in his hand until the dreadful day he chose his wife and career over her. And it was that same man whom she blamed with every sip of alcohol. *My God*, she thought. *What have I done? I'm the one responsible. I didn't know I was pregnant…*

Sarah's mind fought with questions and unforgiving answers. The joy that should accompany a new birth was buried with anxiety. She no longer cared if he was deformed or mentally challenged; she only knew that she wanted to keep her baby alive.

"I won't hear of it! He's mine and I want you to help him." Sarah's voice fell to a whisper, "Please, doctor, I beg of you. Do whatever you can to make my baby well."

Dr. Clark had no recourse but to honor his Hippocratic oath. The child's mother made her decision, now he would do everything in his power to save the baby.

He placed his hands on the baby's head and began applying pressure to the protrusion. He ignored the infant's hysterical cries as he attempted to mold the crown. Pressing and pushing at the baby's capitulum, Dr. Clark shaped it as if it were a slab of clay. He was successful in forcing the point to a smooth curve, although he could not fully round the back of the skull. Dr. Clark had made a vast improvement to the original disfigurement.

Two hours after he was born, the baby was placed in the incubator labeled "Robbins." With multiple tubes inserted into his body, he had the disconcerting appearance of a shriveled old man waiting out his final days. None of the needles bothered the infant now as the warmth of the incubator lamp calmed him. With no more probing or pinching, he drifted off to sleep.

"I want him watched around the clock," Dr. Clark instructed the registered nurse. "I want to be notified if there are any changes, good or bad. Tonight will be critical. If he makes it to morning, then there's hope. I'm gonna lie down for a couple hours. I'll be back at seven." As Dr. Clark scurried through the ER waiting room to a nearby exit, he failed to notice that the ER was vacant. All the victims of the multiple car crash had been treated and released. He had treated none of them; instead, he had dedicated one-hundred percent of his care and skill to the Robbins' family.

"Wake up, Sarah. It's morning. I need to give you a B12 shot. And by the way…I've got good news for you. Your little boy made it through the night without any complications."

Sarah opened her eyes and saw a slender and very attractive woman tapping the syringe filled with B12. She was dressed in the standard white nurse's uniform that buttoned up the front. Boring on most, but on her it fit like a glove. Even the starched white cap looked fashionable. Surrounding it, curly locks of platinum blond hair bounced freely.

"Has Dr. Clark seen my baby this morning?"

"He's examining him as we speak. So don't you worry about him right now. You've got to get better, too, Sarah."

All the while the nurse attended to Sarah, she maintained an angelic smile on her face. She embodied compassion with every touch and word.

"Okay, I hope that didn't hurt too much."

"No, I barely felt it. Thanks for being so gentle, nurse."

"Call me Fran, Sarah," she said while tucking in the bed sheet. "I have a feeling we'll be seeing a lot of each other."

"You are so much kinder than the nurse in ER. She was so rude. I hope I don't have to see her again."

"I know who you mean. Don't worry, you won't have to see her again. She's leaving Monrovia General next week to work in a smaller hospital. She says this place drives her crazy."

"Well, that explains her bedside manner," Sarah laughed.

"Sarah, I'll be back in twenty. If you need me in the meantime, just ring the bell."

"Thanks, Fran."

"Oh, there's just one more thing. Whose name should I enter as the father on your baby's birth certificate?"

"You probably already know that I'm not married. So I'd like it to say 'unknown,' at least for now. I can always change it later, can't I?"

"Sure you can, sweetie. Mum's the word."

Fran winked, leaving Sarah as the sole occupant in the four-bed ward. Alone, she faced a new realization. She was the mother of Henry's only son. She wondered what he would think if he found out. It had been seven months since he broke off their relationship. She remembered the bitter words…

"From a career standpoint, divorcing my wife and leaving my daughters wouldn't look good. I have my status to think about." He added, "And, Sarah, just so we understand one another, I'd appreciate it if you didn't bother me anymore."

It was convenient for the judge to hide behind those words. Much easier than admitting he had received a letter that had threatened to expose their relationship and far easier than trying to discover who had sent the letter, signing it only with the initial J.

"Bother," Sarah said while gritting her teeth. The words still sickened her. Henry thought nothing of sharing her bed for five years, until push came to shove when he dropped her flat. She wondered what her Aunt Gertrude would have thought of her German friend.

Sarah remained hospitalized for two weeks while she recuperated from severe malnutrition. Dr. Clark ordered a diet rich in starches that he thought would nourish her and compensate for the sudden lack of alcohol to her system.

"You'll need to continue this diet, Sarah. I probably don't need to tell you to lay off the alcohol. You're lucky your liver's intact. It could have gone the other way."

"I promise, Dr. Clark. I don't ever want to go through the shakes and vomiting again. Withdrawals, ugh!"

"Good. I'm releasing you today, but I'm keeping you on liquid iron and weekly B12 shots."

"I was starting to go stir-crazy in here. What about my baby?"

"He has a long way to go. I'm not sure how many weeks or months it will be before I release him. Keep praying. Every day, when he opens his eyes, I see a little miracle in him."

Ordinarily, a celebration such as this would have begun with a few rum and colas, but not this time. The thought of a drink made Sarah shudder. She had her walking papers, while her baby held the fine line between life and death.

As Sarah sat in the wheelchair enjoying a last ride through the corridors, she asked the volunteer to stop by the nursery. Peering through the glass, she compared her son to the other babies. He was by far the smallest. Yet despite his size, she could see strength. He was a survivor and she knew that someday, somehow, he would share the ambitions of his birth father, Judge Henry Kinslow. She would see to it.

Sarah lightly tapped the window and whispered, "Mommy is going home today. I'll be back to see you tomorrow, Master William Anthony Robbins."

two

NEIL DVORAK

Detroit, 1950

Neil Dvorak pressed his face against the glass window of the baby ward at Detroit Memorial. Shrouded in blankets of pink and blue, fifteen newborn infants lined up for public viewing. But for this proud father, there was only one that mattered.

"That's my baby over there. Victoria Marie Dvorak. Second row, third from the left. The one with the full head of hair, just like mine. Born yesterday, May 31, 1950."

There was no denying Neil was her father. Wavy hair, wide-set eyes, and dimpled chin, every feature linked the infant to the man who just couldn't take his eyes off her.

"Mr. Dvorak, is this your first baby?"

Neil turned around to face the very young woman standing behind him. Draped in a bulky hospital robe, her bulging stomach had yet to recede from childbirth. She was as eager as he was to point out her offspring.

"That's my son, Jonah. He's our third. We were sort of hoping for a little girl. Actually, that's what my husband wanted. I didn't care one way or another. You know, as long as the baby was healthy."

"Congratulations, ma'am. I'm sure your husband is thrilled about your new son."

The young woman wished that was the truth, because she hadn't seen her husband since she had given birth; however, it would have been awkward to share that information with a stranger. Instead, she asked, "So is Victoria your first baby?"

"Ah, yes she is," he answered.

From an honest man came forth a blatant lie. But, like the young woman, he thought it pointless to tell a stranger that Victoria was his second daughter with his second wife, Anne.

"I've got to get back to my bed. It's feeding time and I don't want to keep my baby waiting. Nice talking with you."

"Yeah, it was nice talking with you, too. Again, congratulations."

As the young woman disappeared down the corridor, Neil rested his forehead against the window. He concentrated on Victoria, but through the miracle of daydreams it was six years earlier and the little baby he adored was Amy. He remembered the day vividly.

"I want to have four more, Jan. Boys or girls, I don't care, just as long as we have a big family. My love, you have made me the happiest man in the world."

With such optimism Neil never imagined that his marriage to Janet would end in divorce. He had been raised in an orphanage and knew what it meant to be alone. Perhaps that's why he believed in the idea of family solidarity, of staying together whether war, illness, or financial hardship intervened. The only reason to abandon a marriage, in his book, was adultery, a transgression that he categorized all on its own as "absolutely unforgivable!"

It was a scorching July afternoon during the heat wave of '47. Neil, a cabinetmaker by trade, had just finished sanding the base of a walnut armoire. He had just turned the sander off when the shop's owner approached him.

"Fine work, Neil, as usual," Bernie Stocker said.

"Thanks. It should be complete and ready to go by the end of the week."

"There's no rush. The customer doesn't need it until next month."

Bernie stepped back and admired the workmanship. It was another masterpiece that he would sell at three times Neil's weekly paycheck. "You know, I'd be a rich man if I only had one more worker like you, Neil. I swear that you've got angels guiding those fingers of yours. You've got a God-given talent. Yes sir, that's what you've got. A God-given talent."

"I don't need an attaboy every day, Bernie. I'm not going anywhere soon."

"Glad to hear that, because a lot of people are talking about your work. I'm just afraid some big prefab company will tempt you with a mother lode of cash."

"Like I said, Bernie, I'm not going anywhere. Besides, I'm your only employee. Where would you be if I just up and quit?"

"You know where. I'd be up that proverbial creek without a paddle."

Neil laughed while wrapping a soft cotton cloth around his hand. Skillfully, he removed wood shavings from the chiseled designs in the armoire. This was the one facet of his job that he usually dreaded, as it was tedious and time-consuming. On this sweltering day he welcomed the task, for as boring as it was, it helped him forget that the overhead fan was broken beyond repair. And with no breeze whatsoever, the shop was rapidly becoming an inferno.

Bernie held out a twenty dollar bill and said, "Put the cloth down, Neil, and take this."

"What's this for?"

"Let's just call it a heat-wave bonus. Why don't you take Janet to some nice place with air conditioning? Have a brew or two on me."

"It would be hard to pass on an offer like that, thanks. I'll go as soon as I clean up my workbench."

"Nah, get out of here. I'll clean it up. Oh, and by the time you come back tomorrow, the new fan will be up and working."

Neil retreated to his car and quickly rolled down the windows. *God, it must be a hundred and ten in here,* he thought. Any other time the windows would have been left open, but he had closed them due to an earlier thunderstorm. The downpour should have cooled the air, but with temperatures soaring, every raindrop that reached the pavement had sizzled into a vaporizing steam.

Neil turned onto the four-lane expressway and for once was able to exceed the posted speed limit. Normally, he would have been competing for road space with the autoworkers from Detroit's big three. But at one in the afternoon there were no traffic jams or fender benders. With the road all to himself, he was home in less than thirty minutes.

The brakes on his 1940 Buick squealed to a halt in front of the Dvoraks' two-story red-brick home. Their house was an exact replica of every other one on the block with one distinction: a rose garden. Unlike the other yards landscaped with lawns of Bermuda grass, theirs boasted a floral wonderland.

Neil peeled himself from the hot vinyl interior and slammed the car door behind him. Across the street he saw their neighbor, Denise, fanning herself with the morning newspaper.

"Hey, Denise! How are you doing in this god-awful heat?" Neil lifted a sagging flower, smelled its fading scent and added, "I'm wilting away, just like this delicate 'Peace' rose."

"Neil, you're home early today."

"My boss gave me the day off. I'm going to surprise Janet and take her out to lunch. Would you mind watching Amy for us? We'll be back before four."

"She's already here. The girls are taking a nap. They wore themselves out after squirting each other with the water hose."

"That's one way to beat the heat. So where's Janet?"

"I don't know. She just asked if I'd babysit today. She left Amy here a couple of hours ago."

"Did she say where she was going?"

"I didn't ask and she didn't say. Sorry."

"Oh, well. I'll check inside. Maybe she left me a note."

Neil unlocked the front door and went straight over to the white-tiled kitchen counter. If Janet had left a note, then that is where he would have found it. But there was no message.

Dripping with sweat, he opened the refrigerator door and leaned inward. The sudden blast of cold air chilled the perspiration embedded in his cotton shirt. He stood there for several minutes before finally grabbing a bottle of beer. *Might as well take an ice-cold shower,* he thought.

Neil trudged up the stairs and wondered where Janet was. But he had to give her credit. Wherever she was, it had to be cooler than in the sweltering house.

Upstairs, the air had a stagnant smell; he noticed that every window was closed. He couldn't remember any other summer day, scorching or not, that they weren't wide open. *No wonder it's so hot in here. What was Janet thinking?* He stepped into Amy's room and unclasped the first lock. He lifted it upward, hoping for a surge of fresh air but found little difference between the suffocating air outside and the stale air inside. He moved to open the second window, but was sidetracked when a reflection of his bedroom door appeared in the glass. It too, was closed. In all the years they had been married, the door was only closed at night and it was always reopened before Amy awoke in the morning. "Oh, Jan, the heat must have really gotten to you," he mumbled jokingly, as he opened the door.

That was the last unprotected moment Neil would remember. Upon entering his bedroom, the world as he knew it was shattered. He swallowed hard and tried to decipher the unthinkable. Janet was sitting erect in bed, flushed from a recent orgasm. But more unsettling was the outline beneath the sheets. A man's face was buried between her legs.

Choking on his words, Neil stuttered, "Get out. Get out. Get the hell out!" But it was Neil who fled the room. As he ran downstairs, he screamed again, "Get out!" Barely coherent, he found himself standing amid the rose garden tearing each petal from its stem. By the time Janet reached him, the ground was covered with a blanket of multicolored buds. Every bush was barren. Every flower destroyed.

"What have you done to my rose garden, Neil? For two years I've nurtured every bush. It was my hobby, Neil. My only hobby."

"What did you just say to me? Your hobby? Are you serious?" He couldn't look her in the face. But from the corner of his eye, he saw the shadow of a man fleeing up the street. "So how do you explain that? It looks to me that you had more than one extracurricular activity."

Caught red-handed, Janet realized there was no point in trying to lie her way out of the situation. "Well, you were bound to find out sooner or later. It's not like this was my first time."

"And what does that mean? You've been with him before?" He hesitated and then asked slowly, "Are you in love with him?"

"Of course, not. But…how can I say this to you?" She searched for less damaging words, but they didn't exist. "He gives me what you are incapable of. He satisfies my every desire."

Anger overcame him. "I don't want to hear this, Janet. You are nothing but a whore!"

Janet bent over and retrieved a handful of petals. She inhaled their perfume before mustering the courage to respond.

"If I were a whore, Neil, I'd be making a lot of money. Much more than you bring home every week. To tell you the truth," she said, her confession turning into a boast, "I've had others. Many others."

Neil could almost taste the acidic words. They parched his throat, rendering a bitter, metallic aftertaste. His will to fight had been stripped. Disheartened, he surrendered as a broken man.

"I can't stay married to you any longer, Janet. It's over. As of this moment, you are nothing to me."

"But Neil, it's just that our sex life…"

While his very soul had been wounded, he remained stone-faced. "I don't need to know why you screw other men. Save it for the court."

If he had let her have her say, it wouldn't have been the first time Janet had expressed a need for sexual gratification. But trying to convince Neil to just let loose had always been futile. His childhood teachings at St. John's Orphanage had set the groundwork for Neil's sexual reticence. To this day he could still hear the priest's lecture.

"Sexual intercourse is an act to be performed for procreation only. When you commit this act, it should be done in the way God intended. Face-to-face. Any deviation thereof is sexual perversion and will be reckoned with in the fires of hell." The daily sermons also explained Neil's aversion to nudity, even between husband and wife.

Neil spat on the ground, just missing Janet's shoes. "Denise is watching us through the window. You better go and pick up Amy. As for me, I'm going back downtown to find a lawyer."

✧ ✧ ✧

"Neil, Janet's on the phone again. Third call today."

"Do me a favor, Bernie. Tell her to take a hike."

Neil never provided Bernie with details about his separation. However, Bernie had a pretty good idea from firsthand experience what had happened. Like so many of Neil's other friends, Bernie had been propositioned by Janet. But the difference between Bernie and the others was that he had declined her offer.

"Janet, he doesn't want to talk to you. You really need to stop calling him here," he said.

"Well, if he doesn't want to take my calls, then I'll have to figure out something else to do. Won't I, Bernie?"

At closing time that afternoon, Janet was waiting outside the cabinet shop. When Neil saw her, his first thought was to turn around. But the vision of Janet, sitting atop the hood of the green Buick and smoking a cigarette from an elongated holder, made him pause. She was such a beautiful, sexy woman. Neil realized that no matter how much he admired her beauty, he could never forgive her for what she had done. Sighing, he decided to get the conversation over with.

"What the hell do you want? I deposited my paycheck into the account yesterday."

"It's not the money, Neil. We have to talk."

Up until then, Neil had avoided all contact with her. He was better able to cope when he had mentally cast her aside. But here she was in his presence, and he didn't know how to handle it. He forced himself to suppress his emotions, but his eyelids refused to cooperate. They twitched uncontrollably.

"You best get out of here, Janet, before I do something I regret."

"What about Amy? She needs her daddy."

Finding the strength to shut Janet out was almost impossible as he still loved her. He just couldn't admit that to his wife—or himself. Maintaining a poker face he said, "I'll always be Amy's father. It is very unfortunate that she has a whore for a mother."

"I really don't care what you call me or what you think of me. If you can't learn to forgive, you will lose in the long run. You could lose Amy."

"I'll never lose her, no matter what you do. Shall we talk custody?"

"FYI, Neil, I intend to fight you for custody," she snapped.

"I figured you would, but there's no need. I'd rather Amy didn't know that her mother is a whore. As long as I'm granted regular visitations, I'll give you full custody. Now, get off my car and get out of my life."

Janet slid off the hood and straightened her red polka-dot dress. Raising her shoulders high, she lifted her head upward. She knew it was over. In her white high-heel pumps, she vamped across the street to the taxicab she had left waiting

✧ ✧ ✧

Neil had moved out of their house and was renting a small one-bedroom apartment near the shop, which is where he spent most of his time. Haunted by loneliness, he sought solace with his hammer and nails. In addition to a hobby and livelihood, woodworking had also become his form of therapy. Day in and day out, he crafted slabs of wood into fine pieces of furniture. For him, it was an escape. For Bernie, whose sales had quadrupled, it was a financial windfall.

This relentless work schedule went on for over a year. But Neil never complained, because his visits with Amy kept him going. During their time together, he put away his tools and devoted every second to her. She could have asked for the world and somehow, someway, Neil would have accommodated her.

But times were changing. Janet had moved on with her life and remarried a police officer named Lars Ingram. Her new husband, anxious to assume the key role as Amy's father, wanted nothing more than to demote Neil to understudy. Suddenly, visitations were canceled, and Neil sensed that his role as Amy's father was in jeopardy. So it shouldn't have come as a shock when Janet telephoned him with the news.

"Neil, we moved to South Carolina three weeks ago. I didn't want to tell you because I was afraid you would try to stop us. Lars accepted a position with the Charleston Police Department." Janet didn't give Neil a chance to respond. Instead, she continued reading verbatim from a script she had written earlier. "The move has been good for all of us. Amy is happy with Lars. He's a good father to her."

Neil couldn't exhale. Just as Janet predicted, he had lost his flesh and blood.

"Oh, there's one more thing, Neil. We don't want any more of your child support. All of the money you've paid was returned to your bank account yesterday with a fair amount of interest. My husband is a proud man. He insists on being the sole breadwinner of our family. I'm sure you understand. Take care, Neil."

Although Janet had already hung up, Neil held the receiver for several minutes before slamming it into the cradle. In his haste for a divorce, he had failed to include specific provisions regarding his parental rights. Without those stipulations, Janet had full authority to move Amy anywhere and anytime she wanted. There was nothing he could say or do to change the outcome.

Once again Neil's mouth was filled with a bitter metallic taste. He desperately needed some form of comfort food to overcome the bitterness. He jerked the cupboard door open and blindly stared at a can of sardines packed in mustard sauce. Next to it was a half box of saltine crackers. "God, I'm sick of sardines and I'm sick of this place! I've got to get out of this hellhole," he yelled, momentarily forgetting that the walls were very thin between his dwelling and his neighbor's. In a quieter, more reserved tone he muttered to himself, "I'll take a quick rinse and go out on the town tonight."

Neil dropped his sawdust-covered pants and stepped into a steaming shower. He bent his head backward, allowing the full force of the spray to beat against his face. Normally, the water would have lifted his spirits; but in this place of solitude, he fell victim to his innermost feelings. The sorrow he had suppressed erupted in a flood of tears. He sobbed, softly at first, but gradually his cries, echoing off the bathroom tiles, became deafening. His little girl was lost to him.

When the water turned cold and his tear ducts were finally emptied, Neil emerged from the shower. It was time to let go of his painful yesteryears and embrace the possibilities of tomorrow. So after donning the only pair of dress slacks he owned, Neil set out on a venture. He walked toward the cabinet shop, yet he didn't hesitate to pass it by. As of that moment, his late-night shifts became a thing of the past. Thirsting for companionship, Neil wished to be part of the world again.

The main boulevard in Detroit harbored a variety of bars and clubs from which Neil could choose. Each one, sporting a flashing neon sign, seemed to personally beckon him. But Neil just wanted a beer and some company, so his selection was easy. He chose the bar whose door was closest.

"What can I get you, pal? The special tonight is Rock and Rye with a twist."

"No, thanks. Just pour me a beer. Whatever you've got on tap is fine."

"Coming right up."

Neil gave the place a quick once-over. It was long and narrow, the bar along one side and red-cushioned booths on the other. At the very back was a large open area. He figured it was a dance floor.

"Here you go," the young bartender said as he placed a mug dripping with foam in front of Neil.

"So do people dance here?"

"Every night. You're just early. As soon as the combo starts playing, it'll be packed!"

"The people who come in, are they mostly couples?"

The bartender, young as he was, could generally spot rookie barhoppers. Whether it was the overkill of aftershave or a fidgety mannerism that gave them away, he always knew. Today it happened to be a man with salt-and-pepper curly hair in his mid-thirties, who had just ordered a regular beer on tap.

"Couples go next door to the Blue Sapphire Club. It's much quieter over there. We get the singles. Stick around and see for yourself. By the way my name is Tony."

"I'm Neil Dvorak. I live around the corner at the Grandview Apartments."

"Welcome to the Viper Lounge. I hope we'll be seeing a lot of you."

Neil tilted his glass of beer toward Tony before plunging into its thick head of foam. Thanks to the young man, he felt comfortable in his new surroundings. Dating might not be as bad as he had originally thought.

"Hey, friend, look what's coming your way." Tony nodded his head at four women, around the same age as Neil, who had just seated themselves in one of the circular booths. "See anything you like?"

Neil swiveled on his barstool to face the only occupied booth in the bar. He noticed that all four women were attractive, but there was only one who really caught his eye. She was the spitting image of his ex-wife Janet. With her dark red hair that bobbed at the shoulders and a curvaceous body with oversized breasts, she could have been her twin sister.

"Tony, would you do me a favor?"

"Sure thing. What do you need?"

"I'd like to buy those ladies a drink, starting with the redhead."

Tony took his cue well. From behind the bar he called out, "Hey, Anne. Mr. Neil Dvorak here would like to buy you a drink. The same goes for the rest of you ladies. What's your pleasure?"

Neil laughed out loud. It was the first good laugh he'd had in well over a year.

"Come over and join us, Neil. We're celebrating. We just took first place in bowling, thanks to Thea's six-twenty series." Anne reached her arm around the brunette sitting next to her and gave her a friendly squeeze. "We couldn't have done it without her."

"And your name is Anne?" Neil asked as he slid next to her in the booth.

"Yes, I am Anne Thompson and these are my friends, Thea, Grace, and Emma."

"Glad to meet all of you. Do you ladies come here often? Are you all single?" Neil asked the question to all four, but he was only interested in Anne's response.

"I've been divorced for over a year," Anne quickly responded.

"Me, too," he answered, while never hearing the answers from the other three.

"Do you have any children, Anne? I have a five-year-old daughter."

"Yes, I have two. A son, ten, and a daughter who is eleven. Right now they are living with my parents, Samuel and Victoria Covaci, on their farm in Marlette, about eighty miles north of here."

"Your children are living with your parents? How do you manage to live without them?"

"My parents needed help with harvesting a few months ago and now they need help with planting. It's an endless cycle, you know."

"How do you survive the loneliness? I could really use the advice." He dropped his head and gulped, "Today I found out that Janet, my ex, moved our daughter to South Carolina. No forwarding address, just South Carolina."

"How very sad. Are you going after her?"

"I don't know what good it would do. I was foolish and quick to sign the custody papers. Janet and her new husband have full custody." He chugged his beer and added, "Maybe it's all for the best. Divorce can play havoc on a child. It's stability they need. It's stability we all need."

"Are you afraid that she'll forget you? You know, out of sight, out of mind?"

"Amy may be young, but not young enough to erase me from her memory. I'll be in her dreams, as she will be in mine," Neil said confidently.

"Banking on dreams that fade is risky," she said negatively.

"You don't know my Amy. Years from now she'll come looking for me. When she does, I'll hand her a box filled with a lifetime of unread letters. Those written by her real daddy. The one who loved her so much, that he let her go."

"So what you're saying is that you intend to spend the next several years waiting for that miraculous day?"

"No, I'm not going to sit on my duff waiting. I plan to get on with my life. Start anew, so to speak."

That was the opportune moment Anne had been waiting for. Talking about children had exhausted her. She jumped in and changed the subject.

"Neil, do you live alone?" Except for him, everyone else heard the anticipation in Anne's voice. She had been searching for a mate for months. To date, there had been no prospects.

"Yes, I live by myself…ever since Jan and I split."

That's all Anne needed to hear. She edged up closer to him. "So why are you still wearing your wedding ring?"

"It's never been off my finger since the day I was married."

"You're not married anymore."

Neil hadn't noticed he had been spinning the gold band around his finger. But since Anne had brought it to his attention, he called to Tony as he yanked the ring over his knuckle and threw it across the room. "Catch this and toss it in the can…where it belongs."

With that one gesture, Neil regained control of his life. "Now, Anne, let's talk. Tell me everything about yourself and then I'll tell you all about me."

After that night Neil returned only once to the Viper Lounge. It was three months later when he dropped by to invite Tony to a celebration.

"Hey, Tony. How you been?"

True to his calling, the bartender had a memory for names and faces. "Well, if it isn't Neil Dvorak! It's been a long time. Beer on tap, right?"

"Yeah, that'll be great."

"So how have you been? I haven't seen you or Anne Thompson since that night you first walked through our door. What have you been up to?"

"There's much to tell you, Tony. A lot has happened in three months."

"I heard that you are dating Anne Thompson. True?"

"You bet I am. That's why I'm here. I want to invite you to a backyard barbeque next Saturday afternoon at my place."

"Backyard barbeque? Don't you live at the Grandview Apartments anymore?"

"Not anymore. I've been renting a house ever since my boss gave me an unexpected bonus. He split his profits for the year right down the middle. It was a hefty piece of change, Tony. Someday it's gonna make a fine down payment on a home of our own, one where Anne and I can raise our family."

"Family? Are you and Anne talking marriage?"

"Yep! That's what the barbecue's for. Next Saturday, May fifth, nineteen-hundred and forty-nine, Anne Thompson will become Mrs. Neil Dvorak."

"Wow! But Neil, you've only known each other for three months."

"Yeah, but time doesn't matter. It's the quality of a relationship. Anne is the perfect woman, respectable and kind. Never raises her voice." He blushed and added, "She's even making me wait until our wedding night for "you-know-what." It makes me respect her even more!"

Puzzled by Neil's wildly inaccurate opinion of Anne, Tony pulled at his chin as if he was stroking a full-grown goatee. With no facial hair in sight, he simply tugged at the outline of his jawline. He was stupefied.

"Anne is everything I could ask for in a woman," Neil continued, oblivious to the look on Tony's face. "When I marry her, I'm getting a ready-made family. Next month her children, John and Rose, will be coming home to live with us. I met them last week, Tony. They are wonderful children."

Tony smiled to prevent his apprehension from showing. The woman Neil described was not the same woman he knew. Except for the night she met Neil, Anne Thompson had never been polite or soft-spoken, especially to the subservient bartender. To him she had always been demanding, impatient, and downright rude.

"Well, Tony, the party starts at one. I know you have to work, so show up whenever you can. Bring a lady friend. There's going to be music, dancing, and a ton of food. I hired Pappy's Famous BBQ to cater it."

"Sounds like you got it all together, down to the last detail." Tony paused and took a deep breath before he asked, "Neil, may I be honest with you?"

"Of course, speak your piece. If it weren't for you, none of this would have happened. You were the one who introduced me to Anne, remember?"

"Yeah, I remember," Tony said as he chewed at his bottom lip. "Neil, do you think three months is enough time to really know someone? Truthfully, I never thought you and Anne Thompson would hit it off the way you did," Tony finished.

"Well, why not? It's a match made in heaven, my friend. I owe it all to you. Here's our address. I've got to get going. I'm off to pick up my lovely fiancée from the beauty salon."

Neil took one sip of beer before flipping a quarter into Tony's hand.

"Until next Saturday, Tony. Until next Saturday."

"I'll do my best to make it, Neil. If something comes up and I'm unable to attend, congratulations and good luck."

"Thanks, but you can hold off with your good wishes. I expect to see you there, Tony. Good-bye."

Tony watched as Neil sped around the corner and out of sight. He knew it would be the last time he would see the curly haired man. As he wiped the counter he mumbled, "A chameleon will change its color to suit its environment. You don't know it yet, Neil Dvorak, but you are about to marry a chameleon. May God be on your side."

✧ ✧ ✧

"What a day, what a day, what a day—a fourteen-hour wedding celebration! We sure know how to throw a party." Neil winked at her and sighed, "Gosh, I love you, Mrs. Dvorak."

"I love hearing you call me that, Neil. There's something that makes a woman feel better about herself when she has the word missus attached to her name."

"It's the same for a man," said Neil with an alluring smile. "When a man has a wife by his side, it tells the world that someone loved him enough to say 'yes.'"

With light conversation and a hint at making love, it seemed appropriate for Anne to unzip her light-blue wedding suit. However, the moment Anne started to strip in front of him, he backed away. For Neil, old habits were hard to break.

Grabbing a robe from the closet he blurted out, "Anne, I'm going to take a quick rinse." He closed the bathroom door behind him and then called out, "I prefer the lights out."

The lights out? What gives?

Oh well, Anne thought. *I've been waiting three months for this night. Lights out or not, I'm going to get mine with or without my new husband.*

Patiently she waited for him to finish his "quick rinse," but after thirty minutes her patience had run out. There was no telling how long he would remain in the shower, and she was sex-starved and needed immediate relief. She decided to take care of herself.

Anne poured herself a glass of champagne that Neil had brought in to toast their union. After replacing the bottle back in the ice bucket, she lay back on her pillows. Dipping two of her fingers into the champagne, she placed them between her open legs. The cold and bubbly nectar dripped into her throbbing chamber. Her body responded with waves of pleasure to the slow, constant motion of her fingers. But the moment Anne heard Neil turn off the shower she increased the movement of her fingers until, seconds later, her body exploded with a thunderous orgasm. It was the perfect masturbation. She was completely satisfied before Neil slipped under the covers and mounted her.

With her self-induced lubrication, Neil's entry was swift and straightforward. And a mere four strokes later, he climaxed. Anne didn't need to.

As they were consummating their marriage, Anne figured that straight sex was acceptable. Days later, it was apparent that straight sex was all Neil knew. It was a squeeze, a kiss, and the same old missionary position until their sixth-week anniversary when an unexpected and unforgettable event occurred.

"Anne, I want to talk with you before I get up and go to work."

"What is it, Neil? It's still dark outside."

"We've been married over a month," Neil stated. "Isn't it time for your folks to send Rose and John home?"

"I was hoping for a couple more months with just the two of us. Can't we just be newlyweds for a while longer?"

Neil sat upright in bed. He was well prepared for a defense.

"Anne, it's been too long for you and your children to be apart. I think it's time we put the children's interests before our own."

This was the dreaded debate that Anne had been expecting. Ever since their wedding, Neil had dropped hints about John and Rose coming home. It was evident that he was anxious to fill the void of fatherhood.

"I want a few more weeks alone with you, honey." Anne was ready to roll over and go back to sleep.

"I don't think we should wait any longer," Neil persisted. "The children will be teenagers soon. You know those are crucial years." Then it occurred to her. Her mouth was next to his genitals. It was the closest it had ever been. She decided to take full advantage of her position.

She ceased paying attention to him and deliberately moved her hand across his thigh and, ever so slightly, over the tip of his penis. It caught him off guard. His body responded with an erection, as any man's would. He tried to ease her hand away, but by then Anne was massaging his testicles; she toyed with them until their malleable texture had become taut and rigid.

"Anne, Anne, what are you doing to me?" Neil's breathing accelerated. He could barely speak when she made her pivotal move. She lifted herself just high enough to lick each of his nipples. Using her tongue as a guide, she outlined the direction she was heading. Lower and lower she lapped him until she reached his pubic hairline.

"Anne, please, don't. I, I can't," he stuttered. "I've never. Please, Anne. This is wrong." But his body, aching from within, was finally winning the internal battle of joy against sin. He rested back against the wall and gulped as she took his engorged organ into her mouth.

If Neil once considered this a sin, he did so no longer. *Why did I refuse this pleasure from Janet? Maybe things would have been different.* This was not the time for logical questions or answers. He was nearing the point of no return. And Anne knew it.

All along she had been monitoring his moans and groans. When she was certain he was about to climax, she suddenly disengaged herself from him. Raising her head just inches from his swollen and yearning member, she whispered, "The kids will stay up at the farm as long as I see fit. Forever, if need be. All right, Neil?"

Defenseless, Neil gave in to her wishes. "Whatever you say, Anne. Whatever you say." He waited for her to engulf him again and when she hesitated, he thrust himself upward and back into her open and oh-so-warm mouth. He felt her tongue welcome the intruder.

Neil would have agreed to anything at that point. At the age of thirty-six, he had at last experienced fellatio and was in thrall to its delights; there was no turning back. Anne had discovered a source of power she would use to preempt any future discussions about the children.

This ploy worked like a charm for two months. Whenever Anne wanted something, she would go down on Neil until he gave in to her demands. She only allowed him to climax after he had screamed, "Yes, yes, yes." Ann manipulated Neil. Until one August afternoon, that is.

Neil and Anne had purchased tickets to see *Adam's Rib*, the latest film starring Spencer Tracy and Katharine Hepburn. As they stood in the main lobby waiting for the balcony to open, Neil made a surprising proposal.

"Neil, you're joking," Anne said as she choked on a popcorn kernel. "A baby? Why would I want to get pregnant? I'm thirty-two. Besides, as you've said before, Rose and John will be teenagers soon, and it's not like my parents will live forever. We could have a full house at the drop of a hat."

Neil persisted, "I want you to have my baby, Anne. A baby from you and me."

This was certainly not in Anne's original plan. She was in the lobby of the Fox Theater unable to use what had become her ace in the hole, the one thing that had given her the edge on so many disagreements—her magical tongue, as Neil so often called it.

Neil reached into his shirt pocket and pulled out a motel key. He leaned over her shoulder and pressured, "Let's skip the matinee, honey, and go across the street. I want to make a baby with you, right now. Anne, this time there won't be any extras for me. This time it's going to be all for you."

There was a strange sense of power that emanated from him. He was hypnotic. His assertiveness caused her eyes to dilate, her knees to weaken. She became wet with excitement.

Neil sensed the pendulum was about to swing in his favor. Using his charismatic smile, he lured her to the eight-room motel that charged its guests by the hour. It took considerably less time to impregnate her.

✧ ✧ ✧

The nurse stepped into the father's waiting room and announced, "You have a daughter, Mr. Dvorak. A healthy seven-pound baby girl. Your wife is doing fine, although the doctor did have to give her a sedative to help her relax. You can see her this afternoon during visiting hours. Your baby girl will be in the viewing area within the hour. Do you have a name picked out for her?"

For the entire nine months of her pregnancy, Anne had refused to consider any female names. So when the nurse asked, Neil took it upon himself to name his baby girl. "Her name is Victoria. We're naming her after her maternal grandmother."

The nurse left Neil in a euphoric state. He had never told Anne, but he had prayed every night for another baby daughter, a second chance to make up for losing Amy. Now his prayers had been answered. "Thank you, God," he rejoiced, until he remembered what Anne had said on the way to the hospital. It was unsettling.

"These labor pains better not be from another girl. I do not want another pain-in-the-ass daughter," she had shouted.

"You don't know what you're saying, honey. If we have a baby girl, you'll regret these words."

"I know exactly what I'm saying, Neil. A daughter eventually becomes a more attractive, more desirable version of oneself. Suddenly men, men just like you, give the young women all the attention. You'd do that with Rose with her perky breasts, I know you would. I'll bet you'd give anything to see Rose naked, wouldn't you?"

Neil was mortified, but tried to reason that those were the words of a woman in labor. Still, he couldn't ignore the brutal accusation. It was imperative he defend himself.

"My God, Anne, she's your daughter! How on earth can you talk about her that way? You have no respect for her, or me, for that matter."

"Don't talk to me about respect, Neil. Jesus Christ, can't you drive any faster? My son, and it better be a son, is ready to come out any second. Hurry up!"

As Neil stood by Anne's bedside, he felt full of love for his wife; he had convinced himself her vitriolic outburst was the result of a woman in labor.

"Mrs. Dvorak, wake up. I'll go get little Victoria. Your husband is here to see you," the nurse said, as she gently touched Anne's arm.

Anne squinted, and then slowly opened her eyes.

"She's beautiful, Anne," Neil said, "She looks just like you. Wait until you see her."

Anne took a deep breath and gritted her teeth as she released the air. "Well, you named her after my mother. Didn't you even think to consult me first?"

"Honey, you never wanted to talk about names for little girls. I remembered that Victor was one of the names you liked best for a boy. I figured you would like the female version."

"Obviously, it doesn't matter what I think or want. I didn't get a son. Well, you seem happy enough for both of us. You've got your little girl, Neil." Anne took another deep breath and turned away from him. She was gazing out the window when the nurse returned with their baby.

"It's feeding time. Baby Victoria is mighty hungry. Let's get you situated. Sorry, Mr. Dvorak, but you'll have to leave now. It's time for mommy and baby to have their first intimate moment together."

"I'll go down to the cafeteria for a smoke and a cup of joe. I'll be back later, honey. Okay?"

"Do what you damn well want, Neil—you've gotten your own way so far."

The young nurse cranked up the bed head to a vertical position. After propping up Anne's pillow, she started to lift the baby from her portable crib. "Let's get you some nourishment, little one," the nurse cooed.

"That won't be necessary," Anne snapped. "You can take her back to the nursery because I've always had difficulty breast-feeding. I'm not even going to try it with this one. You might as well start binding me up right now. God knows these breasts of mine are filling up with every waking moment."

"I'll have to speak with your doctor. Perhaps he can give you something to stop your milk from producing. If only you had mentioned it to him earlier, he could have given you a shot on the delivery table. It would have prevented the milk from flowing in, and then your breasts wouldn't be so sensitive."

"Well, I forgot. Do what you must. I'm prepared to be bound up." Anne rolled on her side, away from the nurse and baby Victoria. There was no way on earth Anne was going to permit a daughter to suckle her.

three

THE DRAKES

Alabama, 1949

Thomas Drake seized a half-pint bottle from his hip pocket and downed the last ounce of rye whiskey. Having just completed his 1948 Alabama tax statement, the consolation he required was in liquid form. *Another year I've got to pay the Fed. Goddamn government. Never shells out to the workingman. Gives it all to the wealthy. And I'm caught up in this bureaucracy. It's nothing but a fucking rich man's world!*

It didn't take much to get the forty-eight-year-old on a roll. Drake was anti-everything, especially when it came to being told what to do. In this case it was the IRS, although anyone in a position of authority could bring out the worst in him. That was the main reason he never held a job for more than a few months. Sometimes he would just up and quit, but more often than not, he was fired for insubordination.

"Thom, how did we do on taxes this year? Are we getting a refund?" He barely acknowledged his wife Dolores, who towered over him by several inches. At five foot eleven, Dolores loomed over most men. Her short cropped hair was dull brown, intertwined with heavy streaks of gray. She was, according to Thomas Drake, a homely bean pole who had managed to snare him as her husband.

"We have to talk, Thom. I have something to tell you."

"Can't you see that I'm busy? Fucking income tax. Just get me a beer and leave me alone." He ran his hand across his forehead, forcing back strands of oily black hair. It had been a week since he last bathed.

"Thom, I know that we are too old to start over. Sonya's seventeen and Brenda's sixteen, and it won't be long before they are off and on their own."

Thom stared down at the paperwork and deliberately ignored her. Dolores, used to his rude behavior, took a deep breath and made an announcement. "Now is as good of a time as any to tell you, Thom, that I am pregnant. I'm forty seven years old, and I'm going to have a baby."

She closed her eyes and waited for a reaction. But he didn't budge. The can of beer she expected him to throw was still in his hand. So she continued, "I'll get a job working swing shift at the garment factory. That should help cover the extra expenses."

Still ignoring her, he moved his finger across to the itemized deductions. There weren't enough to offset any earnings. If only he could find a loophole…Frustrated, Thom looked up at her and hollered, "Are you still here? I told you, I'm busy!"

"I'm filling out an application at the garment factory tomorrow, Thom. A neighbor said she'd put in a good word for me with the lead lady. She said I'm almost a shoo-in for the swing shift."

As if someone had just shaken him, his senses suddenly came alive. "What did you just say? Are you finally getting a real job? Well, it's about time! That bullshit ironing you do for the rich snobs ain't worth a rat's ass!"

"I'm not giving up my customers, Thom. I'll iron during the day and work at night. As for supper, the girls are old enough to help out, if that's all right with you."

Now that was worth hearing. He pushed the chair away from the kitchen table and lit up a cigarette. He grinned, exposing the large gap between his yellow stained teeth. Stroking the stubble of unshaven whiskers, he fell into his own world. *With two incomes* plus the dough she pulls in for ironing, I might taste a bit of the good life. Might even buy me a fancy convertible car or maybe I'll take that vacation to Miami I've always dreamed about. Yeah, get away from this female hellhole and Purvis, Alabami.*

Drake's fantasy was short-lived. Between all the could-have-beens was the one thing that would prevent him from acquiring any one of those luxuries. He choked on his words as reality sank in and he screamed, "BABY? Jesus Christ! Are you fucking pregnant again?"

There was no need for Dolores to repeat herself. Besides, she had more important things to tend to. Like saving the portrait of their children that hung on the kitchen wall. Dripping wet, it was close to ruin from the beer their father had just hurled at it.

◇ ◇ ◇

Some people marry for love. Others marry for companionship. But the Drakes should never have married at all. From the first day they met, their agendas were worlds apart. She was a lonely woman who wanted a partner and he was a clever opportunist.

In June of '32, thirty-year-old Dolores Dobson was rapidly approaching the inevitable title of spinster. Because of her height, few men asked her out on a first date and those who did never asked her out on a second. In their little black books they described her as naive and inexperienced. Some went as far as classifying her as an introvert. That's how Dolores would have been remembered, had she not met Thom Drake.

Sitting at the counter of the town's all-night diner, Dolores had been reading the newspaper. No one paid attention to her because she wasn't the type of woman who attracted interest. But when a dark-haired man bumped into her, suddenly everyone sat up and took notice.

"Oh, sorry I spilled your coffee, ma'am. Can I buy you another?"

Dolores had risen from her seat. She kept her head down and mumbled, "I'm fine. No, thanks. I was about to leave anyway."

"Not so fast," he said, attempting to stall her. "My name is Thom Drake. You've probably heard of me."

"No. I don't think so."

Ah, fresh meat, he thought.

"Please sit down, ma'am. And don't leave until I get to know you. I promise I won't bite. Well, not right away."

Dolores shyly stammered, "Okay, I'll have another cup."

"Well, that's a start. Have you lived here long?" He was staring up at her, noticing her stature. *Never had an Amazon before, but there's always a first time,* he thought.

"No, I just moved here from Atlanta," she answered.

"Oh, yeah? Good city, Atlanta. Been there myself on business, a dozen times or so. Usually, though, my company sends me to New York. Now that's what I call a big city! That's where all the bigwigs go."

That was the first of many fabrications to come. Thom Drake had never been beyond the outskirts of Purvis; and nor had he ever held a job that included travel. However, anyone who knew Thom Drake also knew that lying was second nature to him. But the timid woman sitting beside Drake didn't know him and was utterly impressed with his tales of travel.

"So now that I've bought you a cup of coffee, you gonna tell me your name or what?"

"I'm Dolores Dobson," she answered bashfully.

"Is that miss or missus?" He leaned in front of her, tilted his head, and added, "Well?"

She whispered, "It's miss. I'm not married."

"Okay. Now we're getting somewhere," he said as he rubbed his hands together. "If you don't mind me saying, Dolores, you're a real smart-looking female. Tall and thin, just the way I like 'em. And you're real soft-spoken. I like that, too, in a broad. I mean…woman. I get the feeling a gal like you could bring out the best in a man like me!" Again, he spewed a mouthful of lies, and she had no reason to doubt him.

"Do you like the movies, Dolores?"

"Yes, but it's been a long time since I went to one."

"There's a double feature playing at the Regent. A couple of Marx Brothers' flicks back-to-back. The first starts in fifteen minutes. Care to join me?"

"Oh, I don't know if I should. We've just met," she said coyly.

"No problem there. We'll go Dutch treat. You pay your way and I'll pay mine."

Drake's persona was cool. He tempted her while seeing to it that no strings were attached. He was a real piece of work.

"Ummmm," she paused long enough to get a good look at him. His dark hair was slicked back with pomade. He wasn't unattractive—but he was no prize either. He stood several inches shorter than her and had a gap-tooth smile that was tarnished from years of nicotine. Nevertheless, he was kind enough to ask her out.

"I don't see why not. Yes, I would like to go to the movies with you." She took a final sip of her coffee and added, "Okay, I'm ready."

"Now you're talking!"

Thom threw a dime on the counter and headed out the door. When Dolores raced to catch up to him, heads in the diner turned. But no one said a word. The waitress who was holding the metal coffeepot in midair, appealed to the house full of customers, "Someone should tell her that he's nothing but a lying, lowlife bum. C'mon, folks! Someone have the good manners to tell her."

"She'll find out soon enough. Eventually, everyone does," Sheriff Pete Cornell said. Then he chuckled, "Hey, did you hear the one about Thom Drake, the businessman?"

"Yeah, and he's been to the East coast. What? A dozen times?" The cook giggled along with Pete, until all of the diners joined in a chorus of neighborly laughter.

The waitress, who was the only one who showed concern, had been right on target. Someone should have told Dolores. Everyone else had assumed she would see right through Drake, at least by the intermission. But everyone was dead wrong. By the end of the second movie, Thom, who suggested they go for a drive in his pickup truck, was about to cross over the line of decency.

"Come on. It's still early and I'd like to get to know you better," he cajoled.

"I really don't think I should. The people I rent a room from tend to worry about me," she replied.

"I'd say a mature woman has the right to come and go as she pleases." He opened the truck door for her and coaxed, "Get in."

Dolores slid onto the seat, modestly clutching the folds of her wraparound skirt. Regardless, the skirt pulled apart, exposing her legs covered in translucent nylon stockings. Although Thom pretended not to notice, the rising bulge in his pants proved otherwise.

"Okay, Miss Dobson, where should we go on this god-awful hot night?" He kept the engine running but waited for her reply before shifting into gear.

"Anywhere. I'm just happy to have some company tonight. It's my birthday and I just turned thirty." She thought she'd be afraid to say it, but it wasn't so bad after all. Her chance meeting with Thom Drake changed all that. She wasn't spending her birthday alone in a rented room.

"Thirty, huh! I turned the big three-oh last year. Had a party with my friends in New Orleans. Good time in Orleans. Well, happy birthday, Dolores Dobson. We'll have to celebrate. And I've got just the thing in the back of my truck. Have you ever tried pure grain whiskey?"

"Never," she laughed as she hummed along with the tune on the radio. "I've never tasted whiskey before."

"Well, there's no better time than the present." Thom slammed on the brakes, causing the truck to skid into the dirt shoulder. The ground was drier than usual and a spiraling cloud of dust blew in through the open windows. Dolores coughed to clear her lungs. Thom, who had already exited the cab, was rummaging through junk in the bed of the truck. Rooting among a bevy of empty glass bottles, he cheerfully yelled, "Found it!"

When Thom returned, he was holding an unmarked quart bottle of pale liquid. He unscrewed the top, and, like a wine connoisseur, he smelled the distinctive aroma. It was well-aged and pure.

"I got this from a friend of mine. You won't find better hooch anywhere." He lifted it to his lips, but before he took a drink, he handed it to her. "Hey, it's your birthday. You take the first swig."

Gripping the bottle with both hands, she hesitated before drizzling a few drops onto her tongue. Thom, using his index finger, pushed the bottle upward. Her mouth became flooded with the biting liquid.

"Swallow it fast. Just like this." He bent his head back and drank it like water. Unwillingly, she swallowed the fiery potion, gagging as it burned its way down her gullet.

"That wasn't so bad, was it?"

The caustic substance had gradually dissipated. "No, I guess not, but I don't want anymore. Anyway, I think it's time for me to go home," she said.

Dolores was unused to alcohol, and Thom's moonshine suddenly made her edgy. She whipped her head around and saw that the lights of Purvis barely crested the horizon. Her mind ran rampant. *I don't remember driving this far. Where are the other cars? I don't recall passing any.* "Thom, I really want to go home now," she said emphatically.

"Okay, right after I make a toast. Here's to you, pretty lady. To long, tall Dolores Dobson, the woman who made me believe in love at first sight. The woman I can see myself spending the rest of my days with. Salute!" He belched to remove the trapped air bubbles before chugging another swallow of the hooch.

Love at first sight? It can't be. Suddenly she forgot about the desolate road. No longer anxious to go home, she eased back and relaxed. "I like you, too, Thom. I like you very much."

"You know, Dolores, I feel like I could tell you anything. I'm about to share my biggest secret with you. But only if you swear not to tell anyone."

"Not to worry. I can keep a secret. Besides, even if I wanted to tell someone, I don't know anyone around these parts."

"Okay, then, here goes. I've been working on an invention in my folks' old shed. It's a high-powered gadget that's gonna make me the richest man in Alabama. Maybe in the whole U.S. of A.!"

"You're an inventor? Like Thomas Edison?"

"You might say so. On my next trip to New York City, I'm meeting with the big boys. They want me to demonstrate my…"

Chomping at the bit, she reaffirmed, "Thom, you can trust me, I promise."

"Being it's confidential and all, it's probably not in your best interest to know too much. But if you and I were to end up together, it would be my duty to tell you everything."

Twice in one night Thom hinted at a future with her. And to a woman who wanted nothing more than a mate, she savored the thought.

"Dolores, I'm growing fonder of you by the minute." He slid closer to her and casually brushed the side of her face where her long dark hair shaded her eye. He moved the fallen mane behind her ear. "There. I can see you better now."

He ran his finger down the side of her face, her neck, and onto her shoulder and whispered, "I want to see you tomorrow, and the day after that, and the day after that. Tell me you'll go out with me again. You can't let a man like me down, Dolores."

"Of course, I'll go out with you. Every time you ask, I'll say yes."

"Good," he said as he dropped his hand to the top of her thigh. She was confused. No man had ever touched her there. Somehow his touch unleashed a thousand butterflies that she could feel fluttering throughout her body. She yearned to kiss him. But when she leaned forward to taste his lips, he cleverly maneuvered his hand up under her skirt.

"Thom, what are you doing?" She squirmed to free herself but was pinned against the truck door. The butterflies vanished into a sea of terror. She was not ready for this. Not this way. "Please, Thom, get off me! I'm still a virgin. Oh, God, NO! Please, stop."

A chance to deflower a maiden only excited him more. Half-crazed, he jammed three calloused fingers deep inside her. She struggled to escape, but his hands painfully clutched her hair. He pulled her down onto the seat and brutally tore off her underwear.

"Noooooooooo!" She screamed, but to no avail. She was miles from the nearest human. Only the nocturnal animals heard her terrified pleas; they fled to escape the frightening sounds.

"Shut up, Dolores and just go with it. This is the way two people make love. It'll be over soon. Just go with it!" He covered her mouth, holding her down. With his other hand he unzipped his pants and freed his engorged penis.

He didn't care if it was her first time. All he cared about was satisfying his own needs. He lifted himself up and slammed up against her. But the virginal membrane prohibited him from entering.

Frustrated, he yelled "Fuck," and tried again to shove his penis into her. Still, it wouldn't pass. The entrance was shielded with membrane.

"Goddamn it. I'm going to fuck you if it's the last thing I do."

Rather than torture himself, he thrust his fingers back into her orifice. Over and over he jammed them into her until his hand was covered with blood. Dolores was beyond the reality of pain. She was delirious, nearly unconscious. But Thom Drake wasn't concerned. He grabbed his penis and, with his entire body weight, he thrust himself into her. Finally, he penetrated her hymen. She was no longer a virgin when he collapsed onto her lanky body.

"Here, use this to clean yourself up." He handed her the shredded underwear that he first used to wipe himself.

"So, Dolores, what do you think of making love? I thought it was pretty good myself. Once I broke through that steel door of yours."

She didn't know how to respond to him, as she dabbed her swollen vulva. She never imagined it would be like this. Then again, no one had ever told her what to expect. So when Thom Drake told her he had just made love to her, she believed him.

"It was all right, I guess. It hurt much more than I ever thought it would."

"It won't hurt as much next time. Here. Take another drink. A good buzz will make you feel better."

She grabbed the bottle and took a large gulp. *Happy birthday to me,* she thought.

"Well, let's get you home, Dolores. We wouldn't want your landlords to send the search dogs out."

Four months later Sheriff Pete was waiting in his office for Thom Drake. He had been compressing tobacco into his pipe in a slow, methodical manner, and the scent of sandalwood and blackberries filled the room when Thom traipsed in.

"What's this all about, Pete? I got better things to do than waste time talking with you."

Striking a match, Sheriff Pete lit the pipe and dragged the sweet smoke into his mouth. He was direct and unsympathetic when he said, "You're going to marry her, Thom. You got her pregnant and by God, if I have to put a gun to your head, you're going to marry her."

"You can't force me, Pete, no matter what you say."

"Oh, yeah? Well, how do you feel about doing time for rape?"

"You've got no proof, Sheriff."

"Then I'll make proof. We both know, hell, the whole town knows, that you did this to her. This is one time you can't up and walk out. She's a decent woman, Thom. If you want to stay in Purvis, then you've got to make good by her. If you don't, then I'll make the rape charge stick. That's a guarantee."

Sheriff Pete had a forceful way of getting his point across. The following week Thom Drake, inebriated as usual, asked Dolores Dobson to marry him. And she readily accepted.

✧ ✧ ✧

"God, can't you shut her up?" Thom yelled to his wife of eight months. "All that kid does is cry. Man, she's driving me crazy."

"Thom, what's wrong? Are you upset because the shed burned down? Is it about that invention you told me about? Was it damaged in the fire? You can always build it again. I have confidence in you," she said compassionately.

"What do you know? You can't see the forest for the trees, can you?" He laughed until he spit beer from the gap between his two front teeth. "It was a still, you dumb ass. An old still that funneled the best hooch I ever made. As I recall, you had that hooch one night. The same night you got knocked up with her."

"A still, Thom? Isn't that illegal?"

"For God's sake, woman. Come into the real world and stop being so naive."

"I'm not naive, Thom. So, it was a still! It doesn't matter, because you were the one who built it. That's good enough for me."

"Jesus Christ. Do I have to spell it out for you? Anybody can tell you anything and you believe them. Do you REALLY want to know something of interest, Dolores?"

"Is it going to be the truth?"

"You bet it will be the truth."

"Okay, I'm listening. What do you want to tell me?"

"The truth is, I've never made love to you. Not once. To be honest, if it wasn't for Pete Cornell, I wouldn't be here today. Bottom line, you're not my type. Never have been and never will. But I wasn't about to do time for no broad. So here I am, married with a goddamn kid. And I don't like it one bit."

He stormed out of the house leaving her with the cold hard facts. Holding her infant girl, she grabbed onto the rocker behind her before collapsing into it. She finally understood. Nothing in her life was real—except for the baby girl she held in her arms—and the baby girl she didn't yet know she was carrying.

That was the Drakes' first year of marriage. As bad as it was, it never improved over the next sixteen. It only got worse.

✧ ✧ ✧

"Fuck the goddamn taxes. I can't think straight anymore. You're fucking pregnant again just as the girls are almost grown and out of here. Shit. I'm too old to start over."

"I'm not happy either. Not at my age. It just happened, Thom." Gritting her teeth, she repeated, "It just happened."

"Just happened, my ass." He peered out a cracked window and for a brief moment he quietly watched a blanket of late spring fog from a nearby swamp. It funneled into the room with a foul, musty smell, but Thom didn't detect the odor. "So whose is it anyway, Dolores? You sure as hell haven't slept in my bed since the second brat was born!"

"You know it's yours, Thom. Drunk as you were, I know you remember. You raped me. Same as you did seventeen years ago."

"Is that a fact? Well then, abort the piece of shit. I don't want it."

"As tempting as that may be, I won't have an abortion."

"Fuck you," he grumbled, moving within an inch of her face. She stepped back, but he closed in on her and flung a clenched fist into her stomach. "See if that helps," he yelled as he slammed the screen door behind him.

Dolores buckled over from the impact. It was a violent strike, although not enough to cause her to miscarry. Miraculously, the two-month-old fetus remained intact.

Over the next seven months, Dolores worked nearly every waking hour. If she wasn't sewing at the garment factory, she was in the basement ironing clothes for a nickel a piece, or tending house to Thom's ever-growing expectations. But she never complained, not even when her swollen feet mushroomed over her black-and-white oxford shoes.

"Mother, please let Brenda and me help you," seventeen-year-old Sonya pleaded. "You're too far along to be doing all this ironing. He's asleep right now. He'll never know."

"Absolutely not! He's been in a rage all morning. You know what happened the last time you pitched in." Dolores gently touched the greenish purple bruise on Sonya's left arm. After two weeks it still harbored the imprints of her father's hand where he grabbed her before throwing her across the room. Just because she helped the "goddamn pregnant bitch."

"I want you girls to go to church and then out to the movies. Here's fifty cents," she whispered, as she extracted a lint-covered coin from her sweater pocket.

"We shouldn't leave you alone with him. He's already two sheets to the wind," Brenda said, mimicking the term she picked up from her father.

"You don't need to worry about me. I can take care of myself, as long as I stay out of his way. Now get out of here before he wakes up." She kissed each girl on the forehead and added, "I want you to have a good time. Love you both."

With the girls out of harm's way, Dolores could breathe easier. In the past she had been Thom's only target, but as the girls grew into young women (and as tall as their mother), he began tormenting them as well.

For the next hour Dolores worked on her customers' orders while Thom, who had passed out from a late-morning pint of rye, was asleep upstairs. His snores echoed down the basement stairwell until the sound abruptly ceased. It was quiet, almost too quiet. *Like the calm before the storm,* she thought.

She looked toward the basement's ceiling and prayed that he'd sleep until she finished the last batch of ironing, an order that would pay her ninety-five cents, plus a small gratuity that she'd secretly keep for the girls. Halfway through the work order, Dolores heard rustling from above. *God, he's awake.*

From the top of the stairs he yelled, "Where are you, woman? Get up here and fix me some food."

Dolores unplugged the iron and stashed it on a shelf for safekeeping. Bruises eventually fade, but burns would not. Trudging up the stairs, she mentally prepared herself for what was about to transpire.

"Get up here, I said!" He yelled down the stairwell before he quickly disappeared.

Dolores wasn't sure where Thom had gone as she moved from the last basement step into the kitchen. Standing just beyond her view, he held a cast-iron frying pan over her head, and in a drunken rage he slammed the pan across the side of her face. The force of the assault knocked her off her feet and onto the floor. She was dazed and groggy, but conscious nonetheless.

"Get up, bitch," he yelled.

Dolores didn't dare move. Nor did the baby inside her. Fear coursing through her blood terrified the unborn infant.

Thom stood over her, impatiently waiting for her to fight back. When she didn't, he became enraged. "Get the fuck up, bitch, or live to regret it."

When she didn't move, he inflicted a forceful kick into her womb. Dolores wailed out loud as she rolled away; she curled around her abdomen, using her arms and legs to protect her baby. "I said get up, bitch, or you'll be sorry!" He kicked her again. The rye whisky had blurred his vision; although he thought his aim was true, his kicks missed the baby and landed on her arms and legs. He laughed hysterically and shouted, "That ought to kill the bastard. Yep, that just ought to do it!" He snorted, "Guess we won't need to worry about another mouth to feed."

Thom stormed out and headed to the corner tavern, confident that he had destroyed the unborn child. He figured she'd call the hospital, where they'd dispose of the "piece of shit." A term he'd have to refrain from using until after Sheriff Pete went through his usual litany of questions.

Dripping with sweat, Thom sat down at the bar and acknowledged no one. But the bartender, who detected a strong odor of rye, poured Thom a double shot of the same.

Thom dug into his pants and pulled out three crumpled one dollar bills and thirty cents in change. He placed the money on the bar and said to the bartender, "Just keep the drinks coming until this runs out."

As he waited for the inevitable talk with Sheriff Pete, he thought about what he would say to maintain his innocence. *Let's see. What should I tell Pete Cornell when he comes a-lookin' for me? Hmmm. I'll say we were in a fight. A typical marriage spat. Then out of the blue she came after me with a knife. No, on second thoughts, I'll say she grabbed my double-barrel shotgun. Yeah, Sheriff, she pointed it right between my eyes and threatened to blow my fucking head off. So, Sheriff, what else could I do? I had to protect myself, so I struggled to get the gun away from her. She's a strong woman, Sheriff. Next thing I knew, she fell to the floor. It's a shame she lost the kid, Sheriff.*

He chortled out loud. He had his story down pat. Now he'd just have to sell it to Sheriff Pete.

Thom pounded his fist on the bar to get the bartender's attention. "Hey, old man. Pour me another. I don't have all day!"

✧ ✧ ✧

Unable to stand on her own, Dolores slid across the floor and into the kitchen pantry. As she dragged herself along, she left a sticky trail of blood from the gash on the side of her face and the injuries to her legs and arms.

Dolores rested among the onions, potatoes, and jars of berry jam. There was a strange sort of solace in the dark room. It was only temporary. She knew that Thom would return drunker than when he left.

Using the shelves as support, she dragged herself up inch by inch. Finally erect, she understood the magnitude of the injuries to her left leg. Quivering from welts and broken blood vessels, it rendered little, if any, support.

Dolores limped over and opened the freezer. With her fingernails she scraped a handful of ice crystals and applied them to her swollen face. At first touch, they melted. She scratched another handful and pressed it against the wounds to her leg. Again, the ice turned to water before it provided any relief. "I've got to get away from him. For the baby, for the girls, and for me," she whimpered.

Dolores went into the bathroom and propped herself up against the bathtub wall. With a wad of cotton, she patted iodine to the facial cut. The antiseptic burned on contact. Then she poured the rest of the contents onto her left thigh. The red dye found its way into every welt, every gash. It stung while it fought the onset of infection. But Dolores paid no heed to it. Her mind was flooded with questions. *How can I...? Where can we...? What will happen if...?* Too many questions, with not a single answer. And then she heard the front door squeal open on its rusty hinges. She froze, petrified, anticipating the worse. She held her breath and covered her stomach as the bathroom door slowly opened.

"Mom?" Sonya gasped. "Oh, Mother, what did he do to you?"

"I'm all right and the baby's been moving around the last few minutes." Dolores sighed, "I'm glad you came home early. Didn't you go to the movies?"

"At church the sermon was about the hand of the devil. The minister told us that the devil works his way through the weakhearted, the nonbelievers, and the sinners. It made me think of father. How he treats you and how he's been treating Brenda and me."

Sonya soaked a washcloth in cold water. She gently placed it over her mother's swollen face. "This one's going to be hard to hide. Probably the biggest shiner you've ever had."

"If that's the worst of it, I can live with that. Now tell me why you didn't go to the movies."

"I overheard some people talking about father at church. He got fired from his job last night. I remember the last time he was fired. He broke all the dishes and when Brenda begged him to stop, he stopped just long enough to slug her in the back. I think my father is the hand of the devil."

"At this point I couldn't agree with you more. Your father has more hatred in him than any human being I've ever known." Dolores shook her head and conceded, "I should have left him years ago. But I was afraid of what would happen to us."

Sonya lowered her head onto her mother's tummy. Her long raven mane unintentionally adorned her mother's lap. "But if you left him you wouldn't have...this little angel in here." Sonya smiled, but the wrinkles on her forehead conveyed a different message. "What do we do now, Mom?"

"I'm taking you girls to the garment factory with me. While I'm working my shift, you can quilt. There are a couple of benches in the corridor near the front entrance. No one will bother you in there."

Sonya felt a rush of anxiety. "Mom, your shift doesn't end until one and the tavern closes at midnight. He'll be waiting for us when we get home, meaner and madder than ever. God only knows what he'll do."

Brenda pounded on the bathroom door, which her protective sister had locked behind her. "Sonya, let me in. I want to see my mother. Momma, tell me what's wrong."

"Everything is okay, Brenda. I want you to do exactly what I ask," she said with determination. "Are you listening, Brenda?"

"Yes," she said pressing an ear against the door.

"Quick as you can, I want you to pack your sister's and your clothes. Use the empty potato sack that's folded up in the pantry. When you're finished, empty my bottom dresser drawer. Will you do that for me, Brenda?"

"Yes, Momma. I'll do it," Brenda said as she raced into the kitchen.

"Sonya, do you understand now? We aren't coming back here. No matter where we end up tonight, I swear it won't be with Thomas Drake! Now help me with this scarf. I don't want Brenda to see me like this."

Using an old hickory stick as a cane, Dolores hobbled alongside her daughters to the garment factory. Dolores was in the third trimester of her pregnancy, so her daily journey to the garment factory was already a trial; the injuries Thom inflicted made the journey even more grueling. However, a life with Thom Drake taught her not to complain, so she never did.

"There," she said, pointing to a narrow corridor that housed two wrought iron benches with wooden inserts. She handed them the quilt and said, "Work on this as long as you can. When you tire, use it to cover yourselves. I'll be back later. I've got to punch in now."

Dolores limped past one hundred blaring sewing machines toward her own designated station. She wasn't surprised when every machine she passed suddenly idled. One by one, as her coworkers caught sight of her injuries, their feet slipped off their sewing pedals.

By the look on their faces, she knew that she appeared horrific. The scarf failed to conceal her purple jaw or the gash beneath her swollen eye. This time her wounds were far too extensive to hide. Embarrassed, Dolores quickly fed material into her sewing machine. Her machine was the first to hum. But even as the humming multiplied, she couldn't help but hear the blatant comments.

"My God, she's pregnant. Why doesn't she leave the bastard?"

"It's her own fault. Everyone knows that Thom Drake hates babies, especially his own."

"That man can do anything he wants to her and she just grins and bears it."

"If I were her, I'd get the hell out."

"Yeah, and where would she go? I hear her folks in Atlanta haven't spoken to her in years. Not since she married the SOB."

"Just glad my man doesn't beat the living daylights out of me!"

It went on and on. The gossiping made the women forget they had problems of their own. Mary's son had been recently sentenced to life imprisonment for killing a state trooper in Louisiana. Mrs. Cook, the floor superintendent, had just lost her twelve-room home after her embezzler husband was forced to turn over the deed to their house. Judith Hudson also had skeletons to hide. She had sent her thirteen-year-old daughter to spend a year or so at St. Jude's Convent in Montgomery.

"Sending her to a convent was a decision we made to develop her character; it's like a finishing school. The Sisters will teach her poise and grace. It's quite the rage these days," Judith asserted. When her daughter returned home roughly nine months later, no one dared to question the timing.

In Purvis, stories like these were commonplace. However, no one scoffed at the members of the pinochle or bridge clubs. On the other hand, those who weren't part of the inner circle became fair game for ridicule. Such was the case with Dolores Drake.

During the first coffee break, Dolores swallowed her pride and approached a table of coworkers who were whispering among themselves. Dolores knew she was the topic of their conversation, but she was becoming desperate. She had less than six hours to find a place to live before her shift ended.

Dolores cleared her throat to get their attention, but it wasn't necessary. They had ceased talking to gawk at the hideous bruises on her face.

"Ladies, I know we don't speak very often, but I'm asking for your assistance. I need to rent a room starting tonight. It doesn't need to be much and I'd pay whatever you ask. It's for me and my girls, Sonya and Brenda. You might have noticed them in the corridor."

Sporting her beauty salon hairdo, Judith Hudson spoke. "So you're finally leaving the bastard. It's about time!"

"Does that mean you might have a room to let?" Dolores knew that Judith's home was twice as large as Mrs. Cook's. There would be plenty of room.

"Ah, no. I didn't mean to imply that my husband and I were interested in taking in boarders. I just was making a statement." Judith feigned a smile and turned her head in the opposite direction. Without facing Dolores, the coffee tasted much better.

"Is there anyone else who might be able to help us? I really don't want to go home tonight. The truth is I can't go home tonight. Do you understand?" Her plea was in earnest but no one offered their help, not even for one night. Still, there were seven tables of seamstresses left. Dolores moved to the second, third, and fourth tables and repeated her request to each person. Again, it was to no avail. Knowing she couldn't return to Thom and protect her children, she made one last effort to appeal to her coworkers. She stood in the middle of the room and addressed the entire group.

"I'm Dolores Drake. Most of you know me because we've worked together for the past seven months. Some of you have known me since I married my husband. So what I am about to ask is very difficult for me." She took a deep breath. "Please, would anyone rent a room for me and my teenage daughters? A bedroom, an attic, a basement—we're not particular, anything will do. Just name your price. We'll also clean your house and do the washing and ironing, if you can find it in your heart to put a roof over our heads. Please, I can't take my children home tonight."

Dolores, circling the room, humbled herself to the lowest point of her life. She had pleaded with coworkers; their only response was dead silence. She felt like a fool, realizing she had given these women exactly what they wanted: titillating entertainment that would provide weeks of something to chew on. To the gossip mongers, it just didn't get any better than this.

"I guess that's that," she conceded. "I'm sorry I interrupted your break." It was the most depressing moment of her life. Even after all the beatings from Thom Drake, this blow to her self-esteem was the worst. With no place to go but home, she was defeated.

As Dolores retreated toward the swinging doors to go back to her machine, a voice from the back of the room called out to her, "I got a house for you and yours. There's plenty of room, including a room for that baby that's coming real soon."

"What on earth? Who said that?" Judith craned her neck but was unable to identify the speaker. "Come again?" she asked.

"It's me, Mrs. Hudson. Ruthie Jackson."

The women looked past the tables of eight to a small folding table in the corner. Seated at the "Coloreds Only" table was the garment factory's sole black employee. Ruthie Jackson, small in height—no more than five feet—but obese in girth, a woman whose face was heavily scarred with pockmarks, had made her presence known.

"Whites don't live with Negroes. And you *are* a Negro," sputtered Judith.

"Yes, Mrs. Hudson. I'm as black as they come. Still, there ain't no good reason why Miss Dolores and her kin can't come live with me."

Dolores was speechless. So Judith, appointing herself as white protectorate, spoke on her behalf and without her consent.

"I'm sure that Dolores Drake and her two daughters would not be interested in living on your side of town. I can't imagine that any of us would!" Her sarcastic gibe brought about a frenzy of snickering.

"Well, I ain't asking you, Mrs. Hudson. My offer is for Miss Dolores. It's Miss Dolores that needs to do the talking. What do you say, ma'am?"

Dolores felt a thrill of apprehension from the onlookers as she limped toward Ruthie's corner of the room. In front of every woman who thrived on racial issues, she wrapped her arms around the robust woman and cried, "I say bless you, Ruthie Jackson. Bless you. It would be an honor to move into your home."

"You can't be serious, Dolores Drake! Boarding with the cleaning woman? She's a blackie, for God's sake. A blackie," Judith argued. "Stop and think about the ramifications. No decent white woman would ever dream of living in a blackie's home. And what about your children? Think, Dolores. Think before you make a foolish decision."

"Don't listen to them, Ruthie," Dolores whispered. "What you just did means more to me than anything in this world. You just saved our lives."

Ruthie smiled at Dolores while slowly nodding her head. There was an immediate alliance between them. But to the onlookers their newfound union was revolting.

Judith's belligerent mood worsened as she warned, "You'll be sorry, Dolores Drake. Just wait until our husbands hear about this. Even better, wait until Thom Drake hears about this."

The barely veiled threat meant nothing to Dolores. In a way, she had claimed her independence when she chose not to care about what others thought of her. Like the albatross tied to the Ancient Mariner, Dolores had been burdened for many years. Now she had been set free.

Dolores headed to the entryway where her daughters had been resting. She touched them gently, so as not to alarm them in their strange surroundings. "Girls, wake up. I want you to meet someone. This is Ruthie Jackson. She's the woman we will be living with."

"You pretty young ladies can call me Ruthie. What are your names?"

"I'm Sonya."

"I'm Brenda, and I'm sixteen, and my sister is seventeen," she mumbled, kneading the sleep from her eyes.

"Well, we're going to get along just fine. Yes, we are," Ruthie asserted.

Although they were old enough to understand the racial tension in Purvis, the girls would respect any plan of their mother's. Sonya leaned closer to her mother and whispered, "Momma, is this safe?"

"I know what you are thinking. You don't have to worry. It's me they'll blame for this. By this time tomorrow everyone in town will know that I accepted her invitation. But I promise you, no one will ever blame you girls. Now, let's get going."

The long walk to Ruthie's was tiring for Dolores. Her advanced state of pregnancy made it difficult for her to walk any distance, and in addition her injured leg buckled every few steps. The cane, which had supported her before, had become useless.

Ruthie moved to Dolores's side. "It's good you being a tall one. Rest your hand on my shoulder. I'll be your crutch. You girls walk up ahead of your ma and me. We're gonna talk some."

"Thank you." Dolores sighed, as she shifted her weight onto Ruthie.

"Is that better, Miss Dolores?"

"Yes, but if I become too much of a burden, I'll go back to the cane."

"Won't need to. I'm as wide as you are tall. It's a good balance," she chuckled.

"Ruthie, I have to ask you. Why did you do this for us? You've opened yourself up for hatred and scorn just as much as I have. Tell me, why did you do it?"

"Couple of reasons. First off, I've been alone for too many years. The house needs some life brought back into it. You know, the sweet sound of children's laughter. Not to mention the innocent cries of a newborn baby. Truth is, I could use the company…the company of a good friend. We could become good friends, you and me."

"I feel as though we're already friends. Yet, I've hardly ever spoken to you, Ruthie, just a 'hello,' or a 'good night,' or an occasional 'thank you' for cleaning up my station area."

"That's more than any of those old biddies ever said. Funny thing, I don't think they ever noticed me before this evening."

"So what's the second reason you made us an offer?"

"Well," she laughed. "Did you see the look on their faces? I think half of them spit out their coffee, while the other half gagged on their doughnuts. Now that's what I call great entertainment."

"I bet Judith couldn't wait to get home and tell her husband," Dolores said.

"Yep! The town will be a-buzzin' in the morning," Ruthie agreed.

There was a lull in the conversation as they both reflected on the evening's events. They knew it wouldn't be the last time they heard about it. For now, though, they could forget about the evening.

"Ruthie, I was wondering. Have you ever been married?"

"No, ma'am. Can't say I ever got asked either. I'm fifty-eight and it don't look like I ever will." Her giggle was pure and harmonious and invited more questions.

"Well, then can I ask you how you came to own a home? We, Thom and I that is, could never afford one of our own. We've always rented."

"The house I live in used to belong to the Jessups back in the 1850s. My granddaddy and grandma, Honus and Julene Jackson, had been sold to the Jessups. But the Jessups, good decent people, never treated them like slaves. Even went so far as to build a house out back for my kin. That's where my momma was born."

"Do you have two houses?"

"Not anymore. A few years back a tornado ate that house for dinner. Guess it wasn't hungry enough for the main one," she laughed. "Anyway, after the war President Lincoln said that all the black folk, including my kin, were free to go off on their own."

"They must have been happy to taste freedom."

"No, not one bit. When you already feel free, like they did in that little house of theirs, then there's no point in venturing out into the unknown. So Granddaddy kept the gardens and did the house fixin' and Grandma went right on cookin' and cleanin'. Pretty much everything stayed the same, 'cept for one difference. Mr. Jessup insisted on paying my kin a fair wage."

"That's impressive, considering the social issues back then."

"It don't matter if it was back then or right now. Nothing's changed much. I'd say you proved that today, Miss Dolores."

"Yes, some people still tend to wear their prejudices on their sleeves."

"You can say that again. Anyway, Mr. Jessup died shortly after the war. They say he was shot in a hunting accident. No one knows for sure. Some said he got what was coming to him."

"Do you think someone deliberately shot him?"

"Like I said, no one knows for sure. Right after he passed, the missus hired a city lawyer from the North. She said if anything should happen to her, she wanted her house, land, silver, and gold pieces to be willed to Mr. and Mrs. Honus Jackson. One week after the will was drawn up, Mrs. Jessup joined her husband. Some people said her heart just gave out. Others said she put a tad of arsenic in her jasmine tea. Either way, my grandfolks inherited the whole kit and caboodle."

"I don't think I've ever heard of white people doing that for blacks, at least not around these parts."

"No, and you can bet you won't be hearing that again, *especially* around these parts."

If not for the stories Ruthie shared with her, Dolores would have never made it as far as she had. Her body was tired and about to give out when she asked, "Is it much farther? It feels as though the baby is doing somersaults."

"It's just up the hill, Miss Dolores. A few hundred feet or so."

"Please, Ruthie, keep talking. What happened next? I'm all ears."

"Well, it didn't make folks around here too happy, colored people owning land and a two-story home. But it was far enough outside of town that nobody raised a ruckus. At least they didn't try to force them out."

"So how did you come to inherit it?"

"Granddaddy used the same northern lawyer and willed it to my momma. Momma never had a husband, so when her time came she willed it to me."

"But, Ruthie, why on earth do you work at the garment factory? Scrubbing bathrooms and picking up scraps from women who deliberately throw them down just to see you bend. You don't need the money, why do you work at that awful place?"

"If people 'round here knew all that I own, I think they'd try real hard to take it away. Better that they think I need their copper pennies."

Ruthie stopped and cautioned, "Careful when you cross the tracks. The railroad ties are old and slivered. No one's paying to fix them anymore. No need. Haven't seen a train come through the east side in some twenty years."

They passed one shack after another, dwellings that were one quarter the size of the Drakes' small house. But the manicured yards told of pride in ownership. This was a family neighborhood, right down to the old tire swings hanging from the trees, to the lingering aroma of southern fried chicken.

"That's it," Ruthie pointed. "At the end of the dirt road."

By any standard, the house was enormous. However, it appeared run-down. Most of the windows were covered with weathered wooden panels; the place looked as though a tropical storm could have flattened it with one blow. That is what Ruthie wanted the white folks to think because it was all a facade.

"Come inside," Ruthie said, welcoming her new boarders. They followed her lead, but stopped short of entering the living room. They were in awe of what they saw. Tiffany lamps shed a soft light on the room, natural cane furniture with billowy cushions welcomed visitors, and braided rugs decorated the flawless hardwood floor. In the corners of the room stood matching curio cabinets that showcased exquisite porcelain figurines. It was an interior decorator's dream.

"Miss Dolores, sit down and put your feet up. I'm going to show the girls where the kitchen is. I'll be right back."

Ruthie escorted them to an oversized kitchen where a pine table for twelve sat in the center of the room. "I want you girls to feel at home here. You don't have to ask for anything. If you want something to eat, you'll always find good pickin's in the fridge. I keep it stocked for the neighborhood young'uns who come by nearly every day."

She pointed around the corner to a second staircase. "You girls go upstairs and pick the bedrooms you want. I usually sleep in the one downstairs, but I'm gonna move your momma in there. No need for her to climb those stairs in her condition."

"Where are you going to sleep, Ruthie?"

"For now I'm going to rest on the couch until your momma has that baby of hers."

The girls started up the dark staircase but turned back when they heard their mother scream out.

"Sonya, Brenda, Ruthie, please help me!"

They ran to her side and found her squatting down. Her water had broken and spilled onto the immaculate hardwood floor. Ruthie slipped off Dolores's underwear and acting as midwife checked her progress. The baby's head had already crowned.

"Your baby's coming, Miss Dolores. Sonya, hand me the comforter draped across the ottoman." As she placed the comforter under Dolores, she instructed, "Push now, Miss D. This baby ain't waiting another minute."

Dolores's daughters supported her arms while she forced first the baby's head, then his body out. The pain of childbirth made her forget about the pain in her leg and face. But the pain of labor would also be forgotten the moment Ruthie placed the baby boy on his mother's hollowed stomach.

Deftly Ruthie cut the umbilical cord before using a swab to clear the baby's nostrils, ears, and mouth. It was apparent she had helped many infants into the world.

"Ruthie, I'm so grateful to you that I want you to name him."

"Be my privilege, Miss D." Ruthie didn't have to think long and hard. She already had a name picked out and was glad that she was asked for her opinion. "I've always been partial to the name Ethan."

"Ethan," Dolores repeated. "It's strong, yet sensitive. I like it."

Dolores took hold of her son's little fingers and noticed they were curved just like Thom's. It made her wonder what he was doing right then. And what he had thought when he had walked into the empty house.

Thom, however, never made it home that night from the tavern. He had drunk himself into oblivion waiting for Sheriff Pete. When Pete failed to show, an intoxicated Thom went banging on the sheriff's door.

"I got to tell ya, Sheriff. We were in a fight. She fuckin' lost the…that's all I know." It was a shortened version of his alibi. Thom slurred so heavily, Pete couldn't understand one syllable. It merely sounded like one long grunt.

"I don't know why you woke me up, Thom Drake, but it's going to cost you a night behind bars."

Pulling Thom's arm up behind him, Pete forced him across the street to the small local jail. He opened up one of the two cells and pushed Thom into it. "Sober up and I'll see you tomorrow. Maybe then I'll understand what you were jabbering about."

four

DAVID AND KAREN

California, 1950

David Stratton parked his black Chevy convertible under a tree at the far end of the Bachman Aerospace Industries parking lot. It provided his wife Karen shade, as well as keeping anyone from noticing that he had brought her with him to a job interview. It wasn't that it was wrong. It was just that he knew it wasn't appropriate.

"I'll be back as soon as I can, babes. If it gets too hot, pull the top up. In your condition I'd hate for you to get sick out here," he said with concern.

"I'll be just fine," she said reassuringly. "I brought a package of saltines just in case. Besides, I'm only a month late; I doubt that I'll get morning sickness this soon. Now get going, honey. I don't want you to be late for your first interview."

"Nevertheless, roll it up if it gets too hot," the doting husband said.

David raced across the lot that was filled with American-made cars and pushed the outside intercom. It buzzed continuously until a receptionist finally answered.

"Your name please?"

"David Stratton. I have an appointment with…" He never finished his sentence. The door had been pushed open from the inside by a man in his late fifties clad in a bright yellow golf shirt and white slacks. The man was about five foot five, small-boned, and thin as a rail. David, who was six foot one, thought it was odd that security would be represented by someone with such a small physique.

"Sorry about my attire. I was hoping to play golf this afternoon. Do you play?"

"Yes, when I get the chance. Sir, could you direct me to the reception area? I have an appointment with Mr. Bachman the CEO, and I'm afraid I'm a bit late."

"You're not late, David. You're right on time. Come on. Let me take you to my office."

Did he say my office? Close your mouth David, he thought.

"You're Mr. Bachman?" David could feel the blood rushing to his face, certain it had turned beet red.

"Yes, I am Theo Bachman, David," he said, scurrying ahead.

The hallway leading to the president's office had several smaller offices on both sides. Most were occupied with men in suits who were too busy grinding numbers on their adding machines to acknowledge the passing visitor.

"Here we are, David," Theo said as he unlocked the glass-beveled doors to his office.

David took a quick glance around the room. It was completely unlike his father's austere work environment. The room contained a black lacquer bar, two sofas, a conference table for twelve, and an oversized blond desk that appeared enormous for a man of Bachman's size; the office was a grandiose place to conduct business.

"I was going to make myself a Bloody Mary. Care to join me?" Theo was behind the bar dropping celery stalks into two glasses. David wasn't quite sure how to respond. He didn't want to be a spoilsport and say no. On the other hand, he did not want to give the impression that he thought alcohol before noon was acceptable.

Wondering if his character was being tested, David gambled when he replied, "Ah, sure. If you are having one, I will too."

"Good. Grab a seat, David. Oftentimes when it's a one-on-one meeting, I prefer to do business sitting at the bar."

David stirred the drink with the celery stalk and said, "You have a nice view from up here." Then he noticed that the view also included a bird's-eye view of the parking lot and his wife below.

"Yes, I do. It gives me a heads up on who is coming and going."

David cleared his throat, hoping he hadn't seen that Karen was sitting in the car waiting for him.

"So tell me about yourself, David. I hear you're a newlywed."

"Six weeks and four days, sir."

Amused by David's candid answer, he chuckled, "Still counting the days, huh?" before he added, "Congratulations."

"Thank you, sir."

Theo went behind the bar and filled a glass with water. "Are you still working on that Mary or would you like some water?"

Other than chewing on the celery stick, David hadn't taken one sip of the alcoholic beverage. When given the choice, he quickly opted for water. "Water would be great, sir."

"David, you must know that the reason you are here is because of my good friend Charles Tate. We were college roommates way back when. Tate called me a few months ago and spoke very highly of you. And over the years I've come to value his opinion on up-and-comers. Truth is, he's better than any headhunter you have to pay top dollar for."

"Professor Tate is a favorite instructor around campus. The lecture hall is always filled to capacity whenever he is the keynote speaker."

"Yes, Tate's a good man. Now let's get back to you. I understand that you held onto a 4.0 GPA for four years at Ohio State, graduating summa cum laude, and prior to that you were here in Long Beach at St. Joseph's Parochial School. I heard you played some mean football, even had a couple of opportunities to go pro. I'm a bit surprised that you didn't sign. Offers like those don't come every day."

"Football is a sport just like any other. You ride high for a while, surviving the aches and pains. Then eventually you grow older and your body doesn't mend like it did before. The next thing you know, you're a has-been quarterback who has lost his wide receiver. No, that's not what I want in life. I'm out to succeed on my own and I'll do whatever it takes to make that happen."

Theo folded his hands and touched his two index fingers to his lips. "I take it that succeeding on your own means you want no help from your father…Alfred Stratton?"

Hesitatingly David asked, "You know my father, sir?"

"Everyone who is anyone knows Alfred. He's wealthy, even by my standards, and he's successful in his own right. You look very much like him, but you don't have his English accent.

"Unlike my dad, I was born here. Besides, I'm only half English because my mom is Norwegian."

"Ah, Delilah," he said, as if her name had hypnotized him. "Your mother is a beautiful woman. I see a little of Delilah in you, although you certainly have Alfred's height."

"People usually tell me I favor my mom. Her blue eyes, I suppose."

Bachman appeared to have fulfilled the niceties of small talk, because he now moved on to the purpose of their meeting.

"David, you have the smarts, just like Tate said. God knows, you certainly have the genes. So let's get down to brass tacks. You are fresh out of college, a greenhorn, so to speak. Give me one good reason, other than the fact that you are the son of the business tycoon Alfred Stratton, why I should hire you."

David straightened his shoulders. He wanted to be judged on his own merits and not his father's. He looked Mr. Bachman straight in the eyes and with immense determination stated, "I'm a quick learner, sir. I realize that I am young, but I've never failed at anything that I've attempted in my life. I'm not about to do so now. You mentioned that you valued Professor Tate's opinion. I also value his opinion. If he feels that I would be an asset to your company, then more than anything I want to prove to him that he was right."

"Yes, you have the genes and you have the spirit. Wait here. I'll just be a moment."

Theo left David at the bar and went over to his desk. He hummed as he jotted down a few notes. But David wasn't paying attention.

He was looking out of the windows down at his auburn-haired wife who, only that morning, had told him she was pregnant. She looked radiant as she lay back in the convertible, savoring the salty air. He couldn't imagine that anyone so attractive could go unnoticed.

✧ ✧ ✧

It was January 10, 1946, when seventeen-year-old Karen Allen strolled into English literature for seniors at St. Joseph's Parochial High School. It was midyear and her father had been transferred to yet another naval base. This time he was stationed at Long Beach, California.

"Excuse me. The administrative clerk said I should give this to you." Karen handed her transfer papers to the elderly lay teacher, who was writing *The Merchant of Venice* across the chalkboard.

"Thank you. Ah, Karen, is it? Now let's take a look at your scholastic history. Um-hum, yes, um-hum," the woman mumbled as she read each entry.

"Class, this is Karen Allen. She just came to us from Little Creek where her father was stationed at the naval amphibious base."

"Yes, my father is a lieutenant commander in the navy. He was stationed there for a year before being assigned to Long Beach."

"Before Little Creek, I see you lived in Washington, D.C. Would you care to expound on your knowledge of other places in which you've resided? I see here that you've traveled extensively."

The teacher, who was normally apathetic, now radiated enthusiasm. The sudden transformation amused her pupils, but it didn't faze Karen. Nor did it entice her to expand on her life. Politely she responded, "Oh, I've lived in just about every state in the U.S. May I ask where you'd like me to sit?"

Openly disappointed, the instructor's dull character resurfaced. "You'll find a vacant seat next to David Stratton in the second-to-last row. Consider it yours for the remainder of the year. Now class, let's get back to Shakespeare."

As Karen passed by the rows of desks, every eye was fixed upon her. The girls, visibly hesitant to welcome her, silently critiqued her fashionable clothing. Some of the boys jokingly panted out loud. Karen, whose manners were impeccable, did not judge her audience. Instead, she offered a personable smile, which warmed her reception.

Karen hung her purse on the back of her seat and settled in. From the corner of her eye, she caught her first glimpse of David Stratton. He literally took her breath away. But Karen was the second one to become starstruck. David had already memorized everything about her. He judged her to be about five foot four; she was thin, but not too thin. Her skin was tanned a deep bronze. Her long waves of silky auburn hair glinted with natural blond highlights and swayed to the rhythm of her step. That was what he grasped from a distance. Up close, he noted even more. Her eyes were bluish-green, similar to the color of the Caribbean Sea. Her nose was petite and slightly pointed at the end, and her lips were narrow with a pleasant upward curve. When she smiled, the curve extended upward toward her high cheekbones. David captured all this in less than two minutes before a thump on his back startled him. The boy sitting behind him chuckled, "Close your mouth, idiot." Mechanically, David complied.

"Class, I want to delve deeper into *The Merchant of Venice*. Who can explain the relationship between Portia and Bassanio?"

Since this had been recent reading material, the majority of the fifty students raised their hands. David, who kept his hand down, used the distraction to introduce himself.

"Hi! I'm David Stratton," he whispered. "Welcome to St. Joe's."

"Thanks. It's beautiful here. The grounds resemble a botanical garden. I'm afraid I'll get lost in the maze."

"Have lunch with me and I'll show you around campus. It's easy once you get the hang of it."

"Sure, I'd love a tour," she whispered shyly.

The teacher slammed down the book she was holding and snapped. "Mr. Stratton, do I hear talking back there? I don't appreciate the distraction. If you don't mind, I'd like to continue. Let's see, where were we? Oh, yes. We were talking about the love that Bassanio harbored for Portia. All right, Mr. Quarterback, I'd like your take on the relationship of one of Shakespeare's favorite couples."

David was popular and only the lay teacher mocked him for being the school's star football player. She didn't believe in the game of football nor the time that was devoted to it, so she was harder on David than other students. If David had given her the opportunity, she would have awarded him a C or a D grade, but since his test scores were nearly perfect all year long, she was forced to give him an A.

David, slouching in his chair, answered without hesitation. "I'm not sure if Portia felt the same way, but for Bassanio, it was love at first sight." He lowered his head and repeated to himself, *love at first sight.*

"That is an interesting assessment, David. But you must recall the scene where Portia and her lady-in-waiting reminisce about an earlier meeting with Bassanio. Clearly, Portia had been captivated by him as well." Thinking of Karen, David could only hope.

The teacher turned to the other person who had disrupted her class and asked in a stern voice, "Miss Allen, did you study Shakespeare in any of the schools you've attended?"

Karen stood up to respond. "Yes, I've studied most of his work, including *The Merchant of Venice.*"

"Using a single word, Miss Allen, how would *you* describe their relationship?"

"I would call it destiny."

Karen glimpsed at David, captivated by his Adonis-like features. The half Englishman–half Norwegian had dark hair, intoxicating blue eyes, a tall muscular body, and perfect white teeth. He was the imaginary boy that she had always fantasized about.

"Interesting, Miss Allen. What would you say if one of Portia's other suitors had chosen the lead casket? That suitor would have had her hand before Bassanio had the chance to make his selection."

"That's my point. The others were driven by the temptation of gold and silver. Bassanio, who had the same options, was not influenced by wealth. He selected the least desirable box and consequently won Portia's hand. It just goes to show that sometimes people are just meant to be together," she said with a glimmer in her eye.

"Thank you for your unique perspective, Miss Allen. I'm not convinced that either you or Mr. Quarterback accurately captured Shakespeare's characters. Nevertheless, your points are well-taken. Class, tomorrow we will be discussing Shylock and Antonio. Be prepared for a pop quiz."

In the days and months that followed, Karen Allen's life was changed by David in ways she never thought possible. Overnight she had captured the heart of the "most popular" and "most likely to succeed" student. His popularity suddenly became her popularity. They were two young lovers who had each found their soul mate.

Shortly after Karen was crowned queen on prom night, however, the Stratton-Allen romance ran into difficulty. The young sweethearts had been granted five months of high-school bliss, but college was about to separate them. Karen had selected a local junior college where she planned to major in business administration. David, who had been scouted by five universities, selected a football scholarship from Ohio State to major in engineering. It was a choice that didn't sit well with Karen.

In July, one month after high-school graduation, David and Karen were sitting in the gazebo next to the Stratton's Olympic-size pool. Their parents, who had become good friends, were inside the house savoring after-dinner cordials. The six of them had just finished a New England clambake that Delilah Stratton had flown in for the occasion.

"Babes, you've got to pull yourself together. It's a mere four years of our lives," David said, attempting to console Karen.

"Why does it have to be so far away? You could have picked a college closer to home, but you chose Ohio State. I don't understand why you need a scholarship. Your parents can afford to send you to any school on the West coast," she argued.

"It's not about the money, babes. It's knowing that I earned it on my own. That's what I want for my life. That's what I want for our lives. I don't want success handed down to me just because I'm a Stratton."

"You still haven't answered my original question. Why did you pick Ohio State?"

"Okay, here's the truth. I've been reading about a professor at Ohio for quite some time. Not only is he a masterful teacher, but he sees the future of engineering. I would be learning from the best."

Karen buried her head into his chest and muffled her cries. "It's just that I can't bear life without you. What if you meet someone else? What if I lose you to another girl?"

"Babes! We're meant to be together for the rest of our lives. I want you to think of college as a short detour in our overall plan, and before you know it, we'll be back on track."

She could see that all her pleas were in vain. His mind had been made up and no matter how she argued with him, David was not about to change his mind.

"Let's go back inside," he said lifting her off the bench to her feet.

"I'd rather not be with our parents right now," she said wiping her tears. "I want to take a drive along the beach. Let's go to Laguna and find a secluded cove."

"What are you saying?" he asked, but he thought he knew what Karen had in mind. "We've waited this long, we should wait until we're married."

"Well, I don't want to wait anymore, David. I want to explore every inch of your body. I want to kiss places that I've only dreamed of. Then I want to feel you deep inside me, just once before you leave."

If not for the gazebo their parents might have seen Karen acting out of character. She had fallen to her knees and had wrapped her arms around David's thighs. She begged him, "Please take me to the beach and make love to me."

David lifted her to her feet. He was adamant. "Babes, there is nothing I want more than to make love to you. This is not the time or place, and I refuse to let our sexual urges overcome us. Just think of what happened to the other steadies at St. Joe's. Some of them were thrown into parenthood years before their time. That's not the kind of life I want for us. I'm going to do it right. Believe in me and it will pay off in the end." Using his index finger he wiped away the last of her tears and added, "It's going to be all right. I promise.

Now, let's go inside. My dad wants to take the six of us on a sunset cruise. He hasn't sailed all week and he's getting antsy."

Up until then, David had never demonstrated his iron will to Karen. It came as a surprise to her, since he usually gave her anything she wanted. But in those few moments Karen saw something different in David: He was a man of unwavering convictions.

Delilah called out to the senior servant, "Greta, could you give us a minute alone with our families. Pack the Black Forest torte. We'll take it with us on the *Lovely Delilah*," she said referring to their fifty-five-foot sailboat that Alfred had named after her.

Greta gave a quick nod of her head and quietly disappeared into the kitchen where she rejoined the rest of the Stratton staff. There she would remain until she heard a bell that would summon her return.

David pulled out a high-back Victorian chair for Karen; she sat down obediently, but he did not. Addressing their families, he said, "Up until seven months ago I didn't take life too seriously. Mom and Dad, you can attest to that," he laughed. "Then I met the love of my life," he said taking hold of Karen's left hand. "Mr. and Mrs. Allen, Mom and Dad, with your blessings I'd like to ask Karen to be my wife." In unison everyone gasped, including Karen, who couldn't believe her ears. "Now before all of you panic, let me emphasize that it will be a long engagement. But in the summer of '50, soon after I graduate, I plan to walk Karen down the aisle right here at St. Joseph's."

He knelt down beside Karen and as he placed an emerald-cut, one-and-a-half carat diamond on her finger he asked, "Karen, will you marry me?"

Her eyes, still red from crying, hadn't returned to their twenty-twenty vision. Her mind was equally slow to comprehend. "Did you say marry? Yes," she squealed.

"Fine decision, son!" Alfred declared and then mumbled under his breath, "It's good to see he's not letting his 'Johnson' make decisions for him."

"Alfred!" Delilah promptly admonished her husband. Normally, his fine English upbringing would have prevented him from making such a crude comment.

Quickly changing the subject, Agnes Allen turned to her daughter and said, "Let me see your ring, dear." As she studied the solitaire set in eighteen-karat gold she added, "It's a beautiful engagement ring, David. It is certainly larger than the one I received from John when I was Karen's age. But John couldn't afford such an exquisite gem back then," she said humbly. "We did all our shopping at the military store."

David smiled and then explained, "Mrs. Allen, when I was born my parents bought me some shares in Ma Bell. Over the last eighteen years those stocks split and rose and then they split and rose a few more times. Suddenly, they were worth a small fortune."

"You call that a fortune, son? I disagree. It's only a drop in the ocean compared to what the two of you will inherit after I'm gone." Alfred leaned over the table and touched his brandy snifter to Lieutenant Allen. "Know what I mean, John?"

The Lieutenant had always provided a comfortable, slightly above middle-class lifestyle for his wife and daughter; they had never wanted for anything. However, he had never before associated with anyone as wealthy as Alfred Stratton. Now his daughter was betrothed to Stratton's only son. He was pleased, very pleased. "Yes, Alfred, I know exactly what you mean!"

Delilah rang the crystal dinner bell. Greta arrived promptly from the kitchen.

"Yes, ma'am?"

"Greta, go to the wine cellar. We'd like two bottles, no, make that three bottles of Cristal. One to be opened now in the living room and the other two we'll take with us on the boat. Also, please have the appropriate champagne flutes ready for both venues."

Within minutes, the petite Swedish servant had six heirloom champagne glasses and one bottle of the golden bubbly ready for the Strattons and their guests in the living room. In the west-wing entryway she had placed the other two bottles packed in a cooler with six Waterford champagne glasses.

Delilah smiled at her husband, "Alfred, would you do the honors?"

"Yes, my love. It would be a privilege," he said respectfully.

Alfred poured each glass half-full of the champagne, but the effervescent elixir spilled over the top of each one. He joked, "We better tell Greta to bring up a few more bottles for the boat."

"Now that everyone has their drinks, I'd like to make a toast. To my son David, who has never failed me, in spite of the many obstacles I placed before him. To his future wife Karen, who has captured not only his heart, but our hearts as well. You will make a fine Mrs. Stratton one day, Karen, and in time you will make a wonderful mother to our grandchildren. On behalf of my lovely wife Delilah and myself, I welcome you to our family. Cheers!"

Alfred touched Karen's glass before melodiously tapping the others. In turn, a multitude of tones filled the room. But Alfred saved David for last. He placed his glass on the table and embraced him instead. "From here on out, son, I don't want you to worry about a thing. You just concentrate on your goals. We'll take care of Karen while you're gone. That's a promise."

"Thanks, Dad," he said as he returned the embrace.

"Ship ahoy! Let's get a move on and ride like the wind. It's a great day for sailing," Alfred said, ushering everyone out the west-wing door.

✧ ✧ ✧

The moment David arrived on college campus, the laid-back pace of Southern California living quickly became a faded memory. The summer strolls along the beach were replaced with fifteen credits of class work that required two to three hours of homework every night. In between academics he had football practice, scrimmages, and weekend games. For David there was no rest, but it was just the opposite for Karen. Although she attended early morning classes, her days were void of any extracurricular activities. Less than two months after they were apart, the lull in her life caused Karen to slip into a state of depression.

"Karen, this has to stop now. Coming home from school to hibernate in your bedroom day after day won't bring David home any earlier. Here, I've brought you a plate of shortbread cookies and a cup of cocoa," Agnes said to Karen.

Agnes Allen, the soft-spoken wife of Lieutenant Commander John Allen, sat on the edge of her daughter's canopy bed. It was two in the afternoon, and Karen had already changed into her pajamas and was buried under the down-filled comforter.

"Please, take one sip for me, darling. Your father and I are terribly worried about you. Would you mind if we had a little talk?"

Karen moved the covers aside and obliged her mother with a single taste before placing the china cup on the nightstand. In a low voice she asked, "What is it, Mom? I'm not up to discussing life, politics, or the weather."

"Then just hear me out, dear—and take another sip," she said as she put the hot cocoa to Karen's lips.

"Mom, I just want to go to sleep. That's all. I'm awfully tired." She turned on her side away from her mother and closed her eyes.

"Well, I thought you'd be interested to know that I spoke with Delilah Stratton today."

Karen's eyes flew open as if she had received an electric shock. Just hearing the name Stratton reenergized her.

"Did she mention David? Did she say how he's doing? I haven't received a letter from him in over two weeks."

"She said he called home yesterday. He told her that he has so much on his plate right now that he barely has time for anything else except trying to maintain his 4.0. You know David, he's a mighty determined young man."

"More determined than you know," Karen said, remembering their afternoon in the gazebo.

"He left a message for you," she said with a comforting smile. "He's counting the days to summer break."

It was the shot of adrenalin Karen needed. She reached over to the plate and seized a shortbread cookie. "Go on, Mom. What else did he say?" Karen asked as she took a drink of the cocoa, which left a dark chocolate moustache around her mouth. The sudden transformation from a depressed young woman to the now-vibrant creature in front of her was a welcome sight for Agnes.

"Delilah has invited us to afternoon tea. She would like to discuss something with the two of us. Are you up to it?"

Karen didn't answer. She had already disappeared into the closet and was foraging through her clothes for an appropriate outfit. "Mom, what should I wear?"

"Wear your tangerine dress with the tan pumps. I'll wait for you in the car."

"I'll be there in five. I need to put my hair up in a ponytail. I'll drive, Mom."

The distance between the Strattons and the Allens was a mere six miles but the residences were significantly different. The Allens, who had opted to live off the naval base, had purchased a home across the street from the yacht club. The single-story contemporary house had blue stucco siding with a white trim. It boasted a spectacular view of the marina and was undeniably posh. But in no way did it compare to the dwelling of the Strattons.

High on a hill behind an electric gate monogrammed with the letter "S" was the coveted estate owned by Mr. and Mrs. Alfred D. Stratton. Their home, a vast twenty-two thousand square feet of living space, had been showcased on the front covers of numerous "in-style" magazines. It was touted as one of Southern California's most prestigious properties.

The Strattons enjoyed a sweeping panorama of the Pacific Ocean, making the Allens' view of the marina commonplace in comparison. But it was never the intent of Alfred Stratton to outshine anyone. The tall, gray-haired Englishman had the benefit of his ancestors' wealth, but he had also earned his own millions. Like his other profitable investments, the purchase of this mansion was another opportunity to increase his family's net worth. Before World War Two, Alfred Stratton had started a small sheet-metal company that eventually grew into a two-block factory. Sales doubled and then tripled when he expanded into international sales. It became a thriving business and a large conglomerate made him a lucrative offer. Accepting their bid, he had made a phenomenal profit. But Stratton, ever the savvy businessman, knew better than to let money stagnate in a bank; he reinvested in stocks of blue-chip companies, all of which realized great gains after the war ended.

Karen stopped the car before the gated entry of the Strattons' property and leaned out of the open window to press the intercom.

"Hello, Mrs. Stratton? It's Karen," she said holding down the intercom button.

"Oh, sweetie, drive on in. I'll release the gate."

Before Karen restarted the engine, the gate silently glided open to welcome them to the final hundred feet of pavement. At the end of the driveway was the stunning, tanned brunette, Delilah Stratton, who stood regally in front of her mansion. As Agnes and Karen stepped out of the car, Delilah came forward to greet them.

"Hello, Agnes. It's good to see you again."

"It's good to see you, Delilah. You've got a new hairstyle. It's very becoming!"

"It's called a pageboy flip with puffed bangs. It's the new "do" at Raoul's of Beverly Hills. With your silver hair, Agnes, I think the style would flatter you, too. You should give Raoul a call. Tell him that I referred you and I'm sure he'll fit you right in."

"I'm not that daring, Delilah. I wish I were, but that's just not me. I'll probably wear the same rolled-up bob for the rest of my life. It's the same hairdo that I've worn since the day I met the Lieutenant," she said. "I think he prefers that I keep it this way."

"Obviously John knows a good thing when he sees it. It looks very attractive on you, Agnes. Really, you look lovely," Delilah said convincingly.

Agnes Allen was not the envious type. However, there were times she wanted to be more like Delilah Stratton, who was an outgoing socialite. But that was not Agnes's nature; she was happy being the prim and proper wife of a decorated lieutenant.

Delilah turned to her future daughter-in-law and took both of Karen's hands into her own. "Oh, Karen, you look beautiful as always. Come inside. Greta has prepared Earl Grey with traditional English tea sandwiches, scones, and berry jams."

Delilah led the way up the fifteen flagstone steps that matched the circular driveway and the exterior of the house. As they entered the foyer Agnes couldn't help but look up at the forty-foot ceiling. Even though she had seen it several times before, it was awe-inspiring. Her olfactory sense took over as they made their way deeper into the home and she smelled the rich aroma of Corinthian leather. Clean and woodsy, the smell of the leather suggested a more masculine environment than one would expect the feminine Delilah to inhabit. However, Delilah had decorated her home based on Alfred's tastes. He favored heavy velvet fabrics and handwoven rugs from India. His choice of colors was a combination of deep burgundies, browns, and forest greens that complemented the dark cherrywood wainscoting and classical crown moldings.

"It's so good of you to be able to come on such a short notice. Please follow me this way."

Delilah indicated they should proceed down the north corridor. The walls of cherry were lined with paintings by artists such as Gainsborough, Renoir, Van Gogh, and Georgia O'Keeffe. Above each one was an individual light that highlighted its masterpiece. The beams of light illuminated the way to an annex.

As they walked along the corridor, Agnes and Karen marveled at each piece while Delilah, a part-time docent for the county art gallery, gave a brief history of each artist. She went on to say, "The Stratton family collected art for decades. In fact most of these paintings were inherited by Alfred years before I met him. He nearly lost his right to the entire collection. Alfred's younger brother was the black sheep of the family and died young. His son, Alfred's nephew, contested the Stratton family will, claiming that it had been tampered with. After several legal battles, the case was ultimately thrown out of court and Alfred was awarded the entire estate. Our home went from nearly barren walls to the collection you see today. Quite a transition, I have to admit."

Intrigued by the story of the will, Agnes asked, "Delilah, what ever happened to Alfred's nephew?"

"On the day Alfred won the case, Jack, his nephew, had a menacing outburst in court. He cursed the judge and then threatened Alfred with his life. But you know Alfred; he took it with a grain of salt and just walked out of the courtroom. The judge, however, wasn't quite as forgiving. He fined Jack for contempt of court and ordered him to spend several nights in jail."

"Was that the last time anyone saw him?"

"In the flesh, yes, but for a while I believed that he was stalking us. Alfred told me it was my imagination running amok. To this day I stand by my convictions. From David's first birthday until he turned twelve, he received anonymous birthday cards each with the same bizarre inscription—'Time is on my side, little Stratton.' You can call it a woman's intuition, but I firmly believe those cards came from Jack."

Up until then Karen had been quiet. As soon as the conversation shifted to David, she blurted out, "What did David say about receiving the cards?"

"Oh, sweetie, I never gave those cards to him." Delilah smiled. "Besides, once he turned thirteen, he never received another one. So if they were from Jack, apparently he became tired of harassing us."

Delilah turned into the final hallway. "Well, here we are. Welcome to my little corner of the world," she said opening the French doors to the garden room.

It was a room like no other in the house. The walls, molding, and wainscoting on the masonry side were embossed in white and decorated with dozens of photographs that chronicled David's life from infancy through his high-school years. The remaining three sides, which faced the Pacific Ocean, were floor-to-ceiling, windows. The ambiance was light, airy, and feminine, a perfect room for Delilah.

"I like to think of this place as my quiet room. It's my retreat, so to speak. When David was an infant, I came in here to feed him. This became his favorite playroom when he was a toddler. I can still see him taking his first steps…" Delilah gazed toward the photographs, reliving a treasured memory. The conversation stalled until Agnes came to the rescue.

"Delilah, your floral arrangements are exquisite. Where on earth did you find orchids and lilies this time of year?"

"A woman in Malibu grows them in her hothouse. She's such a dear. She creates these elaborate arrangements twice a week for me. She's been my best-kept secret for years, but I'd be happy to give you her number, Agnes."

"Perhaps I'll call her, but just for advice. I'm having a small greenhouse built for that very purpose. It's always been a dream of mine to grow rare blooms. We never lived in one place long enough to cultivate flowers. This time John says we're here to stay."

"That is splendid news, Agnes." Delilah extended her open palm, "Please be seated."

Karen and her mother made themselves comfortable on the floral divan while Delilah pulled the cord to close the lavender drapes. Usually there was a breathtaking view of Catalina Island in the distance, but today heavy cloud cover, coupled with intermittent sheets of rain, obscured the picturesque view.

Just as the women had settled themselves on the comfortable velvet-brocade furniture, Greta entered the room and placed a tray of tea things on the table by Delilah.

"Allow me to pour," Delilah offered. "Please, help yourselves to the tea sandwiches. You'll find cucumber, minced salmon, and curried egg." Delilah lifted the sterling silver teapot. Handcrafted in Salisbury, England, it was another heirloom from the Stratton family estate. The teapot's companion, a three-tiered serving tray, overflowed with scrumptious morsels of traditional English fare.

"It has been years since I was invited to high tea, Delilah. I wasn't aware that this custom was practiced in California," Agnes said between bites.

"Yes, Mrs. Stratton," Karen chimed in. "Everything is tasty. I especially like the tea with lemon." Up until then Karen hadn't said much. In a world all her own, she had been picturing David as a tot crawling across the floor.

"Well, ladies. Let's get down to business, shall we?"

Simultaneously, Agnes and Karen placed their bone china tea cups onto the saucers. For a brief moment they had forgotten that their visit had an agenda.

"As you know, David called home yesterday. He told me that these first eight weeks have been exhausting. He said that ever since he arrived on campus, he hasn't been to bed before midnight. He's blaming the long hours on football practice and homework. I think it's because he just became a frosh pledge. I'm sure there are antics that go on that he wouldn't dream of sharing with his mother," she said.

"He pledged?" asked Karen, "Where to?"

"Alpha Pi, I think. It was something like that. I just know that their members have the highest GPA on campus. He'll fit right in."

Picturing David attending a fraternity party, Karen forced a smile and said, "Yes, I'm sure he'll fit right in."

"After talking with David, it got me thinking," Delilah continued, "sweetie, what do you do with your afternoons when your classes are over?"

"Except for homework, which I usually do before I go home, I don't do much of anything."

Agnes seized the pause and interrupted. "I can tell you what she does, Delilah. She comes home from school, checks the mailbox, and if there's no letter from David, she goes straight to bed."

Karen couldn't believe her mother would divulge that to anyone, especially to David's mother. Her face reddened.

"Karen, don't be embarrassed." Delilah moved from the armchair to the divan next to her. "You miss him very much. The truth is I miss him, too. He's never been away from home this long. In a way, Karen, we are in the same boat."

Karen's smile was faint, but it was a smile. She felt that someone finally understood exactly how she felt.

"Karen, do you play tennis?"

"I played a little at the base in Little Creek but I'm not very good. I've never been the athletic type."

"You don't need to be a star athlete. You just need to know timing and the right moves."

"John and I have encouraged her to join the beach club and take lessons, anything that would fill the hours in the day. So far, Delilah, she's shown no interest in extracurricular activities," Agnes chimed in.

Delilah moved closer to Karen and asked, "Don't you want to better yourself for David?"

"What does playing tennis have to do with David?"

"Well, did you know David is ranked as a B-level tennis player?"

"No," she said, somewhat perplexed. "All he ever talked about was football and winning a scholarship and the importance of doing it all on his own."

"It's that drive he gets from his father. He's strong-willed and career-oriented. That's my David," Delilah boasted. "Since you are going to be a Stratton, it's important that you take an interest in *his* interests. Take it from someone who knows the Stratton men down to their very souls. You've got to keep them challenged to keep them on their toes."

"So you are saying I should take lessons for David?"

"Yes, but that's only a start. You'll need to know a little bit about everything that is important to him. Football, chess, golf, the stock market, car racing…"

Karen interrupted her. "Car racing?"

"Last year, before David knew you, he joined a backup team at the race track. He was only a volunteer, mind you, but it gave him a chance to work in the pit stop. He said it was one of the most exciting summers of his life."

"We've been together for nine months and he's told me none of this."

"His father did a similar thing to me and I had to learn the hard way. You, on the other hand, have four years to learn what makes him happy. More importantly, you will have time to learn what makes you happy. Believe me, everything you do will enrich both of you. Do you enjoy cooking?"

"Not really. I guess I could make a pot roast if I had to," Karen said.

"That will do just fine for the two of you. What will you do, though, when David calls you at three in the afternoon and tells you that there will be thirty guests for dinner?"

Karen giggled, "Maybe we'll have someone like Greta?"

"Yes, but that is not enough. As the lady of the house, you should be able to create a menu and select the perfect pairing of wine to enjoy with each course. A talent like that requires a gourmet palate."

"I'm certain I don't have that," Karen proclaimed.

"Perhaps not now, but with proper instruction you will."

"Are you suggesting that I take a cooking course?"

"I have a better idea." Delilah handed Karen a leather-bound appointment book that spanned twelve months. "Everything you need, you will find in here. It has been prepared just for you. The mornings have been left blank for college. Let's look at the first few months, shall we?"

Karen leafed through the book. "I don't understand. Who are these people?"

Delilah pointed to the first page and said, "Every Monday afternoon for the next six months you will be working side-by-side with Master Chef Jean Javier from LeRoux of Beverly Hills. As a favor to me he has agreed to provide you with private lessons in the art of French cooking. In no time at all, you will be a culinary expert. Now let's see." Delilah flipped the page and pointed to Tuesday.

"On Tuesdays you'll take tennis lessons at the beach club with Eric Bjorn, a former tennis professional. Eric's reputation for turning novice players into strong competitors has yet to be beaten. I'm quite sure that you won't be an exception."

"I hope not," Karen gulped.

"Then it's off to the country club on Wednesdays, where you'll spend your days with Patrick McTavish. He's a wonderful Scottish lad who will teach you everything you need to know about golf. Oh, on Thursdays I thought you might like to join me at the art gallery.

It will be good exposure for you to meet the patrons who donate their private collections. Do you have any questions so far?"

"Mom, is this all right with you?"

"Of course, dear, your father and I discussed it last night when Delilah called the *first* time," her mother smiled.

"Then I don't have any more questions, Mrs. Stratton. Except, what are Fridays for?"

"Ah, yes, I've left the best for last. Alfred and I are founders for several of the theaters in the area and because we are patrons, we have special seating arrangements. Depending on the venue, we are provided with a private booth, founders' seats in the mezzanine, or orchestra seats. I have access to just about every venue in the area, so I thought we'd make Friday our cultural day."

"Mrs. Stratton, this is overwhelming," Karen said with a mixture of enthusiasm and apprehension.

"Well, I've only gone over the first few months. All of this will change in six months," Delilah said. "You won't have time to get bored, sweetie. We have so much planned for you during the next four years. David will be very proud of your accomplishments, I assure you."

"Then I will be sure to succeed just knowing that," Karen said with a sigh.

Delilah turned to Agnes, who had given her free rein of the conversation. "Agnes, I do hope you join us on Fridays, whenever your schedule permits."

"Perhaps, I will." Agnes, peering over her horn-rimmed glasses, reiterated, "Yes, Delilah, perhaps I will."

It was a rare moment for the lieutenant's wife to hint at female independence. But she couldn't help it around Delilah. The fact was no one could. Delilah Stratton had a way with people. With her exuberant personality, Delilah could charm the devil himself. Yet, if she were entertaining political dignitaries, she could easily portray the refined and delicate housewife. Adapting to any situation was one of the skills that Delilah had passed on to David.

"Wonderful, ladies, so it's all settled," Delilah beamed.

And so it was that Karen's bleak and empty days suddenly became exhilarating and hectic. If not cooking, playing tennis, or golfing, she was dabbling in the stock market. But not without the assistance of her father, Lieutenant John, who was a moderate trader himself. As for car racing, after subscribing to a hot rod magazine, she found that she actually fancied the sport.

For the four years that followed, Karen kept to Delilah's stringent schedule and found that the more she learned, the more she understood the life of the Strattons. And even though scholastically her two-year associated arts degree could never compete with his four-year bachelor of science degree, by the time David graduated from college, Karen had become his equal.

✧ ✧ ✧

With his diploma from Ohio State firmly in his grasp, David shook hands with the line of professors. Graduating summa cum laude, he was presented with an Excellence in Achievement Award. The last professor waiting to congratulate David was Professor Tate, who had taken an interest in David from day one. He was unusually emotional when he bestowed his compliments.

"Well done, Mr. Stratton. It's been a pleasure having you in my classes. I expect your future achievements to be monumental," he said choking on his words while trying to maintain a steadfast demeanor.

"Thank you, Professor. You've been an inspiration to me."

"David, I'd like you to stop by my office after the ceremony. Say, in one hour?"

"Yes, sir," David promised as he stepped off the stage.

Walking back toward his seat among the other graduates, David caught a glimpse of Karen and his parents. Lifting his arm, he waved his diploma back and forth in a celebratory fashion. Delilah and Karen cheered, calling out David's name. While Alfred, more proud than he let on, simply applauded his son.

David sat down and waited for the formal ceremony to draw to a close. To symbolize the end of their undergraduate careers, David and his classmates stood and flung their caps into the air. And although a handful of students would go on to graduate school, most of the graduates, including David, were ready to enter the workplace.

David embraced Karen, and his mom and dad, who had congratulated him several times. Between the accolades he kept looking at his watch under the bulky graduation gown to check the time. Alfred noticed and asked, "Son, we've got all day. Our flight isn't until six tonight."

"Dad, Professor Tate asked to see me before I leave. Do any of you mind if I go say good-bye to him?"

It's fine with us, David," Delilah said. "Sweetie, you don't mind, do you?"

"Of course not," Karen said. She added, "I have the seat next to you on the plane. We'll have plenty of time to catch up then," she said touching her engagement ring to her cheek.

"Then I'll meet you back at the hotel after the baccalaureate luncheon," David said. He then raced across the grounds and into Professor Tate's small office.

"David, I understand that you have a big Californian wedding in the works," Tate said. "When's the big event?"

"First weekend in August, sir, at St. Joseph's in Long Beach."

"So when are you heading out West?"

"I'm flying home with my family tonight."

"Timing, and in this case location, is everything. David, I took it upon myself to set up an interview for you with one of my former colleagues, Theodore Bachman of Bachman Aerospace Industries. Theo asked me to weed through the grads and find an up-and-comer. I told him weeding wasn't necessary because I've had my eye on you for the past four years."

David couldn't find the words to tell Professor Tate that he was the main reason for attending Ohio State. Instead, he asked, "Sir?"

"Theo had headhunters all across the country searching for a young director to run his R and D department. I told him he could stop looking because I already had someone who could fit the bill."

"Sir?"

"David, all you need to do is show up for the interview as a favor to me. By the way did I mention the position is in Southern California? Culver City to be exact, only a stone's throw from Long Beach."

David couldn't have been more appreciative. The professor whom he had considered to be a mentor had been paving the groundwork for his future. Now all David had to do was follow through.

"Culver City? Research and Development Director? You bet I'll be there!"

"Good. Be at the personnel office at Bachman's on September sixth. That should give you ample time for your honeymoon, I'd say. Take care, David. Congratulations and best of luck to you!"

✧ ✧ ✧

"Do you, David, take Karen, as your lawful wedded wife?"

"I do."

"And do you, Karen, take David as your lawful wedded husband?"

"Oh, yes I do."

"By the power vested in me, I now pronounce you husband and wife. You may kiss the bride."

The marriage was sealed with a brief, yet appropriate, church kiss. The organist played "Ode to Joy" as arm in arm the couple glided back down the aisle. Following behind the newlyweds were six bridesmaids, each dressed in a different pastel-colored dress, escorted by six of David's closest friends, who were clad in classic black tuxedoes. The moment they reached the vestibule, the wedding party was guided outside through a side door, where four photographers waited to capture the radiant bride and her adoring husband.

Karen stood still while one bridesmaid fluffed the bride's long auburn hair and another positioned the twelve-foot train to the front of her traditional wedding gown. David took his place alongside her and the photographers posed the guests around the couple. The society photographers, hired by Delilah Stratton, ensured the happy event was recorded for posterity. Cameras flashed from every direction, and by the time the last photograph was taken, the lawn was covered with several hundred discarded flashbulbs.

"Let's get out of here," David said, smiling at his new bride. As the fairy-tale couple raced toward the limousine, the patiently waiting guests threw rice at them. David opened the car door for Karen, but her multilayered wedding dress barely allowed her to squeeze into the passenger seat. As it was, one of the hoops of her dress rose up obstructing her vision. David laughed as he pushed aside the hoop and sat in the car. He turned and waved to the crowd, saying, "See all of you at the reception."

As they drove away from the church David said to the driver, "Jenkins, take a twenty-minute detour along the beach. I don't want to arrive at the reception before seven o'clock. And Jenkins, we do not want to be disturbed."

The chauffeur gave a polite nod and returned his eyes to the highway. David locked the window separating them from the driver and drew the red satin curtain. They were finally alone.

"Cristal, Mrs. Stratton?" he asked after popping the cork.

"It's been four years since I first tasted this, when you proposed to me. Now that we're adults we can drink to our heart's desire," she said with her first sip.

"Yes, we can," he agreed. "But not now," he said as he retrieved her half-filled glass and placed it in the holder. He leaned across Karen, pushing aside the silk and taffeta layers of her gown while bending back the annoying hoops. When he had cleared his way, he ran his hand up her leg to her garter belt. Karen tingled all over.

"Just relax, babes. We're married now. I can finally make love to you."

Karen giggled, "What about Jenkins?"

"He won't bother us. Just relax," he repeated as he removed her silk panties. Karen lay back on the velvet seat. She had waited for this moment for four years. David had not exhibited the same self-control as Karen. He had spent his college days "practicing" with several willing coeds.

Using his hard-won expertise, David circled his finger at the base of her mound. He advanced to the portal with each swirl. Upon reaching the center folds, he inserted his finger into her. Karen flinched from the minor penetration, but her natural fluids encouraged the probe. She raised herself up and kissed him hard on the lips until their tongues danced together.

"I love you. I love you," he panted, while moving his finger in and out of her. With each bore, her body responded with natural lubrication. She oozed wetness.

"I love you, David. I want you now. All of you deep inside me."

David unzipped his fly. His member, seeking a warm dwelling, sprang out of his tuxedo. "I'll be gentle," David croaked. Positioning his uncircumcised penis against her, he slowly entered her inch by inch. Karen squirmed forward to meet him. It wasn't nearly as painful as she had thought it would be. Gradually, he entered her, shallowly at first, but then more deeply with every thrust until he was fully buried within her.

"Are you all right, babes?"

As her hips gyrated to his rhythm she said, "Um-hmm. I like it. I like it a lot."

That was all he needed to hear. He had been given the green light. Instantly he increased his pace until he slammed himself against her. Ten strokes later, David screamed out loud.

"BABY, I LOVE YOU!" Collapsing on her, he spurted his juices into her. Karen closed her eyes and smiled. She thought she could actually feel his sperm swimming up through her canal.

"Do you think Jenkins heard us, David?"

"Think of it this way, babes. We probably just made his day!"

"Well then, can we do it again?"

With youth as an advantage, Karen's request rejuvenated David's spent body. But they were only minutes from the hotel. "We don't have time. I'll have to make it up to you later," he promised.

Just as he predicted, only moments later they were turning into the entrance of the Santa Monica Regency. The quarter-mile-long driveway was dramatically lined on each side with twenty-foot hedges. The greenery limited visibility, but occasionally the couple was teased with a glimpse of the pink high-rise hotel surrounded by monumental palm trees.

David handed Jenkins a one-hundred dollar bill, which he accepted while feigning an "I know nothing" expression.

The newlyweds entered the honeymoon bungalow through a private entrance. Once inside, they gaped at the four-poster bed. David shook his head in frustration. They were already thirty minutes late. "Tempting as that bed is, we'd better get to the reception. Our parents are probably fit to be tied as it is. Babes, how soon can you be ready?"

"Just give me five minutes, darling," Karen said.

"Good, I'll be waiting out on the lanai."

Just like royalty, David and Karen entered the grand ballroom where six hundred guests were awaiting their arrival. The bandleader, right on cue, abruptly ceased the music. Picking up the microphone, he announced, "Ladies and gentlemen, I'd like to introduce to you Mr. and Mrs. David Alfred Stratton." After the applause died down, Delilah motioned the newlyweds to stand at the head of the receiving line.

"You're late, you two," Delilah smiled, "but we forgive you," she said on behalf of the other three parents.

David cleared his throat while Karen blushed a rosy shade of red. Delilah, an astute and liberal parent, noticed a glow in both her son and daughter-in-law. She had no doubt that they had become one, and she approved wholeheartedly.

Between the dancing, mingling, and traditional wedding customs the evening was perfect. After it was over, the couple retired to the bungalow to consummate their marriage a second time, a third, and fourth time until David fell asleep, still inside his new bride. He was shriveled yes, but still connected to her until they woke the next morning.

After their honeymoon in New York, David and Karen moved into their starter home in Huntington Beach, and the start of their married life.

"I've got my interview today, babes. Wish me luck," David said as he stepped into the shower. Karen dropped her robe and followed him.

"Luck, honey," she said as her hands softly caressed his genitals. "Can I go with? I'll wait in the car and read a book."

"No, because I don't know how long I'll be."

Karen wouldn't take no for an answer. She continued fondling his scrotum and then touched his anus with her finger. She toyed with him, watching him rise.

"Okay, you win. You'd better bring *War and Peace* because I don't know how long the interview is going to be."

"I won't mind waiting, but I have another book in mind."

"Oh yeah, what's that?" He moaned, lifting her up against the shower wall.

Panting, she said, "It's called *Your Firstborn*."

"What?" His breathing stopped short just before he came.

"I'm almost sure I'm pregnant."

The shower was beading down his back. Through tears of joy he sucked her neck feverishly, leaving an array of reddish purple love bites. "I love you, I love you, I love you," he murmured.

"And I love you, too, daddy," she smiled.

"Oh, babes, I wish I could stay in here all day, just loving you. But if I don't hurry, I'll be late for my interview. I wouldn't want to keep Mr. Bachman waiting."

"I'm still coming with you. No one will see me in the car. I'll just lean back and enjoy the crisp morning air."

"Okay, but hurry."

✧ ✧ ✧

Theo Bachman followed David's glance to the attractive woman sitting in the black sports car. David hadn't noticed that the CEO was standing at his side. Theo tapped him on the shoulder and showing David the clipboard he held said, "Tell me what you think of this, David."

10K to start

A five-hundred dollar signing bonus

Executive benefits and company stocks

(NB: Twelve-month executive training program with 15K increase upon completion.)

"How does this look to you?"

David's thought that his eyes would fall out of their sockets. It was more than twice the salary he had hoped for.

"I'd like you to start as soon as possible, David. I've made some slight changes, though. I'm not going to put you in the R and D position, not just yet. I'm going to let Connors continue running it. In the meantime you'll be getting hands-on experience. I want you to learn every inch of this business for the next twelve months. Then I'll determine where you'll best fit in. Think you can pull it off?"

"Failing is not in my vocabulary, sir. I'll do whatever you want. Just point me in the right direction."

"Good. That's what I want to hear. Now you'll need to fill out the usual forms and take an executive physical by our company doctor. Today is probably not convenient for you. So come back tomorrow."

"Oh, I've got plenty of time today."

"No. I hate to see your little wife down there waiting all afternoon. Tomorrow will be just fine."

Utterly embarrassed, David gulped. "Sir, I can explain."

"No need to. Just be sure you leave her home in the future. Wives don't fit in from nine to five," Theo laughed. "Welcome to Bachman Aerospace. I have high hopes for you, David."

David shook his hand. "Thank you, sir," he said. "Thank you," he reiterated as he left Bachman's office. When the door closed behind him, he ran through the hall, down the steps, and into the arms of his pregnant wife.

David's customized training program had him working in sales, marketing, engineering, installation and repair, purchasing, and supply departments. He became envied because no other employee had the opportunity to change positions as often as he did. To his peers and subordinates it appeared as though he was riding on Bachman's shirttails. Still, the rumors didn't intimidate him, because each time he proved he couldn't fail, just as he hadn't failed to impregnate Karen.

On May 5, 1951, nine months to the day after their wedding, Karen gave birth to the newest heir to the Stratton fortune. A beautiful, six-pound baby girl named Jenni Lynn. She was, as David put it, an angel among mere mortals.

five

SARAH'S HOPE

Cleveland, 1949–1954

Seven months after Sarah Robbins had left Donahue's, Sam came to realize that without Sarah, he didn't have much of a supper club. Donahue's, which now catered to unfamiliar faces, had not sold out to maximum capacity since the day in January when Sarah had collapsed onstage. The club had gone from standing room only to a few questionable customers, most of whom came in to get away from the elements.

Without his star entertainer, Sam fought hard not to fail. He tried numerous gigs from comedy acts to lounge singers to magicians, hoping to draw in a crowd. But Sarah's regulars, who had been the club's main source of revenue, refused to step inside. As a result of their absence, the sales at Donahue's had fallen to an all-time low.

The news that Donahue's was hanging on by a thread rapidly spread throughout the hospitality industry. Sam's restaurant suppliers were the first to become concerned. It was obvious to them that he was grasping at straws to cut costs. To keep prime rib on the menu, Sam twice lowered the grade of beef. He passed over fresh bakery goods in lieu of day-old breads and pastries. Donahue's bar had once offered the finest liquors, but now its shelves were haphazardly stocked with generic brands of alcohol.

Sam's only hope of keeping Donahue's alive was to persuade Sarah to return. But so far, his efforts had been in vain. He telephoned her every day to inquire about Billy's progress. And each time Sarah would respond with the same words.

"He's holding his own, Sam. He's better than yesterday, but not as great as he'll be tomorrow."

"Glad to hear it, Sarah. By the way, have you thought about coming back to work sometime in the near future?" He would ask the question but learned not to take it personally when she abruptly cut him off.

"No time to think about that now, Sam. I gotta catch the bus to the hospital. Billy's waiting. Love you. Talk to you tomorrow." Before Sam had a chance to press the issue, she'd leave him with the annoying sound of a dial tone.

This ritual went on for days. With no indication of her return, Sam was coming to the hard conclusion that the club might actually go under. His once-famous prime rib wasn't the mouthwatering delight it had been months before. No longer considered top quality, the meat was so tough it was nearly inedible. Even the stray dogs, whose survival depended on Sam's discarded fare, confirmed that its texture was leathery and difficult to swallow. So Sam compromised. He decided to keep the bar open and provide entertainment every other week or so; however, he would close the kitchen until further notice.

But revenue continued to drop. The cheap gigs he hired never amounted to much. For the first time in his life Sam felt he had failed, and he wasn't proud of himself.

It was exactly eight months after Donahue's cash register had last overflowed when Sam was escorting Manny, who now suffered with arthritis, to the exit. Sam took him by the arm, as he did every evening after last call, and helped his faithful bartender as he hobbled to the door.

"It wasn't a great night, old friend. But it wasn't the worst we've seen either," Sam declared.

Manny cleared his throat. "Boss, I got a hunch you can't afford an old bartender like me much longer. I have to say, though, that my life revolves around this place."

"I know what you mean. I feel the same way. I eat, breathe, and dream Donahue's. The way it was, the way it is, and the way I hope it will be again someday," Sam said.

Manny stopped shy of the door and touched a dusty black-and-white photograph on the paneled wall. It was a picture of Sam's parents on Ellis Island taken shortly after they disembarked from the ship that had carried them from Ireland.

"You can sure see the look of joy on your ma's face. Your pa, too, looks pretty damn happy to be setting foot on American soil. I was wondering what they would've done in your place?"

"I've often wondered myself," Sam said as he locked the door behind them.

He leaned up against the streetlamp and looked up at Donahue's flashing sign. The O, the H, and the E were burned out. "What a message I've been sending to Cleveland! Donahue's is slowly dying, bit by bit," Sam declared.

"You shouldn't give up, boss."

"What's the point, Manny? My well has run dry. You were right. I *can't* afford you much longer."

"Since my Mary passed, I'm a lonely old man. It's not easy walking through my front door because every time I do, I remember that she's not there to give me a hug. And when I go to bed I have to remind myself that it's just me now. But by the next morn I'm looking forward to the club and the customers. Even those days we get no more than five or six, it's what keeps me breathing. So you keep your paychecks, boss. I don't need your money. I just need a place to hang my hat."

"Manny, you are a rare gem among a thousand stones. I'll take you up on your offer. But even if things don't pick up right away, I'll find a way to pay you every dime I owe."

"Put it on the back burner. In the meantime you can do something for me."

"Anything, my friend. Name it."

"I want you to tell Sarah how bad it's been since she's been gone."

"Anything, Manny, but that! She's got enough on her plate with her sick boy. She doesn't need any of my problems."

"She's no less a friend to you than I am. If she knew the fix you're in, I bet she'd be right up there singing like a nightingale."

"I can't do that to her. I don't want her back out of pity. Not after everything she's been through," Sam said.

Manny pressed on. "I was thinking about that picture of your parents setting foot on the land of opportunity. If they were living today, they'd tell you to do whatever it takes. They'd tell you to grab the bull by the horns and go for the gusto."

Sam nodded in agreement while Manny churned out cliché after cliché before finally making his point, "Didn't your folks leave their farmhouse to you?"

"Yeah, it was their legacy. Both my parents worked from dawn to dusk to save for a parcel of land. When they finally had enough money, it took them another two years to build a house."

"It's paid for, isn't it?"

"Uh-huh. But the thought of using their house to bail myself out is an insult to their memory."

"Bull crap! The house is not doing them any good now, but the money it would raise could be a lifeline for the club."

"What good would the money be, if in a few months from now I'm back where I am today?"

"That wouldn't happen if you had Sarah back," Manny snapped.

"Enough. If she's not ready, she's not ready. Period."

"Listen to me. People are dying to hear her sing again. They want her and you need her. So maybe it's time you give her a reason to come back. Make her an offer so good she won't think twice about turning it down."

"What do you mean?"

"Give her a piece of Donahue's. Make her a partner. Tell her the sooner she's on stage, the sooner she'll be investing in her boy's future."

Like the peal of a hundred bells going off in his head, Sam finally had a solution. Borrow against the farm and work a deal with Sarah.

"Manny, you're a seventy-year-old genius."

"When you get to be my age, sometimes you can hear the angels talking. I think that your folks up in heaven used me as a conduit to you. Now it's up to you to make it work."

Although he was apprehensive, Sam took Manny's advice. He took a loan out on the farm and then consulted Harold James, his lawyer and one of the club's old regulars. Sam was ready to gamble again. Only this time it was with his inheritance.

"I need to get Sarah Robbins back as soon as possible, Harry. So I'd like a legal contract that would make Sarah one-quarter owner of Donahue's."

"That's very interesting, Sam. As your attorney, I think that a twenty-five percent stake is a bit on the high side for the first year. I suggest you give her fifteen percent to start, double her salary, and throw in an extra perk like a paid vacation."

"Fifteen percent isn't enough! I want to give her twenty-five," Sam stated firmly.

"Then what do you say to twenty percent with a contract that is renewable annually. Every year you bump her stake up a few notches. That should keep her around for a long while."

"You're the expert, Harry. I've got to get her back because I'm losing money by the minute. Getting Sarah to return is my last hope."

"Yes, I heard tell of sorts."

"Come to think of it, Harry, I haven't seen you at the club in months. What gives?"

"The wife doesn't like the night scene, but she was receptive to Donahue's when Sarah Robbins was onstage. There was something about Sarah that kept us all coming in to see her. She was the adhesive that bonded everyone together. Know what I mean?"

"Yeah, Harry, I certainly do. There's no camaraderie now. All we get is a few drifters who pop in for a quick high or a painful low."

"It sounds like time is of the essence. I'll have this drawn up immediately. Come back this afternoon. It'll be ready for your signature."

Sam bit his lower lip. He didn't know if the package would be enough to tempt her back to work. Worse yet, he didn't know how much longer he could hold out.

The following morning just prior to daybreak, Sam camped out on Sarah's porch swing. He was half-asleep when she opened the screen door.

"Sam, what are you doing here?"

"I thought you might need a ride to the hospital, that's all."

"That was thoughtful of you. But it really isn't necessary. I'm used to taking the bus."

"Sarah, it'll give us some time to talk."

Sarah wasn't that anxious to have a heart-to-heart with Sam. Seeing him only reminded her of the club, which up until that moment, she hadn't missed at all. But Sam had been good to her, so she agreed. "Sure, Sam, it's about time we did some catching up."

Sam tore out in front of her to open the passenger door. Bending over with one arm across his waist, he jokingly said, "Allow me, Miss Sarah Robbins, aka Cleveland's Entertainer of the Century."

"Sam before you go any further, you need to know that I'm not sure I'm ever going back to Donahue's. The reason is Billy. I want to spend every minute with him when he gets released from the hospital." She abruptly changed the subject. "Did I tell you that he doesn't need a feeding tube anymore?"

Her hope and enthusiasm were palpable. But as she reveled in her son's progress, Sam's ruddy Irish complexion became dull and listless. He was faced with the realization that the offer, no matter how lucrative, could be in vain. Sam exhaled slowly and surrendered to the potential disappointment.

"Well, I better get you to see that little boy of yours."

In half the time it took for the bus ride, Sam was stopping in the hospital loading zone. Sarah anxiously opened the car door.

"Gee, Sam, I can't thank you enough. It sure beats waiting for the bus." As she stepped out, Sam reached over to stop her.

"Sarah, please don't go. Not yet. Just give me five minutes."

Sarah shook her head, indicating it was useless to beg, but she felt it was only fair that she explain her position to Sam. Pulling the door closed, she sat back down.

"Sam, my life has changed more than I can put into words. I have a beautiful baby boy who is going to be released from the hospital soon. Just the thought of leaving him night after night just tears me apart. Do you understand?"

"I understand, Sarah. Really I do. But how are you going to afford to stay home?"

"I have some money saved. If I'm frugal, it will more than last us through the next several months. After that, I'm really not sure but I'll figure something out."

Sam knew that the window of opportunity was closing fast. It was his last chance. Leaning over her, he opened the glove compartment and extracted the large manila envelope with "Harold James, Attorney-at-Law" typed in the left corner.

"Here, open this up, Sarah."

"What's this? Attorney-at-Law?"

"Just read it, Sarah, please."

The party of the first part, Sam Donahue, owner of the establishment, Donahue's, and the party of the second part, Sarah Robbins…Salary increase to fifty dollars a week…two weeks paid vacation…twenty percent ownership to the rights of Donahue's in Cleveland, Ohio.

Dated September 8, 1949.

"What? You can't be serious." The eagerness in her voice set the tone for a possible deal. He was beginning to smile again.

Sarah was working out the math in her head. For only thirty hours of work, the salary alone beat the minimum hourly rate of seventy-five cents. It was almost too good to be true.

"This is an unbelievable offer, Sam. But what am I going to do with Billy?"

Anticipating the question Sam blurted out, "I've got it all figured out, Sarah. We'll set up a crib behind stage and then we'll make a gap in the curtains. That way you can keep tabs on him. Hey,

I'll even throw in a rocking chair and a sofa so you can spend your breaks with him. What do you say?"

Sarah nervously picked at the cuticle on her thumbnail until it split open. Sam knew he had tempted her; but he didn't want to push his luck. He folded the contract and stuffed it inside her purse.

"Just think about it, Sarah. The offer stands until you tell me otherwise."

"All right, I will. But I am not making any decisions until the doctor gives Billy a clean bill of health. Heck, I'd settle for a semi-clean one."

"That's fair enough, Sarah."

Sarah got out of the car and hustled up the steps of the hospital. At the top she turned and waved back at him. "Go fishing, Sam. It's a beautiful day to spend on the lake."

Sam drove off, but not for a day of leisure. He headed straight for the club. Turning into the parking lot, he read out loud the announcement on the marquee. FIVE NIGHTS ONLY! OSCAR AND THE JAZZ PIGEONS! *I'll be glad when they're gone. Maybe the next gig will be better. Maybe the next gig will be Sarah Robbins.*

✧ ✧ ✧

Four weeks later Sarah was sitting in the hospital breast-feeding Billy when Doctor Clark interrupted her. "Good morning, Sarah. May I have a moment?"

Sarah adjusted the cloth to cover her exposed breast and said, "Oh, Doctor, I always have time for you," she said respectfully.

The doctor brushed the back of the baby's head and thoughtfully said, "You'd never know that under these curly locks he was born with a grotesque protrusion."

"Thanks to you, the lump has really smoothed out."

"Yes. Billy is one medical miracle, if I do say so myself."

Sarah finished feeding her child and turned the baby over her shoulder. She patted his back to displace the milky air bubbles.

"I'm very pleased with his development, Sarah. I have to admit that I never believed he would live much past his birth, let alone progress as he has. Little Billy has proven me wrong. His senses are strong and there don't appear to be any ill effects from the remolding of his skull. And to date there are no signs of mental retardation, as I originally projected. I think it's time I sent him home with you. I'm releasing him tomorrow."

"Tomorrow? Oh my God. I'm not prepared," she said excitedly.

"I'm sure you'll do just fine, Sarah."

While Sarah fastened her maternity bra, she noticed that Dr. Clark had quietly left the room. She wanted to thank him so she scurried up the corridor with the baby pressed against her bosom.

"Dr. Clark, wait. Dr. Clark. How can I ever repay you for all that you've done?"

Up until then, the doctor had kept his emotions hidden. However, Billy had become his sole purpose for practicing medicine. He pulled a handkerchief from beneath his hospital whites and wiped his eyes.

"You just make sure I see Billy once a month as an outpatient. I would like to continue monitoring his progress. Is that a deal?"

"Yes, I promise."

"I've got to make my rounds now, Sarah. I'll talk to you later," the doctor said, anxious to be on his way.

Dr. Clark darted up the hall, covering his face. His coworkers were stunned to see Old Stone Face Clark wracked with emotion. As he turned the corner out of sight, he fell back against a wall and lowered his head. His weak legs were barely strong enough to hold his torso erect. A steady stream of tears cascaded from his eyes to the polished hospital floor. *After all these years of remarkable cures and unwilling failures, why am I so overcome by the recovery of this one child?*

But Dr. Clark was very much aware of the whys. He was haunted by the detestable advice he had given to Sarah Robbins immediately after she gave birth. He had asked her to choose death over life. *What if she had listened to me? What if? What if?* As hard as he tried, he couldn't erase those acidic words: *The best thing for your boy is to let him die peacefully. Die peacefully. Die peacefully. Die. Die. Die.*

Panting for air, he shook his head in an attempt to discard the revolting memory. Resuming his composure, he pushed himself away from the smooth-tiled wall. Although no one would be the wiser, Dr. Clark would spend the rest of his life yearning for inner peace. Something he would never find.

Sarah entered the crowded elevator of the hospital. The floor indicators above the door lit up as each floor was passed: three, two, one. When the doors opened at the lobby, Sarah was the first to exit. Her pace increased as she sped past the pink and white clad candy stripers selling miscellaneous gift items. She pushed the revolving door to exit the hospital and caught sight of the city bus coming up the street. *Just in time,* she thought.

Opening the bus door the driver asked, "What's this, Sarah? Never saw you make the morning 9:20 before. You're usually my last run of the day."

"Eddie, Billy's coming home tomorrow!"

"That is good news. Where are you headed?"

Sarah dropped a nickel in the slot and answered. "Downtown, Eddie. I've got a lot of shopping to do."

The bus was much more crowded in the morning than it was at 10:35 at night when she usually boarded. After passing each row, she finally found an available seat at the back of the bus. As Eddie drove away, Sarah pressed her face against the window and glanced back at Monrovia General. She saw people throwing coins into the koi pond at the entrance to the main doors of the hospital. She smiled because she understood their hopes, their prayers, and their desperation. She, too, had tossed in her share of pennies. And finally after eight and a half months, her wish had been granted. Billy was coming home. As excited as she was, she was also apprehensive. Billy had only ever known the sterile hospital. How would he adjust to her one-bedroom home? The hospital staff had become her extended family; but she knew that after tomorrow it would all change. Although some of the employees, like Fran, would remain lifelong friends, others would become no more than distant acquaintances. But melancholy wasn't an emotion she cared to indulge in. She had shopping to do.

Anxiously enduring the ten-minute drive downtown, Sarah opened and closed the clasp to her purse. And then the letter caught her eye. The manila envelope that Sam had stashed in her purse was suddenly staring her in the face. She seized it and re-read his offer. "I really could use the money," she mumbled as she realized her trust fund was nearly tapped out. Since Billy's birth she had been withdrawing money to make minimum weekly payments to the hospital. However, she knew that his final bill would be substantial and that the hospital would expect more than she had been paying. She had to face the fact that she needed to go back to work.

It's been nearly a month since I've heard from Sam. I wonder if the offer is still good. If he's changed his mind, I sure couldn't blame him, she thought.

Eddie stopped the bus in front of Hill Valley Department Store. He turned around and said with a wink, "Anyone who's going shopping better get off now. The clock's a-tickin'."

Sarah jumped up and gave him a friendly nudge just before she stepped out. "See you in a couple of hours, Eddie."

Hill Valley Department Store had lavish window displays and a black-suited doorman ready to welcome her in. But Hill Valley was entirely out of the question. She had eleven dollars to spend and that had to be enough to cover all of Billy's needs. So she crossed the street and walked down a couple blocks to Prisky's Five and Dime where they carried similar items, noticeably not as grandiose, but at a fraction of the cost of Hill Valley.

"May I help you find something?" The young salesclerk had been folding blankets when she offered her assistance.

"Gosh, yes. My infant son is being released from the hospital tomorrow. It will be his first time home. I guess I'll need three sleepers, two dozen diapers, a couple bibs, and anything else you can think of, as long as I don't exceed eleven dollars."

The girl retrieved the items as quickly as Sarah listed them. It wasn't until Sarah reached the checkout that she noticed all the items were in the newborn sizes.

"Oh," she stammered. "I'm afraid that everything is too small. I shouldn't have called him an infant. He's nearly nine months old."

"Oh, I understand," the clerk said politely, but the frown on her face said otherwise.

"It's a long story. Let's just say he had complications," Sarah smiled.

"Wait here, ma'am, and I'll go back and exchange these for larger sizes. Would twelve months be too big for him?"

"He's small for his age but he can always grow into them. Twelve months will be just fine. Take your time. I'm going to the soda fountain to get a bite to eat."

Sarah walked to the opposite side of the store and sat on the cushioned swivel counter stool. She said, "I'll have a cola, son. But hold the rum, please."

The sixteen-year-old soda jerk looked perplexed. "We don't serve alcohol in here, lady."

"Yes, I know. It's a private joke. I'll have a plain cola," she emphasized, "and a grilled ham and cheese sandwich."

Sam's contract, which protruded from the top of her purse, seemed to beckon. She yanked it out and perused it again. Halfway through reading it she said, "Young man, I'm going to use the pay phone. I'll be right back."

Sarah picked up the handset and dialed Donahue's. After several rings a man, whose broken English was difficult to understand, answered, "Hel—looo, dis is Donhus."

"This is Sarah Robbins. Is Sam in?" In the background she heard music. *A combo must be rehearsing,* she thought.

"Yes, Lad—dee, he in. I go get him for you."

While she waited for Sam, Sarah listened intently to the tune. It was one of her favorites, only more upbeat than the version she was familiar with. She tapped her finger on the side of the telephone in time to the rhythm of the music. She liked the unfamiliar interpretation until she heard a male voice drown out the music. His voice was raspy and his pitch was off-key as he crucified the words. "A rose, yeah man, a rose is like a rose…" Sarah didn't know what to make of it. The singer had converted the classic serenade "To Each His Own" into a jazzy rendition. She wondered if this were the wave of the future.

"This is Sam Donahue."

"Sam, it's Sarah."

"Sarah, how are you? How's your boy?" Covering the mouthpiece he yelled out, "Take five, kid. This is an important call."

"Yeah, man, whatever you say. You're the boss man."

"Boss man! That kid irks the hell out of me, but I'm stuck with him and his insufferable voice for another two weeks."

"Do you have another booking after him?"

"Nothing concrete, but I'm working on getting this trio of folksingers from Akron. I heard they can pack a house and God knows we could sure use the packing."

"But if you don't get the trio, what's your backup plan?"

"Don't have one, yet. Got any ideas?"

"What about me? Is your offer still good, Sam?"

He had almost given up hope of ever seeing the name Sarah Robbins on Donahue's marquee again, but she was finally interested. "Say the word, Sarah, and I won't need a trio."

"Then, yes. I want to come back."

Hesitatingly he asked, "What about Billy?"

"He's being released tomorrow. So if you'll buy that crib, I'll be ready to start in three weeks. What do you say?"

Sam was smiling ear to ear. He could hardly control his enthusiasm. "It'll be great having you back. You've been sorely missed," he admitted.

"There's just one thing I need to know Sam. Do you think the patrons will hold it against me for having a baby out of wedlock?"

"The ones who really care about you will support you. The others will come around eventually, just give them some time. Anyhow, it's nothing you need to worry about."

"Okay, Sam, then it's settled. I'll sign the paperwork today and drop it off at your attorney's office this afternoon."

"That's exactly what I wanted to hear. We'll talk tomorrow, partner," Sam said.

"Thanks, Sam," she said as she hung up the phone.

Sarah rushed back to the counter stool and took two bites of the sandwich. She found that she was overly excited and not really hungry at all. She retrieved her packages from the checkout and headed back up the street to the bus stop. As she stood at the corner waiting for the light to turn, a burly man with an all-too-familiar voice deliberately bumped into her from behind.

"If it isn't Sarah Robbins! What brings you downtown these days?"

"Henry Kinslow! Can you afford to be seen talking to me in public? Someone, including your wife, might see you," she snarled with mounting resentment.

"Oh, Sarah, how I've missed you." He moved closer to her and whispered, "I still love you. I will always love you."

"Stop it, Henry. You are making a fool of yourself," she said as she pushed him away. "Listen, I really need to go. I'm terribly busy these days."

"Yeah, yeah, yeah. What's with all these packages?"

"They're none of your business."

"Well, you've always been my business, especially since Gerty passed away."

"Aunt Gertrude would have disowned us both if she knew how things turned out between us. I was so young when you first approached me. You made me fall in love with you. You promised to always take care of me. And then you left me flat."

"Sarah, let's not hash over that again," he said.

She gritted her teeth and asked, "That's fine, Henry. So what do you want with me now?"

"Can't an old friend be concerned about another friend?"

"I am none of your concern anymore, Henry," she said as she proceeded through the crosswalk to the bus stop. The judge followed closely behind her.

"I heard a story about you a few months back," he said. "I heard that you had a baby and the doc thought it was going to be retarded or something."

Sarah was beginning to feel uncomfortable. *God, does he know?*

"I was wondering, when was the child born, Sarah?"

Sarah saw that he was trying to calculate their last weeks together. But she was certain he couldn't remember the exact date. So she had nothing to lose in shaving a couple weeks off Billy's birth date. "Yes, you heard right. I had a son in February. And no, he's not retarded, and nor is he handicapped. He's actually doing very well, thank you."

"February, huh? So do I know who the boy's father is?"

It was the first time Sarah saw this self-absorbed man take an interest in anyone other than himself. She answered carefully, "No, Henry, you don't know him. He was one of Donahue's regulars. And if you must know, it was only a one-night stand."

Henry was visibly shaken. "So, he's not mine," he said disappointedly. "And after all these months that I thought he was."

"You mean to tell me that you've known that you might have been his father and still you didn't bother to come and see him?"

"I told you. I heard that he was retarded or something."

"Oh, so let's get this straight, Henry. Your sudden interest in my son is because he's *not* retarded?"

"I didn't exactly say that," he stammered.

"Tell me something, Henry. Did you ever really love me? Or was I just a young girl who you lusted for when she grew into a woman? Because when it came down to actually leaving your wife and family or leaving me, you cast me aside like an old pair of shoes."

Although Sarah would never have believed it at that point, there had been times when Judge Henry Kinslow thought he would divorce his wife and marry Sarah. But Kinslow was a coward. After he had received the anonymous letter threatening to expose his adulterous relationship, he couldn't sever his ties to Sarah quickly enough. He wanted nothing to jeopardize his position in the courtroom where he reigned high above the common citizens.

"Now just you wait one minute, Sarah. I had my reasons."

"None of which means anything to me today, Henry. All I was to you was someone to spread her legs whenever you wanted."

Just as the judge started to defend himself, a passerby tipped his hat and said, "Hey, Judge. How ya doin'? And how's the little missus doing?"

"Abigail is fine. Thank you so much for asking."

As the man walked away Henry turned to Sarah and said, "See what I mean? Everywhere I go, someone knows me."

"Yes, Henry, so you've said before. Anyway, I doubt you ever would have mustered the courage to divorce your wife and marry me. I can't see you standing opposite a fellow judge and suing for divorce. I mean, what would people think?" she asked sarcastically.

"Keep your voice down," he hissed at her.

"Still worried about your reputation, Judge Henry Kinslow?" Sarah checked her watch. Eddie was five minutes behind schedule.

"Let's not argue, Sarah. It's a moot point, isn't it? The boy's not mine."

"Henry, just go home and leave me alone!"

"I'm not leaving until I set a few things straight, Sarah. Like how you got the job at Donahue's. I prearranged the whole thing. Sam was opening a fucking smorgasbord for God's sake. I had to convince him to open a supper club and hire you so that I could see you every night. I'd call that love, wouldn't you? And as far as your boy's hospital bill, it was paid in full this morning. Yes, Sarah, I paid the entire bill," he boasted. What he never admitted was that the money he used was money he had stolen from Gertrude; money that was intended for Sarah's trust fund.

"You shouldn't have done that, Henry. I am capable of paying my own way."

"You're right, I shouldn't have. Especially now that you stand before me and tell me he's just the bastard spit of a one-night stand. How could you, Sarah? How could you?"

Sarah wouldn't dignify the insult. The self-serving man, who used his gavel as power, had become a victim of his own vulnerability. As he stared in a trance and jaywalked across the street, he kept repeating, "How could you, Sarah? How could you?" But her ears were finally deaf to him.

Better Days Ahead

✧ ✧ ✧

The hospital staff gathered around as Sarah, holding Billy in her arms, signed the hospital release forms. The moment was cause for celebration. But with the joy came the sadness of departure.

"All of you have left imprints on my heart," Sarah said warmly. "You were there when times were at their worst. And yet never once did you judge me. I appreciate your kindness."

"So where do you go from here, Sarah?" asked nurse Fran.

"I'm going back to work at Donahue's. And while I'm singing, Billy will be just a few feet away behind the stage curtains. Hopefully, he'll be sound asleep, but I'm sure it will take some time for him to get used to the racket, especially since all he's ever known are the quiet whispers of Monrovia General."

"He'll adapt sooner than you think," Fran said as she folded a strand of her platinum blond hair behind her ear.

"Well, I hope to see some of you there. Just call and I'll be sure to save a table for you."

"Well, you can count on me," Fran said. Reaffirming their close friendship she added, "You and I have become too close to ever say good-bye, Sarah."

While the entourage talked about getting together after-hours at Donahue's, the admitting clerk opened the window and handed Sarah the bill. "Here you go. I've itemized the charges. Pediatrics, Neurology, Intensive Care…it's pretty self-explanatory."

Sarah briefly scanned the multitude of pages and noticed each was subtotaled to the subsequent page. She skipped to the last one and looked at the grand total. It was four thousand, sixty-two dollars and thirty-one cents. The amount owing, though, was zero. The clerk continued, "This is for your reference only. Yesterday morning a courier delivered a certified check to be paid directly to the Robbins' account. You owe nothing. It has been paid in full."

Sarah swallowed, pretending to be surprised. She was now just as keen as Judge Kinslow to keep their affair a secret. "Who on earth would do such a thing for us? I can't imagine anyone in Cleveland being so generous."

Unknowingly, Fran came to her rescue. "You never know, Sarah. It could have been one of your die-hard Donahue customers or a windfall from a plain old do-gooder. If I were in your shoes, Sarah, I wouldn't look a gift horse in the mouth."

"You're right. I shouldn't look a gift horse in the mouth," she repeated to avoid any further discussion.

One by one the nurses said their good-byes and dispersed back to their stations leaving Fran and Sarah. Emotionally Sarah said, "You never know what circumstances can bring people together in life. Up until eight months ago the only woman I had ever been close to was my Aunt Gertrude. Then I came to Monrovia General and was befriended by so many wonderful people. But none of the friendships mean as much as the one I share with you, Fran. You never questioned me about Billy and yet you knew from the first that I had no husband. Still, you never judged me or looked down upon me. For that I will always be grateful. I hope that we will be lifelong friends."

"That's a given, Sarah," Fran smiled. "Just save my hubby and me a table for opening night. We'll be there."

"Well, here's my bus," Sarah said wiping a tear from her eye. With Billy in one arm and the night bag in the other, she flew out the revolving glass door in time to board Eddie's bus.

"So this is the little guy! He's a cute one, he is." Eddie reached into his shirt pocket and found a nickel. "I've been saving this coin for a long time." He deposited it into the metal fare box and said, "This one's on me."

Except for settling in with Billy, the rest of Sarah's day was pretty uneventful. But it wasn't so for Sam Donahue. All he could think about was Sarah's return to the club and what it would take to draw the old crowd back. There had been so many changes, none of which he had divulged to Sarah. Nor did he mention that the club she now owned was not much of a club at all. It had become a hole-in-the-wall bar with less than second-rate entertainment.

✧ ✧ ✧

"Number twenty-two. Number twenty-two?"

"Yeah, I'm twenty-two," Sam declared in the waiting area of the Cleveland Herald.

"How can our newspaper help you, sir?"

Sam unfolded a rough draft and handed it to the newspaper apprentice. "What do you think, son, say a half-page ad?"

Sam waited for a sign of approval as the youth tediously studied the layout.

Grand Re-opening of Donahue's
October 23, 1949
Back by popular demand—Miss Sarah Robbins
Full dinner menu with priority seating for dinner guests
Reservations at WE 7-5322

The apprentice positioned his thumb and index finger an inch apart on the draft. He envisioned the size and type of lettering he would recommend. "May I make a suggestion, sir?"

"That's why I'm here, isn't it?"

The young clerk was proud to give his advice to Sam, who was twice his age. "Well, sir, this will cost you a premium. Why don't we insert a picture of the lady right in the middle of your ad?"

"A picture, huh? That's a good idea. But exactly how much of a premium are we talking about?"

"It'll double the price. Triple it, if you go for a full-page ad."

The clerk dangled the carrot while Sam considered the proposal. He decided to cast his fate to the wind. "Let's go for it!" Sam peeled off a fifty-dollar bill from the stack of crisp bills the bank had just loaned him. *Thanks, Mom and Dad*, he thought.

The clerk accepted the payment and said, "If you can get me the photograph this afternoon, I will start running this on Saturday."

"Great. I look forward to seeing the end product."

"You won't be disappointed, Mr. Donahue. I'll get started with the layout right away."

✧ ✧ ✧

From the kitchen Sarah could hear that Billy had awoken and wanted to be fed. Her breasts involuntarily responded with a strong desire to be emptied. She unbuttoned the top two buttons of her blouse and dropped the panel of her nursing bra. Lifting Billy from the maple crib, one of the two that Sam had purchased, she presented him with a moist nipple.

"You look mighty hungry, little one." She rested back on the sofa and enjoyed the relief they both were experiencing. It was so different feeding him at home than it was in the hospital. It was precious. It was private. It was the way it should be for a mother and son.

When Billy had consumed the last bit of milk, he fell into a tranquil sleep. Sarah changed his soiled diaper and laid him down while she lovingly stroked his black curly hair.

"You don't know it, son, but you look more and more like your daddy every day," she whispered. She pushed herself away from the crib and fell back onto the bed.

"Some daddy Henry would have been." Nervously, she bit her cuticle until it bled. She realized that Billy was becoming a constant reminder of the only man she had ever loved *and* ever hated. The fine line between those two emotions was never so blurred as when Henry called her son the bastard spit of a one-night stand.

"Pull yourself together, Sarah," she ordered herself. "He's not worth your tears or anger!" She reached for a glass of water and with each swallow she fought to bury the past. A feat that seemed nearly impossible until the sound of footsteps interrupted her.

Sarah opened the door and placed her index finger to her lips. "Shhhhh, Sam, the baby's asleep. But I am so glad to see you. Your timing couldn't have been better." She dismissed the onset of depression and added, "Come and see him. I've got your crib, thank you very much, set up next to my bed."

"That's one good-looking baby boy, Sarah. And look at that curly hair."

Yeah, look at that black curly hair, Sam thought. *Not like Sarah's, brown and straight. He must be the spitting image of his father because there's not one characteristic that matches any of Sarah's. He has olive skin and that small pudgy nose. Definitely a one-eighty from his mother's pointed one. I don't see one thing that resembles Sarah and yet there's something about his features that look eerily familiar.*

But Sam had much more pressing things on his mind than trying to identify Billy's father. He needed a close-up picture of Sarah for the newspaper.

"I just can't get used to having a baby of my own, Sam. I just can't take my eyes off him."

"I can see that, Sarah. He makes you glow."

"Can I make you a cup of coffee?"

"I don't have time to stay. But do you remember last Christmas when Manny took those pictures of you onstage? You wouldn't let anyone see them. But Manny said they turned out real good."

"Sam, I was terribly fat. I didn't want anyone to see that gut on me. Come to think of it, I was quite pregnant at the time. No wonder," she laughed.

"So did you keep them?"

"Yeah, they're somewhere in the credenza."

"Mind if I take a look around?" Sam bent down and in a stash of age-old magazines he found the pictures. "These are perfect. They are exactly what I need!"

"They're yours, if you want. But why do you want them?"

"You'll see—come Saturday morning. Well, I'm in a rush. I'm meeting with my vendors this afternoon. I'm planning a gala event for your first day back. First class, all the way. And, you may never hear me say this again, but money is no object. This is an all-or-nothing venture."

"What do you mean, Sam? All-or-nothing venture?"

"Let's just say that Donahue's has been in a bit of a slump these past few months. Enough said. You just get that voice of yours humming again. Remember, rehearsals start Monday."

"We'll be there, Sam. Oh, and Sam, I've got a surprise for you."

"What's that?"

"I've written a song. I just need to work with the piano player."

"Yeah? You're a songwriter now?"

Sarah laughed, "Well, I wouldn't go as far as to say that, but I had plenty of time on my hands when I was at the hospital sixteen hours a day—seven days a week. So I started writing lyrics to a song."

"What's it called?"

"Wait till opening night. I'll tell you then."

◇ ◇ ◇

"Sa-rah…Sa-rah…Sarah." The crowd chanted in unison awaiting Sarah's debut performance. It was a packed house with standing room only for latecomers and those who forgot to make dinner reservations. It was Sam's dream come true. He literally had bet the farm and the roulette ball had just landed on his number. And this time it was all without any intervention from Judge Henry Kinslow. This win was all Sam's own doing.

Sarah made one last check on Billy, who was sound asleep. Surprisingly, the noise didn't disturb him at all. But Sarah on the other hand had opening-night jitters. This time there would be no alcoholic crutch to calm her. "Well, here goes," she said, sliding through the opening in the red velvet panels.

The crowd whistled and hollered. Sam, who stood to the left of the bar, yelled, "Break a leg, partner!"

It was a thunderous reception as Sarah squinted into the flood lights. "Could we dim those a bit?" she asked. As the lights faded, Sarah was able to recognize several of her past patrons. And sitting front and center was Fran and her husband. As soon as Sarah saw her, Fran stood up and stepped to the edge of the stage. She handed Sarah a dozen long stemmed roses. "This is from your fan club at the hospital, Sarah. We all pitched in. Good luck."

"Thank you, Fran. And thank all of you for coming here tonight. It's great to be back," she said into the microphone, "I'd like to start this evening off with a song I wrote a few months ago. I dedicate it to you, Sam. It's called 'Better Days Ahead.'"

Using her index finger, she cued the pianist for a slow introduction. He complied by playing a string of melodious chords before Sarah crooned like she never had before. Her voice, absent of the side effects of liquor, had softened to a romantic flutter. It was alluring, somewhat hypnotic.

> We live our lives expecting,
> That hopes are not mislead.
> When dreams surpass our future,
> There are better days ahead.
> There are better days ahead.

✧ ✧ ✧

By 1954, five years after the grand re-opening, Donahue's was thriving. Reservations were required weeks in advance. Gradually, it had become a club for the elite and upper class of Cleveland, who shelled out Ben Franklins like confetti at a wedding.

With all of the money pouring in, Sam was on his way to becoming wealthy. Even Sarah, who by then owned thirty-five-percent of the club, saw her bank account soar. But Sam wanted more for Sarah and her son. So the day before Billy's fifth birthday, Sam handed Sarah another envelope from his attorney. It stated that she was a full-fledged partner of Donahue's. "Just sign on the dotted line and we're fifty-fifty, Sarah. You own half of the club." Sam wrapped his arms around her and gave her a kiss on the cheek. But the kiss lasted much longer than his usual sign of affection.

"Okay, Sam," she said fending off the unwelcome advance. "We've been through this before. You and I will be friends forever. But I won't take our relationship beyond that."

"You can't stop me from trying. As long as you're by my side, I'm going to do everything in my power to win you over."

"Sweet, sweet Sam. You are my prince. But…"

He cut her off, conceding, "Okay, okay. You win. So, what do you think of this new contract?"

Relieved that the topic had finally been changed, Sarah said, "Unbelievable! You are far too generous. I was thinking, Sam. Now that we have a twenty-piece orchestra…"

"That was one of my better ideas," he said unintentionally interrupting her. "You can get a rest while the customers dance up a thirst. It's been good for sales."

"What I was about to say, Sam, is that I'm down to only two shows a night. If I am to be a full-fledged partner, I need to contribute more to the club."

"I'm listening," he said.

"I want to help out in the office. Now that Billy is in kindergarten, I'm bored to tears during the day. So, let me work on the books. I used to do accounts receivable and payable long before I came to work for you. I know it's been a while, but it will all come back to me. So, if you want me to sign this paper, you'll have to meet me halfway."

"I couldn't say no to you, no matter what you asked. If it's the bookkeeping you want, so be it," he grinned.

Sam didn't admit it, but the fact that Sarah would be spending the better part of the day at the club thrilled him. Over the years he had fallen deeply in love with her, although he kept those feelings hidden as best as he could. But now he had hope that the additional time together would give him a chance to win her over. Perhaps she would come to welcome his advances, but only the test of time would tell.

✧ ✧ ✧

"Ladies and gentlemen, I'd like to introduce Billy Robbins. He's my partner's little boy and today is his fifth birthday, so please join me in singing 'Happy Birthday'…" The crowd chimed in, while Billy buried his face behind Sam's leg. He was a shy and timid little boy who had gained strength from his mentor and surrogate father, Sam.

"Happy birthday dear Billy, happy birthday to you," the crowd sang as Sam eased Billy in front of him. "Look over there, Billy," Sam said pointing to Sarah, who was carrying a large sheet cake with five oversized candles. "It's chocolate," he said bending down to Billy's level. "It's your favorite!"

As Sarah walked across the club floor, the candles flirted with the breeze but retained their flames. Midway to the stage, a rugged man in his late twenties scurried up behind her.

"Allow me, ma'am. This is too heavy for someone as petite as you."

The man, coarse in appearance but neatly shaven, spoke with a slight English accent. Sarah liked what she heard and she liked what she saw.

"Thank you," Sarah said flirtatiously, as she handed him the cake. "You're new here. I haven't seen you before."

"I'm just passing through town. A friend of mind told me to stop in, but I didn't have time to make a reservation. So I figured I'd have a quick brew and then be on my way."

It was unnerving to Sam to see someone he didn't know talking with Sarah. Whether it was jealousy or just plain insecurity, it made him uncomfortable.

"I'll take the cake from here," she said at the base of the steps. "Thank you for your help."

"You're welcome, Miss Robbins. It's Sarah, right?"

"Yes," she said, pausing to take a deep breath. "And what is your name?" she asked coyly.

"My name is Jack Stratton, of the California Strattons."

"Well, it's nice meeting you, Jack," she smiled with a glimmer in her eye.

"Believe me, the pleasure is all mine," he said playfully.

SIX

VICKY DVORAK

Detroit, 1950–1958

Within a few weeks of Vicky's birth it was apparent that Anne wanted nothing to do with her infant daughter. However, to disguise her lack of maternal instinct she claimed she had a case of the baby blues. But Neil wasn't entirely convinced. He remembered what she had said to him on the way to the hospital. She had made it perfectly clear that she wanted a son; a daughter was simply out of the question. So it came as no surprise that the infant girl sensed her mother's disdain and screamed whenever Anne touched her. Vicky yearned for warmth and security. She found that security in her father.

Neal leaned over the crib that he had spent months creating for this precious child. He lifted his infant daughter's hand and solemnly promised, "I'll always protect you, Victoria Marie. Your daddy will never let you down. I swear it." Softly stroking her head, he whispered in a tranquil and soothing voice, "Good night, sweet essence."

"Bravo, Mr. Dvorak. Bravo." Neil turned around to find Anne with her back pressed up against the door. In a slow and mechanical way she applauded him. "So you'll always be there to protect her? How fatherly of you!"

Upon hearing Anne's grating voice, baby Vicky became agitated. She whimpered, if not from a bad dream, then from the distinct feeling that an enemy was close at hand.

"There, there, sweets. Go back to sleep. Daddy's here."

As the baby calmed down and drifted back to sleep, Neil turned toward Anne. Normally he would let things roll off his back, but he could no longer tolerate Anne's abnormal behavior toward their child. He grabbed Anne by the arm and forced her out of the room.

"What the hell is wrong with you?" he demanded, "It's been weeks and you still haven't warmed up to her."

"Why should I? You coddle her enough for the both of us!"

"Someone has to compensate for your lack of affection. She's our baby girl, for Christ's sake," he cursed.

"I heard those exact same words from my ex-husband. He was just like you, Neil. He spent so much time pampering Rose that he forgot he had a wife. Now you're doing the very same thing, and I'm getting sick and tired of it."

Lowering his voice he pleaded, "Anne, be reasonable. She's a baby. If you'd just give her a chance, you'd love her as much as I do."

"I don't think that's possible," she snapped.

"Damn it, Anne. How can you be so cruel and heartless?"

"It's just that I can't stand the thought of another female in my house. She may be small now, but she'll grow. And I can't bear the thought of a younger version of myself stealing my husband from me."

Neil's eyes grew wide and his nostrils flared. He had not been this angry since his ordeal with Janet. "That is a despicable thing to say, Anne. You are a contemptible woman!"

"I warned you that I only wanted a son who could take the place of my John."

"Your John? I'd say he was more of a sibling than a son to you. Your parents deserve the credit for raising him *and* Rose. By the way, if you were so gung ho about mothering, why *didn't* you keep John with you?"

Anne lifted her head and looked him straight in the eyes. "It was John's decision. He wanted to be with his sister more than he wanted to be with me. He said that Rose needed him and that I didn't," she said enviously.

"That's probably the first honest thing you've said." Neil shook his head in disgust. "You are a pathetic person, Anne. There are times I wished I had never married you."

"Ah, but then you wouldn't have your sweet essence, would you? So if I were you, I'd watch my back."

Neil squinted his eyes and reluctantly faced her threat head on. "I've been down this road before, Anne. Just spill it!"

"You haven't touched me since the day she was born. So unless you start showing me half the love you show her, I'll divorce you in the blink of an eye."

"Now we're talking divorce?"

"It's not a pretty word, is it? But I've considered it. And do you know what I've decided, Neil? If I go through with it, I'd do it the same as Janet did. Take your daughter as far away from you as possible."

"Okay, you've got my attention, Anne," he said gritting his teeth. "Just tell me one thing. What ever happened to the sensitive woman I met at the Viper Lounge?"

"That woman disappeared the moment she gave birth to your sweet essence…of stinkweed," she said mockingly.

Cornered, Neil had no way out. Anne had won the battle again, hands down. He knew that he would be at her mercy if he wanted to keep his family together.

"Tell me what you want, Anne. I'll agree to anything as long as we remain a family. Just name your terms."

Seeing that she had the upper hand, she softened her approach. "Honestly, I'm not asking for much. All I want is a guarantee that from this day forward I will come first in your life. I want you to love me more than you love her!"

"But, Anne," he tried to reason, "How can you measure the love of a child against the love of a spouse? Those are two separate beats of the heart. Can't you understand that?"

Anne shrugged her shoulders. At thirty-four she still couldn't comprehend the meaning of love. She believed that love should be given exclusively to her and that she had no need to reciprocate. This was proven with the other three men in her life. Not her father, her first husband, or her son were able to provide Anne with the love and affection she constantly demanded. As each one failed her, she cast them aside and out of her life.

"So what do you say, Neil? Do you want to keep your family together?"

Neil stared at the floor for a moment before he answered. Then he looked her in the eye. "I'll show you endless love, Anne, if that's what it takes. In return, I expect you to be a mother to Victoria. I want a fair trade-off."

"Neil, all she does is cry around me," Anne whined.

Trying to remain cool he said, "She hardly knows you because you shuffle her off to a sitter every chance you get. She's confused about who her real mother is. This has got to stop, Anne. You need to form a mother-daughter bond with her. Do this for me and I'll do whatever you want."

Anne barely managed to control the smirk that was about to emerge on her face. She had fooled Neil with the threat of divorce—because that's all it was—a threat. She had no intention of ever letting go of him. The thought of being a single parent and raising Victoria alone made her quiver.

"Neil, let's talk about this later. I need some shut-eye," she said, anxious to change the subject of bonding with her child.

Neil was not about to let her take her usual nap. It was a convenient excuse that allowed her to escape responsibilities and avoid confrontations. "No, Anne, you're not going to lie down right now. Not until I have a commitment from you. I want you to tell me that you will try and warm up to our baby. Please say that you will."

"I can't promise an overnight miracle," she huffed. "It's hard to care for something that you never wanted in the first place."

"Please," he implored. Humbling himself, he kissed her hand. "We can make this work. I know it."

"Well," she hesitated. "All right, Neil. The more love you show, the more I'll be a mother to her." But that was as far as Anne would commit; she never promised to be a good one. She merely agreed that she would be Vicky's mother.

✧ ✧ ✧

For the next three years Neil doted on Anne as much as humanly possible. He showered her with attention. An outsider might have thought she had it made. But the one thing she wanted, he just couldn't give her. Neil had become impotent. So Anne, who had become sexually frustrated, took her resentment out on her young daughter.

"Stop that crying, Victoria. Stop it or I'll…" She pressed her hand across Vicky's mouth, muffling her cries. "You can scream all you want; your father's at the cabinet shop, so no one will hear you! So scream away, VIC-TOR-I-A!" And the child did. Often the toddler would become so hysterical she'd choke on her own saliva, and then regurgitate until the absence of food would render bitter greenish bile. That was the only way the child knew how to cope with a mother who despised her.

This was Anne's treatment of Vicky whenever they were alone; however, in Neil's presence Anne would temper her ever-growing feelings of hostility. And yet it was Neil she wanted to punish, but she held her tongue. Since the day she threatened a divorce, Neil had become impotent. Anne often wondered if impotency was a problem before she had met him. But she never asked; instead she tried to seduce him.

"Relax, Neil. I know if you'd let me, I could make you aroused. Let me touch you," she would say as she fumbled to untie his pajamas. But he'd simply move her hand away.

"Anne, we've talked about this before. It's my condition. As much as I would like to, I can't make love to you."

"But you've had this condition for three years. Why on earth won't you go see the doctor?"

Neil felt no remorse when he turned over with his back toward her. "I've told you before that I don't want anyone poking around my privates."

"Well, this isn't normal, Neil," she snapped. I want you to see a doctor so you can take care of me the way a husband should!"

"Better yet, Anne. Why don't you take care of yourself? Up until now you've been doing a fine job without my assistance."

Anne was caught off guard. She masturbated frequently while she thought Neil was asleep. She didn't refute the statement.

"I'm going to sleep, Anne. I've had a long day." Neil pulled the chain to the bedside table lamp and closed his eyes. He would remain a faithful husband even though his condition was intermittent. It only happened when he was around her.

✧ ✧ ✧

In the summer of 1955 the suburban lifestyle of East Detroit had become the wave of the future. Before the homes were even built, entire housing developments had been sold out. So when the opportunity extended itself, Neil Dvorak purchased a moderate tract house for him and his family on Temple Street.

The Dvoraks were the first to move in. But as the neighborhood filled, it was obvious that Neil and Anne were at least ten years older than any of the other couples. However, six other five-year-olds were ready for kindergarten, just like Vicky.

Catherine Moore, the former Miss Detroit and the Dvoraks' next-door neighbor, invited all of the mothers to her home for an afternoon meeting. Anne was one of the last to arrive, but offered no apologies. She sat down and cattily reviewed the other women. One by one she gave each woman the once-over, scrutinizing clothing, makeup, and hairdo. Anne was the most critical of Catherine; from Anne's point of view, Catherine was just a little too pleasing to the eye. *I bet she went to the beauty salon to get those blond locks styled. And look at those black patent-leather pumps. A bit much for a midweek afternoon,* Anne said to herself.

It was only Anne who felt that way about Catherine. The others found her beauty to be second only to her winning personality.

Standing in front of the living room fireplace, Catherine addressed them warmly. "I've called you here to discuss the kindergarten school sessions. I think that it's important that we choose the same session for our children. That way if there is an emergency, any one of us could help. Personally, I prefer to enroll Lynn in the morning session rather than the afternoon. But I'll go along with the majority. What are your feelings?"

In succession each woman raised her hand and said, "I vote for mornings." When it was Anne's turn she exclaimed, "Mornings will suit us just fine."

"Wonderful. Registration is Monday morning at nine o'clock. Let's ride down together. My mother has agreed to babysit our other children here at my house. Well, this short meeting is adjourned. Please stay to chat so that we can all get to know each other a little better. There are doughnuts and coffee in the kitchen."

Anxious to leave, Anne said, "Catherine, I have to get going. Neil will be home shortly and he doesn't like to be kept waiting for dinner. You know how men are."

"I do understand. Joe's the same way. Then we'll see you Monday, Anne."

"Yes, Monday," Anne said as she stepped out onto the front porch.

She was relieved to be outside and not confined to a roomful of women who were younger than her with the curvaceous bodies to prove it. She remembered having a voluptuous figure, but that was before she had Vicky. Five years later the weight had not come off as it had when she had her first two children. So socializing with these young mothers was not her preference; besides, she didn't think that any of them had gone out of their way to make her feel especially welcome.

✧ ✧ ✧

The night before school started, Neil swung Vicky over his shoulders and carried her to bed while a 78 rpm recording of "Barcarolle" from Offenbach's *Tales of Hoffman* played on the turntable. This was a ritual they had been practicing as long as she could remember. This was father-and-daughter time.

"Now that you're a schoolgirl, you're almost too big to carry," he teased. "Okay, it's prayer time." Neil knelt down beside her and folded his hands like hers.

"Bless Daddy and Mother, Grandpa and Grandma, and Rose and John. And thank you, God, for letting me go to school with my friends. Amen."

Neil folded back the blanket and Vicky hopped in. He twirled her long brown hair around his finger. "You have a good time with your friends tomorrow. I'll be thinking about you."

"Daddy, I want you to wake me up before you go to work."

"No, I'm taking the early bus tomorrow. You sleep in because school doesn't start until nine," Neil said quite certain of his facts. Events would prove to be different.

Just one month prior, on the day of kindergarten registration, Anne was standing curbside when Catherine pulled over to pick her up. Anne was prepared with her excuse. "Hello, ladies. Sorry, I can't join you. Something came up so I'll have to register Victoria later today. Ta-ta," she said as she turned away and walked back to the house.

Catherine spoke to Anne's retreating back. "I'll have them pencil her name in until you can get there, Anne."

Anne was near the front door when she heard Catherine call out to her. Turning around she forced a smile and said, "That would be very kind of you, Catherine."

Later that day just minutes before the school office was to close, Anne showed up to enroll Vicky. "I'm Mrs. Neil Dvorak. I'm here to enroll my daughter for kindergarten." The administrative clerk checked her watch, but politely handed Anne the forms anyway.

"Oh, yes, Mrs. Dvorak," she said enthusiastically. "This should be quick and easy. I see that Victoria's name was added to the morning session. I believe your neighbors on Temple Street reserved a space for her until you were able to come down in person."

The clerk glanced down at the list and added, "Lucky for you a slot was held in her name. The morning session is now waiting list only. Since it was the preference of most parents, we had to call it first come, first served."

Anne patiently let the clerk make her spiel and then announced, "There's been a change of plans. My husband and I have very busy schedules," she lied in part since she wasn't busy at all. "Victoria will need to be placed in the afternoon class. Perhaps there is someone on the morning waiting list who would like to switch with us."

"By all means, Mrs. Dvorak, we can accommodate you. I am very sorry that it didn't work out for your daughter. I do hope she won't be too disappointed."

Anne interrupted, "Thank you for your concern; however, Victoria is rarely disappointed." If only that was the truth. Anne saw to it that Victoria was disheartened as often as she could pull it off.

She wondered how she would justify the schedule change to Neil and the neighbors. *I'll tell them it was a clerical error. I'll blame it on the incapable school clerk who forgot to put Vicky's name on the list. Just to be on the safe side I won't tell anyone until the last minute. That way there's no possibility of it being changed back.*

Keeping to her plan, Anne waited until the morning of the first day of school to announce the changes to Vicky. Vicky had just finished a bowl of cereal when her mother stepped around the corner. In a mocking voice she asked, "So what's your hurry? You don't have to be there until one o'clock."

"But my friends are waiting outside for me. I'll be late," Vicky said in a panicky voice.

Anne savored the look of disappointment that flooded Vicky's face. "Sit down and finish your breakfast while I reason with the neighborhood know-it-alls." Anne ran out of the front door and yelled to Catherine, "I thought I told you that the morning session was all filled up. Victoria was assigned to the afternoon."

"That can't be! I confirmed it myself that Vicky had a morning slot," Catherine declared.

"You know how those clerks are. An error here, an error there, these things just happen."

"We should protest to the school, Anne. Maybe they'll be able to correct it," Catherine argued.

"No, just leave things as they are. Victoria is happy about it and that's really all that matters, isn't it?"

Surprised, Catherine said, "Yes, I suppose so. Well, we'd better get going. We don't want the children to be late on their first day."

Anne slammed the door and retreated back into the kitchen. Vicky was somber, lost in the lie that was told on her behalf. She froze when Anne leaned over the counter and smirked, "I don't want to hear one word from you. And stop that whimpering! You know I hate to hear you whine."

Vicky abruptly stopped her tears. She knew she had to follow her mother's instructions to a tee.

"I'm going back to bed. You can go downstairs and play. If I don't wake up in time, make sure that you wake me when both hands on the clock are straight up. I have to show you the way to school today."

Anne covered herself with the comforter and smiled. A victory over her child was like a sedative to her. It was her secret revenge for not having had intercourse in years. She never penalized Neil for his condition in the hopes he'd eventually be cured. So she did the next best thing; she took out her frustrations on the one she believed caused his sexual inadequacy.

By late fall, Vicky thought nothing of dressing and feeding herself before she walked alone to school. Her mother, if not sound asleep, was usually doing crossword puzzles. Either way, Vicky knew not to bother her.

One particular December day Vicky peered out her bedroom window and saw snowflakes rapidly falling from the sky. They were noticeably different in size and shape compared to the ones that had gracefully blanketed the ground the day before. These were not as fluffy. These flakes were in a frenzy to reach the ground.

She closed the curtain and sighed, "I better dress extra warm today."

After donning two sweaters and two pairs of snow pants, she put on a jacket, earmuffs, and mittens. Then over multiple pairs of woolen socks she forced on rubber boots. The garb was bulky, but the insulation was well worth the restriction.

As she opened the door, the violent wind mustered its strength. Stronger than she anticipated, it blew the door from her hands, slamming it against an adjacent wall. Oh, how she would have relished a car ride today.

Foregoing any further delays, Vicky began the seven-block journey to school. The wind pummeled her face, singeing her cheeks like the flames from a fire. The snowflakes, no longer distinguishable, had joined forces to become surging waves of continuous white. It blinded her when she stopped at the corner of Temple and Vine, only two blocks from home. With the storm beating against her, Vicky weighed the consequences of turning back and facing her mother who had warned what would happen if she ever missed school without permission. Anne had told the child she would call the truant officer who would come and take her to jail. She was only allowed to remain home if she was sick, and even then, nothing short of a fever would suffice. So whether it was the fear of the truant officer or the fear of facing the wrath of her mother, Vicky was impelled to forge on in the bitter cold.

The fierce wind cut through her mittens, freezing her hands and fingers. She pressed her hands over her earmuffs to block the piercing air from her inner ears. It helped, but barely. *Just run,* she thought.

Although every street sign had long disappeared in the sheets of snow, Vicky remembered the way. She knew she had to go straight up, across three streets, then left four blocks. She was out of breath by the time she reached the school parking lot. Certain she was late for school, Vicky prayed she wouldn't be reported to the truant officer. Worse yet, that she wouldn't be reported to her mother.

Vicky treaded up to the double entry doors and found them securely fastened. She was locked out. She *was* too late. Her small hands, tingling with cold, were unable to knock on the door. She called out, but no voice could be heard above the curious bellow of the wind. With her foot she kicked the door over and over until it flew open. Standing before her was the principal, who looked shocked to see so small a child alone.

"Child, what are you doing here?"

Before Vicky could answer, the principal pulled her in out of the storm. "Didn't you see the news this morning? All school districts in the Detroit area are closed because of the blizzard."

The principal signaled to her assistant to gather some blankets. "It's probably too late to catch your mother. I'm surprised that she would have driven in this kind of weather."

Vicky tried to explain, "But, I..."

"Don't worry, dear," she said compassionately. "I know the streets are slick with ice so we'll give her some extra time to get home. I'm sure when she hears that school is closed today, she'll rush right back to get you."

"I'm okay, really," Vicky said, trying to be convincing. "You don't need to call my mother. Besides, I walked here and it wasn't hard at all. My ears don't even hurt."

The principal was mortified that a child, let alone a five-year-old, had walked to school in a blizzard. *What kind of mother would allow her child to be out in this kind of storm?* "We need to get you home. We'll call your mother."

The principal's assistant pulled Victoria Dvorak's file and then made an attempt to call PRescott 3-2561. The dial tone was intermittent due to downed telephone lines. It wasn't until the third attempt that the principal finally heard a ringback tone. But that's all she heard, as Anne slept through the ringing telephone.

The assistant quickly located the files of the other children on Temple Street and, based on the nearest address, she telephoned Catherine Moore. Again, the dial tone was intermittent; however, this time when the phone rang through, it was answered immediately.

"Mrs. Moore, I'm calling from Temple School. I'm trying to reach Mrs. Dvorak. Her daughter came to school in the blizzard. We need Mrs. Dvorak to come and pick Vicky up immediately. We are closing the office and sending the remaining staff home."

"I see her car in the driveway. She must be home. I'll go next door and give her the message. If by some chance she's not available, I will come and pick Vicky up myself."

Catherine rushed to the Dvorak's house and let herself in when no one answered. She found Anne asleep in bed, her snores almost as loud as the wind outside.

"Anne, wake up," Catherine said as she gently tapped her arm.

Rustling in the featherbed, Anne was slow to awaken but when she saw Catherine, she suddenly became alert. She shouted, "What are you doing in my house uninvited?"

"Anne, I'm sorry to disturb you. But the school called about Vicky. They want you to come and pick her up right now."

Angered, she blurted out, "What? Is she sick again? That child is always complaining about something or other. She will say or do anything to get attention."

For the first time in front of a neighbor, Anne had not been able to disguise her insensitivity toward her own daughter. It made Catherine uncomfortable. "They want to know why Vicky was out in the blizzard, Anne. They said this might have to be reported to the authorities."

"Blizzard? What blizzard?"

"It's been on the television and on the radio. This is the worst blizzard we've had in years. Listen, I'll be happy to drive you to pick her up."

"I appreciate your concern, Catherine, but you've done enough already. You don't need to bother yourself with my problems. You can let yourself out, thank you." Catherine smiled yet said nothing, although she knew that Anne had just snubbed her.

Anne changed from her nightgown into appropriate winter wear and headed outside. The temperature was well below zero and the car door was difficult to pry open. When she finally jerked the door open and sat inside the car, she found there was little solace from the freezing temperatures outside. Anne put the key in the ignition and tried several times to start the frigid engine. With every attempt the battery slowed and churned, until it seemed hopeless. However, Anne tried one more time and the engine suddenly took hold, spitting out black smoke from the exhaust pipe. As the engine warmed, Anne went back out in the storm and scattered handfuls of rock salt over the driveway. But the biting chill was more than she could take. She jumped back into the car and turned on the wipers. The friction caused the sheet of ice on the windshield to break apart. Eventually it bore a circle large enough to see out.

Driving less than five miles per hour she had plenty of time to conjure up a story up for the school officials. *There wasn't any reception on the television. Our radio broke months ago. The car wouldn't start earlier so Vicky decided to walk. But I wouldn't dream of letting her walk in a storm, let alone a blizzard.* She rehearsed the story over and over until she herself believed it was the absolute truth. *Besides, no school official is going to tell me how to raise my child. This is none of their damn business.*

A week after the incident, Catherine Moore was gazing out her kitchen window, etched with a new layer of frost. She watched Neil for several minutes while he diligently scraped the ice off his windshield. When he moved to the passenger window, he caught sight of her.

"Good morning, neighbor," he said cheerfully. "It's going to be another nippy one today. Down to the low teens, but I'm glad to see the sun out again." Assuming she didn't hear his weather comment, he moved on to scrape the rear window. Catherine smiled at him before disappearing back into her kitchen.

"Is something wrong, Cath?" Her husband Joe rounded the kitchen table to the coffee percolator. He stopped and kissed her on the back of the neck.

"I just don't understand it," she said as she reached into the cupboard for two cups.

"Understand what?"

"I spoke with Neil the other day. In fact, it was the day after the storm. And he was so bubbly and happy. I asked him how Vicky was doing. He said that she was doing great. Then he went on about how much she loves school. So much so, she wished she didn't have Christmas vacation."

"What's wrong with that? Imagine if Lynn or Bobbie chose school over vacation. I'd be…I'd be…I'd be asking whose family they belonged to," he joked.

"This is not a laughing matter. Neil didn't make any mention of Vicky walking to school in the blizzard," she argued.

"Neil's a proud man. He's probably too embarrassed to discuss it with you."

"But maybe he doesn't know what happened."

"Don't fool yourself, Cath. If Anne didn't tell him, I'm sure Vicky did. God knows that our kids would never keep their mouths shut if something like that happened to them." Chuckling, he parted her long blond hair and kissed her again. "Don't worry your pretty little head about it. The ordeal is over and Vicky's fine. Neil said so himself."

"Yes, but it's just this feeling I have. There's something about Anne I don't trust. I can't put my finger on it, but it's just something."

"Enough about the Dvoraks," Joe insisted. "Let's change the subject. What does my beautiful wife want for Christmas?"

Catherine's instinct was right. Neil was never told about the situation because Anne covered her tracks in all directions. To the school officials, she managed to shed a few tears while pleading, "Honestly, I would never put my child in harm's way. It will never happen again. I swear to you all. There's no need to let this go any further." To the neighbors, whose topic of conversation was Anne's unusual sleeping habits, she kept her story brief. "I took a sleeping pill because of a migraine headache. Then Vicky left for school without waking me. It was a big mistake. There's no point in dwelling in the past. Neil and I decided that we won't mention it again. The whole episode is far too upsetting to our family."

And finally Anne silenced her child, the only other person who knew the truth. Shouting at the top of her lungs the moment Vicky got into the car, Anne ordered, "Under no circumstance do you tell your father that you walked to school. As far as he's concerned, you had a snow day today. Do you hear me, young lady?"

When Vicky didn't respond promptly, Anne repeated herself. "I said, do you understand me?"

Vicky heard loud and clear. "Yes, Mother."

"Good. Now is a good time for us to have a talk. When you were born your father asked me to bond with you. Today I am honoring his wish. From this moment on you are not to break our sacred bond. In other words whatever I say to you is just between us. Never tell anyone what I do or say. And never ask me why. There! We have bonded. Do you understand, VIC-TOR-I-A?"

"Yes," she said submissively.

"Good. Then we'll have no problem getting along in the future, will we?"

Vicky learned at a very young age not to back talk to her mother. Whatever she was told to do, she did so without question. Her secret life required that she obey her mother's strict commands or suffer the consequences.

Vicky was just six years old when she was performing chores that were unheard of for a child of her age. But her mother had schooled Vicky well, so she told no one about her chores, not even her father. If Neil had only known the eccentric demands that Anne placed on her, he would have come to Vicky's rescue. But he never knew what a typical day was for his young daughter.

Vacuum the rugs, dust the tables, scrub the bathtub, wipe the plastic sofa covers, wash and wipe the dishes. And don't forget to wake me up as soon as you see your father coming up the walkway.

At such a tender age Vicky was barely old enough to know the difference between right and wrong. Certainly, she was not old enough to understand the perverse behavior of her mother. Vicky thought that all children were treated in the same way and were at the beck and call of their mothers. It wasn't until she was seven years old that her friends made her think differently.

Vicky had been on her hands and knees scrubbing the kitchen floor when she heard her friends calling her from outside. "Vicky, Vicky. Come out and play. Vicky, Vicky." Children in the neighborhood never knocked or rang the doorbell at any of their homes. They simply chanted out their friend's name.

As much as Vicky wanted to open the door, she knew better than to open it without her mother's permission. Several times her friends repeated Vicky's name while she fought hard to ignore them. Scrubbing the floor more vigorously, she tried to drown out their calls. When they finally stopped calling out for her, as much as she would have liked to join them, she felt relieved that they had finally given up on her. She didn't want their calls to disturb her mother.

Vicky rinsed the scrub brush in the bucket and moved to clean another area. Not once did she look up; if she had, she would have seen her friends peering at her through the kitchen window. They watched Vicky as she worked on a spot that seemed impossible to remove. They observed her rubbing the stain over and over until they became tired of spying on her and left. The following day at school, Lynn Moore approached her.

"Your mother makes you scrub the floors? Gosh, I wouldn't even know how," Lynn said to Vicky. "No kids have to do that."

Vicky was puzzled as to how Lynn knew. "It's just one of my chores," she said, realizing she had broken one of her mother's rules. "I have to go, Lynn, I'm not supposed to talk about my chores with anyone."

"Why not? Everybody has chores. That's how you get an allowance."

"Allowance?" Vicky asked curiously.

"I get twenty cents a week for picking up my room and helping my mom with the dishes sometimes. And me and my brother trade off setting the table every night. But that's about it. My parents say that a kid's job is to get good grades."

Luckily, studying wasn't an issue for Vicky. Blessed with her father's scholastic genes, she had been able to read since she was four. Straight A's were a given.

"I don't get an allowance but my mom says the more I learn, the more I can teach my daughter when I grow up," Vicky said defensively.

"Baloney. Your mom is just mean. When our windows are open, we can hear her yelling at you to do this and to do that. My mom says it just isn't right for kids our age to do the stuff you have to do," Lynn said.

Vicky feared she may have said too much. "I have to go, Lynn. I can't be talking about this with you." Vicky walked away with food for thought. She wondered if Lynn was telling the truth. She wondered if her mother was different from her friends' mothers.

Later that afternoon, Vicky was washing the dishes while her mother worked on a crossword puzzle. She decided that she would ask her mother to explain. It was a bold decision since her mother was in a somewhat hostile mood. Vicky chanced it anyway. "Mother, I was talking to Lynn this morning."

"What did Catherine Moore's brat have to say?"

"She said children my age don't do the kind of chores that you make me do. Why do *I* have to?"

Vicky made the mistake of asking her mother *why*. It was a simple question, but it paved the way for her mother to physically lash out at her.

"You insolent child," Anne shouted as she seized the object nearest her. It was a wooden paddle with a rubber ball suspended by an elastic string. With the newfound weapon in hand, Anne struck Vicky across the face. The impact caused Vicky to stumble back against the cupboard door. She lost her footing and fell to the linoleum floor. She lay on the floor wailing.

"That is what you get for questioning me. Let me remind you," Anne seethed, "if you tell anyone about this, you'll be sorry for living."

Vicky muffled her cries as she massaged her burning cheek. Her mother standing over her was an unspoken threat. Vicky covered her own mouth this time. She didn't want her mother's hand anywhere near her.

"Boo hoo. Poor little crybaby." Anne's eyes were small and cat-like as she gathered the elastic line piece by piece. When the ball reached her hand, she yanked it free before throwing it across the room. Then she took the paddle and just inches from Vicky's face, she waved it again. "You better think twice before you ever question me again, young lady. Do you understand me now, Victoria?"

"Yes," she whimpered. Vicky didn't move. She waited for a signal that her mother was finished with her. When her mother walked away from her, she started to get up only to hear her mother shout again. "Wash your face and then go to your room. I expect you to be asleep long before your father gets home."

As her mother marched down the hallway, Vicky rushed into the bathroom and cooled her face with ice-cold water. She wondered what she had done that was so wrong; hadn't she only asked "Why"?

The wooden-paddle incident was the defining moment in the relationship between Vicky and Anne. With that one strike, Vicky understood that her punishments were no longer limited to verbal thrashings. To be merely scorned was to get off easy.

Vicky's eighth birthday was only a week away when Neil approached Anne about a party. Once again Anne was unyielding to any recognition of her daughter—birthday or otherwise.

"Not this year, Neil. She's just too young to appreciate it. Besides, if we give her one now, it will just spoil her. So let's just keep it small with just the three of us. I'll make a tray of lasagna."

"Anne, I was hoping for a family gathering. I was thinking about inviting your folks, since we haven't seen them in years. It's about time they met their youngest grandchild. To be honest, I'd like her to meet John's wife and Rose's husband."

Anne threw down a scouring pad and spun around to face him. "Well, why should I talk to them now? They don't seem to want to have anything to do with me. Do I have to remind you that I wasn't invited to either of my children's weddings? Me, the mother of the bride, for Christ's sake. As for my son, it just breaks my heart. I should have been the one sitting in the front pew. Not my parents. He should have remembered who brought him into this world. Because I deserved…No, let me rephrase, I *deserve* more respect. They can all go to hell for all I care."

Neil shook his head in dismay. "Anne, are you really that self-centered? Does everything have to revolve around you?" She tried to interrupt, but he wouldn't allow it. "Rose and John should have lived with us all along. Your parents, fine people as they are, should not have been expected to make up for your shortcomings."

"Shortcomings? What do you mean by that?"

"Like it or not, Anne, someday you will have to take responsibility for your actions. You can pretend otherwise, but it was you who severed all ties with your family. In all these years I never have heard you say that you wanted to see your children. It makes me wonder, Anne. If you were given the chance to banish Vicky, would you?"

"I'm not going to answer that. So let's get back to the subject at hand, your sweet essence's birthday. No party this year. But," she paused long enough for Neil to raise his brow in expectation, "I'll let you pick out her birthday present. Buy her whatever you want. Even the roller skates she told me she wanted for Christmas. And I promise not to object. Deal?"

Surrendering once again he agreed, "Deal. But I'm holding you to your word. I will buy whatever I want without your interference."

"Fine!" she retorted.

Vicky's eighth birthday went exactly as planned. With just the three of them, there was little fanfare. There was a cake, although it was devoid of an inscription, not even "Happy Birthday." And the flavor, German chocolate, was coincidentally Anne's favorite. Although Vicky hated coconut, it was a cake, nonetheless.

After a short verse of the standard song, Anne escaped to the living room sofa and sprawled out. When she was gone, Neil handed Vicky her birthday present. "It's from me and your mother."

"Roller skates, thank you. I wanted these for so long." Bending over, Neil winked and whispered, "They are from your mother, too."

Heeding the reminder, Vicky solemnly called out, "Thank you, Mother." But Vicky never heard "you're welcome."

Neil took the skate wrench and started sizing the roller skates to Vicky's feet. "While I'm doing this I want you to open this up," he said reaching into his shirt pocket. Neil pulled out a red velvet box and handed it to her. "This is from me to you," he whispered.

"Another present?"

"Shhhhhh. No need to wake your mother up." But it was too late. The sudden hush in their voices was as disturbing to Anne as the laughter she had heard moments before. *Something's going on with those two,* she thought. She slid off the couch and positioned herself at the end of the hallway. From her vantage point she could see Vicky opening the gift. *So what did Mr. Dvorak do for his sweet essence of stinkweed this time?*

Anne eyed Vicky as she lifted a fine gold chain from the box. Dangling from its middle was a heart-shaped pendant adorned with what appeared to be a crystal.

"It's all real, Vicky. The chain is fourteen-karat gold. And that's a genuine diamond. Almost a quarter of a carat."

"It's pretty, Daddy. What's a carat?"

He chuckled, realizing that maybe she was a tad too young to appreciate its value. But it didn't matter. His deal with Anne had given him the go-ahead for any purchase. And since this opportunity would probably never come again, he had taken full advantage of their bargain while he'd had the chance.

"Let me help you," he said, fastening the clasp. "It looks beautiful on you."

"Can I go next door and show Lynn and Bobbie?"

"Sure. But come home before it gets dark," he said and then he pressed two fingers to his lips and kissed them. He carried the kiss to Vicky's lips.

The second that Vicky was out of the house, Anne made her presence known by charging into the kitchen. "Well, well, Mr. Moneybags. You certainly outdid yourself this time, didn't you?"

"Awake so soon, Anne? I thought you'd be sawing logs by now."

"You wish! I knew you were up to something. But buying a diamond necklace for an eight-year-old? That was utterly irresponsible of you!"

Nonchalantly, Neil continued sipping his coffee while Anne ranted on. "Don't you dare ignore me! Where did you get the money? You know we can't afford a gift like that. It's going back to the store tomorrow!"

"The hell it is! You won't ever take that necklace from her. Besides, if it's any of your business, I made arrangements for monthly payments. Out of my…what do you call it, Anne? My weekly beer allowance?"

Defeated, she stormed out of the kitchen and into the sanctuary of their bedroom, to stew in her own jealously. Other than her wedding band, the only other piece of jewelry that Neil had ever given her was a mother's ring with a single gemstone. It was an emerald that symbolized the birth of Vicky. Naturally, Anne showed it off when he gave it to her, but as soon as the novelty wore off, she tossed it into a shoe box along with other forgettable trinkets.

Anne pulled her nightgown over her head while struggling with the voices within her. *How could I have been so stupid? She gets a diamond pendant and I get a husband who hasn't had an erection since she was born. I've got to get back at him one way or another. And I will.* Her eyes searched the shadowed room as if an answer would present itself. *Think, Anne, think. What can I do to pay him back? Or, better yet, pay her back. She's the one who causes the problems between me and my husband. If it takes me forever, I'll come up with something!*

A week later Anne was pacing back and forth and repeatedly checking her watch. "Any minute now, the diamond girl should be walking through the…" Before she finished, Vicky turned the handle to the screen door.

"Hello, Mother. I hope you had a good day." It was Vicky's canned statement whenever she walked through the door. It was safe enough because she knew the slightest issue could bring out the monster in her mother.

"So what do you think of that, Victoria? Anne with her arms folded pointed a finger at a festive gift box atop the ironing board.

"It's pretty. Who's it for?"

Anne removed the box from its platform and placed it in Vicky's hands. "This is for you. It's a belated birthday present. Like the pendant your father gave you. This one's from me. Go ahead, open it."

Vicky anxiously ripped the paper to shreds. "It's so heavy," she said with mounting anticipation.

"Well then, hurry up."

As the last piece of wrapping paper fell to the floor, the picture on the box unveiled its contents. It was an iron. Vicky's excitement quickly diminished.

Standing above her, Anne displayed a cruel and satisfying grin. Vicky's disappointment was the reaction she had hoped for.

"Well, what do you say, Victoria? It wasn't cheap, you know."

Vicky was blindsided. Her mother had done it to her again. And now, against her will, her eyes began to well up.

Ah, better results than I originally anticipated, Anne thought. Callously ignoring the tears streaming down her daughter's face she said, "I was thinking that it's about time you became more productive and learned how to iron." Vicky took the sleeve of her blouse and wiped her face. Although she was emotionally hurt, she was also determined not to let her mother get the best of her.

"The ironing board is too high for me. Do I stand on a chair?"

Pushing her aside, Anne walked over and released the underside lever. She smirked as it dropped down to Vicky's height.

"Why do you think they make this adjustable, Victoria? It is so children, but not the spoiled ones who live around here, can help their mothers. So every day after your chores I expect you to iron the sheets and pillowcases. In a month or so when you get the hang of it you can start on your school clothes. And then we'll see about you doing your father's work shirts."

Anne placed the first pillowcase across the board. "Do exactly like this and you won't scorch any of my linens."

Vicky picked up the heavy iron and copied her mother's movements. "See, I can do it."

"Good. I'm going to lie down. Don't burn anything."

Moments later Anne's mouth fell open making way for the uniform grunts that would increase in volume. Vicky picked up a second pillowcase and folded it over the board. She focused on the disgusting noise that escaped from her mother's throat. It was deep and gruff, almost masculine in pitch. The repetition seemed unending.

I wish I had a mother like Lynn's or Tina's. As she folded the pressed pillowcase, she couldn't block out the annoying sound that was only a few feet away. It made her think. *I hate her. I will always hate her. Someday when I get older, I'm going to tell her how I feel. Someday.*

Each afternoon when Vicky ironed to the tune of her mother's snores, she swore the same pledge. *Someday she's going to know how much I hate her.* That was the oath that kept Vicky strong, however much she outwardly conformed to her mother's will. It was a promise of the future. What Vicky didn't know was that the future was so close at hand. In July of '58 shortly after her eighth birthday, a chain of events altered the lives of all three Dvoraks.

Neil ran his hand through his salt-and-pepper hair. He had just received his invitation to the annual American Legion Convention in Grand Rapids. Because it was usually for men only, it was the one time of the year that he was granted a furlough from Anne. But this package invitation was unlike any of the others. It was addressed to Mr. and Mrs. Neil Dvorak.

Neil scanned through the packet and found two itineraries. One contained the schedule of seminars for the legionnaires. The other page listed the activities for the ladies, which included etiquette, cooking, candle making, and a fashion show. *God, the thought of a week of Anne's constant nagging. Not on your life!* He took the second sheet and crumpled it before tossing it into the trash can.

"What's that, Neil?"

"It's my invitation to the Legion Convention. It's going to be a good one. One of the speakers used to be Ike's right-hand man. I can't wait to hear him." When Anne didn't question the paper he discarded, Neil released a sigh of relief.

"I hate this time of year. You go off with your old cronies while I sit home with Vicky. It's not fair."

"Anne, this is the only thing I do outside of work," he reasoned.

Referring to his impotence she spewed, "Yeah, you can say that again!"

"I'm going to take a shower, Anne. I don't want to argue with you."

Neil adjusted the showerhead with one hand while he lathered his genitals with the other. No, he wasn't impotent. His penis hardened with each stroke. *If this is impotence, God, let me have more.* In less than a minute he spurted onto the bathroom wall, proving once again that his affliction was strictly related to Anne.

✧ ✧ ✧

Neil entered the overly crowded lobby of the Grand Rapids Intercontinental Hotel. Hundreds of potbellied veterans, many of whom were smoking pipes, cigars, or cigarettes, were waiting for their turn to check in. It was utter chaos, and it took Neil almost an hour before he was finally at the head of the line.

"Mr. Dvorak, will Mrs. Dvorak be joining you?"

"No, I'll just need a single room. She was unable to make it. We have a daughter at home and we couldn't find a sitter." He babbled on and on to a front desk clerk who merely wanted to know if he needed a second key.

"You'll be in room five-sixty-five on the fifth floor. It has a pool view."

"Ah, thanks," Neil said grasping the key.

"Do you have any special requests, sir?"

"Yes, would you have the porter take my luggage to my room? I'm going over there to the bar. I could sure use a cold one!"

"I'll ring the bellhop, sir."

"Thanks, again."

Neil staked his claim on the only table left in the lobby bar. Nestling back into one of the four sable-colored leather chairs, he looked around. Except for him, every other table was filled with veterans and their spouses. Neil thought it should have remained a gentlemen's conference, as it had been every year before.

"Welcome to Beacon's Bar. What's your pleasure, sir?" A perky young waitress placed a monogrammed napkin in front of him. Neil smiled while he gave her the once-over. She was dressed in a green and black costume that pinched her waist and flared out just inches below her thighs. But the eye-catcher was the bodice that barely covered her nipples, allowing her breasts to spill out from the ruffled opening.

"Ah, I think I'll have a draft," he smiled.

She tipped her head and within a minute she returned with a frosted mug overflowing with a thick white head of foam. "That'll be two bits, sir. It's happy hour."

"And happy I am," Neil said, free of his wife. "Would you mind starting a tab for me?"

"I already did, sir." She was a bit giddy, but Neil appreciated the light flirtation.

As he sat alone he daydreamed of better days gone by when he actually had loved Anne. *When was that? Oh yeah, before Vicky was born.*

It had been a long eight years but Neil had kept his end of the bargain to avoid a divorce. *Other than sex, I've been a good husband to her in every sense of the word. I've provided her with financial security and a good home—what more could she want?* Neil was about to be honest with himself when he felt a tap on his shoulder.

"Neil, we didn't know that you were coming this year. Is Anne with you?"

Neil turned around and there stood Joe and Catherine Moore. In a flash he appraised their appearance. *What a good-looking couple they are. Joe, a shoo-in for Stewart Granger. And Catherine. Oh, Catherine,* he sighed. *Simply lovely.*

His concentration returned. "No, Anne couldn't make this trip. Sit down, neighbors, and I'll buy you a drink. Waitress, whatever they order you can put it on my tab."

Joe slid a chair out for Catherine, but before seating himself, he was distracted by an announcement echoing throughout the lobby. "Paging Mr. Joe Moore. Paging Mr. Joe Moore. Please pick up the nearest house phone." After the message, the paging system went quiet.

"Cath, that's the call I've been waiting for. I want to close this deal so that we can enjoy the rest of the week. I'm going to be tied up for a while. You two enjoy yourselves and I'll meet up with you at dinner." Joe shook Neil's hand and then gave Catherine a quick peck on the cheek. "Wish me luck."

"Hey, Joe, don't you worry about your pretty wife. I'll take extra good care of her," Neil laughed.

Catherine was a vision to behold. The sheen from her shoulder-length blond hair danced with every move of her head. She was the opposite of Anne, whose dyed red hair had lost its youthful glow long before Neil ever met her. Catherine was every man's fantasy. With a perfect smile and heavenly blue eyes, she brought men to their feet whenever she entered a room.

"Neil, we never get the chance to talk much. I'm really glad that we're here alone now. I've wanted to talk to you for some time," Catherine said with a smile.

Had it not been Catherine Moore, Neil might have understood this to be a come-on. But Catherine, a beautiful woman from inside to out, exemplified the unity of a marriage. She flirted with no one except her husband Joe.

"How are things going with you and Anne?" She asked as she removed the gin-drenched olive from her martini.

"Pretty well, I guess. Why do you ask?"

She paused to choose her words carefully. "Neil, I know that this is none of my business. And if you tell me to right now, I will button my lip and stay out of it."

"What is it, Catherine?"

"Well, I heard Anne shouting the other day. She was screaming at Vicky." Catherine took a sip of the martini, but she never let her eyes falter from his. She had to know what, if anything, Neil knew.

"Go on, Catherine."

"She was yelling at Vicky because she didn't do a good job wiping the dishes. The day before that, I heard Anne scream at her about cleaning the kitchen floor. To be honest with you, Neil, she scolds Vicky every day for one thing or another. I'm afraid that's not the worst of it."

Neil's eyes dilated. His forehead rippled with deep indentations. "What else? What are you afraid to tell me?"

"I can't be sure, really. But I hear things. Like the sound of pots and pans clanging together. I hear Vicky crying and Anne laughing. And then there's an eerie silence."

"What are you saying, Catherine?"

"Last month I saw a large gash on Vicky's leg."

"A gash on her leg? Vicky has never mentioned getting hurt to me. But if what you say is true, are you suggesting that Anne did that to her?"

"I'm just saying that more goes on in your house than you are aware. Lynn told me that Vicky is very afraid of her mother."

"Did Vicky tell her that?"

"Not in those words. But she did say that Vicky told her that she is not to talk about her chores with anyone. I assume that includes you, Neil."

Neil's forehead furrowed. He was trying to digest everything that Catherine was saying.

"There's one more thing, Neil. I confronted Vicky about her leg and asked her what happened to her. Do you know what she told me?"

Neil could feel his heart palpitating. He swallowed the last ounce of beer but found it was not enough to satisfy his need for alcohol. He signaled to the waitress, who had suddenly lost her appeal. "Make me a double bourbon and seven."

"She first said she slipped on the floor. I asked her how that happened and then she immediately backtracked and said she fell off her bike. I don't think either story holds true, Neil."

"I can't imagine Anne deliberately hurting her," he said, unintentionally defending his wife.

"Well, something is not right, Neil. I can't put my finger on it, but it's this feeling I have. It's the same feeling I've felt ever since the blizzard."

"You lost me there, Catherine. What blizzard? We haven't had one in at least three years."

"Yes, that's the one. When the children were in kindergarten and all the schools were closed."

"What does the blizzard have to do with Anne and Vicky?"

"School was closed, but Vicky went anyway. No one told her to stay home. So she walked through the storm. When she arrived, the principal was outraged and tried to telephone Anne. But she was sleeping and didn't answer the phone, so they called me. I offered to pick Vicky up, but they insisted on speaking with Anne in person."

Rage clouded Neil's eyes. "What do you mean, Vicky walked to school? I remember that day, Catherine. Anne told me the kids had a snow day. She said school closures were announced on television."

"I don't know what to say, Neil. Except that I had to wake Anne up and believe me, she was irate."

Neil was speechless. He pictured his little girl braving the storm, defenseless and unprotected.

"No one knows, Neil, how she managed to walk all that way. It's a miracle that she didn't freeze to death."

"Catherine, I had no idea. Honestly, I had no idea. What else is going on in my own home?" He grabbed Catherine's wrists and involuntarily squeezed them, forcing her to gasp.

"What else, Catherine? Tell me what else!" He released her, noting the deep impression of his fingers. "I'm so sorry. I don't know what got into me, Catherine. I didn't mean to hurt you."

"It's okay, Neil. I know you don't have a mean bone in your body. I should have said something to you a long time ago," she said disappointed in herself.

Neil pushed away from the table. Dropping three dollars into a cash tray he explained, "I'm sorry that I won't be keeping you company, Catherine. I have to be alone right now."

"Will we see you later?"

"No, I don't think so. I've got a lot of soul-searching to do. I wish I could drive home tonight, but there are a couple of thunderstorms heading this way. The weatherman said there's a possibility of multiple tornadoes touching down but he expects it to clear by late tomorrow morning. So I'll stay the night and probably attend the first seminar. But as soon as the weather clears, I'm heading home. I want to get home about the same time Vicky gets home from school."

The following morning Neil was sitting in the main ballroom among several hundred veterans. The keynote speaker appeared to have everyone's attention except for Neil. His body was there, although his senses were dulled. He watched the speaker's mouth move, but he couldn't hear the words. He was consumed with the realization that he failed his child, even when there were signs. Yet he never confronted Anne. And even worse, he did nothing to protect Vicky from her.

Neil glanced down at the pamphlet. The frail man at the podium was speaking about the ordeals of the wounded soldiers in World War Two. This was the one seminar that Neil wanted to attend more than any other. He had been looking forward to lending his support to those veterans who had had it much worse than he. But Neil was drowning in the murky waters of his own guilt.

Locating the nearest exit, Neil excused himself while passing each veteran in the row. Joe, who was seated a few rows behind, followed him. "Neil, wait up," he said as Neil exited out the back door. Joe caught up with him just as Neil opened his car door. "Wow, you are already packed and ready to go," Joe said. As he looked up at the sky, he added, "At least the storm has passed."

"Yeah, it should be smooth sailing," Neil stated.

"Catherine told me what happened last night. Neil, she wanted to say something to you three years ago, but I told her to let it pass. I apologize."

Placing his hand on Joe's shoulder he said, "Thanks, neighbor, but you owe me no apology. If it wasn't for your lovely wife, I would have kept my head buried in the sand. I was afraid, Joe. So afraid of Anne leaving me, I chose to ignore everything. I swear, though, that after today everything will be different. Joe, I won't be seeing you folks for quite some time."

"I see," Joe said pretending to understand. "Well, good luck to you, Neil. If there is anything we can do to help, you know our phone number."

"I may take you up on that someday," Neil said as he drove off in his Dodge sedan.

The drive back to Detroit was a blur. Anxious to implement the plan he had devised the night before, he hadn't noticed that he had been on Highway 96 for three and a half hours. It seemed that he was just in Grand Rapids, but after a few turns after he exited the main highway, Neil was pulling into his driveway at Temple Street, ready to take action.

From the front porch Neil vaguely saw Anne's horizontal silhouette through the sheer curtain panels. Once again she was in a reclining position, fast asleep. Neil pressed his thumb to the doorbell and let it ring several times to rattle her. When Anne didn't budge, he unlocked the door himself. *She can sleep through anything. But not today!* He hurled his luggage across the kitchen floor. But again, her rest went uninterrupted.

He dropped down into an easy chair and placing one hand on each knee, he scrutinized her. *How could I have been so blind? How could I have allowed her to treat Vicky the way she did?* His forehead wrinkled as he glared at her.

Drops of saliva fell from her open mouth to the pillow she rested upon. It nauseated him and he impulsively struck her arm. She finally awoke, stupefied, and demanded, "What are *you* doing home?"

With his eyes fixed upon her, he took a deep breath. It was all he could do to restrain himself from slapping her across the face.

"Why are you home?" Neil still didn't answer and she screamed, "Answer me!"

"No! You damn well answer ME! Why did my child walk to school in the blizzard?"

"Christ, Neil. That was three years ago. So who told you? Was it that blabbermouth's husband? Did you bump into Joe Moore at the convention?" Anne brushed him aside to go into the kitchen. But he pushed her back down onto a recliner.

"Sit the hell down, woman!" Gritting his teeth he shouted, "I want you to tell me about the day that you had Vicky's hair cut. Tell me why you decided to have her long curls cut off within an inch of her scalp. And don't even try to tell me it was her idea. I don't believe you now. I never should have believed you then. Vicky cried for days and when I asked why, she said she missed me brushing her hair. I know that she would never have had it cut if it weren't for you. What was it? Did the heinous act give you pleasure?"

"All you did was baby her." Sarcastically she mimicked him and said, "'Get me the brush, sweet essence. Daddy will comb your pretty hair.' Well, you couldn't comb it after it was all cut off. Could you, Neil?"

Neil's fists tightened. "What happened to the summer jacket I bought her a couple of months ago? Why hasn't she ever worn it?"

"Like the child needs a new coat. I didn't get new jackets or coats when I was her age, why should she?"

"I'll ask you again. What happened to the coat?"

She cackled, "All right. If you really want to know, it was thrown out along with some of the other things you've bought her. All gone. Too bad," she smirked. "So what else do you want to know, Neil? This is ridiculous. And by the way, you still haven't told me why you're home so early." Dismissing a possible answer, she proceeded to lift herself from the chair. But her legs folded when she felt his hands slam down on her shoulders.

"You know I've never struck a woman. But if I do hit you, I swear you'll never get up again. So sit the fuck down!"

Neil was livid. He thought the day he walked in on Janet was devastating, but that was nothing compared to these last twenty-four hours. Standing inches from her face he asked, "Why did Vicky have so many teeth pulled, Anne? What dentist would pull four of her permanent teeth when she was only eight? I want to know the name of the dentist, Anne. Just give me his goddamn name."

"At least she went to a dentist. My parents never took me to one."

Neil could barely keep his breathing steady when he screamed, "I don't give a rat's ass about what happened to you as a kid. But somehow I think your parents did the best they could. What I want to know now is about my child."

"Calm down, Neil. I don't know the name of the dentist. It was a student at the dental college in Hamtramck. And it didn't cost us a dime."

"What a miserable bitch you are. I don't know how I've lived with all your hate and jealousy. As of today we are finished. I am taking Vicky from you. I'm sure you'll get over it." He added bitterly, "I should have done this a long time ago."

"What makes you think I'll allow you to take Vicky from me? She's my daughter. Remember, Neil?"

"Oh yes, I remember. And when the court hears some of the vicious acts you've committed, you'll be lucky to stay out of jail."

It hadn't occurred to her that Neil would ever leave her. She had always had the upper hand. It was perfect. Everyone had been wrapped neatly around her finger. But suddenly she was desperate.

"Don't leave me, Neil. Let's talk like we did years ago. Remember, you told me that we could make this work," she said chasing him down the hall.

"I'm warning you, Anne, get the hell out of my way."

Neil rushed back and forth between the bedrooms and closets. He grabbed a few clothes, a couple of blankets, two pillows, one of which was Vicky's favorite sponge pillow, and the basic traveling necessities and loaded them into the car. He shut out the voice that petitioned him.

"Neil, I'll change. I'll do whatever you want. I'll even change toward Victoria. You'll see. I'll be like Catherine and the other mothers in the neighborhood."

It was much easier than he thought to ignore her. As he slammed the trunk closed, Vicky came running up the street.

"Daddy, you're home!"

Neil embraced her as he had never done before. He looked into her brown eyes and then ran his fingers through her short brown hair. It had barely grown out three inches since Anne had had it cut off. It sickened Neil as he realized how traumatic it must have been for Vicky. He imagined how she had felt as her long locks were being stripped from her. It made him want to lash out at Anne again, but it would serve no purpose. And for one split second he wished that he was holding a pair of scissors and that Anne was just within his reach…

Coming back to reality and the situation at hand Neil said, "Sweet essence, you and me are going on a trip together."

"Isn't Mother coming?"

"Nope, this time it's just you and me," he stated reassuringly.

Vicky was confused but kept on questioning him because she could question him. He never silenced her. "Daddy, how long will we be gone?"

"We'll be gone a very long time. You and I are moving to California, where there are mountains and beaches, dates and oranges, and palm trees. Lots and lots of palm trees. Oh, and they just opened a great amusement park three years ago. You know, the one with the mouse," he teased. "How does that sound?"

Vicky caught sight of her mother standing on the porch and gulped, "So, when is *she* coming?"

"She's not." Neil, stepping away from the car, waited for Vicky's reaction. "This has to be all right with you, Vicky, because you'll be leaving your friends." Neil stopped loading the car and waited for her answer. "Do you want to move to California with me?"

Vicky had never told her father that she prayed for the day that she would be free of her mother. But now, when given the opportunity to speak out, words seemed lodged in her throat. Anne still had a hold on her. Vicky bit her lower lip and glanced up at her mother who stood just a few feet away, glaring down at her. Anne still commanded authority.

"Tell your father that you cannot live without me, Victoria. Tell him!" she demanded.

Neil bent down to Vicky's level. "There's no need to be afraid. I won't let her hurt you anymore."

"Victoria, I said tell him!"

Vicky looked back at the mother who had chastised her since the day she was born. Because of her, Vicky had collected so many unhappy memories. But the one that vividly came to Vicky's mind involved the watermelon vines when she was only six. She had been sitting on the porch with her friends eating summer wedges of watermelon. It was one of the rare days that Anne had allowed

Vicky's friends in their yard. They were giggling while munching on the juicy fruit and spitting out the watermelon seeds on the ground. Vicky remembered how a few months later those same seeds had sprouted healthy vines. Then she recalled the unexpected punishment for growing watermelons without permission. "Get out there and pull every vine. I want it clean and I don't care how long it takes you. I don't want to see one bit of green life. Do you hear me, VIC-TOR-I-A? Get moving!" When Vicky didn't react fast enough to suit her mother, Anne yanked her by the hair. She remembered being dragged down the steps and thrown down on the ground. All because the seeds had turned to vines…

"No, Mother! I don't ever want to be with you. I hate…" As hard as she tried, she couldn't say it. But Anne knew exactly what Vicky wanted to convey.

"How dare you be so insolent to me?" Anne raced toward Vicky and raised her hand to strike her. But as she swung forward Neil intercepted her arm. He squeezed his fingers, restraining any possible movement. Anne squirmed from the acute pain.

"God help you, woman. God help you if you ever touch this child again. You can expect to hear from my attorney."

"Vicky, I packed a bag of clothes for you. There are some flannel blankets in the backseat. Make yourself a place to sleep. Here's your spongy pillow." Closing the car door he added, "I'll be right back." When Neil turned around, he found Anne on her knees.

"Please, Neil, I'm begging you. Don't leave me alone." But her pleas had no effect on him.

"I will send for the rest of my things as soon as we're settled. You can have the house, but I recommend you get yourself a damn good lawyer."

As he clutched the handle to the door he turned around one last time and said, "And get the hell off your goddamn knees."

seven

THOM DRAKE

Alabama, 1950–1958

Thom Drake, coughing up the acidic remnants of rancid whiskey, slowly opened his eyes. He was lying facedown on a cot in Purvis's local jail. As his eyes came into focus, he saw the legs of Sheriff Pete Cornell, who was holding a steaming cup of thick, reheated coffee.

"Wake up, old man, and take a sip of this."

"What am I doing here, Pete?"

"You tell me. You came in ranting about Dolores. I thought you said something about an alibi, or something like it. I couldn't understand much else."

Thom, reeking of sweat and booze, stared at a crack in the floor. His thoughts were less than crisp. Working his way through a foggy memory, he started to retrieve the events of the day before. He pictured himself kicking Dolores harder and harder until he was certain she had lost the baby. Then he remembered waiting at the tavern for Sheriff Pete, but the sheriff never showed up.

"Well, I got some news for you, Thom. I heard that Dolores took the girls and up and left you last night. I heard she ain't coming back to you. Can't say that I blame her none."

"Is that a fact, Sheriff? Where the hell would she go? She doesn't have a pot to piss in." Thom pulled himself erect, but his head was still spinning. Falling back against the cement wall, his head thumped upon impact.

"Looks like you really tied one on last night, old man."

"I got my reasons. Any questions you want to ask me, you better ask now."

"There's none that comes to mind. Why? Is there something you got a-hankerin' to tell me?"

Thom spit the murky coffee on the floor. "Can't you make a better pot than this? It's got to be at least two days old."

"And then some," Pete laughed.

"Well, if you ain't holding me for anything more than a night out on the town, I'll be on my way."

"You're sober enough now; I guess you're free to go. Before you leave, I got some news for you."

"Good or bad?" Thom asked inquisitively.

"It depends on how you take it. Your wife had a baby last night. A bouncing baby boy," the sheriff answered.

Thom spit again, deliberately hitting the Sheriff's boots.

"Bad news, huh? Under the circumstances I'm gonna let this one pass. But if I were you, Thom, I'd be watching my p's and q's. I won't be so lenient next time. Now get the hell out of here."

✧ ✧ ✧

Dolores, her daughters, and baby Ethan had settled in from the moment they arrived at Ruthie Jackson's. They felt safe and secure because they knew Thom Drake would never come looking for them. Thom had lived in Purvis his entire life and had never set foot across the abandoned railroad tracks. People on that other side of town were just too dark for his taste. So he kept his distance, as did most of the other whites in Purvis, save Sheriff Pete. Pete interacted with all the citizens, no matter what the color of their skin.

It was summer of 1950, just a few months after Ethan was born, when Ruthie's accident happened. She was coming into the house from her orchard, and as she climbed the porch steps, she suddenly lost her balance and fell to the ground. Ruthie could never explain exactly what had happened, just that her leg gave out. When she was first told that she had fractured her left lower leg, she had convinced herself that it was the result of being overweight. Yet she knew the mishap was very peculiar, considering that she had only been four feet from the ground when she fell.

Her suspicions were confirmed by the doctor at the county hospital where she was taken after her accident. "Miss Jackson," said Doctor Benson, "I hope you are feeling comfortable. Well, as comfortable as you can be with that cast on your leg."

Ruthie smiled at the young doctor in acknowledgment of his awkwardly phrased concern. When he didn't smile in return, Ruthie's smile turned into a frown. "Doctor, I feel about as good as you'd expect for someone who was fool enough to fall off a porch and break a leg. Do I have any other reason not to feel good?" That's when Ruthie learned she had osteosarcoma, a form of bone cancer that couldn't be treated. Ruthie was going to die.

"I see that you have Dolores Drake down as your next of kin," continued the doctor in a kindly tone, "It's sometimes difficult for loved ones to understand what this disease means. I will speak to Dolores and tell her—"

"No!" shouted Ruthie. She added in a hushed voice, "No, please don't tell Dolores. You don't understand. She's got so much to do with raising her family and keeping clear of that mangy husband of hers." In a stronger voice she said, "I know what I need to do; I'm gonna handle this in my own way." Doctor Benson had no option but to accede to his patient's wishes.

Later that day, Dolores visited Ruthie in the hospital. She was stunned when she saw the size of the cast. "What did the doctor say, Ruthie? What on earth happened for you to require a full-leg cast?"

Ruthie was not forthright with her friend when she answered, "The doc said that I was lucky I didn't break all my bones, cuz I'm as big as a barn. The bigger they are, the harder they fall, he told me!"

"I don't appreciate your doctor's sense of humor. There's got to be another reason."

"Nope! The doc said this is a good time for me to start shedding a few pounds. Now, who's caring for Ethan?"

"Brenda is home with him. Sonya is baking your favorite cherry pie. She thinks that you are coming home tonight. I have to admit, I thought you were, too."

"Doc said I need to rest up a couple of days," she said, still avoiding the truth.

"Then you take his advice and get some rest. You don't have to worry about anything because the girls and I are going to take care of everything. They are going to tend to the house while I go back to work. It's time for us to pay for our share."

Filled with painkillers, Ruthie drowsily reminded Dolores, "I told you before that I've got enough money to last all of our lifetimes. It ain't doing no good rotting away in the storm cellar."

Dolores laughed, "You mean to say that you keep all your money in the cellar?"

Ruthie cracked a smile and said, "I ain't too trustin' of the lily-white bank president. I don't want him knowin' my business!"

"If I were in your shoes, I'd probably feel the same, Ruthie. Still, it doesn't change the fact that we are no longer going to be your charity case. Besides, dear friend, you need *us* now," Dolores asserted.

"But you're family now," Ruthie said. "I'd rather see those dollars spent on you and yours than have it burn up in that old house someday."

Dolores cupped Ruthie's hand in her own. "That is very generous of you, Ruthie, but my mind is made up. I'm going back to work."

"Please don't go back there," she begged. "You don't need that place. You don't need those people."

"I need to help out, Ruthie. Period," she said adamantly.

"When are you planning on doing this?" Ruthie said, her voice lower with each syllable.

"I'm back on swing shift starting two weeks from today. By then we'll have established a routine for helping you get around. The girls will help out with Ethan and the household chores. Between the three of us we'll have it all under control. You have nothing to worry about."

Ruthie never heard the plan. It was the changes in the future that bothered her. "Two weeks…too soon for my taste," Ruthie mumbled as the drugs slowly lulled her into a deep sleep.

✧ ✧ ✧

The long walk from the railroad tracks to the other side of town gave Dolores ample time to remember her last night at the garment factory. She remembered using a scarf to conceal her face and how it did very little to hide the atrocious injuries inflicted by Thom. She remembered how every woman, except Ruthie Jackson, turned away from her during her hour of need. *I wonder what they'll think of me now. No bruises to feed their gossip. I suppose they'll lose interest in me and move on to some other poor soul.*

Dolores shoved her card into the time clock at quarter to five; she was slightly ahead of the bell, but for good reason. She wanted as few people as possible to notice that she had returned to the factory. But word had already spread, and the rumormongers had beaten her to the punch. They were already seated at their work stations waiting for her return.

As she pushed her way through the swinging doors, she noticed that nothing much had changed. There were fans at the end of each row circulating the fumes from the bevy of chain-smokers; several took long drags on their cigarettes the moment they saw her.

She made her way across the floor that was now blanketed with scraps of discarded material. Filthy and cluttered, the room was in dire need of the janitorial services of Ruthie Jackson. The factory owners had been appalled when they heard that a black woman had opened her home to a white family. As far as they were concerned, it was obvious Ruthie just didn't "know her place." Anxious not to allow other "coloreds" to get uppity, the company had tried to hire a white woman. The pay was, however, so poor and the job so arduous that no one applied. Management had shifted the cleanup duties to the seamstresses, but none of them took the job seriously, and the workroom was a mess.

Ignoring the scuttlebutt, Dolores brushed the dust from her machine and began loading the bobbin. From a basket overflowing with orders, she removed a handwritten note.

Dolores, welcome back. We need ten of these by the end of the day. Your choice of colors. Be creative. Before you start, come and talk to me. Sincerely, Mrs. J. Hudson, Floor Supervisor. Dolores reread the title following the signature. It meant that Judith Hudson had been promoted during her absence.

"Judith? I mean, Mrs. Hudson," she said as she closed the glass door behind her.

"Ah, Dolores. Welcome back. How is your baby? A boy, isn't it? How are Sonya and Brenda?"

"Everyone is fine. My son's name is Ethan."

"I suppose that's as good as any name," Judith quipped while fumbling through a stack of invoices. "So, you've decided to come back to work. I'm assuming your home situation is in order."

"Come again? My home situation?"

Appearing aloof and disinterested, she continued to thumb through the papers. "Now, Dolores, I don't want you to get upset, but I think it's only right that you know what your husband is saying all over town."

A somber look came over Dolores's face. She wanted nothing to do with Thom Drake. She had enough with the painful memories of their life together.

"Well," Judith jeered, "Some of our husbands were at the tavern last week when Thom came staggering in. He was cursing up a storm. Said he wished your boy was born dead. Then he said it wasn't his problem anymore."

Dolores didn't want to hear any more. "Is that all, Judith? I'm sure you have other things to contend with other than my personal life."

"But there's so much more. Thom said and I quote, 'It's the bitch's problem now. Her and that nigger she's living with.' Excuse the 'bitch' word, Dolores, but I thought you should hear it the way it was said."

Dolores could feel the air escaping from her lungs. It was almost too much effort to replace it.

"Is it true or was Thom Drake just blowing hot air, Dolores?"

"Yes, it is true, Mrs. Hudson. Thomas and I are no longer together."

"Not about that! I would have left that man years ago if I were you. I mean, are you still living with that colored woman? I just can't imagine that you would subject your girls to those appalling conditions. On the q.t., where do you call home?"

Dolores glared at the disingenuous supervisor. She walked past her to an open window and inhaled a good amount of fresh air. As she breathed out, a tremendous feeling of confidence and exhilaration overcame her.

"Well, Judith, or do you prefer that I call you Mrs. Hudson? It's really none of your business where I live, is it?"

"I see. Thom Drake *was* speaking the truth. You are living across the tracks. That is disgusting!"

"Like I said, it's really none of your concern," Dolores repeated with a smile on her face. "But what is your concern is the fact that I have reconsidered my employment here. I quit!"

Dolores marched past her out of the office, stopping briefly at her station to pick up her personal belongings. As if orchestrated, the sewing machines went suddenly quiet. No one spoke as all heads turned around to the newly promoted supervisor. Standing at her office door, Judith shouted across the room, "Dolores, what do you mean 'you quit'? I need you on line. Productivity has been down since you left. Now that I've been appointed supervisor, we're two down on head count. You can't quit." Although the volume of Judith's voice rose, Dolores didn't flinch as she approached the swinging doors.

"Remember, Dolores, you don't have a husband to support you. Your girls might be grown, but you're going to need money to raise that baby boy. After all, you're not exactly a young woman. You're almost fifty now, aren't you?"

Judith kept yelling at the top of her lungs, but still there was no reaction from Dolores. In a final attempt to humiliate her, she screamed, "Dolores, living with a nigger could have perilous consequences. The people of Purvis don't approve of such frivolous behavior. Now sit down and get back to work before I change my mind about taking you back."

Dolores had ignored Judith until the moment she insulted Ruthie. That was the breaking point for Dolores. Slowly she turned to face a roomful of motionless women. Standing before them, she began tearing her timecard in half and in half again. She repeated this several times until she clutched bits of confetti in her palm. Still, she had not responded verbally to Judith.

The workers found this to be solid entertainment. They knew this day would enliven their coffee breaks for weeks to come. And it didn't matter to them if Dolores stayed or not. This was gossip at its finest.

Judith leaned up against her office door with her arms folded. "Now, Dolores, let bygones be bygones. You're due for a raise soon. I'll talk to personnel and get it expedited. Now sit down. You've got a lot of work to do." Judith was certain Dolores would come to her senses. *Be patient. Just give her a minute and she'll be back on line,* Judith thought.

"Mrs. Hudson," Dolores amicably began.

Here it comes, Judith thought. *She's decided to stay. Just wait until Mrs. Cook reviews how I handled this incident. I just saved the department's most productive employee.*

"I was wondering, Judith, how *is* your thirteen-year-old daughter?" Of course, Dolores did not expect a reply, so she resumed. "I hope everything went well for her at the convent. I hope they found a good home for the baby. That would be your grandchild, wouldn't it?"

Judith's stance crumbled. Withering before her subordinates, the wall behind her supported her weakened knees. To the roomful of women who had yearned for a confirmation of the rumor, Dolores had handed them just that. As for Judith, she was finally silenced.

Dolores scanned the room until she locked eyes with her next victim. This time it was Mary, the woman whose workstation was directly behind her.

"Oh, Mary, how often do you make the drive to federal prison to visit your son?" Dolores smacked her lips together and continued. "It must be heartbreaking to know that he'll never be eligible for parole. But you can't blame the courts, now can you? After all, he shot a state trooper in cold blood. You just don't hear of those things every day, do you? Well, not in Purvis, you don't," she said.

Mary felt as if a knife had pierced her heart. After months of gossiping about Dolores, her own dirty laundry was on display. The crime her son committed was no longer in doubt. Dolores had delivered another devastating confirmation.

Each woman turned her eyes away from Dolores and bowed her head. No one wanted to be next; however, Dolores wasn't quite finished.

"Now where's Mrs. Cook, our respected superintendent? She must be around here somewhere." Mrs. Cook stepped back into the shadows, hoping that Dolores would pass her by. However, Mrs. Cook's position was given away by the women in the last row who turned their heads in her direction. Dolores followed their lead and faced the wall that obstructed Mrs. Cook from her sight. Dolores proceeded to dethrone another one.

"Embezzlement of bank funds, wasn't it, Mrs. Cook? Your husband's defense couldn't match the overwhelming evidence against him. Oh, and you had to lose that spectacular mansion of yours. I hear that you had to move in with your sister and her brood in their small three-bedroom house. She has how many? Is it eight or nine children? I can't imagine how you manage to keep your wits about you." Without conceding to the facts, the embarrassed superintendent retreated to the nearest restroom. There she would remain until the end of the shift.

Dolores made a full turn and addressed the stupefied workers. "You know, each one of us has a cross to bear in one way or another. It may be a disappointment, an embarrassment, or a personal matter that you prefer to keep within the confines of your family life. For some of you it's easy to hide your transgressions because the finger never points directly at you. But if your luck changes and you suddenly become the target, mark my words, ladies, even those you trust will feed off your misfortunes."

Dolores took a deep breath and wet her lips. She was not finished. "For months it was my pathetic life that fueled your coffee breaks. With every new bruise you'd whisper and, oftentimes, laugh. But never once did any of you ask if you could help me. Not even when I stooped so low as to beg you to rent a room to my children and me." Dolores softened her voice and continued. "In spite of your protests one wonderful woman did come to our aid. Her name is Ruthie Jackson and I am proud to call her family."

It was obvious by the look on their faces that Dolores had gone too far with her audience. They were outraged to hear a white woman call a darkie, family. To show their disdain, they hissed at her, but it only boosted her convictions. "To hell with you," Dolores hollered. Triumphantly, she unfolded her hand and threw the timecard confetti into the air. Upon hitting the ceiling fan, the pieces drifted down to the unkempt floor. As she walked out the door, she heard one final threat from Judith Hudson. "Better watch your backside, nigger lover!" There was a thunderous roar of laughter that followed.

After her impromptu performance at the factory, Dolores fled home. She found Ruthie asleep on the porch in the chair where she had left her earlier. On Ruthie's insistence, the girls had not taken her inside. It was a balmy night and she wanted to wait up for Dolores. She had dozed off, just the same.

Dolores rested back in the rocking chair alongside Ruthie. She thought about the earlier events of the evening. In all her life, Dolores had never been so brazen. She started to worry that the outburst would trigger some form of retaliation. Rocking back and forth, she was unaware that her pace had accelerated to an annoying squeak. It had awoken Ruthie.

"Miss D, where you going in such a rush?"

"Ruthie, I'm sorry I woke you. How are you feeling? When did you take your last pain pill?"

"No need to worry about me. The girls handed me my pills right on time. What's troubling you? Did those busybodies put their noses where they don't belong?" Ruthie looked at the moon and saw that it was only halfway up in the sky. She knew that it was well before the factory's closing time of one o'clock. "What are you doing home so early?"

"Ruthie, I think I may have said too much. I don't know what got into me except that I gave the gossipers a dose of their own medicine. I wanted to help out financially, but after an hour with those wretched people, I just up and quit."

"Good! I only wished I could have been there to see it. Now, no more talk about you going to work. I told you, my money is your money. We couldn't spend it all in both our lifetimes. Truthfully, we couldn't spend it all in Ethan's lifetime. There's much more than you know."

"But, Ruthie. I'm worried," Dolores said somberly. "Not about me, but I'm terrified for the girls. Sonya has one year left of high school. Brenda has two. I'm afraid for them, Ruthie."

"You've got two strong young ladies. They can take care of themselves."

"Not after what I said tonight. From now on it won't be safe for them to go to the sock hops or football games. They might be in danger just attending school."

Ruthie removed her granny glasses and asked, "What did you say that is so bad?"

"It really doesn't matter. You know who we're up against now, don't you?"

"I supposed you are referring to those white-hooded monsters!"

Regretting her words at the factory, Dolores shook her head. "I should have held my tongue."

Avoiding the forbidden word Klan, they both knew that the organization had infiltrated Purvis. The local newspaper, *The Gannett,* reported a sudden rash of vile acts against the blacks and the whites who befriended them. Their livestock, if not missing, had been found slaughtered. Their crops, the livelihood for most, were being destroyed. It was a warning to some. It was great reading for others.

Timidly, Ruthie asked, "Miss D, are you thinking of leaving Purvis?"

"I shudder to think of what would happen to you if I did. I'm not going anywhere. Besides, whether you want to admit it or not, you need me, Ruthie. You can't get around on your own with that cast on your leg. And let's not forget what the doctor said when the cast comes off. You will have months of therapy. I am going to be there to help you."

Ruthie inwardly breathed a sigh of relief. She couldn't image losing Dolores and her family, especially six-month-old Ethan, with whom she had developed a special bond. Ruthie asked, "So how do we put out the fire that you see a-blazin'?"

"First thing tomorrow I'm going to talk to Sheriff Pete about the girls. See if he can help them."

The following morning Dolores walked down Main Street; it was filled with early risers who were buzzing about the events of the night before. To show their disapproval, they were downright offensive to her. They called her names and threw small pebbles at her. Her reprieve came only when she escaped into Sheriff Pete's office.

"I'm sure, Pete, you've already heard what I said at the factory last night."

He was anxious and slightly frustrated with her. He, too, wished she had held her tongue. "Yeah, I heard. Man, oh, man, Dolores, you've got the whole town in an uproar. It's gonna take some doing to calm everyone down."

"I'm sorry, Pete. I didn't want to make things more difficult than they already were. In my defense, Judith Hudson brought out the worst in me."

Pete grumbled an expletive behind the pipe resting in his mouth. Then he stretched his neck up to face the tall, lanky woman. "What exactly do you want me to do?"

"I want my girls protected. I'm terrified that they'll be persecuted at school. Just to be on the safe side, I kept them home today. I can't keep them home forever."

"There's no point in shedding useless tears now. The damage is done. I recommend that you move back over to this side of town. I'd say the sooner, the better."

"No! I'm not leaving Ruthie Jackson, no matter who is up in arms about it! She's having a hard time with her leg. I guess age has something to do with healing. Anyway, I'm here to talk about my daughters. You know that they are almost grown so I want to make some kind of arrangements for them."

"My Lizbeth and I would gladly take them in. But it won't do the girls any good if you plan on staying at Ruthie's. People around here aren't too forgiving. Worse yet, they aren't too forgetting. Take a look outside, Dolores. There's a whole bunch of Thom Drakes lurking out there in the fog."

"I gave her my word, Pete. I'm not leaving Ruthie. I'm not letting that asinine group take control of my life. It's bad enough I let Thom do it for all those years."

"Well, if there's no changing your mind, I'll come up with something else. Let me make a few calls and see what I can do. Now you better go out the back way. The sidewalk appears to be overly crowded today."

✧ ✧ ✧

Sheriff Pete tipped his hat to Ruthie as she rested back in the cozy chair. "Afternoon, Miss Jackson." He stared at her leg and added, "Man, that's one heck of a cast you've got there."

"Big woman, big cast, Sheriff. You can go inside. Miss D is expecting you."

It was the first time Pete had ever stepped inside the Jackson home. He, as Dolores had been, was awestruck by the fine furnishings, coordinating floral wallpaper, and the dozens of antique collectibles. He had to admit that the rundown exterior was a clever decoy for the hidden treasures within.

"Hello, Pete. Any luck?"

"I think I figured a way to help out with the girls. My brother and his wife own a small farm about twenty miles outside of Montgomery. They have a daughter about Brenda's age. I mentioned your situation and before I finished, they said the girls could live with them. They said they could come down and pick them up tomorrow if that's okay with you."

"Montgomery? That's three hours from here. I thought you could find a place for them in a nearby town. But Montgomery…" she repeated, having second thoughts.

"I probably could have found them a place in Newton, but the first time you made the ten-mile trip to visit them, someone would be on to you. It would only bring on more trouble. Montgomery is far enough away that no one from these parts will bother them. Bob and Leona are good Christian people, Dolores. The girls will be safe with them and they said you are welcome to visit anytime. So, if you're planning on staying out here with the coloreds…"

He turned around and saw that the window was wide open. He caught Ruthie's eye. "I mean no offense, Miss Jackson. I just need to make sure that Dolores understands the severity of the situation."

"No offense taken, Sheriff."

"Dolores, I think you should consider this offer. Under the circumstances, it's the right thing to do."

It didn't take much convincing, for Dolores realized that Pete was right. She needed to move her daughters to safety. Somberly, she said, "Pete, it would be the first time in the girls' lives that they would be truly safe. No more Thomas Drake." She paused and then as an afterthought she said, "And no white hoods."

"Thom Drake? What does he have to do with this mess?"

"I've never told anyone this before. The week before we moved in with Ruthie, he came home after yet another binge and…" Dolores stopped herself. "Never mind, it's nothing because nothing happened," she emphasized.

"He came home and what, Dolores. I want to know what the son of a bitch did."

She hemmed and hawed, but finally answered him. "Pete, Thom was so drunk that he crawled into bed with Brenda. That was the first time he ever went after the girls *that* way. Thank God, Brenda managed to free herself from him before he…he…touched her, but he slapped her relentlessly. It's just that if we hadn't left, I wonder if he would have tried again. I fear the answer is 'yes.' I believe it was only a matter of time."

"The SOB. You're sure he didn't touch her?"

"Pete, I swear. There's something else, though. The girls have seen him hanging around school. Sonya said she saw him wink at her once. Pete, they are petrified of him."

"With good reason, Dolores. So is Montgomery all right with you?"

"I've always trusted your judgment, Pete. Call your brother and tell them we'll be waiting for them tomorrow."

"Dolores, your boy is only a baby now. What are you going to do in a few years when he starts school?"

"I'm taking it a day at a time, Pete. God knows, maybe things will be different then."

"One can only hope, Dolores. One can only hope…"

✧ ✧ ✧

Six years would pass, but Purvis was no better off than it was when Ethan was born. The Klan alliance had grown so rapidly that the town had qualified for its own chapter. With hatred spreading by the minute, Purvis was becoming more divided than ever.

Oblivious to the racial prejudice that surrounded the town, young Ethan Drake, the blond-haired, blue-eyed boy, saw life as one big celebration. Sharing a home with his two mommas, one white and one black, he was given a solid foundation for equality. His pale skin was never compared to the darker skin of the children living in the same neighborhood.

"What ya doin', Big Jess?" Ethan asked sixteen-year-old Jesse Brown who lived fifty yards from Ruthie's place. "Can I help?"

"Sure, Ethan. Fetch me that wrench over there."

"You bet!"

Ethan Drake loved getting into the thick of things. At six years old, he seemed driven to pitch in and help. If he wasn't stacking wood or cleaning string beans, he'd be working side-by-side picking cotton with Jesse. And it didn't matter that his small fingers bled, he was just happy to be with his friend.

"What's wrong with your pa's truck, Big Jess? Does it need gas or somethin'?"

"No, not this time. Someone put molasses syrup in the tank. Don't look like it's gonna run no more."

"Why would someone put syrup in a tank? Don't it need gas to go?"

"It needed gas, all right. But it doesn't need gas anymore," he said as he closed the hood. "It's broke good, now. It can't be fixed." Jesse forced a smile at the naive youngster who clearly worshipped him.

"Ah, Big Jess, you can fix it. You can fix anything."

Jesse lifted Ethan onto his shoulders. "You know how you can't grow apples on a peach tree?"

Giggling from high above the ground, Ethan answered, "Gee-whiz, everybody knows that! It can't be done."

"The same goes for my pa's truck. It just can't be done. Let's go inside. My ma made some lemonade and I'm real thirsty. You, too?"

"Yes siree, Big Jess. I'm as thirsty as a…" Ethan thought for a moment before adding, "as a possum who just ate a salt brick. Hey, Big Jess, guess what? I'm going to school next week. Just like you. You and me can go together, okay?"

"I'd like that, Ethan, but we can't go to the same school. I go to a special school." It was easier for Jesse to give a half-truth than try and explain segregation. That was someone else's responsibility.

The following week, in the fall of '56, Ethan was about to join the first graders who, unlike him, had attended kindergarten the year before. Dolores had held him back a year, hoping that the racial tension would miraculously dissipate with time. Sadly, it had only worsened.

Ethan brushed his foot across the floor, dragging the pant legs of his oversized denim jeans. "Here, let me roll up your overalls," Ruthie offered. "I don't want you falling on your face and getting all mussied up on your first day of school."

"Shucks, I ain't gonna fall down, Momma Ruthie," he mumbled as he blew the blond locks off his brow.

Ruthie raised his pants while Dolores slapped on a handful of pomade to slick back his hair. He was ready for school; but Ruthie and Dolores were not. This was the day they had been dreading for years—not knowing what was to come, not knowing how to prepare him.

Dolores bent down to his eye level and took each of his arms. "You're a big boy now. I want you to remember that sometimes children say things that they don't always mean. You just keep saying to yourself 'Sticks and stones can break my bones…'"

Ethan looked at his mother with a puzzled expression and said, "I know, Momma…'but names can never hurt me.'"

"Good, boy. Now let's get going. Give Momma Ruthie a kiss good-bye."

Ruthie lifted herself from the chair using one of her two canes to support her left leg. As soon as she was erect, she placed the second cane under the palm of her right hand. After months of declining health, she now needed both canes to walk. "I'm going with you today."

"You aren't well enough to make the walk," Dolores argued.

"If it was just my health to worry about, I'd stay home. But I ain't going to let you make that walk by yourself. Folks have been waiting a long time for this day," Ruthie said adamantly.

"Maybe they've just forgotten about us," Dolores said hopefully.

"Don't fool yourself none. If they got something to say, today's the day they are gonna say it," Ruthie said as she hobbled out the door.

Located on the north side of Purvis, Coolidge Elementary was the all-white school where Ethan was enrolled. That section of town, which was completely foreign to Ethan, was all-too familiar to Dolores. It was there that she and her daughters had shared a life with Thomas Drake. And although there had never been a divorce, she had had no contact with him since the day she left. Nevertheless, the very thought of him made her stomach churn.

At the edge of the school grounds Ruthie and Dolores said their good-byes to Ethan. Both women were a bit anxious, but it appeared that, at least for the moment, no one was paying any attention to them. "Just walk up those steps, son," Dolores instructed. "The woman standing by the front door will help you. Give her this slip of paper. It says that you are in the first grade." Dolores folded the note and put it in his pocket. "Get going, son."

"Be good, Ethan," Ruthie added.

"But I don't want to go to this school. I want to go to Jesse's."

He felt like a fish out of water. There were so many children in so many sizes. And suddenly they were all staring at him.

"I don't like it here. I don't want to go to this school! I want to go to Jesse's special school!"

Dolores was about to offer Ethan encouragement when a leather-clad boy, who appeared to be about twelve years old, bumped up against her.

"Excuse me, lady. You might want to read that sign over there." He pointed to the brick pillar centered in the school's yard. The silver plaque at its base had the engraving Coolidge Elementary School. Scribbled in chalk beneath were the words "Whites Only." "So you best get your mammy out of here real quick, lady."

Dolores eyed him without uttering a word. The youth glared back and brushed up against her a second time. "Do you get my drift, lady?"

"Ruthie, let's get going," she said, reluctantly heeding the youth's suggestion.

"Get going, son. I'll be back here this afternoon to walk you home. Be good."

"We'll be back," Ruthie said emphatically, ignoring the panicky look on Dolores's face.

"Okay, bye," Ethan said, gaining enthusiasm as he neared the door. At the top of the steps and in front of a hundred onlookers Ethan yelled back, "I love you, Mommas. See you after school."

If only the women in his life had not sheltered him from the outside world, perhaps Ethan would have understood the order on the pillar, "Whites Only." As he was white, he should have had no problem; but the moment that he referred to Ruthie as his momma, he not only became an outcast, he became a marked soul. Whether it would be that day or one day in the future, Ethan was bound to suffer the consequences of racial hatred.

"Class, my name is Miss Adams. Welcome to the first grade. I am going to be your teacher this year. We're going to have a wonderful time learning together. I want you to know that first grade won't be as easy as it was in kindergarten."

Ethan, not having had that initial year, sensed a queasy feeling in his stomach. School was new to him. He had no idea what to expect.

"Class, let's go around the room and tell us your name and where you live and a little about your parents and sisters and brothers."

Oh, boy. I can tell them about my family and Big Jess. This is easy. I can do that, he thought.

After the third child told about his father the "'torney-at-law," it was Ethan's turn. "My name is Ethan Drake and I have two mommas and two sisters. My sisters moved away when I was little. Momma and Momma Ruthie and me live on Washington Street. You know, across the tracks by Jesse Brown's house."

"You got two mommas? No one's got two mommas," shouted a freckle-faced boy in the front row. From the back of the room another boy challenged, "Did you say the other side of town, where the darkies live?"

Before he could answer, another one asked, "Who was that black coon I saw you smooching out front?"

Miss Adams interjected, but did so a tad late. "Children, let Ethan finish his story and there will be no more, and I repeat, no more interruptions."

Ethan hung on those last bitter words. *Black coon?* And then it occurred to him. There were no children in his class, or school for that matter, who looked like Jesse. No one had Jesse's dark shiny skin, not even himself. Ethan suddenly felt like he was the odd man out. He didn't fit in there and somehow he knew he wouldn't fit in with Jesse either. Falling to his seat he stammered, "She's my momma."

The children snickered. He was a freak and they weren't going to let him forget it. As he buried his head, the boy behind him whispered, "Ethan is a nigger lover. Ethan is a nigger lover."

He tried to remember the words to "Sticks and Stones" but somehow they wouldn't come to him. He was numb. He never heard the words nigger lover before and he wasn't sure of the meaning, but he knew it wasn't a good thing. By the end of the day, Ethan was sure he was a nigger lover because everywhere he went someone was there to remind him.

That day felt like the longest of Ethan's life. The children at school were cold and callous and refused to accept him. He was hurt, confused, and ready to retreat home at the ring of the bell.

Ethan scuffed his feet down the steps of the school feeling weary and defeated. From behind, a boy twice his size elbowed his side and taunted, "Are you a coon boy or just a plain ass nigger lover?" *Everyone knows I'm different,* he thought. Ethan wanted to run but his legs felt like deadweights. From the steps he could see his mommas waiting for him at the curb, just as they had promised. *I've got to get there before the kids tell them I'm a nigger lover.* But it was too late. As every child passed Dolores and Ruthie, they shouted nigger or coon and then darted off to the security of their own families who seemed to share a bond of racial bigotry.

As Ethan and his mommas made their way homeward, they could hear vitriolic words hurled in their direction, only now the voices included parents as well as their offspring. "Coon! Darkie! Nigger lover! Get out of town or you'll be sorry."

The three of them hustled along, trying to ignore the taunts. But as they moved farther from school, the clamor grew louder. Townsfolk came out onto the streets and echoed the slurs. Suddenly it wasn't about the boy anymore. It was a chance to voice their disdain for any black that still owned land on the south side of town—acreage that the whites were chomping at the bit to procure. "Get out of town, if you know what's good for you, nigger, and take the nigger lovers with you."

Sheriff Pete was sitting behind his station desk when he noticed the swarm of people outside. He grabbed his hat and ran outside and saw Leroy Pentz, his barber of ten years, leaning up against the red, white, and blue spiraled barber pole. Pete called out as he opened his patrol car door, "What's this all about, Leroy?"

"Better stay out of this, Sheriff. This ain't your business."

"Ah but, Leroy, it is my business," he stated as he got into the car.

Pete drove down Main Street with his siren blaring. The influx of people made it appear like a national holiday. Even the local proprietors had abandoned their shops to add their two cents worth. "Get out of town, niggers, if you know what's good for you."

Up until that day, the townsfolk kept racial comments low-key, especially around Pete. Uncertain of his true feelings, they did not want to alienate their one and only peacekeeper. Ignoring the fact that Purvis had an escalating crime rate, the townsfolk rejected Pete's request to hire a deputy. Rather than give him the manpower he needed, they voted to give him a substantial increase in his salary. Pete could only do so much. Incidents that should have raised questions often went unnoticed because he was just too busy. Pete was exactly what some of the townspeople of Purvis wanted in a law enforcer.

As Pete drove through the ever-growing mass of people, he realized that his passive style of keeping the peace may have finally caught up with him. His town had become so prejudiced that the white supremacists were indirectly calling the shots. He knew that on this day the strength of their unity was beyond his control.

Pete pulled up at the front of the school and encountered an angry mob of people. What started out as a few parents and their children now included young mothers with infants, retired people, and business people from the stores on Main Street. All of them were all-too anxious to express their hatred. They held their clenched fists aloft, waiving in unison to the profanities trumpeted through a megaphone. The instigator, standing atop the brick pillar, fueled their hatred.

"Nigger lover," he shouted.

"Nigger lover," they replied.

"Coon nigger move away," he yelled.

"Coon nigger move away," they responded.

Pete forced his way through the thickening crowd. He beseeched them one by one; but it was to no avail.

"Go home, Mary, and put the baby to bed. Get on your way, Howard. You shouldn't be out at your age."

Unable to disperse them, Pete pushed on until he reached the pillar and looked up. He narrowed his eyes and glared at the tyrant stirring up the crowd. It was Thomas Drake, the last person that Pete expected to see. Drake had never before commanded leadership, but today his topic was a popular one. People were thrilled to repeat his hateful words.

"Thomas Drake, you have the right to remain silent. Anything you say will be held against you."

"Who the hell do you think you're talking to, Pete?"

"Get down, Drake. You are under arrest for inciting a riot."

"You hear that folks?" Mocking the law, Thom bellowed sarcasms into the megaphone. "I'm the one under arrest. Not that nigger-loving woman or her bastard boy. Not even that nigger landowner, Jackson."

The crowd booed to show their disapproval of the sheriff's actions; their support for Thom inspired him, and for once in his life he was in a position of power. Although it was self-appointed, Thom finally knew what it felt like to rule. So he ignored Pete and chanted another order into the megaphone. But as the crowd responded, Pete swung his arm and slammed into the back of Thom's knees. Thom's legs folded causing him to lose balance. When he fell off the pillar, Pete was there scrambling to slap the cuffs on Thom's wrists.

"I've been wanting to do this for a long time, you son of a bitch," Pete said while using his foot to keep Thom flat on the ground.

Pete turned toward the crowd and demanded, "Go home now, folks, or I promise that I'll call in the state troopers and have you all arrested, one by one. Go home!"

The crowd diverted their attention from Pete and Thom to search out Leroy for instructions. Standing in the shadows, Leroy nodded his head, telling the crowd to disperse. As the townspeople passed by, Leroy whispered, "There will come a day when it will be our turn. Be patient. I'll go and make bail for Thom Drake."

After that afternoon things seemed to calm down considerably. Thom was given a lenient sentence from the local judge, who suggested he leave town for a year or two. "At least until things get back to normal," the judge said as he winked at Thom before adding, "Know what I mean, friend?"

"Yes, sir. I'm outta Purvis, Judge. For as long as it takes."

Pete's threat to call in the state troopers was enough to keep away even the most notorious hoods. They were the ones who had a list of to-dos on the east side and couldn't afford any interference from a large government agency. So the shrouded rulers of Purvis wanted nothing more than easygoing Pete Cornell. The sheriff had heard about the burning crosses, but often a day or two after the flames had been doused. As for the acts of vandalism, Pete found it nearly impossible to identify the culprits who broke windows, killed cows, or put molasses in gas tanks. Pete just didn't have the resources for those types of investigations.

As a result of the lack of legal protection, several blacks gave in to the whites' demands. They sold their hard-earned land for pennies on the dollar. However, there was a handful, including Ruthie Jackson, who refused to sell out. They were the ones determined to outlive the racial hatred no matter what the consequences.

For the next two years, it was Dolores who walked Ethan to school, as Ruthie had become nearly bedridden. She concealed her illness by blaming her declining mobility on the weight she had added over time to an already ample body. It now took Ruthie considerable effort just to move from room to room. Ruthie initially stayed home by choice, but after several months it became apparent to Ruthie and Dolores that Ethan was teased less and less about his two mommas. After a while, Ethan forgot that he had once been the social outcast at Coolidge. The two women reached an unspoken agreement that Dolores should be the only momma who walked Ethan to and from school. Neither of them ever learned the full extent of the heartache the other experienced because of the decision.

❖ ❖ ❖

It was late October 1958 when Miss Thornton's third-grade class was given the news by the upperclassmen. Her students had been chosen to assist the juniors and seniors with the annual Ghosts and Goblins Party. This was a privilege that came to the younger gradeschoolers only once every few years.

"Welcome back, Bobby Johnson. I remember when you were in my class. Now you're a senior," Miss Thornton said proudly.

"Yes, Miss Thornton, we all grow up eventually. Well, I've got a long list of jobs. Do you mind if I start handing them out?"

"Go right ahead, Bobby. This is exciting, class!"

"All right then. We need someone to make decorations." Every child raised a hand in hopes of being selected. Bobby walked around the room and picked four girls to complete the assignment.

"Okay, great. We've got an enthusiastic bunch here, Miss Thornton. Now we need some of you to set up and take down the folding chairs and tables."

Bobby pointed to five boys; but Ethan, who raised his hand and waved it enthusiastically, was passed over. Bobby requested additional volunteers and each time Ethan's hand went down in disappointment. He was the only one who had not been chosen.

"We have one more job. Is there anyone who didn't receive an assignment?" Seeing that no other child had raised a hand, Ethan partially lifted his.

"Oh, Ethan Drake. How did we miss you?" He asked with a slightly crooked smile.

"Well, we have one job left. It requires one person. So the job is yours, if you want it."

Ethan brushed his blond hair out of his eyes and proclaimed, "I'll do it, whatever it is."

"Okay, but remember that this is the most important job—we can't have you fail. We need you to pick up a bale of hay from Old Man Denton's barn the day before the party and drop it off at the gym. Do you have something to haul it in?"

"I can pull my wagon behind my bike."

"Good. Ethan Drake will pick up the bale next Thursday after school so that the girls can decorate on Friday morning. Now I trust that every one of you will complete your assignment."

"My students won't let you down, Bobby. Don't you worry! It's going to be a fine shindig," Miss Thornton said.

"Oh, I'm not the least bit worried. I'm sure that *everything* will go as planned."

The following Thursday Ethan, who could barely sit still, counted the minutes before school was to let out. His excited behavior disrupted the class.

"Ethan Drake, stop turning around to look at the clock. We still have twenty minutes of class left," Miss Thornton reprimanded the blond-haired boy.

"I'm sorry, Miss Thornton. I have my party assignment today. I gotta pick up the hay so the girls can decorate tomorrow."

"Oh, yes, I do remember. Well, if you stop turning around, I will let you go a few minutes early."

Facing forward, he obliged her and waited until she finally gave in. "All right, Ethan. It is ten minutes to three. You are excused."

Ethan shot out of his seat and raced to the door. Miss Thornton stopped him before he left. "Ethan, be careful riding out to Mr. Denton's. We'll see you tomorrow."

"Yes, ma'am."

He jumped on his bike, pushing the pedals faster than the chain could manage. Every so often he was forced to stop and tighten its slack. This unforeseen delay, coupled with towing a heavy wagon on a dirt road, made the three-mile ride a grueling one. But Ethan was determined to complete his notable task no matter how long it took.

Shortly after five, Ethan dropped his bike at the edge of Denton's lawn and headed straight to the well for a drink. He turned its wheel until he heard the bucket splash into the water. He cranked it back up and filled an old tin cup he found on the well's ledge. The water, with a lingering taste of limestone, tasted exceptionally good after the long ride.

Refreshed, he ran up toward the front door but a frightening sound caused him to come to an abrupt halt. He turned around and saw a large flock of crows flying out of the barn. As they swooped over his head, Ethan covered his ears from the whistling noise they created. It was deafening until they flew out of sight and into the horizon.

Horizon, he thought. *The sun's setting. It's going to be dark soon. I'd better hurry up.*

Ethan knocked on the old man's door for several minutes before peering through a window. As far as he could tell, there were no lights on inside. *Old Man Denton must have wanted me to get the bale myself.*

He walked across the dirt lot to the left side of the barn and opened the latch to the door. As he slid it open, Ethan was overwhelmed by the heavy scent of cow manure from within. Inside, it was almost pitch black, only the fading natural light that slipped in through a broken window from above relieved the gloom.

Cautiously, Ethan walked past the large pen that housed Denton's prize bull. The bull, eyeing Ethan, snorted through its nose ring that momentarily glinted in the light.

"It's okay, bull. I'm just here to pick up some hay," he quavered.

He edged his way deeper into the barn as the light from the outside slowly diminished. Thick ropes hung from the ceiling to the floor. He pushed past them and made his way to the hay. Grabbing the ties to a bale, he started dragging it across the floor. Darker now, it was difficult to find his way back out.

The twilight of the night scared him. His mind began teasing him with the sound of an old familiar chant. "Coon boy, coon boy, coon boy." He pivoted to escape but tripped over the bale and became lost in the darkness. "Coon boy, coon boy," he heard again. He heard it from the left so he darted to the right, but the sound was now directly in front of him.

"Who is it? Who's in here? I'm Ethan Drake. I just came to get a bale of hay," he stuttered.

"Coon boy's come out to play." It was louder now; he knew it couldn't be his imagination. Overcome with fear, Ethan started to whimper. Then he heard someone say, "Do it BJ, do it now!"

Suddenly, the light from a powerful flashlight blinded him. "Please," he begged. "Whoever you are, let me go."

"We'll let you go all right. Straight to hell, you nigger lover!"

Too afraid to run, he trembled with fear. The taunting continued. Just as his eyes adjusted to the brilliant light, the source was extinguished, and he was plunged into darkness again. His tormentors repeatedly turned the light on and off until he became disoriented. "Please, leave me alone," he gasped.

"We'll leave you alone, coon boy. But…" Then everything went silent. No one moved; no one spoke.

Ethan panted loudly. The darkness enveloped him. He couldn't remember the way out of the barn. He was petrified. Urine trickled down his overalls to the straw-covered floor. "Please, let me go home," he begged.

For a brief moment he thought it was over. He welcomed the silence, but just as he did, the back of a shovel was bashed into his chest. The blow was so intense that Ethan fell choking to the ground. But his persecutors weren't finished with him. They cursed him vehemently and with every insult they kicked his head, his back, or his groin. Over and over he was thrashed until someone ordered, "Enough of this bullshit. Let's get this over with."

"Yeah, take this, you nigger lover." It was the final insult that preceded a vicious slash to his thigh from a six-inch switchblade. The pain rendered the eight-year-old unconscious.

At eight o'clock that evening Dolores was pacing the wooden floor. Ruthie, who was just as nervous, rocked back and forth in the wicker rocker. Neither could imagine what was taking Ethan so long.

"I can't take it anymore, Ruthie. I've got to go to Coolidge. I'm going next door to ask Jesse to go with me," she said as she snatched a sweater from the coat hanger and ran next door.

"Jesse, it's me, Mrs. Drake," Dolores said, pounding on the Browns' front door. "Ethan isn't home yet. He left to pick up the hay hours ago. Please help me look for him."

Jesse opened the door and said reassuringly, "I'm sure your boy is fine, Mrs. Drake. He probably got another flat tire on his bike. I'll help you find him."

"Jesse, he should have been home by now. I have this feeling that something is terribly wrong."

Jesse had the same feeling, but skirted the issue. "We'll find him, don't you worry none."

The streets of Purvis were empty by the time they reached the school grounds. All lights had been extinguished except for a small floodlight that illuminated the Coolidge sign. Jesse and Dolores checked the four sets of double doors, but they had all been locked with heavy chains. Clearly, no one had been there for hours.

"Jesse, run and get Sheriff Pete."

Jesse took the shortcut through the field past the swamp. Assuming that the jail was closed, he ran directly to Sheriff Cornell's home, though he approached no closer than the white picket fence. From the fence he cried out, "Sheriff Pete, Mrs. Drake can't find her boy."

Sheriff Cornell, still in uniform, finally opened the door. "Now, what is it Jesse? What's this about Dolores Drake?"

"Ethan is missing, sir. He didn't come home from Denton's farm."

"All right, boy. Get in the car." Jesse opened the back door and slid in. It never occurred to him to sit in the front.

Pete found Dolores sitting on the school steps holding her head in her hands. "Dolores, what's going on? What's this about Ethan?"

"Pete, he didn't come home. He was supposed to ride out to Al Denton's farm and fetch a bale of hay for the Halloween party. He's been gone for hours now."

"Come on. We'll find him," Pete said while cupping her hands in his.

"Why did Ethan have to go all the way out to Denton's for a bundle of hay? It doesn't make sense to me."

"I never thought to question it. Ethan said it was his assignment for the school party. He was just happy to be picked. He doesn't have any friends, Pete." She turned around and faced the backseat of the patrol car. "Except you, Jesse. You are his hero."

Pete Cornell deliberately ignored the comment. Her situation, viewed by the townsfolk as repulsive, would only worsen if that statement was repeated. Even Pete had a hard time accepting the fact that she raised her son among them.

The siren was blaring as the sheriff sped through the quiet and usually peaceful town. There was no sign of the boy anywhere. As they turned onto the road that led up to Denton's farmhouse, the lights from his patrol car lit the way. It was dark, almost too dark. There was no sign of Denton or his faithful hound dog who howled at every visitor.

"I'm gonna check around the house, Dolores. It doesn't look like Ethan ever made it here. You both stay in the car. I'll be back in a minute."

Dolores sat motionless. Jesse, who waited until Sheriff Pete disappeared around the corner of the farm, exited the car. "I'm gonna check the barn, Mrs. Drake."

Jesse crossed the yard under the full moon that had finally freed itself from the cloud that shadowed it before. It provided just enough light to find the sliding doors and see that a heavy railroad tie barred the entry. It suggested that Ethan had never arrived.

Without removing the barrier, Jesse pushed against the warped door. A crack about three inches opened up. He couldn't see or hear anything. It was quiet. Even the bull and his cows seemed to be resting for the night. *Not in here,* he thought. He started back toward the patrol car, but something made him stop dead in his tracks. He didn't know what, but he just knew he had to go inside.

Working the wooden beam back and forth, he managed to loosen it from its support. When it finally dropped to the ground, Jesse slid open the door and stepped inside.

The moonlight had found its way in through a broken window and illuminated a direct path to the hayloft. The bull, woken from his slumber, grunted as Jesse passed his pen.

"Ethan, you in here? It's me, Jesse." Following the scent of manure and hay, he made his way into the main room. But the natural barn odors suddenly changed to a pungent stench of fresh blood. It led him to the boy who barely clung to life.

Jesse shrieked, "Sheriff, I've found him. Sheriff Pete, he's in the barn. Help!" Jesse fell to the ground and wrapped his arms around Ethan. His body was limp, almost lifeless. "Please hurry. Sheriff Pete, please hurry," Jesse yelled.

Jesse laid his ear on Ethan's chest and listened for a heartbeat. It was faint, but it was there. Jesse screamed again. "He's here, Sheriff. He's in here. Ethan is alive."

While Jesse waited for the sheriff, he tore off his shirt and twisted it around Ethan's thigh. The tourniquet slowed the flow of blood oozing from the wound. Jesse held it tight until Sheriff Pete raced in.

"Lord in heaven," Pete exclaimed. "Jesse, I'll take it from here. Go to the car and radio for help. Tell them we need an ambulance at Denton's. Tell them to hurry, we don't have much time."

Fear had paralyzed Dolores, so she had remained in the patrol car, which was parked nearer to the house and away from the barn. She had not heard Jesse's cries. It was not until she saw the panic on his face when he returned to call for help that she knew her fears for Ethan's safety were justified. "What is it? Is my boy in there?" she beseeched him.

Jesse didn't answer her. He couldn't look her in the face. When he picked up the radio and asked for an ambulance, she fled into the barn.

"Please, Pete, tell me he is all right."

Dolores fell to Ethan's side and wiped his hair from his forehead. His blond locks were sticky and matted from blood that had seeped from his head wounds.

"He's alive, Dolores, that much I can tell you."

"It's their retaliation, Pete. The hooded monsters waited years to pay me back. I know it."

Pete didn't argue with her. A white who lived with darkies was bound to suffer consequences. On the other hand, perhaps it was some sort of prank that got out of hand. Pete wouldn't speculate, not just yet.

eight

DAVID STRATTON

California, 1951–1958

In October of 1951 shortly after David Stratton had completed his executive internship, Theo Bachman's secretary spoke to David over the office intercom. As she was with all of Mr. Bachman's subordinates, she was curt and to the point.

"Mr. Stratton?"

"Yes, I'm here. What can I do for you?"

"Mr. Bachman has requested a few minutes of your time. He would like to meet with you in your office promptly at three o'clock. Please clear your calendar."

David glanced at his watch and started shoving papers into a top drawer before he responded. It was a mere fifteen minutes before the CEO would be visiting him.

He pushed the button and asked, "Is there something specific that I should be preparing for?"

"Mr. Bachman is not in the habit of divulging the nature of his meetings to me."

"Of course not," he said into the intercom whose light had already extinguished.

It had been over a year since David had started his career with Bachman Aerospace Industries. During that period he rarely saw the slender, short man who owned the company. Unbeknownst to David, Theo Bachman deliberately kept his distance from him. Bachman wanted his young protégé to learn the facets of the business without his influence. Bachman also knew that the less they saw of one another the rumors that David was riding on his shirttails would have less credence.

Theo Bachman knocked twice on David's door before letting himself in. "Good to see you again, David," Bachman said as he sat down on one of the two chairs in front of the desk. "Where has the time gone? It seems like yesterday when I first welcomed you aboard."

"I can't agree with you more. This past year has been a whirlwind."

"Well, I do hope that we have given you enough of a chance to grasp the basics of our departments."

"The basics, yes, but I couldn't attest to much more than that. Just about the time that I start feeling I know my way around a department, it's time to move on to another. I spent last month working in personnel."

"Yes, I know. Was it one of your favorites?" Bachman questioned him knowing full well that it wasn't.

"I have to say that it was interesting to learn about how a company deals with employee issues."

"But did you find it challenging?"

"Honestly? Not really. There are other departments such as R and D that I still gravitate toward," he said as he hinted about the original position he had been hired to fill.

"Ah, yes, the Director of Research and Development. Well, there's been a slight change of plan. I've decided not to move Mitchell Connors out, since he has finally stepped up to the plate. During the last quarter, Mitchell outperformed every department in terms of meeting his benchmarks. It probably had something to do with him knowing that you were on the sidelines waiting to take over. In light of his improvement, I feel it would be unfair to him to move him out at this time. I take it that you understand."

Although David did not understand, he was not about to take exception to his superior. "Yes, Mr. Bachman," he said. "I know that business is business and you have to do what is right for the company."

"Good. I knew a Stratton could see it no other way than my way," Bachman stated.

At that moment David caught a glimpse of his company badge lying on his desk; but as he went to pick it up, Bachman seized it. David wished he had not forgotten to clip it on.

David watched as Bachman silently studied the badge. The difference between all the other employees' badges was that theirs included an employee identification number, while David's badge was marked "temporary" and only displayed his name and title of junior executive. To date he had not been assigned a permanent number. Preparing for the worst he asked, "Mr. Bachman, are you here to give me notice?"

"Notice, David?" Bachman burst out laughing. "Is that why you think I'm here? To fire you? Be serious, son; I've never fired anyone in my life. You should know that I let personnel handle the dirty work. No, I have other plans for you."

"Whew. That's a relief," David said as he jokingly wiped his forehead.

"Next time you jump to conclusions, David, remember that I play by the rules," Bachman said. "Although, I have to admit that every so often I will bend them a little when it's good for business."

"Mr. Bachman, what can I do for you?"

"You can start by calling me Theo. I remember asking that of you over a tall Bloody Mary on the day I hired you."

"Sorry, Theo," David said uneasily.

"The second thing you can do is stop by personnel tomorrow morning and ask that your badge be reissued. This was an oversight that should have been rectified months ago," he said, tossing David's temporary badge back on his desk.

"I'll take care of it, Theo," he said, anxiously waiting to hear Bachman's plans for him. "What else can I do for you?"

"David, we have an opportunity to take BAI into a new venture—one that has nothing to do with jet engines," Bachman said as he rubbed the palms of his hands together. "Yes, I've been thinking about it a great deal and I've decided that we should give it a go."

David's curiosity was piqued. "A new venture, Theo?"

"Let's just say it could be an expansion of BAI's core business. Of all the departments you worked in, I heard that you thrived the most in sales. I find that fascinating, considering that your forte was engineering."

"I did find sales to be the most challenging and the most rewarding. May I ask who told you?" David questioned him.

"My internal spies have kept me abreast of your development. I know that you spent as little as two weeks in some departments while sales and marketing held on to you for five months. This was part of our strategic planning."

Bachman scanned David's office and added, "I am feeling a bit claustrophobic in here. Let's go back to my office and discuss this further over a drink. Do you like Scotch?"

Before David answered him, Bachman was already scurrying through the maze of corridors to his prestigious corner suite. Just as he opened the door, David had caught up with him. "Ah, this is better," Bachman sighed.

"Did you say you did or didn't drink Scotch, David?"

"I've never tried it before; my father claims that one must acquire a taste for it."

"He is absolutely correct. Speaking of your father, how is Alfred doing these days? I haven't seen him at the club for over a month or so. What's he been up to?"

"He was in Chicago on business, and then he and my mom flew to New York before sailing off to Europe. Right now they are touring England and France before they head off to Italy. I don't expect them back until Thanksgiving."

"Sounds like Delilah Stratton put together quite an itinerary for the old man."

"My mother does love to travel. It's the one thing she does that my father agrees to unconditionally."

"The Alfred Stratton I know never agrees to anything unconditionally. He tends to weigh the pros and cons on every decision even when it comes to a game of golf." Bachman chuckled and then asked, "So how are your wife and baby doing?"

"They're doing just fine. Jenni Lynn is five months old. She's the spitting image of my wife when she was that age."

"So where are you living?"

"For the time being we're living in one of my father's bungalows in Newport Beach. It's small and quaint but it will do until our home is built."

"Where have you decided to build?"

"We found a lot on the beach just north of Santa Monica and hired Stonehenge Architects. As soon as the plans are approved, the foundation will be laid," David answered enthusiastically.

"Glad to hear that you're not overseeing the project yourself. Some things are best left to the pros. Have a seat at the conference table while I make our drinks."

Theo measured three fingers of single malt whiskey into two small tumblers. "Remember when drinking fine Scotch, you never add ice, David. It could dilute its full-bodied flavor," Bachman said, handing David the drink.

"I'll keep that in mind." As David took his first sip, the taste surprised him. It warmed his mouth while coating his tongue with a velvety oak aftertaste. He sipped it again.

"Better take it slow, David. I need you to pay close attention to me."

David set the glass down. It was apparent that this was not the social visit that Bachman had pretended it to be. "I'm all ears, Theo," he said eagerly.

"Okay then, let's get down to brass tacks."

"Should I be taking notes?"

"For now just take them mentally. Have you heard about the Heisen Proposal?"

"I've heard bits and pieces in the executive dining room."

"What exactly did you hear and please be specific? I'd like to know what my men think about the project."

David answered honestly, "I've heard that BAI is being asked to bid on an offshore oil rig. Some of the executives think it's an unusual request for a company that primarily builds jet engines."

"Do they think I'm off my rocker for responding to this request for proposal?"

"No, it's just the opposite. I get the impression any one of them would take ownership of the project, if given the chance."

Bachman was snipping off the end of a Cuban cigar. He moistened it with his mouth before lighting up. As he drew in the first puff he announced, "Here's where you come in, David. I've decided to turn the Heisen RFP over to you."

David was initially flattered, but apprehension soon took over. He knew that as the rookie executive, Bachman's decision to give him the project would not be a popular one. He saw this as an upward battle when he said, "Theo, this is an honor, but…"

"Hear me out, David. I want you to handpick an A-team of about twenty or so managers. I'm sure you came across an ace or two from your tours of duty around the various departments. Choose the best of the best, no matter which department or division. I expect to see a list of names by the end of the week."

"Theo, I repeat that this is truly an honor. I would have thought that a project like this would be given to the vice president of sales," he said, just shy of asking *why me*.

"Ordinarily, it would have been assigned to Angus. But this time I need an up-and-comer, someone who thinks clearly and acts quickly. I can see that you have those qualities. Besides you are the only executive with hands-on experience in every department of the company. It's you I need, because it's the Heisen account that I want."

"But…"

"No more 'buts,' David. I expect you to build in a twenty-two percent profit margin," Bachman said adamantly.

Willingly, David responded, "I'll do my best, Theo." David lifted his glass of Scotch in a toast, just as his father would have done, but the CEO pushed David's glass back down on the table. There would be no celebrating the moment.

"Yes, I expect the best from you, David, because nothing less will suffice. I suggest that you tell your wife that you'll be working late until the Heisen deadline of February 28th, four months from now. Head back to your office and begin choosing your staff. On your desk you will find a complete list of BAI personnel along with the request for proposal from Heisen."

Theo pulled an antique watch on a gold chain from his pocket. Before opening it, he used his thumb to wipe off a fingerprint. "Well, our meeting is over, David. I'm off to another one."

Theo left his office having never touched his drink. David sat there dumbfounded, wondering what just happened. At the snap of a finger the lighthearted conversation about his family had turned into the hottest topic at BAI. This was the business side of the CEO that David had never before been privy to.

Realizing the magnitude of his responsibility, David chased Theo who was running down the corridor. "Theo, wait a minute. Is there anything else I should know? Like when do I start?"

"I thought I made myself perfectly clear. Select your managers and then divvy up the assignments. Believe me, they'll be more than anxious to utilize their own gurus to get the legwork done. However, when it comes to the end product, they'll be by your side all the way."

Bachman stopped in front of the large conference room and pushed open the door. As the door slowly closed in front of David, he overheard Bachman say, "Gentlemen, I've come to a major decis…"

Theo Bachman was shrewd and calculating; he often made decisions with ulterior motives. He paid his people well, but he expected a hefty return on his investment. David Stratton was no exception. After fourteen months of extensive training, it was payback time.

Theo sat down at the head of the conference table and declared, "Gentlemen, I've decided to give the Heisen RFP to David Stratton."

"Theo," Angus interrupted. "He's too green to manage that project. Why not give him a smaller one like the Butler or Anderson account? They're only a fraction of the size, not to mention they are within our core business."

"I understand your disappointment, Angus. I have my reasons."

"But, Theo I'm over sales. What's he over?"

"Angus, I'm about to explain to my staff why I selected Stratton. The reason I did not choose you is another matter altogether. I assumed you would want me to discuss it with you in private. But that's your call. If you prefer not to wait, I'd be more than willing to accommodate you right now in front of your peers."

Angus Bachman, a nephew of Theo's, was the only senior executive who hadn't been headhunted for Bachman Aerospace. In fact, he would have been Bachman's last choice as vice president of sales except that Angus was his sister's only son. As a favor to her, Bachman granted him the position. Weeks later when Bachman realized what a mistake he had made, he protected himself from making another. He immediately added an addendum to the company's practices and procedures that stated nepotism was forbidden at BAI. Luckily for the unimpressive Angus, it was written after the fact.

"We'll talk later," Angus conceded.

"That would be my preference, Angus," Theo said, subtly brushing him off.

"Let's move on with the meeting. You all know that I have invested over one year in the young Stratton lad to be absolutely sure where he would fit in. Now, I know what you must be thinking. You are wondering what happened to R and D. Well, if I had told you a year ago that he wasn't going to fill it, you would have questioned my motives for hiring him." Theo took a drag of the cigar that was now half its original size. "Especially you, Mitch, and with good reason."

Mitchell Connors cleared his throat and readjusted his bifocals. After seven years of running Research and Development, he assumed he would be losing his job to a fresh-out-of-college graduate. But the lack of job security served Mitchell well. Mitchell figured if he was going down, he was going down with phenomenal results, so he made a few risky decisions and ended the fiscal year a half million under budget. With results like those, it was obvious that Theo Bachman knew exactly what he was doing.

"So, Mitch, you've got your department running as it should. The same goes for the rest of you. You know, with the government contract for twenty engines, this will be a banner year for us. As for next year when—not if—we win the Heisen bid, there will be a substantial bonus for each and every one of you."

Bachman circled the room and praised the work each executive had accomplished, until he laid eyes upon Angus. Fumbling with the lock to his briefcase, the awkward VP expected no recognition from his uncle, nor did he receive any. Angus knew his days were numbered. The younger Bachman, who resembled his uncle in body alone, was not a natural salesman. Potential customers intimidated Angus, causing him to sweat profusely in his three-piece suits. The stress eventually became too much for him, so he began sending his subordinates to the bid conferences. When they would return with the win, it was Angus who took credit for the sale, until the day that Bachman learned of his dishonesty.

Bachman cleared his throat to draw the attention away from Angus, who was melting in his own embarrassment. Bachman said, "Over the past year my informants have kept me abreast of David Stratton's progress. I heard that he found ways to cut costs and increase productivity in most of your departments. He's a thinker, that one. He seems to come up with innovative ideas and all the while he draws people to him like a magnet. That is why I decided to give him the Heisen project. Are you with me here?" Puffs of cigar and cigarette smoke filled the room as the board nodded in the affirmative.

"Good. BAI needs Stratton on this venture. We must think outside the box, as this one is different from our usual proposals. Stratton has the business blood of his father and the savoir faire of his mother. And let's not forget his Cary Grant looks. He could wrap any woman around his finger. He's exactly what I need to go up against young widow Heisen."

"I see where you're going with this, Theo," the director of supply said. "I see why you picked the kid. It's his stud qualities," the director laughed while his peers joined in.

Bachman gave a hearty chuckle as well. Then he added, "Yeah, I pity the average Joe who tries to make a half-baked spiel to Jessica Heisen. She'll spit the poor bastard out before he can count to three. So, I take it we are all in agreement, gentlemen."

"Yes, sir. Good decision, Theo!" His staff rarely disagreed with his business know-how because everything he touched seemed to turn to gold. Even Angus agreed; he didn't want to be the one Jessica Heisen would spit out.

"FYI, gentlemen. I told Stratton to pick the best of the best from your departments. That means you might be short on staff for several months, but you can make up the shortfall with contractors. I assume there are no objections." Even if there were, none of the executives would jeopardize his relationship with Theo. Again, they willingly gave him the go-ahead.

"Before we adjourn, there is just one more thing. You can expect to see David Stratton in my staff meetings from here on out. Effective immediately, I am promoting him to Vice President of Strategic Accounts. But don't let the cat out of the bag. I haven't made him an official offer, although I'm fairly confident he won't turn it down!"

◇ ◇ ◇

David trudged up the bungalow's walkway, draping his navy blue suit jacket over his shoulder. His necktie, loosened from its knot, hung carelessly around his unbuttoned Oxford shirt. While he searched for his key, Karen slipped off the chain lock and opened the door for him.

"Mr. Vice President, you look awful. I kept your dinner in the oven," she whispered, not wanting to wake the baby.

"I'm so exhausted, babes, I can barely think. Thank God tomorrow is Saturday. I only have to go in for a few hours."

"You have to work another Saturday? Did you forget that your parents invited us to dinner tomorrow night? They've hired Christmas carolers to sing for us."

"Cancel it. I really don't know how long I will be," he said as he splashed cool water from the kitchen faucet onto his face.

"David, this is getting ridiculous. You haven't been home before midnight in over three weeks. Theo Bachman can't expect you to keep up these hours for much longer."

Exhausted, he snapped back at her for her lack of support. "We've had this conversation before, Karen. The engineers and managers are involved in the dynamics, but I am the one who is ultimately responsible. Period."

"I hate the hours you are keeping. And I hate the Heisen Corporation."

"You aren't being fair, Karen. We've had it made up until now. This is my big chance to prove I was worth the bankroll Bachman gambled on me."

"Shhhh. You're going to wake the baby."

"I wouldn't mind waking her. At least *she'd* be glad to see me."

"That was cold. I wait up for you night after night and I rarely complain."

David felt his blood boil. He wanted to fight back but the headache he had been courting kept him silent. He went into Jenni's bedroom and leaned over her crib. She was now seven months old, and the appearance of a newborn infant had long faded. He had missed out on so many of her firsts. For a split second he felt like the Heisen Proposal was sucking the life right out of him, but the feeling quickly passed over.

"I'm lonely, David. Jenni does take up most of my day, but when she sleeps, all I do is pace from room to room waiting for you to come home. I'm going stir-crazy."

"I can't worry about work and you at the same time. Not now, Karen."

"What am I supposed to do all day long? I'm bored to tears," she whined.

"Why don't you get a hobby? Use the skills you acquired in one of those classes you took when I was in college. Talk to my mom, I'm sure she'll come up with something."

"Why don't I just get a job?" Karen said sarcastically. "That way neither of us would see Jenni Lynn!"

"Karen, what the hell do you want from me?" His voice was hoarse and cracked from exhaustion.

"I want you to tell Bachman that your family is more important than your job. Let me be more specific. Tell him that your family is more important than that god-awful Heisen contract."

"Ah, I see, Karen. You opt for *my* unemployment! If I were to say that to Theo Bachman, I'm as good as unemployed."

"Then talk to your father. I'm sure with his connections he could find you a company that would pick you up in a minute. A company that requires only half of the hours you are putting in."

"What on earth are you talking about? For a year I worked seven, maybe eight hours a day. Now I'm asked to go full throttle and you give me nothing but grief. I'll tell you something right now, Karen. Nothing, let me repeat, nothing, you say will stop me from giving my all to this project."

"I guess it's a waste of my time to complain. You are telling me that for an indefinite period you'll be coming home long after midnight. Correct?"

"Listen, Karen," he said as he placed his hand across his forehead. "When we win this contract, it'll be turned over to operations and I'll be out of the picture. I need you to bear with me until February 28th."

He started to rub his brow feverishly, trying to soothe the migraine that was nearing full force. His vision blurred. Nausea was close at hand.

Karen didn't mean to take out her loneliness on David; when she realized he was in pain her instinct was to make her husband feel better. Sympathetically, she asked, "How bad is it, honey?"

"It's just the usual stress headache," he said not really wanting to explain.

Karen knew David was able to cope with regular headaches. He generally had one or two a week that an aspirin would alleviate. His face was flushed. She knew he was experiencing a headache of the worst kind. It made her stop and think. On his forehead there were deep lines and his chest was sunken. He had lost a tremendous amount of weight and was no longer the muscular football player. His trousers were baggy and would have fallen to the floor if not for the suspenders holding them up. He was clearly exhausted, and probably had been for several weeks, but up until then Karen hadn't noticed.

"I am so sorry, hon. I am so very sorry." She led him to the bedroom and began removing his clothes.

"Here, take this. It'll make you relaxed."

"What is it?"

"A mild sedative," she said as she put the blue pill in his hand.

While she massaged his throbbing temples, he asked, "When did you start taking these?"

"I haven't taken any yet. The doctor gave them to me because I told him I was having trouble sleeping when you're not at home," she admitted.

David swallowed the pill and within minutes he had escaped into a deep and tranquil sleep. The confrontation was over.

As he lay on his side, Karen thought about their verbal exchange of cruelties. It made her think that perhaps she should get a hobby or perhaps a part-time job. She decided that rather than asking for Delilah's advice as David had suggested, she would talk with her own mother and see if they could come up with an idea. After all, her mother had learned to keep herself occupied whenever Lieutenant John had been called for duty. That was the last time Karen fought about the hours David spent on the Heisen Proposal; however, it wouldn't be the last time she'd fight about the project's outcome. Win or lose, the Strattons' connection to the Heisen Corporation would impact their lives in ways they could never have imagined.

✧ ✧ ✧

David unbuttoned his sports jacket and greeted his team as they entered the conference room. Just one week prior to deadline, he had called an emergency Heisen meeting. The timing, they thought, was unnerving.

"Gentlemen, be seated. We need to go over a few critical items."

In front of each man was a brown Naugahyde binder with the letters BAI stamped in gold on its cover. Its contents held the staggering seven-hundred and forty pages of specific engineering solutions to the Heisen requests. From the outside, it was an impressive package.

"Let's start on page twenty-six."

One by one the managers lifted their eyes to catch sight of a peer. Silently, they all thought the same thing. *Page twenty-six? He's got to be kidding. At this rate we'll never make the February 28th deadline.*

David impatiently tapped his finger on the table while waiting for the entourage to find the page. "Let's get started. I think the responses on this page are totally…" He paused and looked at his audience; each man held his breath. They were just as exhausted as he was and the thought of one more change was unbearable. David continued. "What was I saying? Ah, yes, the responses on this page are totally…on target. Just like the other seven-hundred-and-some-odd pages."

David closed his copy and said, "Excellent job, team. This is a winner. This is the package Theo Bachman expected from us."

David turned around and pressed the button to the intercom on the table behind him. "Ladies, please bring in the refreshments."

Immediately, a parade of clerks carrying a variety of delicacies entered. They were holding trays of champagne, Cuban cigars, caviar and blinis, and Belgium chocolates.

"I'd like you to open up the Dom, ladies, and start pouring. Then you are excused," David said. He always maintained a professional relationship with the female workers at BAI. Other executives, who were not as businesslike, often took advantage of the female subordinates. They would have invited the ladies to join them. But not David; he knew where to draw the line.

Each clerk held a bottle of the expensive champagne and in unison they peeled off the foils and metal protectors before forcing the corks free with a popping sound reminiscent of a New Year's Eve celebration. The clerks, who were eager to please the dashing Mr. Stratton, promptly poured the bubbly. But the moment their services were no longer required they quietly exited and returned to their respective offices.

"I want to thank you for all of the hours you've contributed to this project. I know that most of you probably experienced some flack from your better halves. I know I did," David disclosed with a smile.

Recollecting their own domestic quarrels, they grinned along with him, as not one of them could claim recent household harmony. The Heisen project had been a drain on everyone who was affiliated with it.

David lifted his champagne flute and rubbed his index finger around its rim. "You are the finest men at BAI and it has been my privilege to work with you. Your contributions to this stage of the project were overshadowed only by your endless support. I know it would have been easy to oppose my authority, especially since I'm not…well, I'm not as seasoned as most of you."

With their glasses held in midair, his team suffered from a mild case of guilt because David was right. He had been resented in the beginning because of his youth, tenacity, and the fact that he was Bachman's protégé. Yet David never flaunted his clout. He went out of his way to give credit to his people, leaving little for himself. So naturally it was hard to hold a grudge against such a likeable guy as David Stratton.

"To a sensational team," he toasted. "And to the hope of winning Heisen!"

As they were about to take their first sip of the expensive champagne, an engineer at the far end of the table stood up. "Wait a minute, guys. Don't drink yet. I have something to say to Mr. Stratton on behalf of all of us. You were right. Some of us did feel a bit jealous when you took over. We figured you'd be like a certain VP, who for political reasons, I'd rather not name."

Everyone, except David, chuckled at the indirect reference to Angus. David saw no advantage to criticizing his peer. The engineer, sensing David's displeasure, continued. "Anyway, we thought you'd pass everything off to us. You know how it goes. 'Show me the baby, but keep the labor pains to yourself.' We had no idea that you'd work right alongside of us. And then sometimes you'd send us home, but you'd end up working all night. We've never known a BAI executive to roll his sleeves up, pitch in, and get the job done. Mr. Stratton, you've been our inspiration."

Still standing at the edge of the table with his half-empty glass in hand, David blushed. He had been given the greatest honor by his team. He had been given respect.

"To you, sir! Mr. Stratton, break a leg at Heisen's next week. We know you can do it! Down the hatch, everyone."

The following week in the men's room at Heisen Corporation, David splashed his face with water and then straightened his Italian silk tie. His presentation seemed to have gone off without a hitch, although he was given no inclination of acceptance or rejection by Jessica Heisen or her staff. He had been cordially treated and then dismissed, with a request to return at four that afternoon. David decided to drive out to Huntington Beach and wait it out.

When he turned onto Pacific Coast Highway he found himself thinking more of Jessica Heisen than he did of the meeting itself. Aside from the fact that she was a knockout, David's first thought was that she was too young to be running a corporation the size of Heisen; however, that thought quickly passed the moment she spoke. She was in control. She grilled David about BAI; he had to admire her line of questioning, which was nothing short of brilliant. David understood why the competitor before him had grumbled when he had exited Jessica Heisen's office. She had manipulated him into admitting his company's weaknesses. She failed, though, to extract the same information from David about BAI.

"I think it went well, Theo," David said into the pay phone across the street from Huntington Beach. "I'm supposed to go back at four."

"That could be a good sign, David. My informants told me you were the final bid. They've been accepting bids for three weeks now."

"Well, it's too soon to get our hopes up, Theo."

"I'm with you there. I guess I'll hold off buying my new Bentley until we have signatures."

David was anxious to bring up the topic of Jessica Heisen. He wanted to know what Theo thought of her. "You didn't tell me that she was so young, Theo. I'd heard she was a widow, so naturally I expected her to be much older."

"Age has nothing to do with the brains Jessica has. She's one smart cookie. So what did you think of those incredible legs, David? I get a rise every time I think of them."

Talking with Theo Bachman was always a gamble for David. He never knew when a die-hard business attitude would suddenly be replaced by levity. He hesitated to give his opinion so Theo continued.

"And, David, what about those bedroom eyes and that raven hair? She's got quite the package, doesn't she?"

"I can't argue with you, Theo. She's a number, all right. Of course, I have to say that she's not as pretty as my wife Karen," David said as an afterthought.

"Cut the crap," Theo laughed. "Any man would bed her in a second, if he could."

David kept his thoughts to himself, although deep down inside he was instantly attracted to her in ways he couldn't define. Jessica Heisen had an air about her that was more seductive than her infectious smile or her ability to manipulate even the most professional of men.

"Theo, you know that I am a devoted husband," David said.

"That is what I am banking on. But you never know…" Theo said with a slip of the tongue. He quickly added, "When you hear something one way or another give me a buzz. I've got another call. Bye."

David hung up the phone and crossed over to the deserted state beach. Even the local sunbathers who tanned almost all year long shied away from days when the heavy fog blanketed the coast. As for out-of-state vacationers, most of them had retreated back to their normal and, oftentimes, humdrum lives. So the beach had been forgotten.

David leaned up against his 1947 black convertible and removed his two-toned loafers before he rolled up the pant legs of his designer suit. There was no need to lock the car that was only five years old, because he had the beach all to himself. He strolled barefoot on the sand, enjoying Mother Nature's tranquility. As he reached the water, the foam that edged its way onto the dampened beach slowly crept over his feet. There was no splash because the waves had already disintegrated upon impact at the man-made breakwater a hundred feet offshore. This section of the beach was taboo to surfers who took their boards to Newport. But David wasn't thinking about catching a wave today. His thoughts were consumed with the Heisen Proposal.

David stared past the barrier of rocks and into the horizon. He imagined an offshore oil rig just a few miles from the coast bearing the letters BAI. The monstrous contraption would drill beneath the ocean floor to a hidden gusher somewhere below. He pictured a second rig and then a third and then he imagined a multitude of BAI rigs. David stooped down and picked up a piece of beach glass. He stretched his arm back and before hurling it into the ocean, he yelled, "BAI!" At that moment David would have sold his soul just to get the win.

✧ ✧ ✧

Jessica Heisen's secretary, a somber elderly woman, escorted David to Jessica's private office. It was not the general office where he had met her earlier in the day. "Mrs. Heisen will be with you shortly. I will inform her that you have arrived."

The secretary left David in the vacant office and closed the door behind her. This executive office was as extravagant as Theo

Bachman's, only far more unusual. Standing in each corner were free-flowing neon lights that did little to light up the room. In the center of the room was a contemporary, yet functional, metal lamp that hung from the ceiling directly above Jessica's extraordinary desk. The base of her desk was made of huge glass blocks covered with a beveled-mirror top. In front of the desk were three triangular-shaped chairs with pewter rods as backrests. David sat down on one of the chairs and discovered that it was not only uncomfortable, but its slender silver base made it wobble back and forth.

David found this demonstration of unconventionality intriguing. He suddenly wanted to know more about the striking woman dressed in a formfitting white suit who had just walked in.

"I'm glad to see that you've made yourself comfortable, Mr. Stratton." Jessica said, noticing that David didn't attempt to cross his legs. She knew that he needed both feet on the ground to keep his balance. "This is our corporate attorney John Malcolm. He'll be overseeing our meeting," Jessica said curtly.

David stood up and shook their hands. When he sat back down, he struggled again to conform to the chair's irregular shape. This amused Jessica; she had personally designed the chairs as a test of fortitude. It gave her the upper hand in her office.

"Mr. Stratton, I want you to know that there are two other bids that we have been considering. You should know that both of them underbid Bachman's by more than a quarter million." David felt his heart pound. He didn't know where he could cut an additional two hundred thousand. It was the first sign of a potential loss. He squirmed trying to keep his balance in the contortionist's chair.

"A quarter of a million dollars," David gulped. "That's a stretch. Perhaps I should reiterate that BAI is prepared to open an entire division for Heisen. We plan to house a dedicated staff to this project."

"How will this affect the core of your business? We are fully aware that offshore oil rigs have nothing to do with jet engines."

"It won't affect it at all. We're planning to fulfill your requirements in an off-site facility, a stand-alone company, so to speak."

"I'm listening," Jessica said without displaying any emotion. "What are my guarantees?"

"Mrs. Heisen, you already know that BAI prides itself in building the best and most efficient equipment. That pride stems from the vision handed down from Theodore Bachman. It's that same vision Mr. Bachman sees for the Heisen project. It's a new world and a new opportunity. Together, our two companies will pave the way for the future."

"I like your enthusiasm. Theo Bachman is the sole reason we offered BAI a chance to bid. My late husband had the utmost respect for him. That being said, I am going to be honest with you, Mr. Stratton. It would be an injustice to compare the BAI bid to the other bids. In responding to our request, you did not omit a single line item. I cannot say the same for your competitors."

Intently, David listened to her. His heartbeat accelerated with anticipation, not knowing if she was ready to make a decision. He worried that there would be many more meetings such as this, with no confirmation one way or another.

"Your pricing is more than fair, Mr. Stratton. Yet don't think for one moment that we were not prepared to challenge any overage," she said sternly.

David exhaled, only partially. He drew in a deeper breath, waiting the final outcome.

"Consider this a verbal confirmation. I am awarding BAI the Heisen contract for two years. Our legal department will contact yours." She extended her arm, firmly shook his hand, and added, "If everything goes well and all my expectations are met, we will not go out to bid for future phases. BAI will be our exclusive vendor. However, I must emphasize that if your company fails Heisen in any way, I will not hesitate to invite bidders to compete with you again. When they learn the mistakes they made this time, I am certain they won't make them again. So congratulations, Mr. Stratton. We, rather I, look forward to doing business with you."

"You won't be disappointed in choosing Bachman Aerospace," he said cheerfully.

"Since we are going to be business partners, you can call me Jessica and I shall call you David," she said with a smile. It was the first time she had permitted herself to show her feminine side.

Jessica pushed back her leather chair and came around to the front of her glass desk to face David. She turned to the attorney and said, "John, I'll meet you in your office in ten minutes. I'd like a few minutes with Mr. Stratton in private." At her command, the attorney fled her private quarters.

Jessica leaned against the glass blocks just a few inches from David. She deliberately touched her high-heel pumps against his Italian loafers.

"Now tell me a little about yourself, David. I see you are wearing a wedding band. Most men who are out to gain my business usually remove their rings. I commend you for your honesty."

"I've got a great wife. We've been married for eighteen months."

"Counting months, are we? Are you planning on starting a family soon?"

"Starting?" He laughed. "We have a daughter named Jenni Lynn. She'll be a year in May."

Although David was high on the excitement of winning, he momentarily lost his fervor. Karen had called him the night before to tell him Jenni had taken her first step. He missed it because of the final edit to the Heisen contract.

"Yesterday my daughter took her first step. I missed that event just like I missed the day she spoke her first word. She opted to say 'mommy,' but I missed it just the same. I hope those are the only milestones in her lifetime I miss out on. Now that you've accepted our RFP, I plan on spending a lot more time with her."

"I see. Your part with Heisen is finished. You made the sale and now you are handing me off to someone else. How very sad since the two of us have such a good rapport."

"Please don't misunderstand me. I'm not one to drop the ball. I'll be here at your beck and call for the next several weeks. After that there is a team chomping at the bit to take over."

"Well, now. Theo was smart to send you in for the kill, wasn't he? Now I'll be stuck with one of his overage cronies. That's not quite what I had in mind. Not for this venture." She had his attention; even more so as she moved her black pump against the calf of his leg.

"I'm sure that you'll be happy with whomever Theo chooses. I promise you that even though I won't be involved as much as before, I'll always keep my eye on your project. I won't let you down."

"For the time being that is acceptable to me." She glanced at her wristwatch and said casually, "It's early. Join me for a happy-hour celebration drink." With an edge to her voice, she added, "I won't take no for an answer."

David did not have her final signature and wasn't about to say no. Besides he saw nothing wrong in spending time with a beautiful woman, as long as it was business related. "Sure, I have time for one before I have to go back to the office."

"I'll meet you downstairs, David. I have to make a quick telephone call. Pick me up out front," she said.

◇ ◇ ◇

The Bachmans of the world labeled Jessica Heisen the "Italian Black Widow." A stunning young woman in her late twenties, she wore her long black hair stretched tight at the scalp and crimped into a bun at the base of her neck. It was the perfect contrast to her flawless white complexion—earned by forsaking the harsh rays of the summer sun. Her cheekbones were high and sculpted. Her lips were full and shapely, just like her body. The Italian Black Widow had it all, including a lingering reputation as gold digger.

Jessica's reputation stemmed from the day she married Douglas Heisen, a multimillionaire fifty-one years her senior. Many people silently speculated as to Jessica's underlying motive for marrying Heisen, but no one made mention of it. A few months later those speculations seemed to have foundation.

Possessing an unearthly power over the elderly man, Jessica enjoyed the position she was in. Her husband, who was in his seventies and ill of health, was openly insecure when it came to her youth and beauty. Rather than chance losing her to someone half his age, he changed his sedentary lifestyle to suit her fun-filled ways. Overnight, Douglas Heisen's calm and structured life became one of parties, other social events, and monthly jaunts to Las Vegas, and all strictly against the advice of his cardiologist.

The transformation in Heisen's life fed his senses as well as his ego. Having a siren at his side, he was the envy of most men, no matter their ages. He especially enjoyed the attention he received in Las Vegas, so the Sin City trips became more and more frequent. One afternoon just as his plane had landed, Douglas felt a sharp pain down his left arm that gave him little notice of his imminent demise. There, in the middle of the desert on a scorching runway, Douglas Heisen suffered a fatal heart attack.

Perhaps no one would have thought the worse if Jessica had handled his passing in a more compassionate way, but her rush to move forward with her life raised more than a few eyebrows. Jessica acted as if time was of the essence. She had her husband's body cremated just one hour after the Nevada coroner had filled out the death certificate.

"Here are his ashes, Mrs. Heisen. As you requested I have arranged for a memorial service at Beecher Funeral Home in Beverly Hills on Friday. We are terribly sorry for your loss." The funeral executive recited the usual regrets before he smiled suggestively at the very attractive and very wealthy young widow. "Perhaps you may need me or my services in the future," he said as he handed her his business card. "I've included my private number on the back. Don't hesitate to telephone me anytime."

Averting her eyes from the funeral director, Jessica lowered her sunglasses. Ignoring his blatant flirtations she said, "Thank you. I can handle it from here. I have a car waiting outside to take me to the airport."

Three days later the Beecher Funeral Home was filled to capacity with mourners. However, very few mourners chose to accept Jessica's invitation to gather at the Heisen's home after her husband's memorial service. Those who did attend were treated to a rather bizarre gathering.

Acting as if she were at a coming-out party rather than a funeral, Jessica sipped champagne and mingled with the guests. She circled the room chatting lightheartedly about theatre, fashion, and other unseemly funeral topics. She never once mentioned her husband. This behavior went on for about two hours before she ascended one of the two spiraling staircases. Standing midway in the second-floor foyer, she tapped the edge of her glass.

"May I have your attention? Thank you all for coming. I am sure that my husband would have appreciated your kindness, just as I do. I must excuse myself, but you are welcome to stay. There's a buffet in the main dining room. Enjoy. Again, thank you for coming."

The guests, assuming she was weary, were astonished when she made a hasty exit down the steps and out the front door. Speechless, they looked on as she called out to her driver.

"Humbert, take me to Heisen. I'm late for a meeting."

The doors to the Heisen executive conference room were locked when Jessica first attempted to storm the meeting. She shook the brass handles but was still denied access. Irritated, she pressed the intercom.

"Would someone get off his duff and open these doors?" For one startling moment no one budged. "Do I have to repeat myself? I said OPEN THESE DAMN DOORS!"

"What the hell? This is a closed meeting," Arnold Chase, the chief financial officer uttered.

According to the instructions left in the Heisen safe, all board members were to gather in secret upon Douglas Heisen's death to choose a member of the board as his successor. The votes had just been tallied. Arnold Chase had just been unanimously selected as CEO when Jessica interrupted them.

"See what she wants," Arnold said.

The doors opened to reveal a sassy Jessica Heisen dressed in a formfitting black suit with a wide-brimmed Parisian hat. For most women, funeral black would have promoted the image of a grieving widow, but on Jessica Heisen it was just plain sexy.

"Mrs. Heisen, can we help you? We are very sorry about Douglas." Jessica pushed her hand on the man's chest and moved him aside. She walked over to Arnold who was seated at the head of the table.

"Arnold, I believe you are sitting in my seat."

"We are in the middle of a closed meeting, Jessica. Can't this wait until later?"

"No time like the present, Arnold. Now the sooner you move your derriere, the sooner I shall be on my way."

He reluctantly removed himself from the head of the table. Since all the other leather chairs were occupied, he opted for a folding chair near the corner of the room. Without knowing it, he had been dethroned before he had been crowned.

"Gentlemen, I believe you all know who I am, so this won't take very long. As you all know, my husband's death was unexpected. He was a good man. Good to me and certainly good to all of you. So let me just say how much I appreciate that you attended the memorial service."

"We miss him, Jessica," Arnold subtly interjected. He may have lost his seat at the table, but he wasn't about to let her forget he was still in the room.

She slowly turned toward him and raised her hand and silenced him. "As I was saying, I was pleased to see you all there. The floral arrangements you sent, or should I say the Heisen Corporation, sent were lovely." Embarrassed by her accurate assessment, each one took a mental note to erase the flowers from his expense report.

"Gentlemen, I was also very surprised that not one of you accepted my invitation to my home. I should have thought that after everything my husband did for you, you would have wanted to offer your personal condolences." Although she smiled at them, her smile compressed her generous lips into a thin and purposeful line. Not one man felt easy under her gaze.

"Let's get down to business, shall we? I spoke with my attorney yesterday and I was informed that I am the sole beneficiary of Heisen." She paused long enough to enjoy the panicky expressions of her audience. "So today, gentlemen, I am happy to accept your support in naming me to the position of Chairman and CEO."

Except for two or three who gasped, no one made a sound. Speechless, they waited for the next shoe to drop. They wondered if their own positions were in jeopardy.

Finally, Arnold objected. "But, Jessica, we have specific instructions left by Douglas Heisen." He walked over to her and handed her the legal order.

"I see, Arnold. You failed to pay attention to the date of this document. The signatures were dated over ten years ago—eight years before I met Douglas. Would you care to see my document? It is dated June, 1949!"

Arnold turned away from her and returned to his seat at the window. "Italian Black Widow, Genoa must really be missing you," he muttered sarcastically, just loud enough that a couple of the board members overheard. It was the nickname that Jessica Heisen would bear from then on.

"You see, gentlemen, with my original holdings and the ones I inherited from Douglas, I now have controlling interest as the majority stockholder. Effective immediately, a Heisen will continue to manage the company—with or without the consent of the board members. In other words I am here to gather your support or gather your resignations." Having no intention of waiting for an amicable endorsement, Jessica grasped her handbag and with her head held high, she left. "Good day, gentlemen."

Outside the skyscraper, Humbert stood next to the limousine until he saw Mrs. Heisen. He rushed to her side to escort her to the car. "Is there anything you need, madam?"

"Just drive, Humbert, but I don't want to go back to the house right now." She thought for a moment and added, "Take me to Santa Barbara. I'll get a hotel for the night."

"Yes, madam."

As he pulled away from the curb Jessica studied Douglas Heisen's latest will. There was a specific clause that she had deliberately avoided mentioning to the board of directors. It stated that she was to be named CEO for a period of seven years from the date of his death. At the end of that period she would have to prove to the stockholders that she had increased the volume of business by twenty-five percent and was able to gain a productivity increase of eighteen percent. If she failed to produce either result, his stocks would be divided among the board members who would then vote for his permanent successor.

Jessica resented her husband for his lack of faith in her. She felt that by marrying him she had earned the rights of ownership to the company. But since it wasn't so cut-and-dried, she knew she had seven years to use whatever means available and whatever resources necessary to make the numbers work to her advantage.

In the weeks to come, news of Jessica Heisen's "chew 'em up and spit 'em out" attitude spread like wildfire throughout the industry. It was then that Theo decided he needed more than the usual group of gray-haired, balding cronies to go up against her. That was when he decided on David Stratton.

◇ ◇ ◇

David tapped twice on Theo's door before letting himself in. It was nearly eleven o'clock and executives had long gone for the night. David knew that Theo would not leave until he had heard firsthand about the Heisen contract.

"Theo, it's in the bag! Make mine a Scotch."

"Yes, I've already heard. Jessica telephoned me before the two of you went out on the town to celebrate."

"Oh," he said slightly embarrassed. "I, I didn't know how to say no to her."

"No one does, David. Not to the Italian Black Widow."

"Not to the what? Did you call her the Italian Black Widow?"

"That's the term some of the boys call her. She pretty much gets what she wants. Hell, who could say no to someone who looks like that?"

David was too buzzed to pretend otherwise. He had had one too many with Jessica. And although they began the evening at opposite ends of a booth, eventually they slid to the middle and sat side-by-side. This was the closest David had been to another woman since he had married Karen. As much as he tried, he couldn't help respond to Jessica. Her perfume was intoxicating and her laughter contagious. David found himself trapped in the web of the Italian Black Widow.

Bachman poured a drink for David. "Drink up, you're going to need it. Jessica has put a hold on the contract. She's refusing to sign."

"What?" David had a sobering moment. "I have her verbal agreement. She can't change her mind now."

Bachman said, "She won't sign unless I make a major change."

David's forehead was covered with beads of sweat as he remembered all the hours of work he had put in to the project. "Theo, what does she want?"

"In a word? You!"

"I don't understand. My part is over."

"David, I'll spell it out for you, if you feel that it is necessary. Bottom line, unless you continue with the project, the deal is off. So welcome to operations, David." Bachman folded his hands together and preventing any objections added, "I'll have to come up with a new title for you. OPS VP isn't appropriate. Besides, we already have one of those." Bachman watched David who seemed to be in a trance and then tempted him. "I think I'll call you my Senior Executive Vice President—Corporate Ventures. I think that means I've just promoted you…again. It appears that you are on a fast track, David. Considering that you are the son of Alfred Stratton, it's not such a stretch of the imagination."

"Theo, isn't there any other way?" David thought about Karen and Jenni and what this would mean to their relationship. He knew his family life would continue to take a backseat to the Heisen project. "Theo, you've got some real talent out there. There are men who'd give their right testicle for the chance to head this up." He implored Theo but saw that it was useless. Theo was like Jessica. He also got whatever he wanted.

"I know why you're apprehensive, David. She's quite a handful, isn't she? She's irresistible, sexy, and intriguing; you don't know if you can hold on to your sanity with her. But as of today she's your problem, so you had better toughen up. That is, unless you'd prefer to seek employment elsewhere."

"You know me better than that, Theo. I'll figure out a way to keep everyone happy."

"I have no doubt, David. So let's move on to the logistics. You are going to need a bang-up staff. You may want a couple of the top hitters from Heisen, but if I were you I'd go after some of the boys in Texas. Recruit the best drillers, derrick men, roustabouts, crane operators, barge engineers, and subsea engineers. I'm sure you can lure them to come out West with some signing bonuses."

This was not what David had in mind. He was ready to hand the project off; however, taking it to its conclusion would be a thrill. Still, the thought of working full time around Jessica Heisen petrified him. She was more of a temptation than most men could resist. His only defense against her was the thought of his love for Karen and Jenni Lynn.

"I'll get right on it, Theo."

"I knew you'd come through. So how does another 25K added to your base salary sound?"

"Wow, very generous," he said realizing the additional money meant additional responsibility. "That will pay off the lot we bought in Santa Monica. Did I tell you that we start building our house this summer?"

"Good for you. I want you to take a couple days off to refocus. Prepare the family for what's to come. Come Monday, you'll be breathing Heisen every waking minute."

"Heisen is all I've thought about for four months, Theo," David said, knowing what he was going to be up against. Now that the proposal had been won, day in and day out he'd be thrown together with Jessica Heisen. He wouldn't admit it, but the thought of working with her excited him. It excited him much more than it should have.

nine

JACK STRATTON

Cleveland, 1954

As the cake was being served to Donahue's customers on the night of Billy's fifth birthday, Sam took hold of the microphone that was hanging from the ceiling to make one more announcement. He was excited about a new business venture and wanted to share it with his patrons. Besides, he couldn't think of a better place to market it than right there in Donahue's.

"Ladies and gentlemen, are you having a good time tonight?" The crowd responded with applause.

"Good cake, huh!" Again, the crowd responded as he had hoped. "Did you hear the one about…"

Four years ago Sam had preferred to stay behind the scenes, now he made it a nightly habit of taking center stage. When Sam was in the spotlight, it not only gave Sarah an extra break, it also gave him a chance to get to know his patrons a little better. Over time, Sam's fifteen minutes of fame had turned into thirty minutes of sheer comedic energy.

Sarah, seeing that Sam was ready to take over, quietly stepped off the stage. Sam caught sight of her and said, "Let's hear your appreciation for Cleveland's Sarah Robbins." Sarah, heading toward Fran, bowed her heard while the crowd whistled and cheered.

Halfway across the room Sarah was caught off guard when she heard what Sam had to say next.

"Do you folks know what the most requested song at Donahue's is?" A few shouted out some of the timeless tunes, but most called out the correct answer. "If you answered 'Better Days Ahead,' then you are right. So I got to thinking, why not invest some of Donahue's money into Sarah herself? She wrote the song, she sings the song, I know she could sell the song! What do you say, folks? Which one of you is going to be the first in line to buy Sarah's record, personally signed by Miss Robbins?"

Again, Sam received the positive response he anticipated. All he had to do now was finalize the deal. That, and work on Sarah, since he hadn't run it by her before he made the public announcement.

"When the record is cut, I'll let you know," Sam said as he stepped offstage and signaled for the floor lights to be dimmed. It was the time of the night when the orchestra would take over and the mood of the club would change. The patrons were quick to claim their places on the dance floor.

Fran had been standing with Billy against the back wall of Donahue's. As soon as Sarah reached her, she exclaimed, "A record? Sarah, when did all this happen and why didn't you tell me?"

"Fran, I think this is another one of Sam's dreams, just like the time he wanted to open a smorgasbord. Anyway, it's the first I've heard of it. So I wouldn't get my hopes up if I were you."

"I think you are underestimating Sam, Sarah. He seems mighty passionate about you making a record."

"Like I said, Frannie, let's not make too much of it right now. Sam and I haven't even discussed it," she laughed. Sarah looked around the room and asked, "Where did Billy go?"

"He said he was going backstage to see Sam. Sam promised to give him his present," Fran answered.

"I wonder what Sam bought for him this year," Sarah smiled. "Every year he outdoes himself. He spoils Billy so, but I'm really not complaining."

Fran was interested in the record, but she was more interested in finding out other information. "Okay, Sarah, who is that gorgeous hunk of a man?" She, like the other patrons, had noticed the rugged Englishman who had gone out of his way to meet up with Sarah.

"What are you implying, Frannie?"

"Don't BS me, Sarah; remember that I'm your good friend. So tell me. Is he the one you've been singing about all these years? Is he Billy's daddy?"

"Who on earth are you talking about?"

Fran put her hands on Sarah's shoulders and turned her in the direction of the stranger. "You know, the one who jumped out of his seat to help you with Billy's birthday cake. He's sitting at the bar."

"No, he's not Billy's father," she laughed. "I just met him. His name is Jack. Jack Stratton. He's quite a looker, isn't he?"

"I'll say," Fran said while moistening her lips. "What a dreamboat! Boy, if I wasn't married…"

As if the newcomer had read their lips, he tipped his glass of whiskey in Sarah's direction. He gave a wry grin before chasing the shot down with a glass of beer.

"He's staring at you," Fran said enthusiastically.

For a split second Sarah's body experienced a tingly feeling of weightlessness. Sexual desires, which had been dormant for years, had just been reawakened. She felt like a desirable woman again. *He's what I call a real man—lean and muscular with a full head of hair to boot. Henry Kinslow couldn't hold a candle to him,* she thought.

"You'll have to excuse me, Frannie. I think I'll pay him a visit," Sarah said as she strolled over to the bar.

"So, Mr. Stratton, where are you from?"

"Here and there," he said evasively. "Most of my relatives live in Southern California. What about you?"

She was intrigued with his slight English accent. It captivated her. "Oh, I've lived in Cleveland all my life. I've been working at Donahue's for years."

"That's one helluva long gig. Most singers I know are in one town one night and off to another the next." He pulled a barstool out for her and said, "Sit down. I'd like to buy you a drink."

"Thanks, but no. It's been so long since I've had any alcohol my body wouldn't know what to do with the stuff anymore. I quit drinking when my son was born," she said feeling quite proud of herself. "I'm a co-owner of the club so let me buy. You're drinking boilermakers, right?"

In the past Manny would have overheard Sarah's conversation and begun pouring the whiskey. The elderly bartender, whose years had finally caught up with him, was no longer Donahue's finest mixologist. Arthritis that had plagued his leg joints for years had now taken its toll on his aging hands. It made the simplest of tasks grueling. Even more debilitating was his impaired hearing. At seventy-six years old he was nearly deaf, so Sarah wrote the order down on a piece of paper and handed it to Manny.

"You said you are from California, Jack. What brings you to Ohio?"

"I didn't say that I was from California. My uncle and his family live there," he explained. "He is my old man's brother. You probably have heard of him. His name is Alfred Stratton."

Sarah shrugged her shoulders and said, "No, I've never heard of him. Is he important?"

"He's a big shot. You know, a business tycoon who keeps on reeling in the dough."

"He sounds very wealthy."

"Yeah, he got his start from old family money," Jack said before taking a drag of his cigarette.

"Is it your family's money?"

"It should have been, at least in part. There was a glitch in the legal system and I lost out. Someday, when I can afford a good attorney, I am going after my share."

He swallowed the shot and wiped his mouth with the back of his hand. His eyes had dilated, yet Sarah knew it wasn't from the alcohol. It was the subject of money that clearly bothered him.

"I wish you luck. In the meantime how did you stumble upon Donahue's?"

"A friend of mine told me about the club…and about you."

"Your friend told you about me? What did he say?" she asked curiously.

"He told me you had a knockout body with a voice that could tame a jungle tiger. My friend knew what he was talking about. You are everything he said and much more."

As the star entertainer, Sarah had become accustomed to flattery. Sometimes the comments would be sincere and sometimes they were nothing more than come-ons. Either way, realizing that her looks were no more than average, Sarah had never rejected a compliment. "That's very kind of you. So who's your friend?"

Jack disregarded the question and asked one of his own. "I don't see a wedding ring on your finger and the billboard outside reads 'Miss Sarah Robbins,' so I gather there isn't a husband in the picture. Is there someone who shows up for dinner every now and then? You know, a friend of sorts who turns up in the middle of the night just to kick his shoes off."

Sarah felt that he went too far with his probing interrogation. Still, the man was too damn sexy to let get away, so she played along.

"No. There's no husband or any man kicking his shoes off at my house. There hasn't been for quite some time. Why are you so interested in my personal life?"

He took a last drag of his cigarette and deliberately dropped the butt onto the floor. He grinned as he crushed it with his shoe. "I'm not going to lay down all my cards just yet, my lady," he teased, "Not until I see your hand first."

Jack was cognizant of the effect he was having on her. He kept dropping the bait and watching as Sarah nibbled away at it. From a shaded corner near the front of the stage Sam and Billy had been watching as well.

Unable to conceal the hope in her voice Sarah asked, "Jack, is there any chance that we will be seeing a little more of you at Donahue's?"

"Before you know it, I'll be back," he said as he lifted her hand and kissed her fingers.

Sarah felt her heart pound like it never had before. She was definitely being courted. At least she prayed that she was. "Until we meet next time, Jack," she said with a sigh. "I have to go and check on Billy."

"You tell that boy of yours that Jack Stratton is looking forward to getting to know him. I predict that your boy and I are going to become good friends."

That was the best thing Jack could have said. She was physically attracted to him, but mentioning her son was the clincher. Sarah beamed when she responded, "You bet, I will."

◇ ◇ ◇

Sarah had just finished tallying the weekend sales receipts when Sam rolled a chair up next to her. He seemed disturbed; then again, he had been acting that way for several weeks. She finally decided to confront him.

"What is it, Sam? What's bothering you lately?"

"Are those flowers from the infamous Jack Stratton?"

"You know they are. Just like the ones last week and the week before that. What's your point, Sam?"

"There's just something about him, Sarah. I can't put my finger on it but there is something not right about him. Maybe it's the way he avoids eye contact. You just can't trust a man who can't look you straight in the eye."

"I like him, Sam. I like him very much. Please don't try and ruin this for me. He treats me like a real woman."

"You need to pull yourself together before you or Billy get hurt. I swear that man is up to something. I don't know what, but he's got something up his sleeve. Sarah, haven't you noticed the way he's always looking over his shoulder?"

"You're paranoid, Sam!" Sarah argued defensively. "You've protected me and Billy for so long that you don't want anyone to come between us. You see him as a threat to you."

"You know what? I hope you're right—I hope I am paranoid. I'd hate to see you make a mistake and throw everything away at this point in your life."

"Throw what away? Throw my morals away? There's more to me than you know, Sam. I'm not the pure woman that you imagine me to be. Billy's life proves that I once had a lover. And to be honest with you, I'd give anything to have someone share my bed again. It's been much too long."

Angered Sam yelled, "Is that it? That's what you want? Someone to lie down beside you? Is that what will make you happy?"

"This conversation is going nowhere, Sam. Besides, when was the last time you had sex?"

All Sam could think was *touché*. Sam had not been with a woman since his young wife had passed away from tuberculosis over twenty years before. After her death Sam had planned to remain single for the rest of his life; however, that changed the day he met Sarah Robbins. Sam didn't know it back then, but each day he would fall deeper in love with her, yet he couldn't find the words to tell her. Over time, Sarah assumed any slight advance from Sam was merely platonic.

"What does his note card say, Sarah? Does it say 'I love you'?" Sam imagined sending her flowers and writing those words on his note card. Unfortunately, flowers that Sam had sent her in the past had never included the word "love." Those cards usually read "Knock 'em dead, lady."

"No, he didn't tell me that he loves me. But he did emphasize 'Tonight.'"

"'Tonight'? What's that supposed to mean?"

"I know what I hope it means. He's ready to take our relationship to the next level, Sam."

"What about Billy? Where's he going to be?"

"Drop it, Sam! Billy isn't your concern right now, is he?"

Sam pushed his chair away from her. Her words devastated him. For five years he had tended to Billy nearly as much as she did. Every night he'd read him a story at the club. During the day, he'd take him to run errands and when time permitted he'd take him fishing. They were always together. They were like father and son.

"Fine, partner," he said sarcastically. "It's your life and you've made it perfectly clear that it's none of my business." Sam stood up and pushed his chair across the office. When it slammed against the wall he added, "If I don't talk to you later, don't forget to be at the recording studio Thursday morning at ten. There's still hope for 'Better Days Ahead.'" His emphasis on the double meaning of the song title was clear. "I've got to check on Manny. He's been having trouble stocking the bar these days."

As Sam started out the door, Sarah spoke frankly. "I'm sorry you don't like Jack, Sam. I'm also sorry that we argued. But I'm asking for your support because the truth is I do like Jack, very much. And if there is the slightest chance that we have a future together, then I'm going to do everything I can to make that happen. Now do you fully understand?"

"I don't want to hear any more, Sarah." He bit his lip to stop it from quivering. The apology meant nothing to him after she underscored it with brutal honesty. He strode up the hallway attempting to fend off the tears that flooded his eyes. It was useless. His Irish tenacity dripped away with each teardrop.

That was the first night that Sam would fail to show up at the club. He was in no mood to be the jokester, thus there would be no midshow monologue—an event many of the patrons looked forward to. Sam told Manny to tell the staff that he just needed a breather and was taking a few days off, but Sarah knew better. She knew Sam couldn't bear to see Billy and her leave the club with Jack Stratton when taking them home had always been Sam's responsibility.

Jack pulled his station wagon with wood siding onto the small driveway next to Sarah's quaint house. He exited the car and then came around the front to open the door for her. "Here, let me take him from you," Jack said as he lifted Billy from her lap. "Your boy sure can sleep." Jack kicked the car door closed and walked up the flower-lined walkway. "Nice place you've got here."

"It's a bit small for us with only one bedroom. With the profits I've made from Donahue's, I'm in the market for something bigger."

Jack wanted her to elaborate on the profits, but shelved the inquisition for a more appropriate time. "Where should I put your boy?"

Standing at the entrance of her bedroom, Sarah pointed to the smaller of two beds. "Put him over here."

Billy was accustomed to being carted around in the middle of the night. From the time he fell asleep at the club until the following morning he never stirred, so Sarah saw no problem with inviting Jack into her home.

"I'll put on some coffee, Jack. I made fresh cinnamon rolls this morning. They're in the bread box."

"No coffee for me. You got anything stronger?"

"I've told you before that I quit drinking right after Billy was born. I haven't needed one since."

"I forgot," he lied. "But it doesn't matter. I always carry a pint or two in the glove box. I'll be right back."

Sarah watched him leave and reflected that at last she had a man worth fantasizing over. After her breakup with Judge Henry Kinslow six years earlier, Sarah had spent countless nights masturbating to sexual fantasies of him. Sarah was no different than any other lonely heart. She needed to visualize a real person as she pleasured herself. Lately, however, Henry had been replaced with a new intoxicating image. Jack Stratton. Sarah thought that he was what fantasies should be about. He had penetrating hazel eyes and sandy-blond hair that was slicked back and unevenly cut. As for his muscular physique, Sarah could only imagine the treasures hidden beneath his clothes.

"Pull out a couple of glasses. One for each of us," he said as the screen door rattled shut behind him.

"Jack, I shouldn't. I promised myself."

"What's the problem? A little drink never hurt anybody."

Sarah should have disagreed with him. Liquor had consumed her life to the point of nearly taking it away from her. Instead, as Jack unscrewed the bottle top, Sarah gave in. "Okay, but just a little."

Sarah's intention was to take one sip, just to be social and then set the glass aside. She didn't expect that the first sip of alcohol she had had in years would lead to a second and then to a third sip, until she was holding an empty tumbler. Sarah welcomed the elixir like a long-lost friend.

"Would you like a drop more?" Jack asked but didn't wait for her reply. He had already filled her glass to the brim.

Jack touched his glass to Sarah's. "To good times," he toasted.

"Good times," she repeated, forgetting that Billy was only a room away.

"What do you like?" Jack asked as he began kissing her neck.

"I, I don't know what you mean," she slurred.

He placed his hands on her shoulders and gently pushed her down on the sofa. She fumbled back and with her eyes half open, she watched as he removed his weathered jacket. She panted rapidly when she saw his muscular torso bulging out of an undersized tee shirt. She could barely control herself from physically attacking him; it had been so long since she had been touched by a man.

"Are you comfortable?" He asked while he propped a pillow behind her head.

"Uh-huh."

"Good," he said and propped a second pillow under her thighs. "Lie back and relax."

Bracing himself above her, he leaned forward and introduced his tongue into her open mouth. The strong taste of bourbon was masked only by the animalistic pheromones she secreted. He flickered his tongue teasingly and, as he expected, she responded. Together their tongues danced, their juices flowed. This ritual continued for several minutes until Jack eased his mouth shut. She tried to reopen it by licking the wetness surrounding his lips, but he refused her entry. The quest made her even more wanton. But it also made Jack more determined to maintain control. Abruptly, he turned her over so that her back was to him. He adjusted the pillow to lift her buttocks. Then using his tongue he tickled the nape of her neck.

With a man who was just inches from her yearning crevices, and the effects of alcohol, Sarah could contain herself no longer. A musky aroma, released from her juices onto her panties, had filled the room. Sarah had climaxed without masturbation or penetration. She wondered if Jack knew.

"Please, make love to me now," she begged as she struggled to turn around. But he restrained her.

He demanded, "It has to be from behind. That's what I want!"

Sarah was about to make love for the first time in years. It no longer mattered to Sarah what position she was in. Missionary, from behind, or on the side, she'd take Jack Stratton any way she could.

Jack kept one hand pressed on her back while he unfastened his denim jeans and slithered out of them. From the waist down, Jack was in the raw. Next, he unzipped Sarah's floor-length skirt and pulled it off her body to reveal her garter belt, nylons, and moist, if not drenched, panties.

The time was near. However, for a brief drunken moment Sarah remembered Henry and how she would do anything to please him. As she lay on her face gasping for air, the memory of Billy's father faded as quickly as it had emerged.

She felt Jack's hand on the back of her legs. He had unsnapped her hose from the garter belt and removed each stocking. Next he removed her garter belt and last her panties. And then she, too, was naked from the waist down.

With her derriere atop the pillow, he squeezed each cheek. Then he slid his hand down the crack until it reached the folds in front. Resting his hand there, he moved his index finger in and out of her.

Sarah could barely breathe, responding to every move. For more than an hour he masturbated her, bringing her to orgasm after orgasm. But still he hadn't entered her and that was what she craved…penetration. But Jack was in complete control.

"Please, Jack, I can't take it anymore," she whimpered. "I want to feel you…all of you. Please take me now."

Without uttering a word, he removed his finger and ran it back up between her buttocks. As she felt it touch her anus, she stretched up to meet it. It felt like a hundred electric shocks ran up through her body. She wailed with delight.

Fully engorged, Jack positioned himself for a direct, swift entry. In one single motion he propelled his penis between her legs, lunging deep inside her. Harder and harder he slammed, striving for the point of no return. But Sarah didn't want him to come—not just yet. The mini-orgasms she had previously experienced were only a prelude to the magnificent one that was building. Chafed and raw, it felt good to be a complete woman again. But Jack was focused on his own pleasures. Bearing down, he grunted louder and louder with every stroke as Sarah groaned from each impact. She was nearly there. But just as she was about to climax, he gave one final push, spouting his semen inside her. He had climaxed while Sarah was left with an orgasm longing to be released.

Exhausted, Jack fell onto her back and lay motionless. With her face buried in the sofa, Sarah ached for her own matching finale, which he had abandoned. She would just settle to have his gradually softening penis inside her. As long as the two of them were physically connected, she felt desirable.

Sarah felt his sweat as well as her own covering her back. She could have remained in that position for hours. But a muffled whimper broke the moment of intimacy. Startled, Sarah turned and saw Billy crouched in the corner of the living room, sobbing uncontrollably. He had been a spectator to the acts of his naked mother and the man he hardly knew. It was the same man who had acknowledged Billy's presence with a leer and a shameless wink of an eye—just seconds before he climaxed.

✧ ✧ ✧

It was five in the morning when Sam unlocked the back door of Donahue's. As usual, the club was dark with a lingering odor of musty cigars and rancid cocktails. The early morning club aroma would sicken most; however, to Sam it meant the cash registers had overflowed the night before.

Sam had thought he could stay away from the club for a few days. After one night he realized that the club was his life. With or without Sarah, Donahue's meant the world to him so he returned early the following morning. As Sam walked down the darkened corridor, he straightened the row of framed newspaper articles about Donahue's. He reread the review that made his club "the place to be" in Cleveland. When he reached the back office, he noticed a light coming from under the door and assumed that Manny had forgotten to turn it off. He opened the door to find Sarah keying in the sales on the adding machine.

"What are you doing here this early, Sarah? Where's Billy?"

"He's asleep backstage. He doesn't feel good. So I'm keeping him home from school today. As soon as I'm finished, we're going back home. I thought you were taking the week off."

"I changed my mind. I never knew how much I'd miss this place until last night. I guess I'm married to Donahue's," he said.

"Sam, since you're back, would you mind if I took some time off to be with Billy until he gets better?"

"Time with Billy or time with Jack?" Sam said, suddenly wishing that he hadn't.

"Sorry, it was a slip of the tongue. It won't happen again. You want to take time off because Billy is sick? That never stopped you before. He's had fevers, colds, the measles, and the mumps. I've always taken care of him backstage while you were up front." Sam said suddenly suspicious. He knew something had happened, but he'd never ask.

"Let's just say that I need some time with my son. Perhaps I'm spending too much time here, doing the books in the morning and singing at night. I probably should give up some of this."

"Hey, I was doing the books just fine. You're the one who insisted on helping out, partner. Remember? After we went fifty-fifty, you wanted to do more to earn your share. Why this change all of a sudden?"

"Sam, drop it. Like we agreed yesterday, some things are not your concern."

Sarah was angry with herself and was taking it out on Sam. She wished she had made other arrangements for Billy prior to bringing Jack to her home, but she hadn't. Her five-year-old boy had seen far too much for a child of his age—or any age, for that matter.

"So, how's Jack Stratton?"

"Sam! I'm not going to discuss him with you anymore. That's final! I'm going to check on Billy."

She stapled the strip of tallied numbers to the page of daily stats. Grabbing her purse, she dashed out of the office and headed down to the ladies' restroom. It was the only place where she was guaranteed privacy.

Sarah leaned up against the counter and lit up a cigarette. The ingested nicotine calmed her, although she was still ashamed. She had not only put her son in harm's way, there was also the chance she had robbed him of his innocence. She kept thinking that if only Billy hadn't seen what she had done with Jack Stratton, then everything would have been different. Yet, as bad as she felt for what happened, she couldn't help herself. She still yearned for Jack—now more than ever.

She took a final drag on the cigarette and then discarded the butt into the wash basin. *I've got to go check on Billy. God help me.*

Sarah ran up the back steps of the stage to find Billy cradled in Sam's arms. They were both emotionally distraught. As Billy wept, Sam struggled with his own tears. He didn't know what had happened, but undeniably the child had been traumatized and Sam could do little to comfort him.

"I don't know what's going on, Sarah, and you're probably not going to tell me."

She had inadvertently acquired a Jack Stratton trait. It was now impossible for Sarah to look Sam in the eye. Her actions spoke louder than anything she would admit. And Sam knew right then and there that Jack had something to do with Billy being sick.

"Take him home, Sarah. He needs some rest. Take a week off. I'll hire a backup act to cover for you. Don't worry about the books. I'll take care of them. Just do what you can to make sure our boy is healed."

Under the circumstances Sarah didn't correct his deliberate claim to Billy. Instead, she took him from Sam's arms and said, "Yeah, I better take him home. Sam, are we still on for church on Sunday morning?"

"Of course, that's one tradition I hope we never break. Sarah, do you want me to push back your ten o'clock appointment tomorrow? You can always cut a record later."

"I know what you went through to get me into Sunburst Records, so I'll go and take Billy with me. But, Sam, I don't want to rush into anything right now. I'll record 'Better Days Ahead' as we agreed, but let's wait to have it mass-produced. We have plenty of time to sell records. Right now I need to concentrate on other things."

The following Sunday Sam drove over to Sarah's to pick them up for services. Usually, Sarah and Billy would be waiting for him curbside. But on this Sunday no one was waiting. Sam exited the car and went up to the porch. He rang the doorbell twice, but no one answered. He rang it again and called out, "Hey, where are you two? Sarah? Billy? Is anybody home?"

When no one answered, he turned the handle to the screen door. Unlike every other time he had let himself in, he found that this time the door had been locked. "Where the heck are you?" Sam repeated.

"I'm over here, Sam."

From the side of the house Sam heard a faint voice. He peered around the corner and saw Billy leaning against the weathered slats. He was barefoot and wearing soiled clothes. Even his hair, which Sarah usually kept groomed, was matted and uncombed.

"What are you doing outside, son? Why aren't you dressed for church? Where's your momma?"

"She's inside with her boyfriend Jack."

For a child who had been overwrought only days earlier, Sam noticed that Billy now appeared rather indifferent. Somehow Sarah must have convinced him that her behavior was more than acceptable.

"So that's what she's calling him these days, huh?"

"Yeah, they kinda like each other. So what you got in that box, Sam?"

Clearly disturbed, Sam didn't even hear Billy's question. He turned toward the house and imagined what secrets lay within. He could only imagine because as of that moment he knew any hope of winning Sarah was lost. Sam knew there was nothing he could do about it.

Billy asked Sam again. "Sam, what's in the box that smells so good?"

"Sorry, son. I stopped by the bakery and picked up some after-church sweets. There's a chocolate cupcake for you."

"Momma said we aren't going today. She told me to go outside and play. She said God gave us a vacation day."

"I see. Well, then I guess it wouldn't hurt to give you your treat now. Go ahead."

Billy wiped his grimy hands across his blue jeans and scraped a mound off the chocolate cream frosting. While the sugary delight melted onto his tongue, the child forgot about his mother, her boyfriend, and going to church. It would be impossible for Sam to forget what happened next. The sound of a headboard slamming against a partially insulated wall provided him with an unwanted visual of Sarah and Jack's intimacy. The noise was thunderous, almost deafening, until suddenly there was no sound at all. It was over, but the incident embedded itself into the deepest recesses of Sam's mind. He was left with an indelible image, like a photograph, of Sarah and…someone other than himself.

"Come on, son. I didn't hang that old tire from the oak tree for nothing. I'll give you a push," Sam said in a low and dispirited voice.

"Okeydoke, Sam!"

Billy raced to the tire and squirmed inside. Sam, who felt like the wind had been knocked out of him, was slow to follow. Images of Sarah and Jack together crowded his imagination.

Sam drew back the tire as far as the rope would allow before releasing it. Billy giggled, seemingly without a care in the world; Sam was choking on his tears. He used the sleeve of his shirt to wipe away the mist.

"Sam, do you like Jack Stratton?"

Just hearing his name nauseated Sam, but he answered, "I haven't thought about him, son. Why, do you?"

"You won't tell Momma?"

"Not if you tell me not to. It'll be another one of our man-to-man secrets."

"Okay, then. I don't! I don't like him one bit."

Apprehensively Sam asked, "Why not, son?"

"He makes Momma act funny and I don't like that."

Although he was only five years old, he was able to explain his reasoning perfectly. Since the night Sarah met Jack Stratton, she hadn't acted the same toward anyone. Distancing herself from those around her, she suddenly became secretive. This was not the Sarah that Sam or Billy knew; but it was, however, Sarah under the influence of alcohol.

An hour would pass with Sam pushing Billy on the swing before Sarah finally stepped out onto the porch. Draped in a black satin robe, dulled with patches of sweat, she leaned up against the railing and called out.

"Sam, I didn't know you were here. Why didn't you ring the doorbell?"

Rather than admit that he had rung the doorbell several times, Sam avoided the truth. "Me and Billy just wanted to swing for a while. Enjoy the morning sun before the afternoon storm starts rolling in." It was all he could do to muster up a few words for her. The distance across the yard helped him gaze past her and into the horizon. As for Billy, he simply stared up into the oak tree, giggling with every push.

Sarah folded her robe and started walking out to them. Sam was trapped. He couldn't escape her.

"Sam, I should have telephoned you. Billy and I are not going to services today."

"Yeah, Billy told me."

"Here, let me push him for a while," Sarah offered.

"Whatever you say," he said trying to act nonchalantly.

Sam felt he was too close to her and moved a few feet away; nevertheless, her presence could not be avoided. Sarah's floral perfume was unable to mask the overpowering stench of alcohol. The odor contaminated everything and everyone around her.

As awkward as the situation was, to believe it could get any worse was unthinkable. But it did. A strong gust of wind cleverly burrowed its way through Sarah's robe. Finding its way out through the opening, the wind blew her robe wide open. In that moment, Sarah's naked body was fully exposed to Sam. It was another visual that he would be unable to forget.

After years of pretending, Sam was finally forced to accept Sarah as a mere woman and not the saint he had imagined her to be. The cold, hard truth was difficult for Sam to swallow.

Jack pushed aside the handmade gingham curtains and saw Sam and Sarah's awkward body language. Although he couldn't hear what they were saying, he had a pretty good idea of the subject. He fell back on the pillow and laughed, "You tell him, Sarah. You tell Sam Donahue exactly how it is with you and me." Then he smirked and added, "It's all going according to plan."

Seven Years Earlier

"You can call G5 home, J. Stratton, Number 584688. Your cellmate's name is Ben Adams. He'll be your bunkie, your best friend, or anything else you can think of for the next several years," the prison guard said.

Resting on the bottom left berth was a spindly six foot four man who had just turned over on his side. The gangly man in his twenties barely opened one eye to acknowledge the new prisoner. Stratton stared him down, but it made no difference to Ben Adams. He had shared his quarters with numerous other inmates, all of whom had been granted parole before him. To Ben Adams, Stratton was just another face.

The guard munched on his chewing tobacco. "Lights out at ten, Stratton," he said as he stepped outside the metal cage and forced the sliding door into the automatic deadbolt. "Locking cell number G5," the guard announced. "Oh, Stratton, if you have any questions, just ask Ben Adams." The veteran guard, turning his back to the new prisoner, burst out laughing and quipped, "And if you're real, real lucky, you just might get Ben Adams to answer you."

As the guard ambled down the walkway past a dozen metal cells, he exchanged pleasantries with the other convicts. But the newest inmate at Ohio State Minimum Security was not so amicable. Breaking the quietude of the mellowed inmates, Jack Stratton grabbed hold of his cell door and shouted out a multitude of obscenities that were directed at the judge who had sentenced him. The guard, now several cells away, simply ignored him. He knew how most convicts acted on their first night of imprisonment: the moment lights went out and the cell darkened, a prisoner's sentence would play out over and over in his head. For Jack Stratton, the sentence handed down by Judge Henry Kinslow would haunt him.

"First of all, Mr. Stratton, let me say that I never go easy when it comes to rape. It doesn't matter if she consented or not. A grown man has no business with a thirteen-year-old girl. No way. No how. Do you get my drift?"

Berating the accused was typical of Judge Henry Kinslow. He was one of those individuals who savored his own prestige while condemning the faults of others. He was less than perfect himself, but the cloak and gavel kept him at arm's length from what he considered the degenerates of society.

"I don't suppose you plan on marrying this girl, do you?" Stratton found the judge's question humorous. Knowing it was only moments from sentencing, he refrained from laughing out loud. Instead, he shook his head "no."

"No, I didn't think so," the judge growled. "You are nothing but filth and evil. I want you banished from society until you come to your senses. I do believe that through me there is hope for your redemption."

Stratton appeared to ignore the sermon, but he had memorized every word. The more the judge criticized him, the more he saw through the facade. Perhaps it was the judge's condescending nature or that he was just too eager to cast the first stone. Either way, Jack Stratton could see right through Judge Henry Kinslow.

"So for your indecency to the human race, I sentence you to five years in Ohio State Pen with no chance of early parole. Now get him out of here. Next case," Kinslow said as he slammed down his gavel.

Stratton sprawled out on his bunk and vowed revenge. "Someday, Ben Adams, I'm gonna pay the bastard back. One way or another

I'm gonna see to it that Kinslow gets his! I'm in this joint for fucking a girl who told me right out that she was past the age of consent. How the hell did I know she was jailbait? Damn Midwest farm girls. They're as horny as hell," Stratton said as he spat into the soiled toilet that separated his bunk from his cellmate's. "You know what I mean, Ben?" Stratton asked but had learned not to expect a response from the skinny man who shared his cell. It was just as the guard predicted. Since Stratton entered cell G5 over a month before, Ben Adams had not made one audible sound.

"Yep, the day's gonna come when I nail Henry Kinslow for costing me time and money. Two things I don't have right now," Stratton said, vowing retaliation. He cleared his throat and spat again. Still, there was no reaction from Ben who was in a world all his own.

Stratton continued simply out of boredom. "I never should have come to Ohio, Ben. It was a dumb mistake. A while back I got shafted out of some family money. Next thing I knew I was behind bars for mouthing off to some hotshot California judge. After I got out, I hopped on the first train that headed East. Did I tell you that I'm talking about big money? It was money my old man should have got before he died. But his fucking brother ended up with the whole lot and when I tried to fight for a piece of it, the bastard and his hotshot lawyer managed to cut me out. Fucking Alfred Stratton and fucking Henry Kinslow."

Whenever Stratton rambled on, which was almost every night, he was guaranteed a good night's sleep. Venting acted like a tranquilizer to him. It never mattered what he had to say because the nearly catatonic Ben Adams never commented until, that is, one night nearly a year after Stratton was incarcerated.

"Yep, Jack, I know just what ya mean. Cuz I know Henry Kinslow. I know him well." His voice was strained and raspy as Ben spoke his first words in years.

Stratton's mouth dropped open. He had come to the conclusion long ago that Ben was deaf and dumb. So when Ben spoke, Stratton nearly fell off his upper bunk. Not wanting to startle him

Stratton calmly asked, "What do you mean, Ben? Did Kinslow put the screws to you, too? Are you doing Henry Kinslow's time?"

"Yeah, and I get a bunk and three square meals a day. And I don't need to work no more as long as I'm in G5," he said, sounding gravelly.

"Are you crazy?" A question posed in jest; however, in Ben Adams' case it was closer to the truth than Jack Stratton knew. "So tell me about Kinslow, Ben. Exactly why are you locked up?"

"It's a long story, Jack. But I'll tell you if you got the time," Ben said as his voice became less labored.

"I've got all the time in the world, Ben. I'm all ears."

"I was Kinslow's groundskeeper. I did the mowing and edging. Come spring and fall I pruned the trees and the hedges. I was damn good," he stated confidently.

"Ah, you were on his payroll. You must have been on his good side at one time. So what did you do so bad to end up here?"

"Never said I was on his good side. I just did the mowing, is all. But I didn't steal no car, even though the judge said I did," he said adamantly.

"Yeah, yeah, and I didn't screw the Bradley girl. Go on."

"I said, I didn't steal no car! But I did see the judge with his lady friend—Miss Sarah."

Stratton, who had been stretched out on his bunk, sat straight up. "What did you just say? Miss Sarah who?"

"Miss Sarah Robbins. She was his woman. Not his wife, mind you, his woman," he asserted.

"Kinslow's married?"

"Yep, but you'd never know it when he was with Miss Robbins. I know cuz I followed him when he wasn't looking."

Ben used his finger to trace a pattern on the cement wall. He seemed to be outlining a vivid picture of something he had once seen. But the memory seemed to slow his faculties. He was quiet again, reliving a moment somewhere in time.

"Don't stop now, Ben. Tell me more." Jack flung his legs over the edge of his bunk, yearning for the story about the judge and Sarah

Robbins. *If only I could journey through the mind of this dumb ass,* he thought.

A few minutes had passed and Ben was still tracing a pattern on the wall. He was no longer communicating with Jack. So Jack reclined, expecting nothing more. Then out of the strange silence, Ben began to tell his story.

"Did I ever tell you 'bout the day the judge caught me hanging on the window ledge?"

Jack wasn't sure if Ben was talking to him or back in a world of his own. He didn't answer.

"I had just finished eating my dumpling stew. Hm-mmm. Hot, juicy chicken dumpling stew." Ben licked his lips while his taste buds frantically searched for the stew. He slurped and smacked, certain there was a home-cooked meal within reach. When he found none, he continued.

"Anyway, I was washing out my soup bowl when I heard some rustling in the backyard. I looked out the kitchen window, but didn't see nothin' at first. I thought it was a stray cat or a possum come begging for some of my dumpling dinner. Then I heard the bushes move, real loud and close to the window. I had to squint some, but then I saw this judge trying to squeeze past my evergreen hedge. He didn't know I was watching him so when he got to the alley, I snuck outside. I followed him all the way to Miss Sarah's until he disappeared through her back door."

"Is that all? You saw him go into her house?"

"Nah, Ben saw. Ben saw everything," he said, suddenly referring to himself in the third person.

"Now we're getting somewhere, Ben. What happened? I want to know every smut-filled detail," Stratton said, impatiently pressing Ben. "Ben, I want to know more!"

Ben did not answer Stratton, as he had retreated back into his private world. Staring unblinkingly at the wall, Ben no longer heard Jack.

"Are you still with me, Ben? So what happened next?" When Ben didn't answer him, Stratton grumbled, "Damn, I should have kept my mouth shut."

The following night cell G5 was back to normal. Jack was cursing Alfred Stratton and Judge Kinslow, while Ben Adams did little more than blink his eyes. The only difference was that Jack knew the judge's Achilles' heel—someone by the name of Sarah Robbins. Unfortunately, since Ben hadn't uttered a word since the night before, Stratton figured her name was the only thing he'd ever know. That is until the guard announced, "Lights out."

Like a director who called "action" on the set, Ben stood up and, without reference to the hours that had passed, took up where he left off. "It makes me laugh when I think of the judge hurdling over Miss Sarah's picket fence. That old fart; he was mighty old for a young one like her. But Miss Sarah didn't care. No, sir! She just welcomed him in like he was Clark Gable. Anyways, I crawled down low to the ground until I reached her front porch. I might have stayed there all night, but then I heard Miss Sarah handing out that sweet talk. She told him she was gonna pull the rattlesnake out of his pants and swallow it whole. Well, I just had to see for myself. Know what I mean?"

Jack didn't dare say a word. He remembered that the last time he opened his mouth Ben clammed up. He wasn't about to jeopardize the tale now that it was getting good.

"Man, oh, man could that woman put out. And the judge? He didn't even have to pay for it. Goddamn, some men have all the luck. Anyways, I could see the back of Miss Sarah's head bobbing up and down. So I moved up a little closer, just under the ledge. I crouched down and pushed up against the wall until I had a bird's-eye view. Man, you should have been there. She was licking his rod and all he had to do was lay back. The son of a bitch. She sucked him a couple of times and in between takes she'd asked when he was gonna leave his wife. He'd tell her 'real soon.' The son of a bitch," Ben repeated. "After a while he asked her to turn over. Man, oh, man was he lucky. That round ass of hers. Nice and full. Yeah, she had a real nice round ass. Well, I kinda got my own thing going on. You know what I mean, Jack? I'd been listening to that sweet talk and watching him slam up against that fine ass of hers. I just had to finish my own affairs, right then and there. That's when I fell against the windowsill and sort of startled all of us. The judge yelled and Miss Robbins screamed, I just…Well, all I wanted was to spill my seed and get the hell out of there. But it was too late. The judge saw me and told me I was gonna have to pay for my sins. I pulled up my pants and went home to eat more stew. Next thing I knew, I was arrested for stealing a car. Don't know whose car I stole," he said, less certain that he had not committed the crime.

"So that's it, Ben? You got caught spying on the judge and his woman while you were yanking your crank? For that you're stuck in here?"

Using his name in the third person a second time, Ben said, "Ben gets thirty years with three squares and a bed."

"Holy shit, Ben. Thirty years? Are you appealing?"

Stratton was stunned by the inflated sentence. He was even more surprised that Ben displayed no anger or emotion. To Ben the sentence was just a number. In fact, Kinslow could have confined him to a year and it wouldn't have made any difference. Ben Adams was mentally disabled and incapable of understanding the magnitude of his sentence.

It all started to make sense to Stratton. Judge Kinslow pointed a finger in every direction, but never at himself. He had even framed a half-wit to protect himself.

If Stratton was honest with himself, he would have seen that he was no different than Kinslow. Taking advantage of Ben who was mentally challenged, Stratton manipulated him into sharing the story of Judge Henry Kinslow and Sarah Robbins countless times thereafter. And always, the unsuspecting Ben responded the same.

"Did I ever tell you 'bout the time…"

Ben Adam's tale, retold word for word, never altered. Even the occasional pauses, as well as the twenty-four hour interruptions, were identical. For Ben, whose memory lapsed from day to day, each recollection was a first. As for Jack Stratton, Ben had supplied him with the best entertainment behind bars. So by the time

Stratton's five years were up in cell G5, he was bound and determined to bed Judge Kinslow's woman.

✧ ✧ ✧

Sam glanced past Sarah and noticed that Jack, who was barechested, had stepped out onto the porch. Even from a distance Sam could see that his hair was mussed and that golden stubble covered his face. It was obvious that Jack had spent the night. "It looks like you've got company, Sarah," Sam said, trying to act surprised. "I'm going to take Billy to the lake with me. There's no reason that he should give up our Sunday picnic."

"I was hoping that Jack and Billy could get to know each other a little better today. I was just getting ready to shower before making the three of us breakfast."

"The two of them will have plenty of time to bond, Sarah," Sam argued. "Let me take Billy for the day. We'll catch some catfish before the storm kicks in. Afterwards I'll take him back to my place for a fish fry. It'll give you and your friend some time to yourselves."

"That's a tempting offer, Sam," she said and added, "Actually, I could use a free day."

"Couldn't we all? So I'll keep him overnight and take him to school in the morning."

Billy had already jumped out of the tire and was running back with his tackle box and fishing pole. Sarah smiled and said, "Okay, you two. Have a good time. I'll pick you up from school tomorrow, Billy," she said as she bent over and kissed him on the forehead.

Sam barely lifted his eyes to meet Sarah's. Between the stench that permeated from her body and her snarled hair, the mere sight of her disgusted him. Pointing toward the porch he added, "He doesn't look like the type of man who likes to be kept waiting. You better get going."

Sarah turned around and smiled at Jack. Without displaying any sign of embarrassment, Sarah sighed out loud. Leaning against the wooden railings Jack Stratton was half-clad in a skimpy towel, smiling like a Cheshire cat.

"Let's go, Billy," Sam urged. "The catfish aren't gonna wait all day for us."

As soon as Sam and Billy drove out of sight, Sarah rejoined Jack on the porch. "We've got all day and night. Billy's staying with Sam."

After hours of marathon sex, Sarah rolled off Jack's chest and said, "Tell me about yourself, starting with this bizarre tattoo on your arm."

He lifted his arm and showed off the custom design that was permanently marked into his suntanned skin. "What do you think of it?"

"It's so unusual. It looks like a snake and a mythological goddess. What does it mean?"

"It's a cobra snake being devoured by Venus."

"What does the G5 underneath it mean?"

"G stands for Grace, my mother's name, and five is my lucky number," he lied.

"Well, I've never seen one like it."

"And trust me. You never will again," he said arrogantly.

Jack glanced back at the masterpiece and remembered the cost for the artwork. Three packs of cigarettes. But for such intricate detail, it should have cost ten to fifteen dollars—the usual cost if you went to the corner tattoo parlor. But at Ohio State Penitentiary, a smoke was worth its weight in gold. So at three packs, it was more than a fair deal.

"Jack, where did you get it?"

"Oh, I got it in Dayton. I was there on a weekend trip a few months back," he rambled, making it up as he went along.

"Why a cobra and Venus?"

"It's a story I heard a long time ago. It's about the goddess of love and how she bit off the head of a cobra, the king of snakes."

"Why would Venus eat a snake? I don't get it."

"Like I said, I don't remember the story," he said, remembering only too well the tale told by Ben about Sarah and the Judge.

"Most of the tattoos you see these days are patriotic. You know, eagles, flags, and anything else pertaining to the USA. Did you serve, Jack?"

"Just missed out on WWII," he said. "I did serve the government, but I'd rather not talk about it," he said disingenuously referring to his prison time.

"Most men don't want to talk about the armed forces, unless they are talking with other men. So were you in the army or navy?"

Fiercely, he repeated, "Listen, Sarah, I really don't want to talk about it!"

For an instant there was a tone in his voice that scared her. She quickly changed the subject to accommodate him. "Billy is really fond of you, Jack. I can tell."

"He's a good kid, all right. Considering that he doesn't have a daddy. And why is that, Sarah? Why doesn't Billy have a daddy?"

"The man who is Billy's father does not deserve him. He never wanted Billy in the first place. And because of that, I never wanted him in our lives. Like you, Jack, there are some things I'd rather not discuss," she stated. Sarah brushed her hair from her eyes and added, "Besides, Sam's always been there to help out with him. He's been like a father to Billy since he was a baby."

"How come you and Sam never got together? Or did you?" Jack asked meaningfully.

"Sam and I never had that kind of relationship. We value our friendship too much to let love ruin it," she said unaware of Sam's true feelings.

"That's good to know, Sarah. You know, I've been thinking a lot about you. I feel like I've known you for years. In fact, I even knew what it would feel like the moment you put your wet lips on my cock."

"Jack!" Sarah blushed. "You are not supposed to talk about such things," she said, mimicking what the Judge had told her years before. When Kinslow had first coerced her into the act, she was just a teenager and had found it repulsive. As she became older, she came to appreciate the intimacy she shared with the judge. So by the time Sarah had taken Jack's penis into her mouth, she found it sexually exciting; however, she still didn't want to talk about it.

"God wouldn't have made something feel so good if he didn't want you to do it," Jack said in his role of the considerate lover.

"You're probably right," she said as she fondled him again.

"I think there is one thing that we should do and the sooner, the better."

He paused and stroked her forehead, "Let's get married."

"What?" Sarah had hoped to hear those words, but she never expected to hear a proposal so soon. "You are asking me to marry you?"

"Do I have to get down on my knees, bare-ass naked and ask you again? Marry me, Sarah."

"Yes, I'll marry you!" she said elated. "When?"

"Let's get our blood tests tomorrow. We'll get married as soon as the results are in. But…"

"But what? Jack, what is it?"

"Let's keep it our secret. After we're married, you can tell the world," he said as he kissed her breasts.

"Are you asking me not to tell Billy?"

"Not Billy, not even Sam," he said kissing her breasts again, while slipping his hand between her legs.

"But Sam is like family," she said as she responded to his touch.

"Maybe, but I'm the one who is going to be your husband, so what I say takes precedence."

"Oh, what the heck," she conceded. "I'm going to be married. I know he'll be happy for me," she said as she kissed the tattoo on his arm.

The following week Sarah and Jack stood in a line of ten couples waiting to be wed at the courthouse. The line itself took twenty minutes; the legalities of wedlock took only five. There were no wedding frills, no special honors. It was the most basic of packages. But nonetheless, with a simple "I do" Sarah Robbins became Sarah Stratton.

"Jack, I have to call Sam. I can't keep this from him another moment. Besides, I need him to be there when I tell Billy."

"You can tell him tonight at the club. You are planning on singing, aren't you?"

"I hadn't thought about it, but you're right. Wedding night or not, it's too late for Sam to call in a replacement for me. I'll only do a couple of short sets, okay?"

"Good, but I'm coming with you to the club. Now that you're my wife, I want every Tom, Dick and Henry to know it."

"You mean, Harry, don't you?"

"Ah, yeah. Every Tom, Dick and Henry should know that you're my wife."

Sarah dismissed what she thought was no more than an error. But hearing Henry's name made Sarah think. Although Billy's biological father had no claim to him, neither did Jack. In a hurry to exchange vows, Sarah had forgotten to talk about adoption. Somehow it just didn't seem appropriate to bring it up now.

"I'm glad you want to come with me, Jack. We can tell Sam and Billy at the same time."

"I couldn't agree with you more, Sarah."

✧ ✧ ✧

Sam tapped the microphone and, after a brief feedback squeal, introduced his partner Sarah Robbins. It should have been a night like every other, except this one was different: Sam no longer felt the same about Sarah. However, his warm introduction gave no indication that things between them had changed.

"Thank you, Sam. As always, you are too kind," she said sincerely. "Tonight I'd like to sing a song to someone very special to me. He's in the audience. Jack, this one is for you."

Sarah sang a romantic ballad and held the last note for several seconds. It was long enough for Jack Stratton to lift his glass in honor of her. The audience joined in cheering, whistling, and clapping their hands. When the applause died down, Jack stood up and ran up to the stage. It was obvious that Sarah welcomed the interruption.

"I'd like to make a toast. Billy, are you still awake? Come on out here and join your mother and me on stage."

Hearing his name, Billy parted the velvet curtains and shuffled over to her. First he looked at Sarah, then Jack, and finally he rested his eyes on Sam. Only then did he feel secure again.

"My name is Jack Stratton and you all know Sarah Robbins and her boy Billy. Well, tonight I want to make a new introduction."

Sam didn't know what was going on. He knew that Sarah could not have been thinking clearly or she never would have allowed a guest to come onstage. It wasn't in the program.

"I want to introduce you all to my wife Sarah Stratton."

Waitresses, busboys, and patrons alike stopped dead in their tracks. For a few moments the only sound came from the air-conditioner vents. But the silence was broken when a high-ball glass slipped from Sam's grip. As its pieces shattered across the floor, Jack yelled out, "Hey, Sam. I only married her; she's still your partner. And speaking of partners, Sam, maybe we should get better acquainted."

Sam couldn't move. In the midst of gasps and surprises, Fran began to clap her hands. One by one the others joined in until the entire club was shouting "Congratulations." Everyone, that is, except Sam Donahue. The shock was too much for him. His jaw tightened while his face twitched. He appeared to be having a convulsion, but the reality was Sam had just suffered a stroke.

ten

NEIL'S FRIENDS

California, 1958–1960

Neil had never been more determined than he was the moment he drove off with Vicky from their home in Detroit. In the rearview mirror he could see Anne throwing stones at the car as she chased after them. To avoid another altercation with her, Neil eased off the gas pedal and ran the red light at the corner.

Eight-year-old Vicky, kneeling on the back seat and facing the rear window, was watching her mother's antics. Vicky couldn't remember a single day when her mother had been desperate or had lost control. She was almost relieved when her father insisted, "Vicky, I want you to turn around and face the front. Don't look at her anymore. I want you to concentrate on California and all its wonders. I want you to think about the mountains, the ocean, and the orange groves. And just wait until spring when you first smell the orange blossoms. It's a perfume like nothing you've ever smelled before. Vicky, you're going to love it out West." Neil patted the cushion adjacent to him and urged, "Climb over the seat and sit up here with me."

Vicky took one final glance at her wailing mother and swung her leg over the green tuck-and-roll seat. Her mind was filled with questions, but she was too young to know where to start. She only knew that her father had just left her mother behind and that he was unusually calm, even though he could still hear the hopeless, yet fading, cries of her mother.

Vicky needed reassurance that in choosing to live with him, her mother couldn't punish her in the future. She almost dreaded her father's answer when she asked, "Daddy, if Mother comes to California will she have to live with us?"

She stared up at her father and began scrutinizing the lines that accented his eyes. Barely noticeable at first, each one deepened, becoming more pronounced. Vicky was delighted to see they were the result of a smile that developed into hearty laughter.

"Nope, honey, she's never ever coming to live with us. Mark my words. It's just you and me, kiddo, from here on out," he chuckled.

Her father's outpouring of enthusiasm was completely out of character. Then again, the whole afternoon had been one surprise after another. Her normally reserved father, who rarely raised his voice, had relentlessly chastised her mother. He reminded Vicky of the way her mother had reprimanded her all her life. Initially it was unsettling, but Vicky found it strangely gratifying to finally see her mother on the receiving end.

Less jovially he said, "Vicky, we need to have a heart-to-heart talk. I need you to be honest with me."

"Okay," she said nervously. "Did I do something wrong?"

"No, but I did. When you were a baby, I promised never to let anything or anyone hurt you. Yesterday at the convention I learned that I've been failing you for years. I didn't know how your mother treated you."

"I'm okay, Daddy. You don't need to worry about…"

Midsentence, he interrupted her. "Wait, I'm not finished. I learned about you walking to school in the blizzard when you were only five. My God, you were only five."

Neil felt an eerie chill pass through his body even though it was nearing summer. The chill gave him a vivid picture of the incident three and a half years before. While Anne slept, Vicky was forced to walk to school in a blizzard. He wondered what other evil deeds his wife perpetrated on his child. The thought inflamed him. He clenched the steering wheel until his fingers turned white.

"Vicky, I have to know why you didn't tell me. I'm your father," he said emotionally.

Hesitatingly, Vicky explained, "I was afraid that I would get into trouble. Mother warned me never to tell anybody, especially you."

"Well, there's nothing to be afraid of now. I want you to tell me everything that happened between the two of you—everything that you can remember."

Not knowing where to begin, Vicky stammered. She thought long and hard before letting it spew out. She told him how her mother pulled her down the steps by her hair just for growing watermelon. She told him about the wooden paddle and how her mother had hit her countless times across the face. Vicky told her father more than he wanted to know.

"What kind of father have I been to you? I let you down just like I let Amy down a long time ago," he let slip.

"Amy? Who is Amy?"

Neil took a deep breath and confessed, "Since we're not going to have any secrets between us, you might as well know that Amy is your half sister." Neil saw the perplexed look on his daughter's face and added, "Just like your mother, I was married to someone else a long time ago. It also didn't work out."

"Well, where is Amy? How come I don't know her?"

"To be honest she lives with her mother and her stepfather." It was the first time Neil said it out loud and actually accepted it as a fact. He no longer felt disdain for his first wife; however, his animosity toward Anne was only beginning.

"Daddy, can Amy come and live with us in California?"

"No, she's very happy living with her mother. You know, I hadn't heard from them in years until a few months ago. Amy's mother sent me a picture taken on Amy's fourteenth birthday. Here," he said taking his wallet from the dashboard and flipping it open. "She looks like you, doesn't she?"

Vicky stared at the picture and wished she did look more like her half sister. Her sister didn't have buckteeth like Vicky's. She handed him his wallet back and exclaimed, "Amy's mother loves her! So why didn't my mother love me? Why am I so different?"

Neil had an opportunity to deny it, but Vicky had spoken the truth. From the day she was born her mother had despised her—simply because she was a girl. Neil decided to be forthright. "Sometimes people love themselves so much that they have nothing left to give. Your mother is one of those people."

Sympathetically, Vicky stated, "She didn't love you either."

"I don't know. Perhaps there was a time way back when; but that changed many moons ago."

"Are you going to get another wife, Daddy? Am I going to have a stepfather, I mean, a stepmother?"

"I'm not making another mistake, Vicky. No, I doubt I'll ever marry again. It's just you and me," he sighed.

After hours of emotions, painful memories, and new revelations there were no secrets left between Vicky and her father. Vicky edged up closer to Neil and quietly they both watched the last hint of sunlight disappear beneath the horizon. Shortly after, the sky revealed its pageantry of glitter. Stars that were normally shadowed by city lights would provide the Dvoraks with a panorama that inspired wonder and awe.

Vicky finally broke the silence and asked as she pointed low in the sky, "What's that one called, Daddy?"

"That's Mars. Over there is Sirius the Dog Star. Can you see the Big Dipper? Keep an eye on it and watch how its position will change as the earth rotates."

If anyone could distinguish a planet from a star, it was Neil Dvorak. He was fascinated by heavenly objects. When Russia launched Sputnik, Neil woke up every morning around two o'clock just to locate its whereabouts in the sky. To the average man it was a lackluster event; however, to an astronomy enthusiast like Neil, tracking the man-made object was a triumphant feat.

The neighbors back on Temple Street had always respected Neil's appreciation for the stars. On the night when the sky emitted waves of pink and blue, it was Neil whom they petitioned to explain the strange happening. As usual, he had provided them with an explanation.

"There's nothing to be alarmed about," Neil had told his neighbors. "That's what you call the aurora borealis, better known as the northern lights. It's the moon reflecting off the polar ice caps, but you usually don't see that kind of phenomenon in Detroit. Farther north in Canada you see this all the time."

Neil shared his knowledge of the stars with any willing listener. On the first night of Neil and Vicky's cross-country jaunt, Neil would have loved nothing more than to pass it all on to Vicky. However it would have been futile, for as much as Vicky had battled to remain vigilant, her body had refused to cooperate.

She was exhausted when Neil asked, "Are you tired, sweet essence?"

"Um-hum," she uttered with a yawn.

"Crawl in the backseat and make yourself a bed. Your pillow is under the blankets."

"Aren't you tired, Daddy?"

"No, not at all. I might as well keep on driving. I can go another couple hundred miles before I need some shut-eye. Tomorrow night we'll pull off at a motel. As for the rest of the week, we'll just stop off at rest stops. My goal is to reach California by Friday so that Saturday I can find us a place to live. The sooner I find us a home, the sooner Joe Moore can send my tools and table saw. Good night, sweet essence."

"G'night, Daddy," Vicky said half-asleep.

With no one to stimulate conversation, the hours were gradually catching up with Neil. He was mentally and physically drained and wished that he could pull off the road and snooze for an hour or so. If he were traveling alone, that's exactly what he would have done. But on that barren stretch of highway it was far too risky to stop with an eight-year-old child. He did the next best thing. He rolled down the window and faced his head into the brisk night air. It was revitalizing. Good enough to bring on a hearty thirst.

From the cooler packed with staples he grabbed a brew and opened it with his key-chain bottle opener. The lager that he consumed in less than ten minutes refreshed his faculties. Few people had Neil's stamina for alcohol. While most would have yielded to the hypnotic white lines of the road, alcohol didn't faze Neil in the least. The cold beverage acted like an amphetamine. Suddenly wide-awake, Neil turned on the radio. It was on nights like these, when the road was void of oncoming headlights, that the sounds of a radio made Neil feel like he had company. He knew that on some deserted highway, perhaps hundreds of miles in any direction, there was a fellow traveler zeroing in on the same broadcast.

As he turned the dial to the right, Neil began scanning every station beginning at the lowest frequency. The unclouded airwaves offered an endless selection of music, news, and late-night entertainment. Moments of clarity were followed by distorted sounds, but he managed to pick up several stations. Crackle…"and the weather in Des Moines will be sixty-five…" *Iowa. That's a few states away. That'll do just fine.* He adjusted the knob to receive a better transmission. However, the reception faded in and out, finally conceding to a more powerful broadcast. "News at Four on WXYZ, Detroit, Michigan."

"The last thing I want to hear about is anything about Detroit," he said. Just as he was about to change the channel, he heard a familiar name mentioned.

Late this afternoon in a Detroit suburb, a woman set fire to her garage, minutes before ingesting an overdose of sleeping pills. Anne Dvorak, who was apprehended by authorities, was admitted to the psychiatric ward at Detroit Memorial Hospital. Police say concerned citizens contacted the authorities when they witnessed her bizarre behavior. Using the butt end of a shotgun, she shattered the windows of her home and then fled into the garage where she set fire to a woodworking area. The neighbors were able to douse the flames before the fire department arrived; however, the damage to the garage was extensive. Witnesses say her actions came just hours after her husband requested a divorce from her…And in Ypsilanti the extent of the damage was revealed in the aftermath of yesterday's tornado…

"Are you awake, Vicky?" *Please, God, don't let her answer.* Luckily, the only trait Vicky shared with her mother was her ability to sleep anytime, anywhere. This night was no exception.

Neil tried to recapture the news segment, but all he could remember were bits and pieces. *What am I going to do?* He glanced at Vicky in the rearview mirror, relieved she was still asleep. *Think, Neil, think. Anne's been admitted to a hospital. Boy, they are going to have their hands full dealing with that mouth of hers.* Picturing her restrained in a straightjacket, he had to chuckle. But the laughter was short-lived as he recollected more details.

God, if the garage is gone, so are my tools. With all that wood it must have been a roaring fire. That bitch! That unbelievable bitch! I'm not turning back, Anne Dvorak, no matter what you did. I'll keep Vicky as far away from you as possible. But what am I going to do now? We were almost free. If only I hadn't turned on the radio…

Although Neil sought for answers, it was fruitless. He couldn't dismiss the burden that fate, or Anne, had forced upon him. *One way or another I've got to get this resolved before we get to California.*

He ran his fingers though his curly salt-and-pepper hair. *I should call Joe and Catherine. On second thought, they don't need to be involved. Maybe it's time I call her parents. Yeah, that's what I'll do. I'll drive to Edda's Cafe and call Victoria and Samuel from there. Maybe, just maybe, there's a sliver of a bond left between them. But I'm not turning back!*

Just about the time that the morning sun touched the skyline, Neil was turning onto the dirt road to Edda's Cafe. The smooth hum of the paved highway abruptly gave way to grinding spits of rock. The rumble jarred Vicky from her sleep.

Rubbing her eyes, she squinted from the sunlight that bored through the windshield. "Achoo."

"Bless you, sweet essence. Are you hungry?"

"Uh-huh. Where are we? Is it morning already?"

"Yeah, it's a little past five. We're stopping off at Edda's to get some grub and gas."

"Who's Edda, Daddy?"

"She's a real nice lady who owns a restaurant. Back in the forties, long before you were born, I used to travel across the country as much as I could. One day I was passing through Lake Town, Missouri, and asked this fella where I could get a good home-cooked meal. He told me about Edda's Cafe. He said truckers come from all over the U.S. to chow down on Edda's porterhouse steaks. So I decided to give it a try and it was the juiciest piece of meat I ever had."

"Are you gonna have a steak for breakfast?"

"No, I'm not very hungry right now. I'm just going to have a cup of coffee. You need to get something in your stomach, though. Did I tell you that Edda makes the best fried-egg sandwiches this side of the Rockies? I'll probably get a couple to go."

"I have to go to the bathroom, Daddy."

"That's another good thing about Edda's. She's got clean restrooms, so you can take care of things."

Vicky looked out the side window at a dirt parking lot that was filled to capacity. Beyond the lot, she saw a large billboard on the restaurant's roof with a picture of a heavyset woman in a chef's hat. The legend below read: Welcome to Edda's. Serving good people, good food since 1936.

"Ah, here we are. Just as I remember it. Honey, grab your bag and get some fresh clothes and undies. I put a washcloth, your toothbrush, and toothpaste in a sack under the seat. You'll find the ladies bathroom just inside, off to the right."

"I can't find my socks."

"That's okay. Wear your penny loafers without them. We'll find them later."

Vicky jumped out of the car and scurried to catch up with her father. He was standing at the entrance of Edda's, holding open the screen door. Vicky took hold of her father's hand and together they walked in.

"Well, lookee here." A raspy but jovial voice was heard from across the room. Vicky recognized the lady to be the real-life version of the replica on the billboard.

"My, my, my. It if isn't Neil Dvorak in the flesh. How long has it been?"

"It's been far too long, Edda. Good to see you."

Edda bent down and rubbed her warm pudgy fingers across Vicky's face. "This can't be…"

"No, Edda, this isn't Amy. This is my younger daughter, Vicky." Neil pulled out his wallet and proudly showed Edda the picture of Amy. "She's fourteen now and living with her mother in South Carolina. Janet remarried shortly after our divorce."

"My goodness gracious, where has the time gone?" Edda wasn't one to dwell on the unpleasant things in life; her ample cheeks almost buried her eyes when she smiled and asked, "So, I take it that you are also remarried?"

"That's a whole other story." He patted Vicky on the head and added, "Vicky, don't you want to freshen up before breakfast?"

Vicky took the hint and excused herself. "Where is the bathroom?"

Neil nodded his head toward the ladies' room. "Over there. Don't forget to brush your teeth. That means the back ones, too" he grinned.

The moment Vicky was out of sight the smile on Neil's face faded. His disposition, which was carefree at first, abruptly became agitated and nervous.

"Edda, I've got to use the pay phone. It's urgent. I need lots of change—quarters and dimes," he said, handing her a ten-dollar bill.

"Is everything all right?"

"No, it isn't. I'll explain later. In the meantime, if Vicky comes out before I'm done with my call, give her a glass of orange juice and whatever else she wants for breakfast." He followed Edda to the cash register. "Just give me a roll of dimes and the rest in quarters."

"The telephone's around the corner. Take your time, friend. I'll keep your little girl busy."

"Thanks, Edda. I knew I could count on you," Neil said, as he disappeared around the corner and picked up the receiver.

"Operator, I want to place a call to Marlette, Michigan. The number is Jeffrey 8-7421."

"Please deposit two dollars and twenty-five cents for the first three minutes."

Neil dropped each coin into its designated slot, it returned with a chime of acceptance. When the full amount had registered, the operator placed his call.

"Hello, Victoria, it's Neil. I know it's been a very long time and I really don't know where to begin."

"Neil, what's wrong? How are Vicky and Anne?" Her Romanian accent was strong.

"That's why I'm calling. Anne is in trouble."

"I don't understand. What do you mean Anne is in trouble? Where is Vicky?"

"Vicky is fine. She's with me. We're in the lower part of Missouri. Victoria, I want you to know that I've left Anne and am filing for divorce. I don't have time to go into details right now, but Vicky and I are moving to California."

"She wasn't good to Vicky, was she? That is why you are leaving her."

Neil could hear her voice crack with anxiety. He was stunned by her candidness.

"How did you know?"

"She wasn't good to Rose or John either. She was never a caring mother to her children. That was the reason why Samuel and I never sent the children back to her. Tell me, Neil, is Vicky all right?"

"She is now…and she will be from here on out. For years I was blind to Anne's deceit. I didn't know what was happening to my own child." Overcome by his own admission, a sudden cascade of tears gushed from his eyes. He wiped them on the sleeve of his shirt.

"That's not why I'm calling you, Victoria. I need your help with Anne."

"Go on," she urged him.

"I hate to do this to you, but you and Samuel are the only ones I can turn to."

"I said, go on," she pressed. "What is it about Anne that you are hesitating to tell me?"

"Anne is…"

"Please deposit seventy-five cents for three additional minutes."

"Hold on, Victoria, I need to add more money."

Victoria covered the phone and called out to her husband. "Samuel, there's something wrong with Anne. I don't know; he's putting more money in the pay phone."

After the last coin was inserted the operator said, "Thank you," and removed herself from the call.

"I just heard on the radio that Anne set fire to the garage and then took an overdose of sleeping pills."

"A fire? Is she burned? Did you say she tried to take her own life? Is she alive?"

"Yes, she's alive," he said. "The news station said she was taken to the hospital. She's in the psychiatric hospital."

"Do you know which hospital?"

"She's in Detroit Memorial."

"You are in a curious predicament, Neil. I sympathize with you. We know the kind of person Anne is. The kind of person she has always been. She always demanded attention. We tried to give her what she needed, but it was never enough. Nothing we did could make her happy."

"I've learned more about the kind of mother she was in the last forty-eight hours than I did our entire marriage."

"Samuel and I believed that once she had children of her own, her maternal instincts would grow. But we were wrong. Behind closed doors she was spiteful and cruel, especially to Rose. She was not so harsh with John, except when he stood up to her and defended his sister. That is when Anne became just as mean to him. We learned this terrible truth when Anne sent the children to live with us. That is why we chose to raise them ourselves. We did not want Anne to do any more harm to them than she already had."

Neil understood how difficult it must have been for Victoria to say those things about her own child. He said nothing while she unburdened her heart to him.

"Neil, we never worried about little Vicky. We knew that you were there and would protect her. Now we learn that Anne was cruel to her, too."

He swallowed the bitter taste of truth. "Victoria, you are a wise woman. Only you can speak the words that I can't even bring myself to admit. I need to be honest with you. I don't want to turn back to Detroit. Not now, not ever."

He waited for her to object, but she said nothing. So he continued. "Under the circumstances, Victoria, I can understand if you think I am abandoning your daughter. But I am merely saving my daughter from yours."

The words that he uttered were far too harsh for this gentle woman. He wished he could have retracted them. He was angry and confused, but determined not to have mercy for Anne.

There was a pause of silence before Victoria spoke. "Move forward, Neil. Samuel and I will take care of everything here. We know you'll take good care of our granddaughter and make a fine life for her. Perhaps someday we will come see you in California. You need not worry about Anne. She is no longer your business."

"I wish there was another way, Victoria. You really don't need this burden."

"Anne is our burden and we'll make do."

Samuel, who had been sharing the receiver, seized the phone from his wife. "Neil, it is Samuel. You have a safe trip to California. When you are settled in, let us know where you are. Take care."

"Thank you, Samuel. Good-bye."

Neil placed the receiver on the cradle and leaned up against the knotty-pine wall. His face, still wet with tears, needed to be blotted dry. Grabbing a handkerchief from his pocket, he erased all remaining evidence of his emotional meltdown. Still, his conscience challenged him. *Perhaps I should call the hospital just to check up on her progress.* Picking through the last of the coins, he counted out another two dollars. Just before he fed them into the pay phone, he suddenly dropped them back into his pocket. *What am I thinking? I have her parents' blessing. Besides, this was probably another one of her attention-getters. She shatters windows to attract a crowd, starts a fire, and only then does she take an overdose of pills. Well, Anne, if suicide was your real intention, you wouldn't have sent up so many red flags! No, I'm not buying your crap this time. You've made your bed, now lie in it.*

Through this rationalization Neil could literally feel the shame releasing itself from his body. With each exhaled breath, he liberated himself of all his liabilities. Truly, he was experiencing an inner cleansing of his second wife.

"Problems at home?" Edda asked, as she handed Neil a glass of freshly squeezed orange juice spiked with vodka that she kept hidden in a small flask. "You better drink it back here. I don't have a license to sell liquor, my friend."

"Edda, I think I'll pass. Where's Vicky?"

"She's in a booth eating a waffle and playing the jukebox. I gave her a handful of nickels to keep her busy."

"Thanks. Edda, would you mind grilling up a couple of your famous fried-egg sandwiches to go? I want to get on the road as soon as possible."

"Consider it done." Turning toward the kitchen Edda yelled out to an apprentice cook, "Two yellow eyes a-movin' and heavy on the mayo. Make it snappy."

Neil joined Vicky who was flipping the pages to the miniature jukebox on the table. "Vicky, you've got enough music lined up to keep this place rocking all day. But I want you to finish your breakfast and drink your milk. I'd like to get going as soon as my sandwiches are cooked."

To oblige him, Vicky stuffed her mouth with the syrup-drenched waffle. Just as she swallowed the last piece she heard the cook yell out, "Order's up."

"That's mine," Neil said. "Come on, Vicky. Let's go."

Edda followed them outside to their car. Vicky had already climbed into the front seat and was waiting for her father, who was suddenly not in such a hurry. He was having a difficult time saying farewell to Edda.

"I don't know if I'll ever pass this way again, Edda, but I will always remember you. You're been a good friend on my journeys. It's been a pleasure knowing you."

"Likewise. Drive carefully and good luck to you and your little girl," she said, as Neil sped away.

The cloud of dust that erupted behind his car eclipsed Edda's silhouette. Even though she could no longer see them, Edda kept waving good-bye until the Dvoraks turned off the gravel road onto the main highway. They were westward bound.

"I like her, Daddy."

"Yeah, she's one of those lifelong friends. You always feel at home at Edda's. So what do you say to covering about four-hundred-fifty miles today? Then we'll stop and get a motel."

"What state will we be in?"

"Oklahoma. I know of this motel where we can sleep in a genuine teepee. If I remember right, they've got an outdoor swimming pool," Neil said.

"I don't have a bathing suit. Can I go in my shorts and top?"

"Sure you can. Now pass me one of Edda's egg sandwiches and a soda."

"You got it, Daddy."

Except for that one night in the rustic Oklahoma hotel, Neil drove straight through to California pulling off only for an occasional shut-eye. Following this rigid schedule, by late Friday night they were ready to cross the state line several hours earlier than expected.

When Neil pulled up to the state agricultural inspection booth, the agent leaned into the open passenger window and asked, "Are you carrying any fruits or vegetables, sir?"

Neil handed him two black-skinned over-ripe bananas. "Take these. The heat has turned them to mush anyway."

"Yeah, it's a hot night, all right. Where you headed, sir?"

"Me and my daughter, that's her sound asleep in the backseat, are moving out here. Well, not exactly here," Neil clarified. "The desert is too hot for my taste. We're planning on settling in nearer to the coast, perhaps Santa Monica."

"Well, then stay on Route 66 all the way. The road ends just north of the pier in Santa Monica. You should be on the coast in about five hours, sir."

"Thanks," Neil said to the agent who saw few people cross the border during the wee hours of the night.

Neil followed the agent's directions and ended up in Santa Monica at six o'clock in the morning. As he drove up and down Pacific Coast Highway he searched for a property while getting a feel for the area. He noticed that people were not in the market to rent out their beachfront homes. So Neil turned back onto Santa Monica Boulevard and began searching for a place further away from the oceanfront.

Santa Monica is home, he thought. *If I can't find a home to rent, then I'll have to settle for a decent motel with kitchen facilities—at least for the time being.*

"Sweet essence, wake up. We're here. See the palm trees that are lining the street? They're pretty, huh!"

"Um-hum," she yawned. "Why is it so foggy?"

"That's what you call June gloom. It's the morning fog that rolls in off the ocean. Later on in the day it will burn off."

"Where are we?"

"We're in Santa Monica. This is where I'd like us to stay. As soon as a store opens, I'll get a newspaper and check out the rental ads. If I can't find a place to rent, we might have to stay in a motel for a short time. I haven't noticed any motels with vacancies, so we might have to go inland a few miles. We're probably too close to the beach."

Vicky sat up and pressed her head against the window. She yawned again and asked, "But what about that place over there?"

Neil had been concentrating on the "Sorry No Vacancy" signs of the motels. He missed the sign on the lawn of a little white cottage that read "For Rent or Lease."

Without thinking, he shifted into reverse gear and backed up in the middle of Santa Monica Boulevard. Fortunately it was early and there were no other vehicles on the highway. Neil pulled on the brake and parked in front of the quaint dwelling.

"This has to be too good to be true," Neil said, salivating at the prospect of two bedrooms with a detached garage. "It's furnished and only one block from the beach. What more could we ask for?"

Neil jotted down the phone number. Checking his watch, he knew it was too early in the day to bother a potential landlord. He restarted the engine and turned onto a side street.

"I'm not going to take a chance of losing this place. If it's still for rent, we're going to be the people who rent it."

At eight o'clock, Neil pushed open the door to the phone booth. He hadn't slept a wink for fear someone else would beat him to the house. "Hello, I'm calling about the house you have for rent on Santa Monica Boulevard. Is it still available?"

A woman with a refined voice answered, "My husband just put the sign up last night and you are the first to call. Would you care to take a look at it? I can be there in twenty minutes."

"Wonderful. My daughter Vicky and I will be waiting out front. I'm Neil Dvorak."

"I'm Mrs. Benedict. I look forward to meeting you, Mr. Dvorak."

"The same here—we'll see you in twenty."

Neil started back toward the car and caught sight of Vicky stretching her arms in the backseat. He held up his right thumb to indicate so far, so good. She grinned at him, showing off her two front teeth that protruded over her bottom lip. Neil smiled back, although he didn't want to be overly optimistic. He knew the cottage was ideal, for instead of living in a motel and doing under-the-table odd jobs for quick cash, he could build a business again. He imagined converting the garage into a workshop, just like the one he had in Detroit. Neil hoped his luck was changing.

Vicky, still tired from the cross-country ride, staggered out of the car. "Daddy, I need to use…"

"Use the restroom next door at the gas station. I already checked it out. It's clean enough. You can wash up in there and don't forget to brush your teeth."

"I know. I know," she said as she ran her tongue across her two bucked teeth.

While Vicky freshened up, Neil rested up against one of the two date palms that adorned the front yard of the beach cottage. He guessed by their height that they had been planted about the same time the house was built—about forty years ago.

"Okay, they're clean," Vicky said when she returned a few minutes later. Plopping down next to him, she wriggled her feet in an unintentional imitation of Neil's nervous habit.

"Daddy, if we don't get this place, we'll find another," she said encouragingly.

"We'll know soon enough," he said as the roar of a new '58 Cadillac Brougham turned onto the side street. The car parked immediately behind theirs.

"It must be her," Neil said as he anxiously inhaled a deep breath.

Neil jumped to his feet and raced to open the elderly woman's car door. She allowed Neil to take her hand and help her from the car. "Mrs. Benedict?"

"Yes, and you are Mr. Dvorak," she said warmly. As they walked toward the cottage, Neil took hold of the genteel woman's arm and escorted her up the three cement steps. Again, she graciously accepted his assistance. "Thank you. Let's go inside." She unlocked the deadbolt that secured the white French doors and invited them in.

"The furnishings have all been newly replaced; however, if you prefer your own, we could have everything removed."

"No, Mrs. Benedict, we need a place that is completely furnished. I have to say, your decorator has done a magnificent job," he responded while admiring the blue silk draperies and matching throw rugs.

"Thank you. I did the decorating myself to resemble our cottage in Bordeaux, France."

"Then I take it you don't live here," Neil speculated.

"Our home is three miles up the coast just north of Santa Monica. Except for spring in Bordeaux, we are Californians through and through. What about you, Mr. Dvorak? I notice that you have Michigan plates on your car."

"Yes, my daughter and I are from Detroit. I no longer have a wife." His brief explanation was interpreted to mean deceased wife. Mrs. Benedict didn't pursue it further nor did Neil offer to clarify himself.

"I see," she smiled compassionately. "Let me show you the rest of the house." She proceeded up the short hallway and pointed to two bedrooms, one on each side. Between them was a wall with a painting that resembled a Monet.

"This is very interesting," Neil said as he stared at the large hanging.

"I see you appreciate art, Mr. Dvorak. This piece was painted by one of the local artists in Laguna. I feel he really captures the intense beauty and color of the wildflowers. Don't you agree?"

Neil blushed. He hadn't noticed the proliferation of flowers nor its likeness to a Monet masterpiece. He was, instead, fascinated by the hand-carved mahogany frame that bordered it.

"I'm embarrassed to say that I was looking at the frame. Several years ago I carved one just like this," he said. He had recognized his work immediately. He touched its satiny surface and remembered the hours he labored in creating the piece. "I believe that a chisel and a pelican knife were used in the process."

"You are familiar with woodworking, Mr. Dvorak."

"I'm a cabinetmaker by trade, although I've tried my hand at carving a few artistic pieces in the past. I once carved a bust of the actress Jeanne Crain out of sycamore wood. I was really proud of that."

"You must be very talented."

"I've been called a jack-of-all-trades. The truth is that I'm a master of none," he chuckled. Neil's hands had continued to caress the frame. Mrs. Benedict recognized that a craftsman had been reunited with his work.

"This is your work, isn't it, Mr. Dvorak?"

Neil placed both hands on the frame and asked, "May I?"

The tilt of her head gave him permission to lift the oil canvas from its hanger. He turned it over and using his handkerchief he brushed away a dozen years of dust particles. The still-legible initials, NCD, were carved at its base. He remembered the day he finished the piece. It was to be mounted over a family portrait.

"Things have a way of turning up when you least expect it!"

"Oh, my, you are the one!" she exclaimed. "Funny, I didn't make the connection with your name. Dvorak isn't that common. My aunt searched for you for years. She even placed an ongoing ad in the *Los Angeles Herald* that ran until the day she died."

"Why was she looking for me?"

"Sweet Aunt Lorraine, bless her soul, was a bit eccentric. Mr. Dvorak, you left an impression on her. She would never settle for anything less than a Dvorak piece."

"Come again?"

"She purchased an estate in Beverly Hills with the intent of having you custom build all the furniture. When she failed to locate you, she refused to have it furnished with anything second best. Her home was virtually empty when she passed, save her bed, a few chests of drawers, and this one frame that she treasured."

"It's a small world, isn't it?" Neil placed his hand on Mrs. Benedict's shoulder and swore, "If I had seen the want ad, I would have done my best for her. I'm a man of my word."

"I have no doubt, Mr. Dvorak. I believe that you and this picture frame belong together. The frame used to hang in my aunt's bedroom. It framed an oil portrait of her husband."

"I never framed an oil painting, Mrs. Benedict. If I remember correctly, it was made for a photograph taken in the eighteen-hundreds. I believe it was a picture of a man and woman with their two small children standing in front of a carousel."

"I recall the photograph. It was a picture of my grandparents with my father and my aunt. It's been years since I saw it last. Tell me, Mr. Dvorak, do you still do cabinetry?"

"Yes. It's what I plan to do here as soon as Vicky and I get settled in. I was thinking that your garage would make a splendid place for me to set up shop."

Mrs. Benedict chose her words carefully. "I would like to lease this cottage to you and your daughter, with one condition."

"I'm open for any condition. How much do you want?"

"What do you say to a little bartering, Mr. Dvorak?"

"I'm all ears," he said pointing to his own.

"I would like to refurnish my own home up the coast. There are seven bedrooms, eight baths, and a few extra rooms I have yet to count. I would like to hire your services on behalf of Aunt Lorraine. We'll forego rent while you're working for me. I will pay you in addition to providing the materials. Please tell me that you'll agree to my terms."

"Live rent free? Who could pass on an offer like that? But I promise to cover only my expenses and not charge you more than I need."

She lifted her aristocratic head and surprised Neil when she said, "Horsefeathers! I insist on paying you exactly what I would pay if I were shopping at a fine furniture retail store. That is the deal, Mr. Dvorak, and it's final."

Neil shook his head in disbelief. "I won't let you down, Mrs. Benedict."

"Of that, I have no doubt. We can work out the details later. Here are the keys," she said trusting him wholeheartedly.

✧ ✧ ✧

David Stratton stooped to pick up the afternoon edition of the newspaper lodged between the hedge and the driveway. Skipping the headlines for August 20, 1959, David went directly to the sports section. There was talk that the LA Rams had been considering a new coach. He wondered where that would leave Sid Gillman.

Seeing his wife's purse on the counter he called out, "Karen, I'm home."

"I'm in the pool."

"Okay. Just give me a minute. I'll change into my trunks and I'll join you."

Karen closed her eyes and relaxed on the floating lounger. Her tanned body glistened from the ample coating of cocoa butter that she had smoothed onto her exposed skin. Lifting her Valentino sunglasses, she inspected the dramatic tan line at the base of her floral bikini. The contrast was well worth the hours she had spent sunbathing. She leaned back again and allowed the breeze of the ocean, less than three hundred feet from the edge of their property, to navigate her about the pool. She was drifting off to sleep when she heard the sliding-glass door open.

"I'm making myself a champagne cocktail. Do you want one?"

"I'm game. Make mine with three sugar cubes, okay?"

It was a simple, yet redundant, request. Whenever David made champagne cocktails, he automatically added extra sugar cubes to Karen's glass. Unlike him, Karen had never acquired a taste for the bubbly.

When David returned with the drinks, Karen asked, "So what brings you home so early? I thought you'd have another late night with the infamous bitch, Jessica Heisen."

"Karen, I don't want to fight about her again. Just give me a break, will you?"

"But you still haven't told me where you were till three o'clock the other morning."

"I told you, I was working. That should be enough for you," he said skirting the issue.

"Well, were you working with her?"

"Damn it, Karen. I didn't come home to argue with you. So change the subject or I'm going inside to do paperwork."

"You win," she said to keep him from heading back inside.

There was a brief moment of silence between the two of them. Karen floated about the pool while hiding her emotions behind the wide-framed sunglasses. But David was relieved that she had backed down and the subject of Jessica Heisen had been dropped. In his role of caring husband he asked, "So how was your day, babes?"

"Mom and I had our monthly breakfast meeting at the diner this morning and decided to hire three more girls. The Bikini Hut is doing better than I ever expected," she boasted.

"Who would have thought that you and your mother would sell more than a few bathing suits to some friends? I'm a bit surprised you're still in business."

"Am I supposed to thank you for that backhanded compliment? No, I don't think so," she said, answering her own question. "Anyway, did I tell you that we started selling the tops and bottoms separately? It's a great selling point for women whose breasts are not in proportion with their hips."

"How is your mom handling the working side of life? I thought she'd be bored to tears by now."

Defensively, Karen asked, "What do you have against my mother? She's been nothing but sweet to you from the first day she met you."

"I meant no harm, Kar. It's just the thought of dignified Agnes Allen persuading women and teenagers to buy the latest styles; well, it's almost laughable. On the other hand my mom would have been strutting around the shop modeling the suits," he said sarcastically.

"Well, this wasn't a Delilah Stratton project, was it? This was a Karen Stratton undertaking. So who better to ask than my own mom to help out? Okay, I will be honest with you, David. I never imagined that Mom would enjoy working as much as she does. Lately she's been kicking me out at noon and telling me to take the day off. She absolutely loves managing the salesgirls by herself. In fact, Mom would like to open a second Bikini Hut."

"A second shop? That'll be the day," he said, still picturing the struggling swimsuit shop that he had visited just once, when it opened fourteen months before. Since then David had been too involved with the Heisen projects and his own career to keep abreast of Karen's small venture.

"David, what do you think of this? I am considering a mail-order business. I bet there are thousands of girls across the country who would be interested in our California designs."

David didn't offer much encouragement when he answered, "Babes, I think you had better stick to the basics. You never know when bikinis will become a thing of the past."

"It's a good thing that I'm finally above asking you for support. I can and will do anything I want with my company, no matter how small or insignificant it is by your standards," she said. "However,

David, if it makes you feel any better, I'll put my idea on the back burner for now."

"Babes, I'm just trying to protect your interests," he said, trying to sound convincing.

"Okay, enough about the Bikini Hut. Tell me about your exciting day," she said, also trying to sound convincing.

"You know, the usual. Bachman presses for higher profit margins while Jessica fights to get them reduced. And I'm caught in the middle of them both." David regretted mentioning Jessica by her first name only. Although Karen did notice the slip of his tongue, she didn't harp on it. He quickly continued, "Enough about work right now, babes. God, it was hot today. It was over one hundred in the city," he said as he handed her the drink from the pool's edge. "I wish I could have come home earlier to try out my new board on the waves. Did you see those curls?" David eased his way down the mosaic-inlaid steps until he was waist deep in the water. "Where's Jenni?" he asked.

"She's spending the night with her friend from dance class. In other words we've got the house all to ourselves tonight."

"What friend?"

"You know, Vicky Dvorak. She and Jenni have become inseparable these past few weeks."

"I don't know who you're talking about, Kar. Have I met her?"

Karen wanted to chastise him for not being home long enough to know his daughter's friends. Again, she let it pass. "You know, the girl with the curly brown hair. She lives on the corner of Santa Monica and Twenty-third."

"I still can't place her. Have you met her parents?"

"We met her father at church several months ago. He's the cabinetmaker from Michigan. His name is Neil. Remember now?"

"Yeah, he's a nice man. Where did he say his wife was?"

"He didn't. I assume she passed away and that's why they moved out here."

"That's got to be hard on Vicky," David said, wondering how he would take care of Jenni Lynn under the same circumstances.

"It doesn't appear to be. Neil has taken on the roles of father and mother admirably. He attends every dance class, rehearsal, and recital with Vicky. He also volunteers at school. Last month he gave the children an astronomy class. He even donated an eight-inch telescope."

David was feeling a bit inferior when he asked, "How can he be so involved and still hold down a job?"

"He works from home. When they moved here last summer, he opened a small cabinet shop in his garage. Turns out, he's quite the genius with wood."

"How do you know this?"

"One of the mothers at Jenni's dance class was raving about him. She said she hired him to build a dining-room hutch and when it was finished, it was way beyond her expectations. So she referred him to a few of her Beverly Hills friends who in turn referred him to theirs. They call him the Wood Virtuoso of Santa Monica."

"Maybe I should talk to Neil about building us a new bar. Something with a drop ceiling, double sink, and back shelves. You know, the works."

"Why would we want a new one? There's nothing wrong with the one we had built with the house."

"That was five years ago, Karen, and I need something bigger now. I need a bar that will seat ten comfortably," David said as he stepped out of the pool and climbed onto the diving board.

"Okay, I can understand why you'd want a more modern one, but why would you want one so big? We rarely entertain anymore since you've been traveling so much on business."

David took two jumps on the board before diving in. When he came to the surface he said, "Karen, the second-in-command at BAI should have a decent place to entertain his clients. Don't you think?"

"There you go, again, David. Wishing and hoping. It's been six years since Theo gave you your last promotion and since then he's just been dangling a carrot."

"Not anymore, Karen. Theo just served that carrot on a silver platter. And all because of the profits we've received from all the Heisen projects."

"I hope this means much more money," she said, failing to congratulate him.

"Since when did money become your first priority, Karen?"

"When I realized that I deserved it for putting up with all the late hours, the missed dinners…and Jessica Heisen." Subtly, Karen got her point across. But rather than argue, David dived under the water and toppled her floating lounge chair.

Karen made a splash as the silky, cool water chilled her singed skin. She turned toward her husband and pressed her prom-queen body against his. After ten years, Karen's body was still flawless. David wiggled closer to her and then lowered himself into the water. With teasing touches of his hands and legs to her inner thighs, he managed to weaken her spirit. "Let's go inside," he whispered into her ear.

Karen stepped out of the pool and reached for their matching monogrammed robes. She wrapped herself in the smaller one before delivering the oversized one to David. His member, protruding from the wet trunks, significantly handicapped his immediate escape from the pool. As he covered himself with the robe he said, "I wonder what it would be like to live in the hills without a beach full of voyeurs."

"Honey, if we had ordered the brick enclosure instead of the clear glass you insisted upon, we would have had plenty of privacy," she lightly scolded him.

"Yeah, but it would have blocked our view of the ocean. So for the most part, it's a fair compromise."

David fumbled with the terrycloth tie and urged, "Let's hurry. I can't wait to strip off your Bikini Hut original and do some early celebrating. Afterwards, we'll take a walk to Joey's Fish House on the beach." David grabbed her by the hand and rushed to their bedroom where he pulled her body on top of his. "In spite of all our bickering, I do love you, Karen. Please know that I love you."

That was the truth. David was still in love with Karen, but he had not been exclusive with his body. Since the day Jessica Heisen signed the first multimillion-dollar contract with BAI, his body and, oftentimes, his soul were possessed by another. But on that hot afternoon, David belonged only to his wife. There was no Jessica Heisen to contend with.

Later that evening David and Karen were nestled in a corner table at Joey's Fish House, their favorite neighborhood restaurant, feeling like honeymooners again. David handed the menus back to Rocco the waiter and placed both their orders. "Rocco, I'll have the crab Louis salad with extra dressing on the side. My lovely wife will have the halibut; hold the capers, and bring her a dinner salad with oil and vinegar. We'll take two glasses of the '57 Chardonnay. By the way is Joey in tonight?"

"Not tonight, sir. Would you like the wine served with your dinner?"

"Tell you what, Rocco. Instead of two glasses, just bring us the bottle. You can serve it now."

"I'll be right back," Rocco said, aware that these customers were in the habit of leaving a generous gratuity.

David ran his fingers several times through his dark hair. He appeared suddenly anxious and Karen recognized the signs. He was about to give her bad news, the counterpart of the good news about his promotion. "I need to talk to you about Aspen, Karen."

She stared out the window at the golden rays across the ocean. The glimmer of light brought out the highlights of her long auburn hair. She sighed, "We're not going this Christmas, are we?"

"Well, I'm not. With the company's year-end restructuring, it's important that I be around during the transition period. Bachman is leaving for Europe next month, and that's probably why he didn't wait until next year for my appointment."

"Oh, honey," she said disappointedly. "Our parents are counting on us being there. This will be the second year in a row that we've missed Aspen."

"That's why I'm insisting that you and Jenni go."

Karen took a long drink of water. The thought of having to make an excuse for David's absence at yet another family gathering was embarrassing. "Honey, I won't complain if it is truly the transition period that is keeping you from going," she said, hinting at the possibility that something else was keeping him at home.

"Babes, I have to be here. With the restructuring and the riggers' union negotiations beginning in November, it's important that I hold down the fort. Remember I'm at the very top now."

Karen appeared naive when she questioned him further. "Why would someone at your level need to be involved in negotiations or restructuring? That doesn't make sense to me."

"It's more than that, babes," he said cupping her hand in his. "All we've done is answer to the government since the last contract was awarded to us. It's politics, you know. The more you get, the more they want to investigate. As for the union negotiations, I need to be here in case it ends up in arbitration, for moral support if nothing else."

Karen wouldn't allow herself to ask if Jessica had anything to do with his decision to remain behind; although deep inside she did wonder. And yet, there was something different about David earlier that afternoon. She felt he truly came home to her when they slipped into bed together. Their lovemaking wasn't the usual five-minute act that she had become accustomed to after his long day at the office. It was tumultuous, playful, and exciting.

Wrestling beneath the sheets, they had tickled, teased, and probed each other's orifices. David had grasped hold of both Karen's wrists with one hand and slid his tongue down her tanned body. With short pecks, he had kissed every inch of her until he reached her pubic line. Then for one brief moment he lifted his head to look up at her. "My God, babes, you are so beautiful," he muttered before burying his face between her legs. But Karen did not lie still. Instead, she maneuvered her body until they were positioned toe-to-head, head-to-toe, and when she found his organ, she feasted on it. They licked and sucked and then licked again, fulfilling each other's rawest desires. As they looked into each other's eyes at Joey's Fish House, it was obvious that they were both remembering their afternoon delight.

After the waiter uncorked the Chardonnay, he poured one ounce for David's approval. David swirled the Chardonnay in the glass, inhaled its perfume, and allowed his taste buds to be the final judge. "It's crisp and light with a hint of vanilla," he exclaimed, showing off his wine expertise. "Yes, Rocco, this will do just fine. Go ahead and pour."

"Honey, I'll go to Aspen without you. I couldn't disappoint Jenni, although she is going to be devastated that you aren't going to be with us," Karen said trying to maintain a positive attitude.

"Babes, just because I can't go in December doesn't mean we can't take a family vacation. Jenni still has six weeks left before school starts," he coaxed her.

Enthusiastically, Karen asked, "Do you mean we could take a vacation now?"

"We leave two weeks from tomorrow," he said proudly. "I've scheduled the time off. As for your shop, it sounds like your mom can handle it just fine," he said.

"Honey, you've already planned a vacation?"

"Planned and paid for."

Karen twirled her hair like a teenager who had just fallen in love for the first time. "Where are we going, honey? Someplace far away from BAI, I hope."

"We're taking a fifteen-day transatlantic cruise to Europe. I purchased a two-bedroom suite on the promenade deck."

"A cruise?" Karen immediately thought about her wardrobe. She needed several more formal outfits for a cruise of that length. "I have so much shopping to do for Jenni and me," she said excitedly.

David laughed, "I figured that would be the first thing you'd say. You can go shopping tomorrow."

"Honey, I was just thinking about Jenni. If she could bring a friend then you and I could spend more time together," Karen suggested

"I know just where you're going with this. Let's talk to Vicky's father and see if he'll allow her to join us."

Karen sipped on her Chardonnay and confessed, "You know, honey, just when I think I've given up on you, you have a way of reeling me back in. You are a good father and I'm lucky to be married to you," she said lovingly. "Honey, it's high time I said 'congratulations.'"

"I was wondering when or if you were going to say it. Thanks, babes. I know that there are times BAI takes a toll on us both. But I'm going to try…"

"Sir, I hate to interrupt you, but you have a telephone call on line one," Rocco announced.

"Babes, it's probably Theo. I'll be just a minute, okay?"

Karen pressed the wineglass to her lips and made no comment about BAI's demands on David's time. She was so happy at the thought that their afternoon together could be repeated on a cruise ship. She fluttered inside with the memory of his groping tongue. "Take your time, honey. I know, I know, business is business," she said, only this time she actually meant it.

David picked up the phone and wasn't surprised to hear Jessica Heisen on the line. He had called her earlier in the morning and had mentioned that he would be dining out with Karen; Jessica was the only person who knew of his whereabouts.

Scornfully, Jessica said, "You can't be serious. You leave me a message that you are taking your family on a cruise and you expect me to be fine with that? That's utterly absurd."

"Jessica, I can't talk long. I'm juggling my life the best I can and I am in no mood for a fight. I wanted to tell you before you heard it from Theo. I have to do this for my family. Christ, I need to spend time with my daughter."

She snapped, "And do you want to spend time with your wife?"

David kept the truth to himself. He did want to spend time with Karen. But he needed to be far enough away that there could be no distraction from Jessica Heisen. A cruise was the perfect solution.

"Please, not now, Jess. I'll make it up to you later. Besides, we've got Christmas together. I'm not going to Aspen with the family."

"Well, you're going to have to pay for this, darling. One way or another, you're going to pay."

"Jess, I've said I'll make it up to you. I've got to go. We don't leave for two weeks. So I'll see you before I go."

"All right," she said abruptly. "Go on your fam-i-ly vacation, but come December, you are all mine," she said as she slammed down the phone without saying good-bye. David expected as much, because hanging up on people was something Jessica Heisen did quite frequently. And despite their intimate relationship, David was no exception.

David pulled up his chair and found Karen gazing across the ocean. There were a few clouds on the horizon, which the sun painted in shades of pink, orange, and crimson. It was going to be a breathtaking sunset.

"Let's order another bottle of Chardonnay, babes. It was Theo, but I was able to take care of everything," he said with a sinking feeling. "Now, let's celebrate my promotion."

✧ ✧ ✧

With Karen at his side, David rang the doorbell to the Dvoraks' cottage home on Santa Monica Boulevard. It was so small and quaint in comparison to the Stratton's beachfront estate, yet it was warm and inviting, nonetheless.

"Hello, Mr. Dvorak," David said when the door opened.

"You can call me Neil. It's David, right?" Neil turned toward Karen and said, "Ah, but I do know this lovely lady. Good to see you again, Karen."

"It's always a pleasure, Neil," Karen said.

Neil held the door open. "Come on in. The girls are out back practicing on their stilts. I made Vicky a pair and Jenni liked them so much, I made her a matching set. In the past few weeks they've pretty much mastered the technique."

"I had no idea Jenni could walk on stilts. I guess she never got around to telling me," David admitted.

"Don't take it personal, David. It's the young kids these days. One minute you are a hero and they want to share everything with you. The next minute you've been replaced by that Elvis lad and you're just too darn old to understand. I laugh about that all the time."

"Yeah, they sure grow up quickly, don't they," David said, while managing to avoid any guilt for his recent absences. "My wife tells me that you run a cabinet business out of your garage."

"I do custom woodworking on cabinets, crown moldings, counters—you name it, I build it."

"So how does someone like me get on that wait-list of yours? I'd like you to design and build us a bar. Do you do that sort of thing?"

"I built a bar of my own when I lived back East. It had a yellow tufted cushion across the front with a rustic knotty pine top," Neil said, suddenly missing his old bar.

"Neil, I'm interested in having one built that can seat eight to ten."

"Wow. That'll be about twelve feet long using a wraparound drop shelf."

"Can you do it?"

"Building it isn't the problem. I have such a backlog of work that I probably couldn't start it until spring. With all of Vicky's activities, I'm only able to put in a twelve hour day. I wish I could work a few back-to-back eighteen-hour days just to get caught up. Unfortunately, Vicky would be the one to lose out. So, I work when I can, sometimes until three or four in the morning."

"I guess that is the sacrifice a single parent must make," Karen said sympathetically.

"It's not a sacrifice, I assure you. Besides, I do a far better job than her mother. Truth is, I don't want her mother anywhere near Vicky."

Karen glanced at David before speaking out. "We thought your wife was deceased."

"No, Anne is in Michigan; we're divorced. Without boring you with the details, she was somewhat of a neurotic person." He paused briefly and added, "It wasn't a healthy environment for Vicky or anyone for that matter."

David asked, "Did you come to California to start over?"

"Yes, sir," Neil happily answered.

"Neil, Karen and I would like to ask something of you. It's about Vicky and Jenni. We hope you'll say yes."

"How can I help?"

"In two weeks we're leaving on a fifteen-day transatlantic cruise to Europe."

Neil lit up and said, "Say no more. Of course Jenni can stay with us. Vicky and I would love to have her. We'll take good care of her."

"No, it's just the opposite. We would like to take Vicky with us. She'll be home before school starts."

Neil took a drag on a cigarette. It was the only action he was capable of in his dumbfounded state. Their offer was beyond his wildest imagination.

He allowed the smoke to slowly seep from his mouth. "I don't know what to say. But…" Without embarrassing himself, Neil was assessing his financial situation. He had never cruised on a ship or flown in a plane before so he had no idea of the associated costs. But Neil did know that this kind of opportunity offered itself just once in a lifetime.

"I have some money set aside for emergencies. Far as I'm concerned, this is one of those emergencies. If it's okay with you, I'll write you a check."

David felt badly for misrepresenting the offer. "Neil, everything has been taken care of. We have a two-bedroom suite that is all paid for. There are no additional expenses for Vicky," David said. "All you need to do is rush the paperwork for a passport for Vicky."

"I've always paid my own way," Neil persisted.

"Not this time. Jenni will have a much better time if she has a companion. What do you say, Neil?" David, surprised that it was such a hard sell, watched as Neil hemmed and hawed.

"Okay, Vicky can go. I insist that you accept one-hundred dollars for miscellaneous expenses," Neil said, extracting from his wallet the bill that he kept hidden for a rainy day.

David reluctantly accepted the bill. He understood there was fatherly pride involved. "Thanks, Neil. This will be Vicky's spending money."

"So be it. Since I'm going to be able to work those eighteen-hour days, I want to do something special for the two of you. I'm going to build your bar and have it completed by Thanksgiving. My labor is free to you; you need only pay for materials. In fact, from this day forward any work I do for you will be under the same terms." He smiled exposing his broad teeth. "Fair enough?" Neil asked.

"Fair enough," David said to one of the most proud and strong-willed men he had ever met.

Neil leaned out the kitchen window and called out to the girls in the backyard. "Vicky, Jenni, put down your stilts and come inside. Boy, do we have something to share with you!"

eleven

ETHAN DRAKE

Alabama, 1958–1959

Doc Edward Jones had intercepted the emergency call from Sheriff Cornell and had arrived a few minutes before the ambulance. He grabbed his medical bag and rushed to the barn that housed a few mice, a prize bull and eight-year-old Ethan Drake who was in critical condition. "Let me take a look at him, Pete," Doc Jones said to the sheriff.

"I've got to give Jesse Brown credit. If it hadn't have been for him we may not have found Ethan in time," Sheriff Pete said.

Jesse had already retreated to the far end of the barn. He knew his place and it wasn't with the white doctor who he knew wouldn't acknowledge him. Like Ruthie Jackson, Jesse's family was one of the few remaining black families who refused to be intimidated into leaving Purvis. So rather than stay by Ethan's side, Jesse put distance between himself and the doctor.

"Yeah, the boy might be the one who saved Ethan's life, although I wouldn't be making a point of telling folks." Doc Jones bestowed a rare compliment on the black teenager; however, with a quick glance at Dolores he went on to say, "Of course, none of this would have happened if people had done the right thing years ago."

Dolores knew exactly what the doctor meant. Doc Jones was one of many townspeople, including Pete, who thought she should have left Purvis years ago. Sending her daughters away to Montgomery was not enough; Dolores should have provided the same protection for Ethan. Instead, she had defiantly fought the townsfolk and continued to live across the tracks with Ruthie Jackson. Now her young son was paying for her decision.

Pete nervously asked, "How's it looking, Doc? Is he gonna make it?"

"He's been beaten pretty badly and he's lost a hell of a lot of blood. And I can see flesh protruding out of a deep wound in his thigh. I'll know more when I get him into surgery."

"What can I do to help, Doc?"

"Pete, I need you to apply pressure while I start an IV." The doctor turned to Dolores and said, "Mrs. Drake, it would sure help if you went outside and flagged the ambulance. It'll save us time if they know exactly where to find your boy." He nodded his head toward Jesse on the far side of the barn and added, "Take him with you."

Following instructions Dolores pulled herself away from Ethan, whose body was limp and unresponsive. She would do anything the doctor asked as long as it would help her son. "Come on, Jesse. Come outside with me," she called out.

The second that Dolores and Jesse were out of the barn, Doc Jones rushed to say, "Pete, we need to talk. I had a feeling something like this was gonna happen. Leroy and his men have been acting real strange this week. If I knew they were up to something, why didn't you?"

"What are you saying, Ed?"

"I'm not telling you how to run your business, but I'd start asking some hard-hitting questions. Get my drift?"

"Yeah, I hear ya, Ed. I won't let this one pass. I give you my word."

"We'll see, Pete. I'm sure that whoever did this to the boy is banking on your usual method of investigation."

"What the hell does that mean?"

"Hell, Pete, there are times that a hound dog could wrap up a case better than you. What I'm trying to say is that this time you might want to give it your all. Whether I agree or disagree with his mother's choice of residence, the boy didn't deserve this."

Pete was fired up and ready to defend his worth; however, the siren they had heard in the distance was now wailing at the barn door. The sense of urgency had resumed.

"Pete, you'll need to put out a call on the radio. He'll need blood…lots of blood. We have a couple of pints in the blood bank, but they'll have to be replenished."

"I'll donate, Doc," Pete said willingly.

"That's a start, but we'll need more, Pete." Doc Jones heard the drivers open the barn door. He yelled, "Get a move on, men. I want him in OR in thirty minutes!" When the drivers didn't respond as fast as he demanded, Doc Jones yelled again. "I said, move it!"

Dolores climbed into the ambulance and rode to Taber Hospital with the doctor and Ethan. Jesse went with the sheriff, who this time insisted that Jesse ride in the front with him. As he pulled in front of Jesse's house he said, "Jesse, I want you to go next door and tell Ruthie what happened. Tell her I'll keep her updated on Ethan's progress. Will you tell her that, Jesse?"

"Yes, sir, Sheriff," Jesse responded politely as he exited the patrol car. Jesse closed the door and then turned to face the sheriff. Ducking his head through the open window, he said, "Sheriff, I know you'll find the varmint who did this to Ethan. Ah, thanks for the ride, Sheriff."

On the way to the hospital Pete radioed for blood donors for Ethan. "I want you listeners out there to spread the word. Ethan Drake is hurt real bad. Doc Jones says he needs blood right away. No need in punishing the boy for something he never done. So all you churchgoing souls, I expect to see you at Taber. Ten-four."

Pete's plea fell on deaf ears; it turned out that he would be the sole donor. Whites refusing to aid Dolores's kin stayed clear, while the blacks who wanted to help didn't dare step inside a white hospital.

Pete, ready to part with a pint of his blood, was slumped in a chair in the vacant hallway of the hospital waiting for the nurse to call him in. But it was Doc Jones and not a nurse who approached him. "Pete, we need you in the operating room. You've got type O negative which makes you a universal donor. We don't have much time; we need to put your blood directly into Ethan's during surgery," Doc Jones said.

Pete was a bit apprehensive and asked a rapid succession of questions. "You can do that, Doc? Shouldn't he be receiving his mother's blood? Is this procedure safe?"

"Yeah, Pete, it's safe enough, it just takes a bit longer. Dolores's red cell blood count is too low; she's anemic. As for Thom Drake, I doubt he'd lift a finger for the boy. So I need you to put on this hospital gown and then lie down on the gurney straight away."

"Anything you say, Doc," he said nervously.

Pete disrobed and donned the flimsy cotton gown that tied in the back and barely covered his middle-age paunch. A minute later, the nurse came in and rolled him into the operating room. It was the first time Pete had seen the extent of Ethan's injuries. His face and body were covered with bruises and oozing red welts. His eyes, both blackened, had swelled beyond recognition. And there on his thigh was a large metal clamp that held together a gash that was more than eight inches long.

"Let's get started," Doc Jones announced.

Needles were inserted, first into Pete's arm and then into Ethan's. It intimidated Pete, but for the sake of Ethan, he did exactly what was asked of him. He was instructed to pump his fist and then release. Pump and release. It was a slow, monotonous process.

"The knife went in clean, but came out on an angle. It took a heap of meat with it," Doc Jones murmured to himself. "The kid's real lucky, though. It could have been his artery that got slashed. His thigh muscles are a mess, but they should heal."

"Doctor, his BP is dropping. Sixty over forty," said the intern, whose sole responsibility was monitoring blood pressure.

Doc Jones frantically sutured the thigh wound. He then pulled back the drape covering Ethan's upper body. He noticed a slight bulge to his abdomen that was not there upon his first examination.

"Doctor, his pulse rate is rapid, yet very faint," the intern said.

"Something else is going on in there," Doc said hurriedly. "I've got to get inside and find out."

Ethan, whose unconscious state was aided by anesthesia, was now hanging on by a thread. Doc Jones took the scalpel and made a new incision across his abdomen. He discovered that Ethan was bleeding internally from a ruptured spleen, the result of one of the many kicks he had received. Doc Jones clamped the torn tissue and prepared to remove the spleen. All the while he kept talking to Ethan as if he were wide-awake. "Come on, boy. You've got the strength. With your ma's headstrong will and your daddy's spit and hellfire, all you have to do is grab hold. I know you can make it."

"I don't think he can hear you, Doc," Pete said.

"He hears me all right. He just won't remember that he did."

Pete asked, "Doc, what did you find in there?"

"His spleen has been ruptured and I have to remove it. He has internal bleeding. Pete, I just can't fathom how horrendous the blow must have been to rupture his spleen."

"Can he live without his spleen?" Pete asked, sounding distressed.

"He can live a normal life after the splenectomy; however, he'll be more susceptible to infections." Doc Jones turned to the intern and nurses and declared, "I'm ready. Let's get this over with."

The following morning, Pete awoke in a private room of the hospital. He was finally free of the needle and fully aware of the tender and slightly discolored area on his arm. He scratched the sleep from his eyes and focused on the newspaper stashed at the end of his bed. The headlines read "SEVERELY BEATEN BOY LIVES." In smaller headlines it said, "SHERIFF PETE CORNELL A HERO." He picked it up, wondering how *Gannet* got the scoop so early. *This just happened last night and the Gannet Tribune already has it in the headlines.* Pete read on:

Last night eight-year-old Ethan Drake was found in Al Denton's barn; he had been severely beaten and stabbed. Sheriff Cornell and the victim's mother, Dolores Drake, searched the property and found the boy lying in a pool of his own blood. *No mention of Jesse,* he thought. Al Denton was in Mississippi visiting his sister. *Oh, that's where he's been.* Sheriff Cornell will begin his investigation as soon as he's released from the hospital. See article on HERO below.

"Okay, Sheriff, I see that you're finally awake. Here's your breakfast. I brought you some extra orange juice. You need it after last night," nurse Mabel said as she placed the tray on his table. "Have you read the newspaper? You're quite the hero today."

"Mabel, how is he? How's Ethan? And why am I still here?"

"You're here because you passed out. Maybe we took too much of your blood," she said certain they had not; she didn't want to embarrass him for fainting. "Doc Jones wanted you to rest up. He said you're gonna need it. As for the boy, the doc said he's gonna pull through, as long as there's no infection."

"That's a relief, Mabel," Pete sighed.

"I got to say that the poor kid is sure gonna suffer. Along with all the contusions, he's got five broken ribs. I don't think I've ever seen so many bruises on one little body. Sad sight, he is. Now eat your breakfast, Sheriff."

"No thanks, Mabel. I made a promise to myself last night. I gotta start working on this case. Gotta find out who did this. Is Ethan awake? I want to see him."

"You ain't leaving this bed until you drink your orange juice."

Pete huffed at the heavyset nurse and said, "You're one stubborn woman, Mabel." He downed the juice in one swallow.

"That's better. The boy is awake off and on. Doc's got him drugged to keep the pain at a minimum. But the way he moans, I don't know if any drug could help."

"What room is he in, Mabel?"

"He's in intensive care, Sheriff. That's where he'll be for quite some time."

Pete raced down the hall and pushed open the door that read "No Admittance." All of the beds, except one, were unoccupied, and that had its curtains drawn for privacy. Pete slid through the opening and found Dolores clutching Ethan's hand. He had tubes inserted into his nose and mouth. He was still receiving blood, but now it was from the glass bottle above his head, labeled "Red Cross." The blood dripping into Ethan's arm made Pete involuntarily rub his sore arm.

"Has he said anything yet? Anything at all, Dolores?"

"Hello, Pete," she said slowly. She hadn't slept in more than twenty-four hours. "No, nothing that makes any sense. Last night I thought he said something like 'Beeyay' or 'Bejay.' I don't know. He was probably just dreaming."

"Do you think he said 'BJ'?"

"I don't know, Pete. Maybe I was the one who was dreaming. Why do you ask? Do you know someone called BJ?"

"Not off hand, but you never know. I'm going to Coolidge Elementary today to talk with the children. In the meantime, if he wakes up, I want you to ask him if he knows who did this. Tell him not to be afraid because whoever is responsible is going down. I swear to it. I'm going to make sure that nothing like this ever happens again in these parts."

"Do you blame me, Pete? Do you blame me for staying with Ruthie?"

"What good would it do to place blame, Dolores? Besides, if anyone is pointing a finger, they could point it at me. I'm just as much to blame. I lost control of the town many years ago."

"Pete, I could never find fault with you. You helped my girls."

"And I failed your boy," he said remorsefully. "Dolores, what we're dealing with now is downright attempted murder. I've got to get to the bottom of this. Now you get some shut-eye. You're gonna need your strength."

Sheriff Pete began his investigation with the determination to pursue it until he saw justice done. While he had little to go on, the tip from Doc Jones, coupled with the initials BJ, gave him ample questions to ask. He headed straight to the barbershop to find some answers. As he walked through the barbershop door, the bells at the top chimed. Pete noticed that even though the shop was filled with customers, not one person was being served.

Sarcastically, Pete asked, "Can you squeeze me in, Leroy? I'm in dire need of a shave and a trim off the sides."

"Yes sir, Sheriff Pete. Looks like you ran out of the house this morning and forgot to razor that stubble," Leroy said gritting his crooked tobacco-stained teeth.

"I think we both know I didn't go home last night, Leroy. I was at the hospital giving blood, in case you hadn't noticed the gauze wrapped around my arm. I have a strong notion that the bandage caught your eye the moment I walked in."

Leroy cleared his throat and flipped the cotton drape over Pete. "I don't know what you're talking about, Sheriff," he uttered while resisting eye contact. Upon extracting the scissors from the drawer, Leroy caught sight of Pete's reflection in the mirror. Almost waxlike, the sheriff kept an unwavering grimace on his face, ultimately locking eyes with him. The gaze caused the lanky, six foot barber to push back his shoulders and straighten his spine.

"Is there a problem, Leroy?"

"Ah, no sir, Sheriff. Should there be?"

"Guess not," Pete answered with skepticism.

The sheriff rested back in the barber chair and used the mirror to scrutinize the fifteen customers, some standing, some sitting, who lined the wall. Each one, feigning the need for a haircut, duplicated Leroy's apprehension. They knew that as long as Pete Cornell was among them, their meeting to discuss the barn incident would have to be delayed.

Facing the row of customers, Pete bored his eyes into first one man and then the next. For once, they could feel the magnetic force of the law in Purvis. As if they were choreographed, each man lifted a newspaper to obstruct the sheriff's view. No one wanted to face him that morning. At least not before discussing alibis for their sons, whose overzealous acts had landed Ethan Drake in the ICU. However, the teenagers were not the only ones who needed alibis. Their fathers, who were now gathered at the barbershop, had given the orders. "Give him a couple black eyes. Kick him where it hurts. In other words, scare the hell out of him. Tell him that his nigger mama better sell her land. If she refuses, tell him he'll come home someday and find his house burned to the ground…with both mamas in it. The bottom line, boys? Put the fear of God in him!"

That was the plan orchestrated by the Elders and turned over to the teenagers who were more than willing to comply. But in an effort to prove their worthiness as future Klan members, the boys did more than slap Ethan Drake around. They beat him relentlessly until one blow was no longer distinguishable from the next.

These infractions went far beyond the instructions of the Elders. They knew that persecuting a WASP was forbidden by the "Neutrals." They were the townsfolk who were politically quiet, yet who were quick to forgive any methods used in coercing a Negro family to sell. That was until today. There would be no amnesty from the Neutrals for what they did to an innocent white boy.

✧ ✧ ✧

The pressure to oust the blacks came when the proprietors of Mackelroy Feed and Grain decided they wanted the rich land across the tracks. Although the plots of Ruthie Jackson's neighbors collectively equaled a mere three acres, she owned the mother lode with over one hundred acres. It was this prime earth that the Mackelroys needed for their company's expansion; a venture that lured investors from four surrounding counties.

Ruthie's situation was unique. With Dolores and Ethan living with her, she had been somewhat protected and the Mackelroy Company had been forced to make legitimate, although meager, offers. But to no avail, for not only did Ruthie decline their "pennies on the dollar offerings," her indignant refusals became downright embarrassing. So they made one final offer, upping their bid a few cents an acre. Still, Ruthie thumbed her nose at it, using the contract as kindling for a backyard bonfire. It was an inferno that signaled yet another rejection.

After weeks of failing to procure the property, the expansion of Mackelroy's had to be put on hold. Consequently, their near-term earnings had to be adjusted down, causing investors to bail out. This negative domino effect was the last straw for the Mackelroys. They requested the assistance of the Elders, whose clandestine persuasions would convince a targeted family to sign over a quitclaim deed. On rare occasions when a family refused to sign, they vanished into the night. No one knew if they willingly fled Purvis or if the powers-that-be had something to do with their disappearance. Either way, the moment the property was evacuated, the land was seized by the Mackelroys.

The threat-and-sign process rapidly changed the demographics on the east side of the tracks. One by one, the black families moved on. There was only a handful left when Mackelroys went up against Ruthie Jackson, but forcing her to sell was more difficult than anyone first thought.

It was one week prior to Halloween when the Elders held a roundtable meeting. It was there that one of the members came up with the idea of passing the Ruthie Jackson assignment over to their teenage sons. They thought the idea was brilliant, but they also had to admit that they were taken aback by the Elder who had proposed the scheme.

"I say we let the boys handle it. Have them work the Drake kid over. If it's done right, it ought to scare his bitch mother out of town. Then if the nigger doesn't follow suit, we'll deal with her properly after they've gone," Thom Drake declared.

Leroy, hunched over a chair, took a drag on his cigar.

"What do you say, Leroy? Don't you have a boy hankering to join up? I've heard he wants to run his own chapter someday."

"Yeah, he just might do that, Thom," Leroy said proudly. "But speaking on behalf of my Klan brothers, I am surprised that you would do that to your own blood. It is your boy we're talking about, right?" Leroy paused and waited for some type of reaction from Thom. He remained stone-faced.

"First of all, let me remind you, Leroy, that business is business. Second, it ain't my blood we're talking about. Don't know the bastard and don't care to. Now, let's get on with it. I've come back to Purvis for one reason only—to find out why your chapter has been slacking off. This town should have been clean by now. As for that Jackson nigger, she should be long gone. I spoke with the Mackelroy family and they told me they made their request months ago. What's the holdup, gents?"

"You know the rules, Thom. We can't touch a WASP, no matter what."

"Yeah, well, I say we bend the rules. Tell your boys to punch the bastard around. Make it look like a fistfight. Just make sure he has enough black-and-blues to bring home to his mommas," he smirked. "It's about time those bitches know what they're up against."

Drawing on his musty cigar, Leroy blew smoke rings as he pondered the idea. After the last ring floated through the air he said, "Okay, gentlemen, I agree with Thom. It's a go. We'll take the boys fishing tomorrow and let them know what's got to be done. They can take it from there."

"Now that's the kind of spirit I like to hear from a small chapter like this," Thom cheered.

"Then it's settled," Leroy said. "Halloween morn we'll all gather back at the barbershop to touch base and make sure that everything went as planned. Thom, will you be joining us?"

"Yeah, I can stick around another week. I'd like to hear that the boy went home bawling to his mommas. Hell, you never know. They might up and leave Purvis right then and there. Problem solved."

"You can count on my boy, Thom," Carl Logan spoke out, but as usual, no one paid heed to the farmer. Carl wasn't a leader, nor was he the first to follow. He was just a "do what you're told" kind of man, at least among his peers. It wasn't so in the confines of his home. There he was king over his domain, where his wife, son, and daughter catered to his every wish.

Carl repeated, "I said, Thom, you can count on my boy! He'll do the kid up right. Do ya hear me?"

"Yeah, yeah, Carl. Your boy," he laughed not expecting much results from an offspring of Carl Logan.

✧ ✧ ✧

Facing a lineup of fifteen *Gannet* newspapers, Pete took the hand mirror and inspected the back of his shaven neck. "Looks good, Leroy. Here's four bits," he said as he tossed two quarters on a tarnished tray. "I've got to get going. I've got to find out who bloodied Ethan Drake," Sheriff Pete said.

"Sure thing, Sheriff. See ya next week. Oh, Sheriff, I'll spring for your next trim."

Pete was nearing the door when he pivoted to face the barber; his face bore the same steadfast grin. "Yeah? Why's that, Leroy? I've been coming here for more than a decade and I can't recall a time you ever gave a cut for free. Why now?"

Pete returned to the center of the shop and hovered over the empty barber's chair He gave it a swift spin, startling the men camouflaged behind the *Gannet* newspapers. Each one slowly lowered his paper and peered over the top.

"You know, as long as I'm here, I might as well ask some questions," the sheriff said, not admitting that he had had no intention of leaving. He slammed his fist on the spinning stool, halting its motion. It was an attention-getter. Leroy, like every man against the wall, felt the hair on the back of his neck rise. Their chance to prepare for a community alibi was gone.

The sheriff reached inside his jacket and removed a ballpoint pen and notepad. He clicked the pen open and closed, open and closed, open and closed. Everyone held his breath, not wanting to be first to be questioned.

"Should I start with you, Leroy?" He paused and then toyed with the rest of the group. "Perhaps you should be first, Carl. Or maybe I should be talking with Adam, Ned, or Bart." He pointed to the center and baited them, "What about you, Jeb? Well, I want you all to know that unlike the half-ass inquiries I may have done in the past, this one's going to be investigated inside and out. I'm going to find out who's responsible for what happened to Dolores Drake's boy, come hell or high water. You can mark my words, someone's gonna do time for this one."

"Do your asking, Sheriff, we got nothing to hide," Leroy declared adamantly.

"That's good to hear. So, Carl, when was the last time you were out at Denton's farm?"

Carl, Sheriff Pete's first choice, nervously stirred in his seat before he answered. "I guess about three or four weeks ago, Sheriff. He's been out of town for the last couple weeks." As if his response warranted a notation, Pete scribbled something on his pad.

"Carl, did Al Denton tell you he was going out of town or did you read it in the *Gannet* this morning?"

"Well, ah, kind of both. The *Gannet* only reminded me he was out of town." Again, Pete jotted two more pages of notes. With each stroke of the pen, the tension in the room escalated. No one could figure out what he was extracting from the brief answers to his simple questions.

"Mr. Jeb Gannet. First of all, thanks for the write-up on me. I've never been called a hero before. I appreciate the kudos!"

"Well, Sheriff, you deserve the recognition. Few people would donate blood to the likes of that boy."

"Oh, that's where you're wrong, Jeb. Every last person across the tracks would have been willing to help the boy, given the chance."

"Now that's where you're right, Sheriff. I'm sure the coloreds were itching to pump their blood into a white. For the rest of us, we aren't going to pollute our stock to a kid who been raised by one of them!"

"It didn't hurt me none," Pete declared. "I just got to thinking, Jeb. How did you manage to scoop the story and get it printed by this morning's paper? It was almost like you already knew what was going to happen. You've sure got one helluva nose for the news," Sheriff Pete said suspiciously.

"That's what a good reporter does, Sheriff. You get wind of a story and then you run with it. Of course, I can't reveal my sources," Jeb answered smugly.

The sheriff scrawled notes on page after page. Occasionally he paused before continuing his interrogation. "So, Ned, can you tell me if Al Denton sold his prize bull last month?"

"I don't know, Sheriff. How could anyone pass up an offer like that? I know I wouldn't!"

"I have to agree with you there, Ned. The bull is worth his weight in gold." Pete's notepad doubled in size with the ink-printed pages. Laughing out loud he said, "Good thing I brought a few more of these here notepads, because I wouldn't want to miss anything. You men are really helping me with the investigation."

What on earth is he writing about? Nobody's said anything that's noteworthy, Leroy thought.

The interrogation lasted more than an hour with elementary questions about Al Denton, his barn, the bull, and the hay bale. It appeared as though Sheriff Pete had finished with them when the bell chimed again from the opening door.

"Sorry, I'm late," Thom Drake said upon opening the barbershop door. "How did it go last night?"

The newspapers flew up once again shielding the fraternity. Without a similar camouflage, Leroy made an about-face. It left Sheriff Pete staring directly at Drake.

"How did what go last night, Thom? Do you care to expand on that?"

Without flinching Thom responded, "If it ain't Pete Cornell! It's been a long time, Sheriff."

"Yeah, the last time I saw you was two years ago, Thom. You were doing some preaching on the school grounds and damned near caused a riot. As I recollect, your mouth landed you behind bars."

"Sheriff, I calls it as I sees it," he answered in defiance.

"So, Thom, where you been keeping yourself?"

"Don't see that's any of your damn business," he said as he spat on the floor.

"Speaking of last night, Thom, you might want to know that your boy got beat up pretty bad last night," Sheriff Pete said as he waited for Thom's reaction.

Thom took two steps closer to Pete and stabbed his index finger into Pete's chest. "Let's get something straight, Sheriff. I fathered two daughters. You know, I can't rightly say where they are right now. But I'm telling you once and for all, I ain't got a son. If you're referring to that scrawny tow-headed kid, he ain't no relation to me. Best I know, he's the bastard of the fucking bitch I used to be married to. Enough said. Now, do we have an understanding, Sheriff?"

"Back off, Thom," Pete said as he squeezed Thom's finger, bending it backwards.

Thom squirmed before he could jerk his finger away. He tightly clenched his fists and prepared to strike back, but Leroy, fending off the altercation, put himself between the two. Laughing he said, "Hey, hey, hey, men. There's no need for this." He pulled a hot towel from the steamer. "Sit down, Thom," Leroy said, gently forcing Thom into a vacant barber's chair.

"We know who the boss around here is, don't we Thom?" Pete grinned, irritating him even more.

"What the fuck do you want, Sheriff?"

"I have just a couple questions for you, being that the boy's last name is Drake."

Pete fanned the contents of the first pad in front of him. "Wow. Looks like I'm out of space in this one." He pulled out two more and flaunted the pages of scribbles. "No room in these either. I sure can't thank you all enough for your help with my investigation, but it looks like I'm plum out of paper. Thom, I'd appreciate it if you'd come back to my office. It won't take long."

"Whatever you say, Sheriff," Thom said pretending to be amicable. "I'll stop by after I get a shave and a cut."

"It's important that I talk with you right now. By the looks of this place, Leroy has his hands full with a dozen or so ahead of you. It seems like everyone needs a bit of grooming today."

"Ah, Thom made an appointment with me, Pete," Leroy interjected. "Everyone else is on a drop-in basis. I can send him over to you in twenty."

Sternly, Pete repeated himself. "Like I said, I'd like to talk with him now. You got a problem with that, Leroy?"

Leroy was caught in the middle, to either accommodate the sheriff's request or brief Thom, which was far more important. However, Leroy was in no position to rile the sheriff. Reluctantly he agreed. "Thom, go with Pete. I'll fill…I mean I'll fit you in as soon as you return."

While Leroy was bargaining with Sheriff Pete, Thom kept eyeing the notepads. *What did those sons of bitches tell him? Did they betray the sacred trust of the members? When I find out who did the talking, there's going to be hell to pay!*

With every thought of treachery, the red color of Thom's face deepened its hue. To him there was nothing worse than showing your hand to the law. He wondered who had been the backstabber.

"Okay, Sheriff. Lead the way. This better not take long," he grumbled.

"It shouldn't take but a few minutes, Thom," the sheriff said coolly.

The moment they left, Leroy motioned for the rest of the men to exit out the back. "I think we need to split up for now."

"Yeah, Leroy. Looks like the sheriff is onto something," Jeb stated.

"It's not the sheriff I'm worried about. It's Thom Drake. None of you saw the look on his face. But I did. He thinks that we ratted."

"Nobody said nothing, Leroy. It was just Sheriff Pete asking stupid questions—pretty much par for the course," Jeb said reassuringly.

"But Thom doesn't know that!" Leroy closed his eyes and shook his head. He imagined the repercussions. "The last thing we need is someone of Thom's rank putting the finger on us. Know what I mean?"

They knew exactly what he meant. When Thom left Purvis two years ago, he planned to be gone only until things calmed down. However, shortly after he had arrived in Birmingham he had located one of the largest KKK chapters in the South and decided to move lock, stock, and barrel for the cause. Starting out as a grunt, he worked his way up through the ranks. Ultimately he reached a level that earned him respect from every Klan member—even Leroy.

In a way, it was ironic. Of all the jobs Thomas Drake held in his lifetime, none was more suited to him than this. All it took was his strong racial hatred. It was the one trait that Thomas Drake never concealed from anyone.

"Okay. I want everyone out of here, except Jeb. You stick around. We need to discuss tomorrow's *Gannet* before the Neutrals start asking questions of their own," Leroy ordered.

"Good idea," Jeb concurred, stepping back into the shop.

"Leroy, what about me? It's my boy Bob we have to protect. It was his knife and all," Carl Logan stuttered, as Leroy shoved him outside.

"Yeah, it was his knife and all. But who the fuck told him to bring a knife in the first place? I don't recall that being part of the plan, Carl!"

Leroy didn't wait for Carl's defense. Instead with one final push, he slammed the door in his face and turned the deadbolt. It kept Carl from reentering, although he tried several times.

"You have any suggestions, Jeb?" Leroy asked nervously.

"As soon as the sheriff is done questioning him, we need to cover our bases with Thom. I think you need to pay him a visit at the motel. In the meantime, I'll write an angle on the original story. I'll mention that boys will be boys. Fistfights happen all the time. Shit like that."

"Okay, Jeb. We have no choice. To be honest, I wish you had never printed it at all."

"Leroy, if I didn't print something, Sheriff Pete might have gotten suspicious."

"Like he's not already? The kid's in the hospital for Christ's sake. It's only a matter of time before the Neutrals come snooping around. If that ain't enough, we've just pissed off Thom Drake. We're in a bad spot, Jeb."

Pete unlocked the door and both he and Thom walked into his office. Pointing to a straight-backed wooden chair, Pete said, "Have a seat, Thom."

Thom shook a Cuban cigar from a metal container. He flicked his lighter several times before it finally ignited. Leaning back, he inhaled before belching out a long tail of smoke.

"Wherever you've been, Thom, you must be doing all right for yourself. That's one expensive weed you've got there."

Thom was relaxed and seemed to be enjoying his exchange with Sheriff Pete. The insolence Thom had displayed minutes before had disappeared. Even the color of his cheeks had faded from red to their natural flesh tone. He was almost too relaxed for the sheriff's taste.

"Okay, Sheriff, what do you want from me? I thought you got everything you need from the goddamn double-cro…" He was about to say "double-crossers" but he stopped short, realizing it was a poor choice of words. Pete got the drift anyway.

"Thom, can you tell me what you know about the incident in Al Denton's barn?"

"I heard that some of the boys got into a fight. The runt kid got a couple of black eyes."

"Um-hmm. So do you know who was involved? Say, for example, were there any out-of-towners involved or just a few of the locals?"

Thom was positive that the barbershop brood had already divulged the information. He resented Pete for asking and narrowed his eyes in contempt. "It was the local boys, but you already knew that, didn't you, Sheriff?"

When Pete ignored his piercing expression, Thom resorted to theatrics. Forcing the last plume of smoke from his lungs, he slowly blew it into the sheriff's face. Again, Pete disregarded the feeble insult and welcomed the discarded smoke into his own lungs.

"Yep, that's some fine weed you got there, Thom. And you're absolutely right, Thom, I already learned that the local boys were involved," Pete lied, as it wasn't until he tricked Thomas Drake that he had a confirmation.

"Well, Thom, that's all I need today. I've got a shitload of paperwork to go through. Everyone has been so helpful. I sure do appreciate it when ya'all cooperate with the law."

Thom was infuriated and the crimson shade of his cheeks resurfaced. Certain he was betrayed, droplets of sweat ran down from his hairline. He used the salty liquid to slick back the oily strands of his graying hair.

"Well, between you and the men at Leroy's, I've got everything I need right now. If I have any other questions, I'll stop by your motel."

"So, that's it, Sheriff? Cuz I didn't say much of anything. I was wondering, though, what exactly did you hear at Leroy's?"

"It wouldn't be right, repeating their statements, Thom. You know, it's all part of the investigation," he teased.

Thom grunted but managed to keep his composure. "Guess I'll be on my way."

From the window Pete watched him head straight back to Leroy's barbershop. "Looks like I put enough bait on the line," Pete chuckled out loud. "Yep, from here the fishing looks pretty damn good today!"

Pete wasted no time in transferring his notes into a manila folder labeled "Drake Assault/October 30, 1958." Ignoring the scribble he had written to intimidate the group at Leroy's, he placed asterisks alongside three key points. The first was BJ. That was the only clue from the victim himself. The second was "local boys," which would narrow the search. Third was the reference to "double-crossers." It was Thom Drake's slip of the tongue that supported the doc's allegations.

At Coolidge Elementary, Pete started with the children that were Ethan's age, although he doubted that a crime of this magnitude was committed by any eight- or nine-year-old. Still, he was more likely to get information from the younger kids than he would from the boys at Grant High.

Pete headed straight to Ethan's third grade class. As always, whenever the sheriff came to visit them, the children stood up respectfully. Ordinarily, he would have told them a knock-knock joke. Sheriff Pete wasn't in a joking mood today.

"Sit down, children. I haven't come for a social call. I need to talk to you." They obediently nestled back into their desks.

"Do you know why Ethan Drake isn't at school today?"

As he looked around the room, the children did the same. They were looking for someone who knew the answer to the question. In unison they said aloud, yet slowly, "No, Sheriff."

"Nobody, huh?" Again he perused the room, but their blank expressions reaffirmed his original conclusion. These children were not involved.

"Well, that's all I need for now. You kids get on with your work. If any of you hear something about Ethan, let me know. You might be a hero of sorts."

As he turned to leave, Carl Logan's daughter removed her finger from her nose and stood up. A shy child who was twenty pounds overweight, she rarely spoke to avoid drawing attention to herself. However, she was the only one who knew something, so it made her feel proud.

"I don't know what happened to Ethan, but my big brother does," she boasted.

"And why do you say that?"

"Cuz I heard him talking this morning with the other big boys. I heard them say Ethan was in the hospital. My big brother is in high school. If you go over there, he'll tell you all about it."

"Yeah, I know your brother. His name is Bob, right?"

"Not anymore. The big kids call him BJ for Bob John. That's his secret name. I don't think he'd mind if you called him that, Sheriff."

"If it's his secret name, I won't mention that you told me. That goes for the rest of you, okay? Today you are my junior deputies. So anything we've said in this classroom needs to stay in this classroom. Okay?"

"Okay, Sheriff," they shouted.

"Mum's the word," he reiterated with his finger pressed to his lips. "I'll see you kids later."

"Out of the mouths of babes," Pete said to himself as he climbed into his patrol car and drove back to his office. *BJ. Carl Logan's kid, Bob. It was staring me right in the face. But I'm not going to arrest him just yet. I need to find out who was the mastermind behind this crime.*

Just as Pete turned on Main Street, he caught sight of a mob of townsfolk attempting to squeeze into Leroy's barbershop. *It didn't take them long to reconvene,* he thought. *They must have called another meeting.*

"Sheriff, get over here quick," Jeb called out.

Pete pulled on his hand brake and stopped the patrol car in the middle of the street. If it was a meeting, he was surprised to be invited.

"Blood everywhere, Sheriff. Leroy and Thom. It's a mess, Sheriff."

Pete pushed aside the crowd to find the scene just as Jeb Gannet described. The mirror he gazed into earlier was splattered with chunks of flesh and murky with blood. Adjacent to the mirror was Leroy, who had collapsed at the foot of the leather chair. His eyes, permanently wide open, reflected the terror he had felt before he died. Pete bent down to examine him. In the middle of Leroy's forehead was a single bullet hole—a clean shot that had tunneled its way through his skull, leaving remnants of his brain on the wall behind him. Pete gasped at the sight. Even though he had seen combat wounds in France during the war, there was nothing that could have prepared him for the carnage he was now witnessing. "Everybody get the hell out of here," he yelled. "Jeb, call the morgue."

Pete then stepped over Leroy's body to inspect the corpse of Thomas Drake. He was lying facedown in a pool of his own bodily fluids. The holes in his jacket revealed four shots that penetrated his back and lodged in his chest. Although the first bullet had hit its target, three additional ones had been fired. It was a guarantee that Thomas Drake's heart would never beat again.

Pete then stooped down next to the still body of Ruthie Jackson who was lying face up near the entrance. Ruthie had kept her incurable bone cancer a secret. She knew her days were numbered; yet she was defiant to the end when she limped from her home across the tracks to confront her enemies. Ruthie was determined not to surrender her life to the likes of the Mackelroys. She chose, instead, to end it as judge, jury, and executioner.

Pete pulled a handkerchief from his pocket and removed the pistol that Ruthie still clenched in her hand. The six-shot cylinder was empty—five bullets had taken the lives of Leroy and Thom. The sixth and final bullet Ruthie had saved for herself. It had been expelled into the roof of her mouth. Her death had come within seconds of the other two.

✧ ✧ ✧

As Pete escorted Dolores Drake from the real-estate office he asked, "Well, Dolores, what are you going to do with all that money? That sure is a lot of dough!"

"Yes, it is. I still wonder what Ruthie would think. Selling her property after everything she went through to hang on to it."

"You did it the way she would have wanted. It's one thing when the Mackelroys offered Ruthie a pittance for her land. It's a whole different thing when there's a bidding war between two multimillion dollar companies. The clincher is that the Mackelroys still lost out. Yeah, I think Ruthie would be pretty happy with the outcome."

"Pete, how long had you known about her will?"

"From the day she asked me to be a witness—a few days after you left the garment factory. She said it took guts for you to stand up to them. She said she hoped the day would come when she could do the same. I guess she got her wish."

"I miss her, Pete," Dolores said warmly. "She would have been proud of you and all that you've done to improve Purvis."

"I've still got a long way to go, Dolores. Did you hear about young BJ Logan? He got sentenced to two years in juvenile hall. The others got off with probation until they turn eighteen."

"That's not much time considering what they did to my boy. What about their fathers? They all had a hand in this."

"It's hard to prove, Dolores. Besides, Ruthie stopped them in their tracks with Leroy and Thom. And now there aren't any leaders."

Dolores sighed, "Still, I often wonder why she had to go and do it."

"I think she wanted to put an end to the virus that was infecting our town. I'll never agree with what she did, but you have to admit that there's been a change around here for the better. I just heard the local Klan chapter has been dissolved. It must have been due to all the interrogations."

"You never know, Pete. I may regret not living in Purvis."

"What do you mean? After all this, you're not thinking of leaving now, are you?"

"That's exactly what Ethan and I are going to do. First we're going to Montgomery to see my girls. You know, Sonya is getting married soon and I'm sure that Brenda won't be far behind. I'm going to share some of the money with them and then I'm going to use a portion to buy a home somewhere on the West coast. I was thinking of Los Angeles."

"But there's enough money for you to build a mansion here. Won't you reconsider?"

"No, Pete, we need a fresh start. I want to bring up Ethan in a place where life is not as segregated, where whites and Negroes are civil to one another. I want to enroll Ethan in a school where they don't care about the color of your skin."

"It's hard to imagine a place like that," Pete said.

"Trust me, Pete, places like that do exist. Anyway, the doctor said Ethan is well enough to go back to school as long as he stays clear of sports. He can't risk getting an infection, you know. But nevertheless, I wouldn't consider sending him back to Coolidge or any other school around these parts. Word travels fast and I wouldn't want a replay of the events of the last year."

"My hat goes off to you, Dolores. You've demonstrated you are a strong-willed woman and I respect you for that. Good luck to you."

Dolores hugged the sheriff before she gave him a kiss on the cheek. "Thank you for everything. Good-bye, Pete."

"Good-bye, Dolores. And may Godspeed."

twelve

THE CHILDREN

May–September, 1963

Thirteen-year-old Billy scurried down the hall of Cleveland Convalescent Home, tipping his baseball cap to the nurses as he passed. His destination, as it was every Saturday, was Ward A, where his most beloved companion was housed with three other patients.

"I'm here, Sam. Billy boy is here."

Sam opened his eyes and with a great deal of effort tried to smile. As always, it was a futile attempt; his lips simply refused the request. His eyes, however, welled up with emotions. His son, if only by proxy, was kneeling beside him.

That was the extent of Sam Donahue's ability to communicate since suffering a massive stroke ten months earlier. A second, recent blood clot in his brain had not only cost him his speech, but had left him without the use of his limbs. Sam was paralyzed on both sides of his body.

Billy took Sam's limp hand into his own and gave it a squeeze. Sam could not tell Billy that he couldn't feel his touch, but it didn't matter. Sam's eyes were enough to convey his appreciation. "I prayed for you extra hard this week, Sam. You're going to get better."

Tears cascaded down Sam's pallid cheeks that once boasted a rosy hue. Over the past few months, his complexion had deteriorated to a lifeless shade of gray. It was obvious to everyone except Billy that the once robust Irishman was failing by the minute.

"I have a lot to tell you today, Sam. So I want you to listen real good. Okay?"

Billy never expected Sam to answer, but out of respect for him, Billy spoke as if he could. There was no handicap between Billy and Sam's relationship, just a pure bond between a boy and the closest thing he had to a real father.

Billy began, "I remember when I was a sprout and you used to read to me until I fell asleep. Remember, Sam? Remember the days back at the club? Mom used to sing out front, and you and me, well, we'd be backstage telling tales. Those were the days, huh, Sam! Oh, and remember when you taught me to fly-fish? I was only five, but you taught me real good."

Sam lowered his eyes and fell into a comforting memory. He pictured driving over to Sarah's to take her and Billy to church. He remembered the afternoon picnics, the laughter, and the family love between them. Then Sam's face suddenly soured. He remembered the nightmare of Jack Stratton. Again, Billy understood what he was thinking.

"Don't fret about him, Sam. That's what I want to tell you."

Sam wasn't ready to hear any news about his nemesis. Since he had no way of preventing it, the most he could do was delay the news a minute or two. Sam smacked his lips together signaling that he wanted a drink of water. Billy obliged him and inserted the paper straw into his mouth.

Sam slurped a few swallows as best he could, but most of it dribbled down his chin. Whether he was frustrated or had just had enough, he turned his head away when he was finished.

"You've had enough, huh, Sam?" Billy said while using the bib liner to blot the drool.

"Okay, first things first, Sam. I want to apologize again for Mom not coming to see you. She still can't forgive herself because of you-know-who…and how he swindled you out of the club."

A last lingering tear fell from Sam's eye to his chin. It hurt him more to know that Sarah was still punishing herself, because there was no need. He had settled his score with her many moons ago and had forgiven her for everything: the club, their disagreements, and that she had married Jack Stratton. The fact was, paralyzed or not, Sam was still in love with Sarah.

"She'll come one day, sooner than you think." It was Billy's way of keeping hope alive. "Sam, please listen to me. Two months ago Jack Stratton left Mom. I know that sounds like good news, and it is, but there's more I have to tell you."

Although Jack Stratton had left his mother, Billy avoided telling Sam that she had reverted to drinking every night. Rarely was there a morning that she didn't lace her coffee with the previous night's liquor-of-choice. The alcohol caused her to vomit frequently; her skin had turned to a rancid shade of yellow. Sarah was sick, and this time it wasn't a simple hangover. Billy had become his mother's caretaker.

"Anyway, Sam, I waited for you to feel better before I told you about Jack. Besides, I wanted to be extra sure that he wasn't coming back."

Sam's eyes flew open, wider than they had in weeks. Like a shot of adrenaline, he felt life surge through his body. Perhaps by some miracle, if he could recover, then the three of them could be together again like the old days. They would go on a Sunday picnic on the lake and he and Billy would try and catch the monster bass he'd been fishing for all his life. Sam felt optimistic for a brief moment until Billy pressed on.

"We were right about him, Sam. Remember last year when you got real sick and Jack sold Donahue's?"

Although his body was unable to move and he was unable to speak, Sam's mind was intact. There were things from the last seven years that he remembered all-too well. When Stratton married Sarah, who by then owned fifty-percent interest in the club, she signed her share over to her husband and Stratton had legally become a full partner. After Sam had suffered the second stroke a year ago, Stratton wasted no time in putting Donahue's up for sale. It sold in less time than it took Sam to make the first renovation to the never-realized smorgasbord.

"Anyway, Sam, when Jack sold the club he got a bunch of money. He swore that he would put one-half in the bank for you and he was gonna keep the other half for Mom and him." Billy shook his head back and forth and said, "You probably already figured out that he didn't do that."

Billy didn't wait for Sam to ask for more water. Instead, he placed the straw back into his mouth and paused until he took another drink. "Take a sip, Sam."

Sam took a quick drink and then forced the straw out of his mouth with his tongue. He wanted Billy to continue.

"It all happened in March. Jack didn't come home until four in the morning and boy was Mom mad. She wanted to know where he had been all night, but he wouldn't tell her. She screamed at him, but he never said one thing back to her. That was weird cuz usually he'd be calling her all sorts of names, only all he did was pack his clothes. The next thing we knew, he was gone. That's when the crying started. Boy, oh, boy, I didn't know that Mom could cry that much." Billy stopped and helped fluff up Sam's pillow. "There that's better," Billy said and then continued. "I was glad he was gone. I hated him and I hate him for how he hurt Mom. Anyway, Mom didn't even think to check the bank account for a couple of weeks. Sure enough, he had cleaned it all out—your money, Mom's money—Jack took it all. He couldn't take Mom's house, though. She never put it in his name," Billy grinned briefly.

Billy reached for a tissue and wiped the saliva dripping from Sam's mouth. He said, "Last week Mom got a letter from Jack. He didn't say where he was, but the return address read 'Los Angeles, California.' He told her that he was filing for divorce and wanted it finalized as soon as possible." Billy stopped short of telling Sam that his mom hadn't been off the bottle since. He only admitted, "The letter came at a bad time because Mom hasn't been feeling good lately. She called in sick every day this week."

Sam, whose eyes darted back and forth, appeared confused. Billy picked up on the cue and elaborated. "Remember, Sam? Mom got a job at the phone company after Stratton sold the club. She's an operator and works on one of those big 320 switchboards."

Sam turned his head aside. He tried to remember Sarah doing something other than working at the club, but he couldn't. All he could see was her onstage in a full-length gown captivating a loyal audience. It was a consoling memory for him.

"So now I have to tell you something really important, Sam. It's killing me," he said with tears in his eyes. Billy took a deep breath and straightened his baseball cap. His somber look frightened Sam.

"Here goes," Billy swallowed. "Mom put the house up for sale yesterday. She said she wants to move to California, too. She wants to find him. For what? I don't know. Here, take another sip."

Sam lowered his eyes and focused on the blanket that was draped over him. He realized there would be no more weekly visits with Billy nor was there any hope of seeing Sarah again. Paralyzed and condemned to his hospital bed, Sam felt there was nothing left to live for.

"Sam, I've got to get going," Billy said emotionally. "I'll be back next Saturday and just maybe I can talk Mom into coming. See you next week, Sam," he said as he trudged out the door.

The following Saturday Billy showed up as usual, but before he made it to Ward A, one of the nurses stopped him at the elevator. "I'm sure the men would love to see you today, Billy. Before you go in, there's something you should know."

His voice cracked with apprehension. "What is it? Is Sam all right?"

"I'm very sorry, Billy, but Mr. Donahue passed away in his sleep last night."

In disbelief Billy fell to his knees crying, "NO, not Sam! It can't be Sam, please," he begged as he tugged at the nurse's uniform. "Not Sam." The shrill cry of his pain echoed throughout the hospital corridors. Everyone knew then that Billy's best friend had died.

✧ ✧ ✧

The August heat beat down on Billy as he jumped off the trailer and propped up the tailgate to secure their belongings. The trailer was fully loaded and difficult to lock, although he managed, just as he managed to pack everything without the help of his mother. The evening before, she had drunk herself into oblivion and had passed out next to the floor radiator. Sarah had become a useless human being.

"Please wake up, Mom. Everything is ready to go. I backed the car up and attached it to the trailer hitch," he boasted.

"You're not old enough to be driving," she mumbled.

Billy bent down and lifted her off the floor. Her body was a deadweight. "Let me help you. Hey, that was some going-away party you had last night. Fran stuck around and helped me clean up."

"God, I don't remember saying good-bye to Fran. She has been such a wonderful friend," she muttered, her foul breath wafting over Ethan.

"You did, Mom. Over and over, you told her good-bye. That was some crying jag you two were on!"

Sarah had very little recollection of the night before. She remembered her friends walking through the door early in the evening, but then she remembered nothing else until waking up just a few minutes ago. The entire party was a blur to her.

"Did I ever tell you that Fran and I became friends the day after you were born? She was the nurse that took care of me in the hospital. Anyway, when I gave birth to you, I gave people a reason to talk; however, beautiful Fran gave them a reason to understand."

Billy had heard the story many times, usually when Sarah was having bouts of guilt after a night of bingeing. "I already know the details, Mom. I'm a bastard!"

"Billy, don't you ever let me hear you say that again! You always had Sam, and Jack for that matter, even though the two of you never saw eye to eye. I don't ever want you to forget that," she lightly scolded.

"Yes, ma'am."

"Now would you pour me a glass of orange juice because I need a screwdriver for the road."

"Sorry, Mom, but the realtor told us to clean out the fridge for the new owners. Fran helped me do it last night."

Referring to the liquor bottles stored on the top shelf, she added, "Did you throw everything out?"

"It's all gone, Mom. Down the sink," he said happily.

"I figured as much," she groaned as she staggered into the bathroom. "I'll be out in a minute."

Sarah sat on the edge of the bathtub and faced the beckoning commode. Without the hair of the dog, she knew that the sudden alcohol withdrawal would be gut-wrenching. To hasten the inevitable, she stuck a finger down her throat until she gagged and vomited. This grueling ordeal lasted over twenty minutes. When there was no liquid left to regurgitate, Sarah slowly pulled herself up to face a strong dose of reality. The medicine cabinet mirror reflected her image and was merciless. From flaky day-old pancake makeup to smeared mascara, she was a disgusting sight.

"I've got to do better than this," she vowed. She turned on the faucet and using the last of a roll of toilet paper rubbed off the remnants of makeup. When she was finished and looked almost presentable, she went into the barren living room and found Billy sitting on the floor. He had been staring at an old picture of Sam standing proudly with a prize catfish. When Billy saw his mom, he quickly stashed it into his shirt pocket.

"Let's get out of here, Billy," she said taking one last glance at her Aunt Gertrude's house. "There's nothing for us in Cleveland anymore."

Consumed with bittersweet memories, Sarah and Billy were quiet as they drove away. On the outskirts of town they turned onto the route that took them past the place where Donahue's had once thrived. Shortly after the club had been sold, the owners had leveled the structure and had replaced it with a store that sold everything from groceries to clothing to gardening tools. The one place that was synonymous with Sam was Donahue's. It was heartbreaking to know that now there was no Donahue's and there was no Sam.

Sarah, filled with emotions, made a U-turn and took a detour. She backtracked a few blocks and stopped in front of the cemetery where Sam was laid to rest. "Show me where Sam is, Billy. I want to say a few things to Sam before we go."

Billy knew the location of Sam's final resting place. He had replaced his Saturday visits at the convalescent home with weekly visits to Sam's gravesite. When he exited the car, Billy rushed ahead of Sarah and knelt down. He used his handkerchief to wipe the dust from the headstone and then brushed away the wilted petals from the roses he had left the day before.

"If I had known that I was coming today, Sam, I would have brought you more flowers. The seeds I planted last week should start sprouting out any day now. Well, Sam, like I told you, the day would come when Mom would visit. She's here today, Sam. She has something to say to you," he said, as if his friend could hear him.

Sarah reached the edge of his grave and tried to smile. "We came a long way, partner, didn't we! Oh, Sam," she sighed. "Do I apologize for not coming to see you at the hospital? Do I explain why I didn't go to the funeral? No, I guess not," she said bowing her head. "It wouldn't do any good now."

Billy looked up at his mother and saw that she was truly sorry. Many times she had said the word before, but this time he knew she meant it. "Mom, should I wait for you in the car? I said good-bye to Sam yesterday," Billy offered.

"No, son, stay right here. You've been by my side when I was at my worst. I'd like you to be here when I try and redeem myself, even if it's a little late."

"Sam would have said that it's never too late," he said, reminding her of one of Sam's clichés.

Sarah bent down next to Billy and took hold of his hand. "Sam, if you can hear me…"

"He can!" Billy interrupted her.

Sarah smiled and continued, "Billy has assured me, Sam, that you can hear me. So here goes. Sam, I wish I could turn back the clock to the day I met you. I wish we could have figured out a way to take our friendship to the next level. Perhaps then things would have been different. There would have been no Jack and maybe, just maybe, you would still be on this earth with Billy and me. I am terribly sorry for the mistakes I made and what it cost you. Please, Sam, forgive me."

Sarah paused as a gentle breeze stirred the air. It transported three oak leaves that landed on Sam's gravesite. She picked them up and touched them to her face. "I miss you, Sam. You will always be in my heart."

She stood up, adding, "I know that I've broken promises to you in the past. This time it will be different." She looked at Billy and repeated, "This time it will be different. Let's go, son."

As they drove off from the cemetery, a warm and consoling feeling suddenly overcame them. It was as if Sam's Irish spirit had hitchhiked along for the ride to California. It made Billy smile. It made Sarah take a hard look at herself. For her, there was much work to be done, starting with sobriety.

◇ ◇ ◇

Billy scratched another day off his NBT—no booze today—calendar. Including the week-long move across country plus the twelve days boarding in a Santa Monica motel, his mother had not indulged, although the temptation was always there. There wasn't a moment a bottle didn't call out to her, but Sarah refused to give in. She was determined to feel good again, as good as she did after Billy was born and before Jack Stratton stepped into her life.

"Guess what, son? I got a job at General Telephone. I'm going to be an operator and because of my past experience, they are starting me at a higher pay level. With the money I got from the house and a few months on the job, I should be able to qualify for a home of our own real soon. I figure we'll only be moteling it for a couple months longer."

"I knew you could do it, Mom," Billy said supportively.

"Well, I have to pass a physical next week, but it's just a formality. It's to make sure that you don't have something contagious, like TB. Hey, do you want to go to the department store with me? I need to buy your school clothes," Sarah said enthusiastically.

"I guess. I'll go, if you want me to," he reluctantly agreed.

"I get the impression it's not the way you want to spend your last Saturday before school begins. Am I right?"

"Well," he paused. "I was hoping I could go to the beach today."

"Then I want you to go and try and make a new friend today. Someone you can walk to school with."

Billy nodded, but only to please her. Deep inside he didn't have the know-how to meet someone his own age. He was a loner. Stemming from his lifelong relationship with Sam Donahue, his comfort level resided with adults.

After he changed into a pair of shorts and tee shirt, Billy headed down toward the beach. It was a warm morning and temperatures were predicted to be in the high eighties by early afternoon. So he took off his shirt and tied it around his head. It was just enough to keep the sun from beating down on his curly black locks. In doing so his bare white chest would suffer a blistering sunburn by the day's end.

As Billy neared Pacific Coast Highway, he rested in front of a beach cottage and removed his sneakers. While he was tying the shoelaces of his sneakers together, a middle-aged man approached him. The first thing Billy noticed was that the man's hair, salt-and-pepper in color, was as curly as his own.

"You best get your shirt on, son. It's going to be a scorcher today," the man said as he sat down beside Billy.

"Oh, I'm fine. I'm going to get a California suntan!"

"Then I take it you're not from here."

"No, me and my mom moved from Ohio last month," Billy answered.

"May I ask the whereabouts in Ohio?"

"Cleveland."

"Is that so? My daughter Vicky and I are from back East, too. We came from Detroit. So, what's your name?"

"Billy, Billy Robbins."

"I'm Neil Dvorak," he said as he extended his arm and shook the youth's hand. His grip reminded Billy of Sam's once-firm handshake, long before the paralyzing stroke.

"It's nice to meet you," Billy said as he flung the tied shoes over his shoulder.

"What's your rush? Do you have big plans for the day?"

"Nah, not really," Billy answered honestly. "I'm going on the pier to watch the fishermen pull in their catch. 'You can tell a lot about a man from the way he reels 'em in,'" he said, quoting an old adage from Sam.

"So you are a fisherman?"

"Yep, I've been fishing since I was four," Billy boasted.

"That's another thing we have in common. I'm not much of an ocean fisherman, but back East, I used to fish all the time. One year I made my own nine-foot fiberglass boat." Neil wiped his forehead with his sleeve. "That's the one thing I miss about the lakes in Michigan. It's that solitary moment when you become one with nature. Picture this, son. You're out on a tranquil lake early in the morning and the sun is just coming up over the horizon. You swing your pole back and cast your line out fifty feet or so. When the weight hits the water, it creates little ripples in every direction until they slowly die away and the lake becomes calm again. Then you wait, ever so patiently, for that first nibble. Suddenly, it happens. The line darts out, the reel spins, and the chase begins. What a feeling of exhilaration!" Neil said with a deep sigh.

"I know what you mean, sir. When I used to go fishing with my…" Billy bit his lip trying to describe his relationship to Sam.

"Your father?"

"He wasn't my father; he wasn't my stepfather either. He was my best friend in the whole world and if I could have picked a dad, it would have been him." Billy's eyes welled up. He choked adding, "He died three and a half months ago."

"I'm sorry to hear that. It's hard when you lose someone you really love, son," Neil said sympathetically.

"That's what Sam used to call me—son. You kind of remind me of him, except that Sam had red, straight hair, not curly like yours and mine."

Up until then Neil hadn't noticed the similarities between them, but he had to admit that they definitely resembled one another. In fact, Billy could have passed for his biological son.

"Well, I guess I better get going," Billy said as he stood up to leave.

"Wait a minute, Billy. I was just wondering if you like to work with your hands? Have you ever carved something out of a piece of wood?"

"Nah, I never learned how."

"All you need is imagination and a few carving tools. Like the ones I have out back in my cabinet shop," Neil answered.

Billy felt no need to rush anymore. He wanted to know more. "Neil, do you build cabinets?"

"I build cabinets, frames, dining room furniture, bedroom sets. I even did custom wainscoting on a couple mansions."

"Wainscoting?"

"Inlaid wall paneling. It gives a home its own signature."

"Will you show me some of your stuff?"

"I'd be happy to, Billy, but I can't today. I'm delivering dresser drawers to my good friends. They have a house on the beach, a couple miles north of here. My daughter Vicky spent the night with their daughter."

"Oh, well, I guess I better get going then," he said disappointedly.

"I'll tell you what, Billy. You come back tomorrow afternoon and I'll show you what a pair of hands can create. I've always wanted to hire an apprentice."

"Did you say hire? Like a real job?"

"I'm offering you fifty cents an hour after school to work by my side in the cabinet shop. In the meantime I'll teach you the trade."

A day on the pier suddenly wasn't so inviting. "I wish I could start today."

"No, you go on and enjoy the sun, but don't forget to put your shirt on. It's gonna be a scorcher."

"I'll see you tomorrow, Neil," he said foregoing the pronunciation of Dvorak. "I won't be late."

✧ ✧ ✧

"Hi, Neil, come in," Karen Stratton said, as she opened the hand-carved mahogany door. It was another Neil Dvorak creation. "The girls are in the pool."

Glistening from a thin layer of cocoa butter, Karen's skin reflected the efforts of a summer-long tan. No longer was it a natural hue, instead, her skin appeared leathery brown beneath the butter. Still, she refused to pass up a day of basking in the sun.

"So how's David, Karen? I haven't seen much of him lately."

"Neither have I. I suppose the infamous Jessica Heisen doesn't have the same complaint."

"Excuse me? Jessica Heisen?"

Karen had her suspicions but sharing them with Neil was unfair to him and to David. She rephrased her comment, "I just meant that the Heisen Corporation sees much more of my husband than I do."

"He's a hard worker, Karen. Look at this beautiful home that he had built for you."

"Every cabinet, every piece of woodwork, and most of the furnishings have been custom-made by Neil Dvorak. This house should really belong to you, dear friend."

Neil cleared his throat at her strange response. "I could never afford a layout like this. Unlike your husband, I'm not the executive VP of a large corporation."

"You underestimate your worth, Neil. With all the work you've been doing, you could be a very wealthy man if only you charged appropriately. All you need to do is raise your prices, at least in line with the competition. You really should consider stretching your margin of profit."

"What's this? Has David's business savvy been rubbing off on you lately?"

Karen lifted her head up high, indicating she had developed her own business know-how without the help of her husband.

"Ah," he laughed. "It's the creative genius of Karen Stratton. So how are Bikini Huts One, Two, and Three doing?"

Excitedly she replied, "In a million years I could never have imagined that I could have designed a line of bikinis that would actually sell. I only did it to pass the time when BAI acquired the first Heisen contract. I had to do something before I drove David crazy." Karen glanced across the room as if she was trying to place the date. "When was that? Eleven years ago? Goodness, so much has changed in that time."

"You can say that again," Neil said, briefly reflecting on life with his ex-wife Anne.

"Neil, can you keep a secret?"

"You know me, Karen, mum's the word."

"My mom and I finally started a mail-order business two months ago and business is booming," Karen said proudly. "Last week we hired a staff of fifteen. We're getting orders faster than we can fill them. Yesterday I spent the entire morning looking for a warehouse. I'd like to keep the inventory in the same facility as the workers."

"Wow, Karen, good for you! What's the secret?"

"I'm not ready to tell David yet. He hardly said anything when I told him I opened a third retail shop. He's been so busy with the Heisen projects that my small venture is of little interest to him. Besides, he tried to talk me out of the mail-order business three years ago."

"Ah, the truth comes out," Neil chuckled. "You up and did it anyway. You're a woman after my own heart, Karen."

"I shouldn't be admired for going behind his back, Neil, but I do appreciate your support. Things are not the same with David and me. There was a time he gave me a calendar with his daily itinerary. I always knew where he was and what he was working on. These days he keeps his business very much to himself. Take last night, for example. He called me at nine o'clock. As usual, I thought he was going to tell me he was running late. It turns out he had a last-minute appointment in New York. Imagine, David forgot to mention that he'd be three thousand miles away for the rest of the week," she confided.

Neil would have preferred that Karen kept that information to herself. He cared about his two friends equally and to take sides with either one of them would be a disservice to the other. He responded neutrally, "Like I was saying, he must be a very busy man. Just like his father, I suspect."

"Ah, like his father. Except that when Alfred worked, he kept Delilah informed. I don't seem to deserve that same consideration," she snapped.

This biting, sarcastic tone unnerved him. It was a relief to him when she abruptly changed the subject. "Enough about my woes, Neil. When are you going to raise your prices?"

"It's not my style, Karen. Besides, ever since Mrs. Benedict sold me the bungalow, Vicky and I have all that we need."

"Dear, sweet Mrs. Benedict…she drops your name as much as I do."

"Don't think I don't appreciate your referrals! Between the two of you, I've got enough orders to keep me busy for the next couple of years," he said as he stepped back outside. "I've got a surprise for you. Jenni's dresser drawers are finished. I'll carry them in."

"Another order finished weeks ahead of time. You are too good to us, Neil."

He stopped and reiterated, "If I've told you once, Karen, I've told you one hundred times, that's what I do for friends. I will be ever indebted to you and David for taking Vicky along on your cruise to Europe."

"That was four years ago, Neil. You've repaid us tenfold."

"Not the way I see it. I'll be back in a jiffy."

Clad in a one-piece bathing suit and a turquoise skirt cover-up, Karen leaned up against the beige stucco on the porch. Her spirits had been lifted as she watched him unload the drawers. She admired him because he had chosen a simple life and was proud of it. It wasn't for lack of ambition; it was that Neil didn't worship the almighty dollar.

"I'll put these in Jenni's room," Neil said as he carried the drawers down the hallway.

She praised him and said, "You've outdone yourself again, Neil. They are beautiful."

"Only the best for the best," he smiled.

When Neil returned from Jenni's room, he pulled aside the drapes in the dining room and watched the two girls bobbing up and down in the pool.

"With those matching flamingo bathing caps, I can't tell them apart," he laughed.

"Neither can I," Karen agreed, if only to be kind.

Side-by-side without the bathing cap camouflage, there was no question who was who. Twelve-year-old Jenni Lynn, born with English and Norwegian genes, was the perfect specimen of a child. Her waist-length sun-streaked hair was thick and flowing. Her eyes, aquamarine like her mother's, were bold and full, and her teeth were white and straight. There was no doubt that when age permitted she would follow in her mother's footsteps and reign as prom queen as well.

Thirteen-year-old Vicky's ethnic heritage was Czech and Romanian, neither of which was the blueprint for a future beauty queen. Her eyes, although an exotic deep brown, were waiflike and far too large for her face. Her drab brown hair was long like Jenni's, but its mousy color rarely stole a highlight from the sun. As for her mouth, she had an overbite that made it impossible to smile without exposing her large buckteeth. By the following spring, Vicky would have her teeth covered with braces and rubber bands attached to a headgear contraption. Unfortunately, until she turned fifteen and the headgear was removed, the orthodontia would be as unsightly as the crooked teeth it covered.

Karen joined Neil at the window and said, "There's that boy again."

"What boy?"

"Over there, the one with the blond hair," she said as she pointed him out. "He's the one with the rolled-up pants and long-sleeved shirt. I swear that if it wasn't for the glass enclosure surrounding the pool, he wouldn't know where the beach ends and our property begins."

Neil peered through the curtain again. The girls had come out of the pool and were standing next to the six-foot tempered-glass wall. Running toward them was a skinny boy, shorter than both girls, with stringy, long blond locks.

"What do you know about him, Karen?"

"Only that he lives in Torrance."

"Torrance? That's a ways up the coast. How does he get down here?"

"I have no idea. I've tried to meet him, but every time I go outside, he hightails it up the beach. He's a bit strange, but the girls seem to like him."

"Like him? The girls are too young to be mingling with boys. I told Vicky she has to wait until she's sixteen before I'll allow her to date."

"I don't think the girls are making dates, Neil. I think they're just making friends," she laughed.

"Well, mind if I go out back and meet him for myself?"

"It won't do you any good. The moment he sees you, he'll make a run for it. He seems to be afraid of people."

"I'll go around and come up from the beach," Neil concluded.

Deep in conversation the girls hadn't noticed Neil's approach. That is, until his hand landed on the boy's shoulder. "Hey, what's going on?"

Vicky couldn't help but act guilty in front of her father. "Daddy, where did you come from?"

With Neil's hand firmly resting on Ethan's shoulder, there was no quick escape for the youth. He said anxiously, "I've got to get going, girls. I'll talk to you tomorrow."

"What's your hurry, son?"

"I just have to go, sir."

Unlike Billy, this boy appeared jittery. He squirmed to be free of Neil's grasp. It was as if he didn't want to be touched by anyone.

"Really, I have to get going," he stammered without looking directly at Neil.

"Not so fast. What's your name?"

"It's Ethan, sir, Ethan Drake," he stammered.

"Do you live in Santa Monica?"

"No sir. I live in Torrance."

He was a polite lad, but Neil noticed he was overly cautious. Neil pressured him. "That's quite a jaunt from Torrance to Santa Monica. How does a young boy like you, about eleven or twelve, get all the way down here?"

"I'm thirteen, sir!"

"Okay, thirteen. So how do you get to Santa Monica from home?"

"I thumb it with the surfers. Sir, may I go now?"

"Ethan, do your mom and dad know that you have been hitchhiking?"

"I really have to go," he said as he lowered himself just enough to break free of Neil's grasp. And even though Neil was just beginning his interrogation, the youth had already fled into the beach crowd.

"You scared him off, Daddy."

"Why's that?"

"He doesn't like to be questioned."

"What does he have to hide?"

Jenni threw down her towel and jumped back into the pool, doing a cannonball. When the splash subsided and she resurfaced, she yelled back, "He's not hiding anything. He just doesn't trust people if he doesn't know them. That's why, Neil!"

Still standing on the deck, Vicky expanded, "It's because something happened to him in Alabama. I think someone hurt him real bad."

"What makes you say that, honey?"

"He said that there are people in Purvis that do terrible things to you, just because of where you live and who you live with."

"Come again, Vicky? I don't understand."

Vicky reiterated, by emphasizing each word, "SOMEBODY HURT HIM, REAL BAD, DADDY."

Jenni who was confident and more outspoken than Vicky blurted out, "It's because he has two mothers, Neil." Jenni dove under and then thrust herself up from the shallow end of the pool. "He has a white one and a colored one, but the colored one is dead."

Utterly confused, Neil seized the moment to correct her vocabulary. "Don't use that word. It's disrespectful to Negroes."

"Anyway, Daddy, he doesn't let anyone get too close to him. He likes me and Jenni, though."

There were few times in his life that Neil was ashamed of himself. This was one of those rare occasions. He had misjudged a boy, a boy who was unquestionably troubled by his past. Neil felt compelled to put things right.

"Girls, the next time he comes around, I want you to tell him I have an after-school job for him. The pay is fifty cents an hour and I'll provide his transportation. Tell him he won't need to hitchhike anymore."

"What kind of job, Daddy?"

"He'll be my second apprentice in the cabinet shop. I already hired a boy this morning."

In unison they dived under the water. When they came up for air, they said, "Okay. We'll tell him."

It would be two weeks before Ethan had the nerve to come back to Santa Monica. When he did, he found the girls floating quietly on inflatable loungers, enjoying the weekend off from school.

"Hey, girls, what ya doing?"

"Ethan! Where have you been? My dad wants to talk to you."

Completely dry from the sun, the girls rolled over, immersing themselves in the cool water. After the initial shock, they swam to the pool's edge.

"What does he want me for? I didn't do anything."

Jenni said sarcastically, "Neil doesn't think you did anything. He just wants to offer you a job after school. It pays fifty cents an hour plus transportation to and from."

"Doing what?"

Vicky answered, "You'll be working in his cabinet shop behind our house. He'll teach you how to use the electric saw and boys stuff like that."

"I don't know," he said hesitatingly. "Your dad asks a heap load of questions."

"I'll tell him not to. Besides, you're not the only one. There's another boy named Billy; he's fourteen."

Ethan was inquisitive about meeting a peer. He asked, "What's he like?"

Vicky fibbed when she answered, "About your size, maybe a little bit taller, but not that much."

The truth was Billy Robbins had already sprouted, although he would quickly peak to his adult height of five foot nine and there he would remain. Ethan, however, had not yet started to develop. It would be three years before he would finally take after his lanky mother and grow to just under six feet. Unfortunately, at age thirteen Ethan thought he was destined to be a runt.

"Listen, Ethan," Jenni interjected. "What do you have to lose? If you don't like the job or the company, just quit! Anything's worth a try. That's what my dad would say if he were here."

"I didn't know you had one, Jenni," Ethan said as if the one thing he had in common had just been taken away.

"A dad? Of course, I do! It's just that my dad is a busy executive," she bragged.

"He travels all across the country and to Hawaii, too. I don't see him that much but that's because he's making a lot of money for my mom and me. Why, Ethan, don't you have a dad?"

"Nope. My mom and him split up before I was born. He died when I was eight," he said with no sign of regret.

Jenni asked, "Of what?"

Ethan shrugged his shoulders, answering, "I don't know. I really don't know anything about him."

That was an understatement. Dolores had always protected Ethan from the truth. She never explained to him that his own father, Thom Drake, had ordered the brutal attack on him. She never told him that Momma Ruthie had retaliated against Ethan's tormentors by killing Thom Drake and then taking her own life.

"Well, I sure would want to know," Jenni pressed on.

"Not me," he lied. "Vicky, how do I get a hold of your dad? I could use the money."

Vicky glanced up toward the house. "Oh, here's my dad now," she said as Neil stepped outside through the sliding glass door.

Neil walked up to the tempered-glass wall that separated the Strattons' property from the public beach and said, "Ah, girls, I see that you've found your friend. Good to see you again, Ethan. Did the girls tell you about my proposition?"

"Yes, sir," he answered shyly.

"Are you willing to listen and learn and work real hard?"

"Do you really pay fifty cents an hour?"

"You bet I do. I'll pay you at the end of each week."

"Then, I'd like to try," Ethan said. The tone of his voice revealed his lack of confidence, and Neil's heart went out to him.

"Good, but we need to ask your mother's permission first. Go around to the front of the house and get in the green sedan. I'll give you a lift home."

Obediently, Ethan answered, "Okay." He turned to Jenni and Vicky and added, "See you later, girls."

As Neil pulled up to Dolores's modest three-bedroom home, he saw her staring anxiously out of a window. When she saw Ethan, she disappeared from sight only to reappear a split second later as she flung open the front door. As Ethan approached her, Dolores protectively wrapped her arms around her son, and only then did she look at the man who had driven Ethan home. It was obvious that Dolores felt threatened by Neil. "Who are you and what were you doing with my son?" she demanded. "What is going on?" She asked of both Ethan and of Neil. "I want an explanation!"

Neil placed his hand over his heart in a gesture of apology and bowed slightly as he introduced himself. "Mrs. Drake, I should have come over and spoken to you before I hired your son to work at my cabinet shop. My name is Neil Dvorak and I met Ethan a few weeks ago at the Strattons' home in Santa Monica."

Dolores wiped beads of sweat off her forehead and looked completely bewildered. "Santa Monica? What were you doing in Santa Monica, Ethan? And how on earth did you get there? You know that you aren't allowed to go to the beach without me."

Ethan stared at the ground refusing to answer her questions. Dolores could see that he was embarrassed, so she released her hold on him. The moment he was free, he darted into the house and closed the door. Neil and Dolores were left facing each other.

"Mr. Dvorak," Dolores said stiffly, "Perhaps I seem overprotective to you, but believe me, I have good reason to be." Neil could see

Dolores struggling to maintain her composure. The expression of compassion on his face conveyed that he understood this woman's pain.

"Mrs. Drake, I understand only too well the need to protect a child." Neil hesitated before he continued, "When my daughter was younger, I failed to protect her, so I understand your fears." Dolores visibly relaxed. She looked at the man in front of her. His sincerity reminded her of Sheriff Pete Cornell.

"I know Ethan thinks I baby him," she said, "But I keep remembering what happened to him and how I almost lost him." Dolores wiped away a tear at the memory of the brutal attack on Ethan. "Ethan has recently become more independent, and he's started to keep things to himself; that's probably because he knows I would be upset at what he's doing." Her anxiety for Ethan spilled over again as she said to Neil, "And now I hear that he has been to Santa Monica. How did he get there—and who are the Strattons?"

"The Strattons are good people. They have a daughter just like I do. In fact, the girls, Jenni Stratton and Vicky, were talking to Ethan the day that I met him on the beach. The three of them have been friends for quite some time."

Dolores brightened at the news. "It's been several years since we moved here from Alabama, and I have never known Ethan to have a friend. It's nice to hear that he is talking to someone. You say that you hired Ethan? Doing what?"

"I intend to teach Ethan and Billy, another boy Ethan's age, the craft of woodworking. Billy has lived here for six months and still hasn't made any friends his own age. I think he and Ethan will have a lot in common."

Dolores felt a confidence in Neil that she had not felt for many years. She took a deep breath and told Neil what she had never told anyone in California. "You should know that Ethan is a very special child. I find it painful to go into details, but when Ethan was only eight years old, he was attacked and left for dead by a group of teenagers."

"My, Lord," said Neil, shaken by the terrible story.

"The doctor thought Ethan wasn't going to make it. Ethan's spleen was ruptured and had to be removed. So for the rest of his life he can't risk getting an infection."

Neil patted Dolores on the shoulder. "It's all the more reason that he needs people like Billy and me to lean on. Mrs. Drake, I'll…"

"Please Neil, call me Dolores."

Neil smiled and said, "I'll take good care of him. You can count on me to pick him up after school and then bring him home after we have finished in the shop. I think he's much safer being with us than when he is trying to make his own way down to the beach. Don't you agree?"

"I don't even want to know how he managed to get there."

Neil smiled and said, "Let's just say that the surfers lost a passenger."

For the first time since they had arrived in California, Dolores found that she could trust someone. She knew that Neil wanted only the best for her son.

"Neil," Dolores said hesitatingly, "In all this time, Ethan has never mentioned the attack. I'm not even sure if he remembers it. Please promise that you'll never bring it up."

"You never had to ask. Just know that I'll be keeping an eye on him, in and out of the shop. Well, I should be on my way. I have to pick my daughter up from the Strattons'. Those two girls are inseparable."

"Thanks, Neil. I'd like to come by tomorrow and see where my son works."

"You're welcome anytime, Dolores. Here's my address and phone number," he said as he handed her his business card. Dolores stood on the grass and waved good-bye as Neil drove off. She realized that not only had Ethan made a new friend, but she had made one too.

✧ ✧ ✧

Billy had skidded up Neil's driveway before slamming on his brakes. The bike was a new one, but he was too impatient to use the kickstand. Instead, he let it fall to the ground.

"Hey, Neil! What are we building today?"

Having just shaved an inch off a piece of plywood, Neil didn't hear him over the table saw. When he did, he removed the safety goggles and switched off the saw. Still buzzing, the blade softly faded to a hum before it came to a full stop.

"You're early today, Billy. Why aren't you in school?"

"My mom had another doctor's appointment, so she picked me up early."

"Another one?"

"Yeah, she said they have to run more tests. She said it's nothing to worry about, though."

"Good," he said trying not to show his concern. "Tell her I can pick you up from school from now on. There's no need for both of us to go, since I have to pick Vicky up anyway. Besides, isn't your mom about to start her new job?"

"She has to get through the tests first. She needs a green light from the doctor, whatever that means."

"Oh, I see," Neil said, forcing himself to show only a nonchalant expression.

"Neil, can I assemble frames today? There are eighteen left to do."

"Sure. The wood glue is on the bench and the clamps are hanging on the wall. Do you want me to help you get started?"

"Nope, I'll do it like you showed me last week."

Pleased, Neil pulled the goggles over his eyes and flipped on the table saw. There was no need to micromanage, because like himself, Billy was a perfectionist. Thriving on attention to detail, he was a natural when it came to woodworking. All Neil had to do was show him once, and Billy would take it from there.

This mutual understanding provided a harmonious work environment. Both had learned at a very young age that if something was worth doing, it was worth doing right. Neil learned it at the orphanage. Billy learned it from Sam Donahue.

Not all personalities meshed as quickly as Neil and Billy's had, a fact that was proven when Ethan joined the team and the easygoing atmosphere suddenly became strained and tense. Ethan kept to himself and struggled with even the simplest of tasks. It became obvious that he couldn't pound a nail into a piece of wood without bending it. Ethan's lack of ability and his reclusive nature created a difficult time for all three.

"Ethan, today I want you to help Billy assemble those picture frames. I've chiseled the wood and numbered the pieces. There are four numbers to each frame. Understand?"

"Yes, sir," he responded formally.

"I appreciate your helping Billy out, Ethan," Neil said supportively.

Billy didn't want Ethan working with him. He would rather Ethan worked with Neil, but Neil had other ideas. He saw two polar opposites with the potential to become friends. Only time would tell if that was remotely possible.

With his head facing the door, Ethan rested up against the workbench while Billy squeezed the tube of wood glue. "So, what do you want me to do, Billy?"

"Find the number two pieces. You can glue and I'll clamp them."

"Okay," Ethan mumbled.

That was the only word he said all afternoon until he saw Vicky pass by the open garage. Showing off, she was walking on her eighteen-inch stilts when he called out to her. "Hey, Vicky, how are you? Where's Jenni Stratton?"

Billy swallowed and then swallowed again. *Stratton?* Without thinking, he let go of the freshly glued piece of frame, which dropped into a pile of sawdust.

"Good thing the vise is holding up the other three," Neil laughed, making light of Billy's first botch up.

"Neil, did he say 'Stratton'?"

"Yeah, why?"

"I suppose there are a ton of Strattons in California, but it sure is a coincidence. That's my mom's last name."

"I thought your last name was Robbins."

"Mine is, but not hers. When I was five she married a creep named Jack Stratton. Man, oh, man was he a creep! A few months ago he left us and moved out here."

"Oh, is that why you came to California?"

"Yeah, at first I thought my mom wanted to get him back. Now I'm not so sure. She hasn't mentioned his name in a long time. Jack Stratton wasn't good to her."

"How did he treat you?" Neil asked, cognizant of how some parents treat their children.

"Like I said, he was a creep. He wanted no part of me and I wanted no part of him."

"Did he ever hurt you?"

"It didn't matter what he said or did, cuz I hated him too much," Billy said defiantly. "I was sure glad when he was gone."

Neil was also glad when he was free of Anne, but it made him think. It had been three years since he called the psychiatric ward at Detroit Memorial to check on Anne's progress. And it wasn't that he gave a damn about her. He just wanted to hear that she had moved on with her life. Instead, he was informed that at that very moment she was being given her thirteenth shock treatment. He never called again.

"Sweet essence," Neil called out. "How about whipping up a pitcher of lemonade for me and the boys? I think it's about time for a break."

After hearing Billy's story, suddenly Ethan didn't feel like the odd man out. Ethan picked up the sawdust-covered frame and offered, "Let me wipe this off for you, Billy. If there's one thing I *do* know how to do, it's cleaning. You learn real good when you live with women," he chuckled. "So where's your father, Billy?"

"I don't know. My mom never married him." Without mentioning that his mother only told him when she was drunk, he added, "My mom said that my real father is a judge in Cleveland."

"Wow! A real judge?"

"That's what she said," Billy said indifferently. "She also said I'm much better off without him."

"That's funny," Ethan grinned, "My mom said the same thing about my old man, whoever he was. The only difference between our dads is that mine is six feet under."

The particles of wood scattered through the air as Neil continued sawing. By then the boys were deep in conversation. From Neil's perspective it was refreshing to see them come together so soon.

Ethan asked, "Billy, do you know the judge's name?"

"Nah, Mom says when the day comes that I need to know, she'll tell me. Anyway, it's too late now. He's in Ohio and I'm in California."

"So what? If he's not dead, then it's not too late. Someday, perhaps when you get older, you might want to meet him. If you do, I'll go back to Cleveland with you."

"I never wanted to meet him," he said trying to sound convincing. "But you never know, someday I might change my mind." Billy's forehead wrinkled and he added, "Right now I have bigger fish to fry. I don't know if I should tell my mom about Jenni Stratton. She might go crazy or something."

"Ask Neil, Billy. He'll tell you what to do."

"Yeah, you're right. Neil, Neil?"

Neil's focus was on the blade of the electric saw as he rounded the edge of a table leg. He didn't hear Billy calling him, and nor did he know that Ethan had come up behind him. "Neil! Billy needs your advice."

Startled, Neil jerked the table leg. For the first time in his life he had removed his eyes from the razor-sharp blade. It was in that millisecond that the blade split his middle finger down to the knuckle. Too stunned to scream, Ethan did it for him.

"Turn the switch off, Ethan," Billy shrieked. Grabbing a batch of polishing cloths, he quickly wrapped Neil's hand. "Ethan, tell Vicky to call an ambulance." Ethan couldn't move because he was in shock. The blood that oozed through the cloths brought out repressed memories. They were memories that he had buried long ago in Denton's barn. Fearing the worst, he trembled.

"I'm sorry, I'm sorry, I'm sorry," Ethan incessantly repeated. Under his breath he whispered, "I'm not a coon boy."

"Ethan, it's okay. It's not your fault. Just stay calm. I'm going to be all right. They'll put a few stitches in and I'll be fine." Neil stretched his free hand toward Ethan and pulled him closer. "It's okay, son."

"Daddy, what happened?" Vicky screamed as she dropped the pitcher of lemonade.

"I'm okay, honey. Dial 0 and ask for an ambulance."

Although Neil had reassured the children, he wasn't convinced about his condition. His face paled, but not so much from the excruciating pain. It was the uncertainty. He didn't know the extent of the damage, and he worried how it would affect his livelihood. Still, he wouldn't let the children see his fear.

After the ambulance drove away with Neil and Vicky at his side, the two boys were left alone in the driveway. Billy, the stronger and bigger of the two, wrapped his arm around Ethan. It was at that moment that each boy had found a brother. They would be brothers for the rest of their lives.

thirteen

FAMILY BONDS

California, 1963

"Good morning, Gloria. Is my son in today?"

The executive secretary had been typing a letter, transcribed from her shorthand notes, when Delilah Stratton walked in. Gloria welcomed the interruption. "Hello, Mrs. Stratton. What a surprise to see you today!" Scanning the appointment book, she added, "I must have failed to pencil you in. Mr. Stratton is leaving for New York as soon as the driver arrives out front."

"I didn't call for an appointment," Delilah emphasized. "I'll only need five minutes of his time, dear."

"Yes, Mrs. Stratton." Pressing the intercom button Gloria announced, "Sir, your mother is here. She'd like a moment of your time."

Knowing that his mother could hear his response, David simply replied, "Send her in."

"There's no need to get up, Gloria. I'll see myself in," Delilah said, adjusting the five-mink wrap that was draped around her neck.

"Son, off again to New York? That's what? Four weeks out of the last six?"

"Mom, what are you doing here? You know that I've asked you to call before you drop in," he said impatiently. "I don't have time today; I've got a flight to catch and the driver should be here any minute."

Delilah didn't care if the driver waited. She sat down on the couch and slowly removed her elbow-length white gloves. While David paced back and forth anxiously, she retrieved a cigarette from an engraved holder. She held it in midair until David picked up the lighter on the table and lit it for her.

"It's good to see you still have some manners," she said.

"Mom, what brings you here? It's important that I don't miss my flight." He hesitated and then added, "Is Dad all right?"

"He's fine, except for high blood pressure. His doctor has increased his dose of medication."

"And how are you feeling?" He asked, as a concerned son should ask.

"I'm of sound mind and body." She exhaled the cigarette smoke into the air and stated, "I wish I could say the same of my only child."

"There's nothing wrong with me," he declared.

"Not physically, but I do believe your mind is in trouble."

David huffed, "Mom, I don't have time for this. So, I'm going to ask you one more time. Why are you here?"

Sternly she answered, "All right. I've come to tell you that you have not been as discreet as you think."

"I don't know what you are talking…"

"Hear me out," she snapped. "You've never lied to me before; don't attempt to do it now. You know exactly what I'm talking about."

Like an obedient child, David dropped down into the plush leather chair. It was useless to argue with her. One way or another, Delilah would have her say.

"Thanksgiving is three weeks away. As you know, Karen has invited us, the Allens, the Dvoraks, as well as two additional friends of Jenni's and their single parents."

"I knew that Neil and Vicky were coming, but I wasn't aware that she had invited the others," he said, hoping that a slight detour in the subject would shut her up. "Mom, I don't see that adding Jenni's friends is a problem."

"At face value there isn't a problem unless of course, something or someone interferes with our family holiday. Do you get my drift, David?"

"I can't say that I do." He glanced at his watch and said, "Mom, I've got to go. Can this wait until later?"

"I'm not quite finished," she said, drawing on the cigarette. "Jessica Heisen has been dropping your name all over town. It's only a matter of time before your father gets wind of it, or worse yet, before Karen discovers your indiscretions." She set her cigarette down in the ashtray and said, "You might as well know that Karen called me last week and questioned me about Jessica Heisen. I find that very interesting since she rarely calls just to chitchat anymore. She has been so busy with her mother at those swimwear shops that I don't see much of her these days."

It was obvious that Delilah disapproved of her daughter-in-law's newfound independence. She had groomed Karen to be the wife of a wealthy executive, not an entrepreneur who owned her own business. She was disappointed that Karen did not follow the same route she had taken with Alfred.

David raised his voice and shouted, "Mom, this is none of your concern."

Composedly, Delilah said, "It is when it could affect my granddaughter's life. As a Stratton heir she deserves the same foundation we gave you: respect, prestige, and honor."

"I give my daughter all that and more," he argued defensively.

"I repeat, Jessica Heisen has been dropping your name as if she knows you in the biblical sense. Apparently, she is receptive to the dissolution of your marriage with no regard to the consequences it would have on your daughter. She isn't a woman you can trust, son."

"I don't want to hear any more about Jessica," he yelled. "We're not having an affair, if that is what you're saying!"

Again David tried to lie to his mother, but Delilah ignored his feeble attempt and continued. "Stop this foolishness, son, while you still have the chance. I know that you don't intend on making a life with the Italian Black Widow, so sever the ties now. It wouldn't hurt for you to spend more time at home with Karen. Perhaps then she would give up this nonsense of trying to succeed on her own. Karen's duty is to take care of you, but since you haven't been there, look what she has gone and done. You need to change your lifestyle before she has no desire to tend to you at all. Do I make myself clear?"

"Mom, you can't come in here and tell me how to run my life. I'm a grown man, for God's sake," he said trying to maintain his cool.

"Then act like one! Be a man to your wife and a respectable father to your daughter. There's still time to rise above this situation, as disturbing as it is," she said as she blew one final plume of smoke into the air. Delilah crushed the cigarette butt into the mosaic ashtray. Clasping her handbag, she added, "I've said enough for one day. I only hope that you take heed of what I've said." She reached up and kissed him on the cheek. "Have a safe flight and I'll see you on Thanksgiving."

When the door closed behind her he said under his breath, "Shit!" He pushed the intercom and shouted, "Gloria, has my driver arrived?"

"Yes, Mr. Stratton. He's waiting for you in the front entrance."

✧ ✧ ✧

Jessica propped up the goose down pillow and rested up against the headboard. Cushioned with tufted gold satin, it coordinated well with the duvet, sheets, and her custom-made negligee. She had exquisite taste in everything, including the man she had been screwing for the past several years.

"Darling, either call your wife or don't call her, but please don't sit by the telephone all night!"

With his elbows on the table and his hands cupped under his chin, David had spent the last twenty minutes pondering whether to make a call home. After the uneasy conversation with his mother two days earlier, he couldn't summon the courage. He had waited two days and knew that if he did call, Karen would hit him with a barrage of questions—none of which he could honestly answer.

"Just call her and get it over with so we can get on with our night. I made late reservations at Bernard's. You promised to make love to me again and I'm holding you to it. I want to screw before we go out."

Always in control, Jessica had never learned how to play the helpless woman. It wasn't necessary. She knew how to call the shots while having people eat out of her hand at the same time. David had become one of those people.

"Do you hear me, darling? Call the little wife," she reiterated sarcastically.

"Yes," he sighed. "I hear you loud and clear, Jessica."

This was one of the rare instances when David's conscience took over. Up until then he had justified his behavior as a way to advance at BAI. He convinced himself that it was good for business and then shifted the blame onto Theo. He was the one who had encouraged his relationship with the Italian Black Widow. And although Theo never told him to have an affair, David insisted on interpreting it that way.

"Darling, say something. What is wrong? Why are you acting so strange?" Jessica demanded.

Plagued by his mother's comments, he said, "I shouldn't have come to New York; the timing wasn't right. Karen has been asking me about you more than ever. She wants to know how often you show up at the projects, meetings, and business dinners. Basically, she doesn't trust you."

"If I were her, I wouldn't trust me either, especially with a man like you," she flirted. "Let's be rational, darling. She doesn't know that you are with me right now, does she?

So just pretend that you're all alone in the Big Apple and call her. I'd like to make love sometime tonight," she said reminding him of her wants and needs.

David looked past Jessica at his face reflected in the floor-to-ceiling windows. It was early evening and the sun was just beginning to set behind the skyscrapers. The view from Jessica's penthouse on Fifth Avenue was breathtaking. However, it wasn't the view he was staring at; it was a powerless man who was about to be unfaithful to his wife for the umpteenth time.

David shoved the phone away. "I'll call her in the morning," he avowed.

Temporarily relieved, he poured a double Scotch and downed it in two swallows. It still wasn't enough. He poured himself another and downed it in one. His guilt faded about the same time the alcohol reached his bloodstream. California suddenly seemed a million miles away and life there surreal. But the woman lying across the bed just a few feet away from him was here and now. This was reality.

David unfastened the sash to his black silk robe. His member stretched forward. It was weighty, yet rising by the second.

"Oh, darling, drop the robe. I want to admire you—your chest, your shoulders, and that heavenly body…" Before she finished her sentence, his robe was crumpled on the floor and he was stark naked. David's penis was now fully engorged, and his body glistened in the waning sunlight.

"God, how could any man ever say 'no' to you? You're so fucking irresistible," he said, as he was about to slide under the comforter, but Jessica stopped him.

"Not just yet. You know what I want first. It's been such a long time. Over there by the window."

He knew exactly what she wanted. She enjoyed being a voyeur. Obliging her, as well as himself, he placed his hand on his throbbing organ and began to massage himself ever so slowly. Muffling his groans, his breathing became heavy and irregular. Simultaneously, Jessica's breathing accelerated.

"David, darling, come to me. Let me take it from here."

Masturbating felt good, but David preferred Jessica's touch and promptly pinched the end of his penis to prevent ejaculation. There was an instant of pain for which he was rewarded when he slid under the covers to find her hand waiting for him. She grasped his penis, but only until she slipped down to take him in her mouth; she sucked and licked him, her passion mounting as David writhed in ecstasy. He refused to ejaculate in her mouth. Instead, he lifted her buttocks above him and eased her body over him. She lifted her legs over his shoulders and using the bed as traction, she rode him. With every buck, she forced his organ deeper and deeper inside of her. Seconds later they both wailed as they climaxed together. Salty and wet, they were mutually satisfied.

For a brief interlude, they lay motionless trying to catch their breath. Then nature took its course. David's organ shriveled until he was no longer inside her. Their bodies disconnected, so she rolled off him and reached for the cigarette box on the nightstand. Her nicotine habit was the only thing he openly disliked about her.

"I've asked you a thousand times not to smoke in front of me. It reminds me of my mother."

"You say that to me every time we finish," she snarled.

"Well, you smoke every time and I'm tired of it," he shouted.

These were two executives who had fine-tuned their lovemaking into a perfect symphony. With a drawerful of sex toys from handcuffs to lotions to vibrators, they were on the same wavelength. That is, until that awkward period right after copulation when they remembered that they didn't belong to one another and then the bickering would begin.

"I got a letter from the union the other day, David. Did you know that we have a problem with the offshore workers? I expect you to be abreast of those issues," she chided.

"Yes, I'm aware of it, Jessica. I've got two managers working on it as we speak," he said trying to remain calm.

"Well, I don't need a work stoppage. Are you planning on meeting personally with the union stewards?"

"Jessica, I said I've got it under control," he stated commandingly. "BAI will be meeting with them on Monday. Does that meet with your approval?"

"Of course, darling," she sighed. "Except that it's unfortunate we have to deal with a middleman. Every time I'm notified of a problem I have to turn it over to BAI. It just seems redundant." She sat up against the plush headboard and said, "It's time you switched gears and came to work for the Italian Black Widow."

Clearing his throat, he skirted the Black Widow comment. "You know, I would never do that to Theo. He's been good to me all these years."

"Theo's getting up there in age, darling. I haven't heard that he's willing to turn it all over to you, has he? He still wants to maintain control."

"And you don't? Let's be serious, Jessica. Karen would divorce me in a heartbeat if I went to work for you."

"One could only hope because frankly I'm getting tired of our little trysts. I'm to the point where I want the world to know about us."

David finally understood what his mother had been trying to convey to him. He jumped out of bed and put on his robe. He hollered, "Know what, Jessica? That we've been fucking each other since the first contract? Remember? You wouldn't sign unless I came with the package. And I do believe you meant that literally."

"You needn't be so crass, David. Besides, isn't fucking what you do to that little wife of yours just so you won't have to deal with the Big D?" She said hinting at divorce.

"You're treading on thin ice, Jessica. I told you that I will never divorce Karen—not under any condition."

"Then perhaps she'll have a good reason to divorce you!"

There was a calculated tone to her voice, almost an implied threat. He was outraged. "Don't you dare do anything stupid, Jessica."

Still reserved, but believing she had the upper hand, Jessica responded, "Do you really think she's that naive, darling? She's had two days to make inquiries at Heisen and learn that I am also in New York."

"Karen wouldn't stoop so low," he said, hoping it was the truth.

"Ah, but she is a woman and the daughter-in-law of in-the-know Delilah Stratton," she sneered.

"Leave my mother out of it, Jessica," he fumed.

"Okay, peace. Let's not argue," she purred. "We only have two days left and I want to make the most of them."

David was furious when he realized that Jessica believed she had total power over his life. Knowing that she was manipulative, he speculated on what actions she would take to get her way. David was suddenly confronted with a major crossroad in his life. Unfortunately, it had taken his mother to point it out to him.

"No, we don't have two days. I'm going to the airport tonight to get a room and I'm taking the first flight home tomorrow."

Jessica glared at him and said very slowly, "I wouldn't do that if I were you. You will regret it!"

"Finally, a bona fide threat! You'll do what, Jessica? Have me fired? I think Theo would back me before he'd back you. If you're insinuating that you are going to tell Karen, I intend to beat you to the punch. So you do what you have to do. It's over between us."

"I wouldn't be so cocky about Theo Bachman. You should know by now that he's only interested in who can butter his bread."

"He has more class than that," he argued as he packed his suitcase.

"Oh, does he now? I wouldn't be so sure about Theo if I were you, darling. As for telephoning your wife, it is a tempting thought. I could give her a heads-up that her husband is crawling back to her because we had a premarital spat, so to speak."

"Do what you have to, but let me put it this way, from this day forward it's business only. If you want anything else, you'll have to find someone else."

Jessica laughed and said, "Do you honestly think that you won't get a hard-on the next time I'm sitting across from you in the boardroom? Before you know it, you'll be begging to come back to me. Your little wife is incapable of making love to you the way I do."

"Don't bet on it, Jessica. You've been a masterful teacher," he said as he slammed the door behind him.

✧ ✧ ✧

"Sir, am I to drive you to the office this afternoon?"

"No, take me straight home. Do you have the address?"

"Yes. Gloria, your secretary, gave it to me this morning."

Having changed his flight plans, David was not met by his regular driver. An alternate driver, who was new to the team, had waited in the baggage claim area for over two hours holding a sign that read "Mr. Stratton." It was a sign that David easily spotted since he had flown first class and had deplaned well before the droves of coach passengers.

"So you're one of the new hires at BAI. What's your name?"

"Call me Jay."

"Well then, Jay, take Pacific Coast Highway. I need a breather before I go home," David said as he loosened his tie.

"So where are you from, Jay?"

"I've lived here and there, but most recently Cleveland. Have you ever been to Cleveland?"

"Not intentionally," David laughed. "I did go to Ohio State."

"I'm not a college man myself. Never went for that uppity kind of life. Guess that's why I drive for people like you and your father. He's Alfred Stratton, right?"

David didn't appreciate the comment about his lifestyle. He looked at the driver's eyes through the rearview mirror as he asked, "And how do you know my father?" David saw the driver quickly avert his eyes.

"I heard my old man mention his name before," he replied. "He told me that Alfred Stratton had more dough than any man ought to."

David had had enough. He found the driver to be unpolished, rude, and utterly unprofessional. He was not the caliber of employee that should be employed by BAI. David closed the divider between them, preventing any further discussion.

Leaning against the window, David faced the ocean. With the Santa Ana winds in full swing, the water was rough and choppy. Somehow the weather was in sync with the uncertainty of what he was about to face at home. He welcomed every stoplight that slowed his arrival, but nothing could delay the inevitable. The driver pushed back the divider and announced, "We've arrived at 411 Ocean Boulevard."

"Home," David said. "No need to take my suitcases to the door, Jay. You can leave them here."

"It's my job. I'll carry them inside for you," the driver insisted.

Emphatically, David reiterated, "I said, no, thank you. I'll take them in myself." David handed him a ten dollar tip and added, "Perhaps you'll be assigned to me again."

It was a courteous, though dismissive, farewell. David had no intention of ever again using Jay. The driver's unshaven appearance, distinct body odor, and inappropriate remarks were all less than suitable in a subordinate. If David had more time to contemplate it, he would have wondered who made the mistake of hiring him in the first place. But at the moment his mind was preoccupied with what was waiting for him behind the front door. He hadn't spoken to Karen in three days.

Taking a deep breath, he picked up a suitcase in each hand. The winds, which had captured grains of sand off the beach, pelted him as he trudged up the walkway. Somehow he felt deserving of it.

From the master suite above, Karen had been watching him forge his way through the winds. Any other day she would have raced down the staircase to greet him. This time she was in no hurry to welcome him home. She let him ring the bell several times before she finally unlocked the deadbolt.

Calm and unfazed she said, "You're early. I thought you were coming home on Friday."

"I got everything taken care of. I figured I'd surprise you and Jenni. God, it's great to be home."

"Well, that's something you haven't said in a long time."

At least she's talking to me, he thought. As he bent over to kiss her, she deliberately turned her head away. She pulled a tissue from her pocket and vigorously wiped the table in the foyer.

"The housekeeper forgot to dust this morning," she explained, although there was no dust to be found. It was simply idle chat. That's when David knew one of two things had occurred. Either Jessica had made contact with her or she was still angry that he hadn't called her all week. He prayed for the latter.

"Where's Jenni?"

"She's spending the night at Vicky's. There's no school tomorrow so Neil picked her up."

"Well, I'd like to see my daughter. Let's drop by Neil's first and afterward we'll go out for a romantic dinner. I'll order a nice bottle of wine and we'll relax—just the two of us."

"I don't feel like dining out tonight, David. As for you seeing Jenni, it's not likely. Neil took the girls to Hollywood to see *Gypsy* again."

David felt that he was getting nowhere with her. If only she would yell and scream at him, he'd know then where things stood. But somehow Karen managed to maintain an aloof composure.

"I'm going up to take a bubble bath. I'm sure you wouldn't mind doing your own unpacking."

That in itself was a sign of her mood. She usually did his packing and unpacking. Today Karen wanted no part of it.

"No problem, Kar, I can do it myself. Just tell me what goes to the dry cleaners."

"Figure it out for yourself," she finally blurted. "You seem to do just fine whenever you are away from me!"

"Okay, spill it, Karen. You obviously have something to say. Now would be a good time."

"What, the fact that you didn't call all week? I guess I'll have to get over it, won't I?"

He was ready to apologize when she promptly added, "Or that you may have been in New York with Jessica Heisen?"

"Karen, I…"

"Are the rumors true? Have you been sleeping with her? David, please don't answer that. I don't want to know what a fool I've been, or how long I've been one. Weeks, months, or are we talking years? That, too, is a rhetorical question. Please don't confirm my suspicions."

"Karen, honey, you are backing me into a corner. I don't know what you want me to say."

"Your lack of defense just said it. You needn't worry; I won't seek a divorce. I refuse to make Jenni another statistic of a broken family.

As for our marriage," she sniffled, "I don't know where we go from here. To say 'I'm sorry' is not enough."

"Honey, I'll do anything you ask." Groveling for her mercy, he begged, "Just name it, Karen. Anything you want. I do love you more than anything in the world and I promise to prove it to you. I swear to it."

"It's a little too late for Valentine promises."

"Listen to me, Karen. I can explain."

"Please don't insult my intelligence. Remember our college days? While your mother was preparing me to be the wife of a Stratton, you were in Ohio having your fill of coeds. Are you surprised that I knew? Well, don't be! Word travels, even across the country. The bottom line is that I eventually got over it. Hopefully, someday I will get over this."

There was nowhere for him to look but down. "I...I don't know what to say. How could I have done this to you?"

"If you're looking for pity, David, you've come to the wrong place. I won't allow you to make me feel sorry for your transgressions."

"Please forgive me, Kar," he cried.

"For such a tall order, those are simple words. I'm going upstairs to take a bath."

"Let me draw the water for you," he said, trying to be accommodating.

"No, I don't want any favors from you, except that you give me the space I need."

As she walked up the staircase she reached behind her and pulled the rubber band that had been holding back her hair. At thirty-four she still wore it long. "I'm getting my hair cut tomorrow."

"Don't do anything drastic. You know that I've always loved that you wore it long. You look so young, honey."

"I'm not young anymore. I'm going to get a Jackie Kennedy cut. It's going to be part of the new Karen Stratton image. That way, women like Jessica Heisen won't think they can move in on husbands like mine—not without a fight."

After years of having it all go his way, David's perfect world had turned upside down. His marriage was suddenly on the brink of collapse, and he knew that he would have to avoid Jessica in the boardroom as well as the bedroom. To do that he needed to remove himself from Heisen's offshore oil drilling projects. He hoped in doing so it wouldn't jeopardize his career with BAI.

David went behind the bar and made himself an extra-dry martini. He would have gone outside, but the winds were even more intense than when he first arrived home. Through the window he saw that the pool was murky with sand and debris. Ironically, there was little difference between the storm outside the Strattons' home and the storm inside.

David slouched on one of the ten cushy barstools and tried to refocus his thoughts. All alone, he stared into the smoked-glass mirror behind the bar. His reflection was somber and forlorn—a contrast to better days when client negotiations were held on that very spot. However, none of those in-home meetings had ever included Jessica Heisen. David had deliberately kept her as far from his home life as possible; although it was, ironically, Jessica's lack of attendance that triggered Karen's suspicions in the first place.

Chewing on a green olive he mumbled, "I've got to talk with Theo. First thing tomorrow, I'll set up a luncheon with him. He'll figure out a way for me to keep my position without being directly associated with Jessica."

The next afternoon Theo Bachman, sporting a red bow tie and gray pin-striped suit, waived off the concierge and went directly into the lounge at the Balboa Sands Club. This exclusive club was "gentlemen members only" and had been the site of many productive as well as ill-fated meetings.

"I'll have a Rock and Rye on the rocks," the CEO requested.

"Are we having lunch today, Mr. Bachman?"

"Yes, later on. Right now I am waiting for Mr. David Stratton."

"Will Mr. Stratton be joining you for lunch?"

"No, I don't think so. Have my table set for one."

"Yes, Mr. Bachman."

Theo rested against the leather armchair. The wingback chairs, designed for much taller men, dwarfed him; his feet only touched the ground when he leaned forward. Otherwise, they dangled freely several inches from the floor.

David walked up to the podium and asked, "Has Mr. Bachman arrived?"

Although David had asked the host, he could have questioned any one of the staff. Every employee at Balboa Sands was required to know which members were present and whether they were in the lounge, the library, or the formal dining room. To be uninformed would be grounds for dismissal.

"Yes, Mr. Stratton. Mr. Bachman is waiting for you in the lounge. Would you like me to show you to his table?"

"I'll find him, Jonathan. Thanks anyway."

David scanned the lounge and saw several familiar faces who nodded to acknowledge him. But that was the extent of their welcome. Unless they were personally addressed, the men usually kept to themselves.

"Theo, don't get up," David said, knowing that it would have been an effort for Theo to maneuver out of the throne-like chair.

As David sat across from him, a waiter returned tableside. David said, "The usual, please."

"Yes, Mr. Stratton. A single malt Scotch and a glass of ice water coming right up."

"David, why did you want to meet with me at the club instead of the office? This isn't quite your style; it's more like your father's."

"I wanted a place where there would be no interruptions."

"Ah, let me guess. You need a place where the Italian Black Widow couldn't buy her way in!"

David grinned. Theo knew him better than he thought. "You're right, Theo. I can't handle her anymore. It's all gotten out of control." David's drink was unobtrusively placed on the table next to him.

"Sounds like you've got trouble on the home front," Theo said as he twirled a cherry stem in his mouth.

"Like I said, things have gotten out of control."

"Don't be naive now, David. You were under Jessica Heisen's spell the day you finalized the first deal. What has changed?"

"For starters, I refuse to divorce my wife."

"And…"

"Jessica asked me to leave BAI and take over Heisen. Don't get me wrong, Theo. I told her both requests were out of the question." David was anxious to divulge Jessica's proposition. He thought Theo would praise him for his honesty. He thought wrong.

"Interesting," Theo said acting surprised.

"Theo, I could use some sound advice. As my friend, my mentor, call it what you will. I'm caught between a rock and a hard place. How do I maintain my position at BAI while not being involved in our number one account?"

"That's a problem with not much of a solution. So I'm going to make this easy for you. Up until now your personal life has been none of my concern. However, when it starts interfering with the progress of BAI, then it becomes my concern."

"I guess an apology is in order, Theo," David said humbly.

"No apology's necessary because, David, you are off the hook. I received a call from Mrs. Heisen yesterday morning—an enraged Mrs. Heisen, I might add. That must have been one hell of a fight because she demanded that I remove you from the account immediately. She said she will work directly with one of your subordinates, young Bill Mattes in particular. For the record, I readily agreed."

With a jolt to his ego, David fell back into the chair. He had assumed that Theo would take his side no matter what the situation. Then David remembered Theo's motto: Anyone at anytime can be replaced. Unfortunately, he never thought it would apply to him.

"Theo, are you eliminating my position? Am I out of a job?"

"In a nutshell, yes," he answered unsympathetically.

David's mouth dropped open as he realized he had just been fired. In shock he began rolling his glass back and forth between the palms of his hands as Theo watched and waited for his reaction. A minute would pass before David closed his eyes and smiled.

"You've been good to me, Theo. Working for BAI has been a highlight of my life. It's time for a real change."

"I agree with you. Your time here was well spent, but it's time that you moved on."

Although David was taken aback by Theo's eagerness to let him go, he kept that to himself. With confidence he said, "I'm going to take some time off, and then I'll get back into the rat race. I may even try a different industry."

"Bold decision, David, and I believe a good one. You've been an asset to BAI and you will be missed. I feel I owe you an explanation about my special alliance with Jessica Heisen."

"You have an alliance? I didn't know it went that far."

"I expect your complete confidence with what I am about to tell you. There's been discussion about a BAI-Heisen merger. We are in the early stages, mind you, but lately it's been heating up. That's why I'll kowtow to the Italian Black Widow and give her whatever she wants. Right now she wants you out of the picture."

The realization that he had been used by Theo was slowly dawning on David. The knowledge made him feel ill; all these years he had thought he was in control, a business wunderkind, but he had been nothing more than a puppet.

"Well, David, let's not beat a dead horse. It's been fun, but it's over. I'll ask Gloria to pack your personal belongings and have them delivered to you on Monday," Theo said unemotionally.

"Yes, Theo, I guess that's how it should be. No fanfare, just a low-key departure from BAI."

"Then you understand, I'm sure, why I won't invite you to lunch, David."

David inwardly seethed, but maintained his composure as he rose from the chair. "Suddenly, Theo, I have lost my appetite. Working with you has been an experience; I certainly learned more than I expected to—this meeting was an education in itself. I'll see you around, Theo."

As David quickly walked past the podium toward the front door, he heard, "Son, I haven't seen you at the club in months."

"Dad," he said with a surprised look on his face, "I thought you and Mom went to Palm Springs for the week."

"We had a change of plans. I had to tie up some loose ends. Just business, you know," Alfred said vaguely. "What brings you to the club?"

"I had a rather interesting meeting with Theo Bachman. I'll fill you in later with the details; right now I want to go home and see Karen and Jenni," David said anxious to leave the building.

"Then we'll talk later, son. Where is Theo? I'd like to give him my best regards," Alfred stated with dignity.

"He's in the lounge, the table nearest the piano," David said as rushed out the door.

Alfred walked through the lounge and nodded his head to several members. He would have been welcomed at any one of their tables, but his destination was the table next to the piano bar. Without asking he pulled out the chair across from Theo and sat down.

"Alfred, you're looking fine today. Did you see David? He left a few minutes ago."

"We spoke briefly," Alfred answered politely, and then turned to the waiter who was now at his side. He said, "Nothing for me today, I won't be staying long."

Theo asked, "Did David tell you that he is no longer employed with BAI? We both felt it was time for him to move on."

"Timing is everything, Theo," he said, relieved that David was disassociating himself from the company.

"I don't understand what timing has to do with it, Alfred. However, I've never believed that a person should spend his entire life working for one company, unless of course, the person owns the company," he laughed. "So how was the golf tournament last week, Alfred? I was sorry I had to miss it. I was working on a new business venture."

"A new business venture," Alfred repeated. "Anything to do with the Italian Black Widow?"

"Are you referring to Jessica Heisen?" Theo asked, although he knew exactly who Alfred meant. "No, nothing to do with her," he lied.

"Theo," Alfred paused and then continued, "I'm onto the two of you. Heisen and BAI's profits may have been good, but not that good. You two did a magnificent job of cooking the books so she could meet the provisions in Derrick Heisen's will. Unfortunately, the true numbers are going to surface soon and Jessica Heisen will lose control of Heisen. And where does that leave BAI?"

"You must be joking, Alfred," he said sarcastically. "I thought you were above spreading gossip."

Alfred stared at him and said, "Mark my words, Theo, you and Mrs. Heisen are riding for a fall."

Theo glared and asked, "Who would believe such rubbish?"

"I have already sent the damning evidence to both the Heisen and BAI boards as well as the Securities and Exchange Commission," Alfred stated emphatically. "There's going to be a grand jury investigation. I hope you are prepared for what is about to transpire," he said as he stood up and walked away, leaving Theo shocked and open-mouthed.

fourteen

THE CALIFORNIA GATHERING
November 28, 1963

It was early Thanksgiving morning when Karen rolled over and opened her eyes to face David. He was still asleep and did not feel her gently rubbing his arm. Since his resignation from BAI three weeks prior, he had not mentioned the company, Theo Bachman, or the Heisen account. David felt a renewed commitment to his marriage, although Karen had yet to fully forgive him for his affair. But the shocking assassination of President Kennedy six days before had brought unity to many divided marriages.

"David, wake up."

Although in a sound sleep, her voice roused him. He had become sensitive to every fluctuation in her voice. "What is it, honey? What's the matter?"

"I think we should cancel dinner. We should have canceled as soon as we heard about Kennedy."

"Life has to go on, Karen. Yes, we lost a phenomenal president and things may never be the same, but it is Thanksgiving and time to find a reason to give thanks." He pulled her closer to him and kissed her forehead. "God, I am so very thankful that you've given me a second chance."

"Let's not talk about that right now, David," she said, referring to his infidelity.

"Okay, okay. I can take a hint."

Karen sat up in bed and said adamantly, "Anyway, I think we should cancel dinner."

"Kar, before we do anything so drastic, let's rationalize it. Tomorrow will be one week since the assassination and three days ago President Kennedy was laid to rest. We've had time to grieve; now it's time to move forward. Besides, canceling Thanksgiving dinner at this short notice would be utterly unfair to our guests."

"The truth is I'm not up to it. All I keep thinking of is Jackie and her two beautiful little children. I just can't imagine what she must be going through."

Karen started to whimper, although her tears were not so much for the Kennedys as they were for herself. She shuddered to think what life would be like if she were to lose David. The thought humbled her.

"Perhaps you're right, David. Jenni's friends don't need any more disappointments. All three of them had tumultuous lives before moving out here."

"Neil shared with me about Vicky and the abuse she encountered from her mother. I'd like to know about the two boys and their situations. What are their stories?"

"Billy, the boy from Cleveland, was raised by his alcoholic mother Sarah. There was a time, right after Billy was born, that she quit drinking. A few years later she met a rogue who swept her off her feet. They were married shortly thereafter. It was he who enticed her to start drinking again."

"Did this "gentleman" adopt the boy?" David asked, with an ironic emphasis on gentleman.

"No, he wanted no part of Billy, although Sarah loved the man in spite of his flaws. That is, until he cleaned out her savings."

"Let me guess. He took the money and ran."

"Yes, but it wasn't just her money. It was the profits from a supper club originally owned by her friend who had given Sarah half-ownership. She was the club's main attraction; she's a singer. Anyway, the scoundrel took the profits from the sale of their business."

"Why didn't they just have him arrested?"

"After she married him, she signed her half of the restaurant over to him—perhaps it was her idea of a wedding gift. Legally, Sarah didn't have a case," Karen paused and added, "although she did file a report on behalf of her partner."

"Why didn't her partner file charges?"

"He had a massive stroke and died a few months ago. I heard that he was the only constant in Billy's life."

"Oh, so that's why they moved to California—to get away," David said, certain he understood Sarah's motivation.

"It turns out that the bastard is living somewhere in Los Angeles."

"Ah, so she moved out here to find him."

"I suppose so. But I get the impression she's been too ill to do much of anything, let alone search for a man she may or may not want to find."

"What's wrong with her?"

Karen shrugged her shoulders. "I don't know. I wouldn't be surprised, though, if it was alcohol related. She drank for years up until the day they left Ohio."

"You mean to say she hasn't had a drink since? Wow, that's commendable!"

"I don't think that she can have one even if she wanted one. Doctor's orders."

"What about the other boy? Ethan, isn't it?"

"Sweet Ethan," Karen sighed. "He's still a mystery. All I know is that he was raised by his mother and her Negro friend. Both of the women acted as his parents. Ethan's mother, her name is Dolores, brought him out here after her friend passed away. I understand that just prior to the woman's death, something unspeakable happened to Ethan."

David thought about Jenni Lynn and was relieved that her only ordeal was having her tonsils removed at age four. Other than that, she had a carefree and happy life. "The poor boy, what happened to him?"

"I don't know, but he had to be hospitalized for quite some time. To this day if you even mention the word 'Alabama' to him, he quivers. I can only imagine that whatever it was, it must have been horrific."

"What's Ethan's mother like?"

"I only met her in passing at Neil's. She's very tall, nearly six feet, and I'm guessing she's in her early sixties. Dolores doesn't drink, doesn't smoke, and spends most of her time volunteering at church."

"Karen, how on earth do you know all this?"

"Who is the only one who knows all of us? It's Neil, of course. The boys have been working for him in the cabinet shop after school. Neil says he's not quite sure how it happened, but somehow he's taken them under his wing. My opinion is that he enjoys being a father figure to them."

"Leave it to Neil," he smiled. "Well, that settles it. We can't let them down by canceling Thanksgiving dinner."

"Your point is well-taken. After talking about those children and what they've gone through, it makes me realize how much we really have to be thankful for," she stared at the floor and continued, "Not that we haven't had our own bumps in the road…"

"I know, I know. I'm the one who caused those bumps, but from here on out our road has a fresh coat of asphalt."

His admission of guilt was an invitation to caress his wife. "You feel so good, babes," he whispered into her ear.

It had been over three weeks since David had had sex and longer than that since he had made love with Karen. He needed to be reassured that she still loved him. Holding her close to him, he became fully aroused. Yet David knew better than to act on the opportunity; Karen hadn't forgiven him quite that much.

"I'm getting up," she said, easing out of bed and away from David's caresses. Karen opened the television cabinet and turned the television on. As it warmed up, a picture of a newscaster came into focus.

"Turn it off, Karen. It won't do either of us any good to see another replay of little John John saluting the casket. I'll turn on the hi-fi." While the record dropped onto the turntable he added, "Babes, do you mind if I take Jenni to Newport? I'd like to get a couple hours of surfing in before we have a houseful this afternoon."

They were interrupted by a knock on their bedroom door. It was their housekeeper holding the newspaper. "*Hola*, Mr. and Mrs. Stratton," Rosa said.

"Thank you, Rosa. You can start preparing the dressing for the turkey. I'll be down in a few minutes to help you," Karen said as she closed the door.

She glanced at the headline "Should We Be Thankful?" and then just as she set the paper down she noticed two photos on the bottom of the page—Jessica Heisen and Theo Bachman. "David, look at this," she said handing him the paper.

He started to read the article in which JFK asked for understanding in a Thanksgiving message that he had written two weeks before his death. "I told you that I didn't want to see any more of this today, Karen."

"Not that," she said as she pointed to the bottom of the page. "There."

David saw the solemn pictures of Theo and Jessica; they looked haggard and distressed. "This can't be true. I don't believe it. They're being investigated for falsifying company records." He read on and said, "And they are being accused of illegal trading of stocks. There is going to be a grand jury investigation. They could both be indicted."

Hesitatingly, Karen asked, "David, are you involved in this mess?"

"Karen, I swear on my life, I had no part of this," he stated honestly. "I wonder if I'll be called as a witness, though."

Karen yanked the paper from his hand and tossed it in the wicker wastebasket. "You are right, David, we don't need anymore of this today. Tell Jenni that her bathing suit cover-up is hanging in the laundry room. Hang five," she said with a smile.

Better Days Ahead

Although David pretended to Karen that he was fine with his termination from BAI, it wasn't until that moment that he realized what a lucky break he had had. Now he could actually be happy about the events. It put distance between him, and Theo and Jessica. Relieved, he sighed, "I'll hang ten today."

✧ ✧ ✧

Karen sat in front of the vanity keeping her eyelids motionless while the glue dried on the just-applied false eyelashes. Facing the mirror, she didn't like what she saw. Her hair had been colored and styled like Jackie Kennedy's and was inappropriate under the circumstances; however, there was little time to experiment with other hairdos. It was after three o'clock in the afternoon and the guests would be arriving any minute.

"Damn it. Why did I get it cut this way?" She said out loud although no one heard her. David and Jenni, whose skins glistened from a touch of the morning sun, had returned from Newport and were already waiting downstairs for their guests.

Karen continued to primp, trying several styles. The doorbell had just rung twice so she quickly rolled her hair into a French twist. While she slipped into her brown satin dress, the doorbell rang again. It rang for a fourth time as she put on the matching pumps. Taking one last glance in the full-length mirror, she mumbled, "This will have to do."

Karen, elegant as always, despite her misgivings, descended the staircase. Almost regal in her bearing, no one looking at her could have known the heartache she suffered the month before, save Delilah Stratton. The grande dame took special interest when it concerned her son and his wife.

Waiting for Karen in the foyer were the Allens, the senior Strattons, and David, as well as Neil Dvorak, Dolores Drake, and a very pale Sarah Robbins. The four children were nowhere to be found. They had already retreated to the family room to try out the newest board games compliments of David.

David turned to Neil and asked, "Got any feeling in that hand yet, Neil?"

"Not yet. The nerve endings were severed. I'm patient," he said optimistically.

Neil's right arm was still in a cast and shoulder sling after the shop accident nine weeks earlier. After two surgeries the doctors managed to save his hand. His middle finger had taken the brunt of the saw and whether it would ever be functional again, only time would tell. Luckily, he had the boys to assist him.

"Karen," Neil shouted, as he used his free arm to push his way through to the front of the group. Taking her by the hand he added, "You look beautiful as always. Let me have the pleasure of introducing everyone."

Up until then Neil was the only common bond between the entourage. He had done work for the Allens and Strattons, so he knew them well. Through his relationship with the boys he had befriended their mothers.

Neil's introduction was informal, yet effective. With his palm up and hand extended he presented each couple. "Delilah and Alfred Stratton, Lieutenant John Allen and his wife Agnes Allen, and our hosts David and Karen Stratton. This is Dolores Drake, Ethan's mother, and this is Sarah Robbins, Billy's mother."

No one had noticed that Sarah's mouth had fallen open after Neil introduced the first couple. Dumbfounded, she was stunned to learn she had shared a last name. And it wasn't Robbins.

There was an exchange of handshakes and small talk. Agnes mentioned the overwhelming success of the Bikini Huts to Dolores, Alfred shared his latest stock picks with Lieutenant John, and Delilah told Karen how much she admired the autumn wreath that decorated the door.

Neil and Sarah, who were on opposite sides of the room, came together. Compassionately, Neil asked, "How are you feeling, Sarah?"

"Very well, Neil. Thank you for asking," she said as she saw her reflection in the mirror over the foyer table. Her skin color bore a sickly yellow pallor instead of a healthy pink hue. She understood why Neil had asked.

Sarah turned to Delilah, who was now standing next to her and said, "Is the name Stratton an English name by any chance?"

"Ah, you haven't spoken to my husband Alfred, have you? He has a strong English accent. He is a descendent of a long line of ancestors who hail from West Sussex. Are you familiar with the area?"

"No, but it's a coinci…"

Sarah was about to bring up Jack when David interrupted the chatter, "Now that everyone has met, let's all go into the living room, shall we?"

As they were escorted down the corridor Sarah walked alongside Neil and whispered, "They think my last name is Robbins."

"They know that you're Billy's mother. That's all," he whispered back.

The formal living room, built on a separate tier from the base of the house, was elevated high enough to provide an unobstructed view of the ocean. Each guest found a cozy place and sat down. Neil was the first to address the crowd and introduce the delicate subject that everyone had been avoiding. "I have a feeling there is much more to Kennedy's death than meets the eye. I don't believe that Oswald acted alone. My gut tells me there is a conspiracy of some sort."

Everyone, except the Lieutenant, had an opinion. He sat back and listened to theories and accusations—with which, for the most part, he privately disagreed.

Alfred Stratton asked, "I'd like to hear your take on all this, John. You were in the military. So, what's this all about? Was it the Bay of Pigs or payback for the senior Kennedy's bootlegging days? Tell us what you think."

The Lieutenant was filling his pipe with tobacco when he answered, "It's too early to draw any conclusions. It's going to take months, perhaps even years, to complete the investigation. I will say two things. Firstly, under any other circumstance, Lyndon B. Johnson would not be president. You might say he was the major beneficiary of Kennedy's assassination. Secondly, you can bet that whatever is uncovered in the federal investigation, those of us living today will never know the whole truth. Oh, they'll come up with a grandiose theory and do their best to sell it to the public, but my guess is that the facts won't be unveiled for another seventy-five to one hundred years."

"Sounds like you know something, John," Delilah interjected.

"You flatter me, Delilah. I wasn't that high up in the ranks."

"Well, we could discuss this till dawn," David stated. "It is Thanksgiving so why don't we give it a rest." He turned to Sarah and Dolores and asked, "Would either of you ladies like a tour of the house?"

Dolores had hoped for the invitation. "Oh, please, yes!"

Sarah wasn't up to the long walk. She replied, "Maybe later? Right now I think I'd like to get some fresh air. Neil, would you join me outside?"

"Of course," he said, opening one of the two identical sliding-glass doors.

"Dad, while I show Dolores around, would you do the honors? Make mine a double."

"I'll help you out, Alfred," John offered, as they made their way toward the bar.

The calm, warm air felt good on Sarah's skin. She stretched her face to the sun to capture its rays. Neil noticed that she was weaker than when she first arrived. He pulled out an Adirondack chair for her.

"Let's take a breather. I don't think we'll be missed."

"Neil, I think today would be a good time to tell you how much I appreciate everything you've done for Billy. He loves woodworking and wants to follow in your footsteps."

"Billy's a good boy. He's always willing to take on more of a load than he ought," Neil said.

"He half blames himself for the accident. He thinks he should have been working closer with Ethan," Sarah confided.

"It was an accident, Sarah, and I can't complain. I've had many close calls in the past. My luck just ran out this time. What about you? Billy tells me that the phone company job fell through. I was sorry to hear that."

"I couldn't pass the physical. I'm thinking of looking into another field of work."

"Is that so? Billy told me that you have quite a voice."

"Oh, it's been so long since I've sung anything. I don't know if my larynx could remember how."

"You shouldn't let a gift slip away."

Sarah drew the salty air into her lungs. She expelled it slowly. "Neil, I asked you out here for a reason."

"I'm listening."

"I haven't told Billy this," she took another breath and continued. "It turns out I have cirrhosis. It went undetected for such a long time that my liver has irreparable damage. To be frank," she looked him in the eye and explained, "I've got cancer."

"My God, Sarah, are you receiving radiation treatments?"

"No, there isn't enough radiation to make up for the damage I've caused myself. It's all because I couldn't go a day without my ration of Cuba libres."

"Oh, Sarah, I don't know what to say. I'm in shock," he said, trying to imagine how Billy would handle the news.

"There's nothing you can say that will change the inevitable. Let me finish, Neil." She opened her purse and handed him an envelope. "I fear I don't have much time left in this world. Should something happen to me, I would like you to know the name of Billy's biological father. His name is Judge Henry Kinslow. I don't expect you to memorize it so I've written it down in here."

"Why do you want me to know?"

"Just in case the day comes and Billy wants to know. I can't bear the thought of leaving him to wonder where he came from for the rest of his life."

"Do you expect this judge to take custody of him?"

"I convinced him a long time ago that Billy was not his. To this day I still believe I did the right thing." Sarah bit her lip and added, "He was married to someone else."

Neil understood that she was tying up loose ends. "Sarah, what provisions have you made for Billy's care?"

"It's a work in progress, Neil."

"I think you know that I have grown fond of him. I wouldn't want to see him be made a ward of the court. If you give me permission then I would take care of him in the event something unforeseen happens."

"Neil, something is going to happen. I think much sooner than I had hoped." She licked her parched lips and asked, "Are you sure that you would want to take on another child?"

"I grew up in an orphanage and I could never let that happen to Billy. So, rest your mind, Sarah. It's a done deal."

"Billy has keen intuition about people," Sarah said. "He liked you from the start and has since grown to admire and respect you. The contents of this envelope are based on Billy's intuition. Not only have I given you information about Henry Kinslow, I requested that you become Billy's legal guardian. It was notarized yesterday. It was a gamble, Neil, but it just paid off."

"You are a wise woman. I promise to be a good father to him."

"I know you will. But if for any reason you change your mind, you have my blessing to destroy this document. No one will ever know."

"I've given you my word, Sarah. There's no need for further discussion."

"Thank you, Neil. From the bottom of my heart, I thank you."

"Sarah, can I ask you something?"

"Of course; we're family now."

"Are you afraid?"

"At first, I was. But lately I've been dreaming about a friend who is waiting for me. In my dreams he has opened a club in heaven and is looking for a lead singer. I plan to apply for that job."

Neil knew she was referring to Sam Donahue. It was a poignant moment.

The sun was falling in the sky. Sarah imagined it disappearing into the Pacific Ocean. It would be the same ocean where she would request the ashes of her withered body to be scattered.

She sighed and said, "Well, I've had enough sun. Should we join the others?"

Neil took her by the arm and helped her from the chair. Walking back into the house, Sarah's steps were slow and labored but her physical condition no longer mattered to her, as the burden of finding a home for Billy was now resolved. Sarah had much to be thankful for on this, her last, Thanksgiving.

"Your home is beautiful, Karen," Dolores said upon returning from the tour. "It must be wonderful living just steps away from the ocean."

"Thank you, Dolores. We enjoy living here."

Rosa was in the formal dining room putting the finishing touches on the table. At each setting a small porcelain cornucopia held the guest's name written in calligraphy. The adult setting also included six different wine glasses, which would be removed upon request. When Rosa placed the succulent turkey in the center, the table became a scene out of a housekeeping magazine.

"David, please tell the children dinner is ready. Would the rest of you join me in the dining room?" Karen asked her guests.

When everyone was seated, David stood up and tapped his Baccarat glass with a spoon. Filled with a Napa Valley Chardonnay, it rang a pure C note. "On behalf of Karen, Jenni, and myself, we'd like to thank you for spending Thanksgiving with us. Now if you wouldn't mind, everyone please join hands. I'd like to thank the Man up Above for this day."

In unison they bowed their head while David prayed. "Lord, thank you for the bounty we are about to receive with our friends and family. Thank you for the gifts of life that we carelessly take for granted. And finally Lord, please shed your grace on Mrs. Kennedy and her young children. Only you can ease her pain so that she may face another day. Amen."

Karen looked up at him and saw compassion. It was what she needed. With her hand still clenched in his, she kissed his wedding ring. "That was beautiful, David" she smiled.

"Rosa, you can begin serving the first course," Karen instructed. The soup, an autumn squash drizzled with cream and toasted almond slivers, was a recipe Karen perfected. It was sweet and buttery with a nutty aftertaste. But as delectable as the soup was, the courses that followed were each more delicious than the last. Overall, it was a culinary experience for the most discriminating of taste buds.

"That was outstanding. The best Thanksgiving dinner I've ever had," Neil said as he consumed the last morsel of chocolate profiteroles. The rest of the guests followed his lead and praised Karen and David for the cuisine and hospitality. With their stomachs full and every sweet tooth satisfied, the youngsters became fidgety. It was apparent that they were anxious to return to their unfinished board game. Karen, noting their impatience, gave them permission to leave the table. "You children may be excused."

"Jeez, thanks, Mrs. Stratton," the boys said almost in unison.

"Thanks, Mom," Jenni said as she placed her folded napkin alongside her dessert plate. Vicky, who was not schooled in etiquette, left her soiled napkin on her chair and leaned over to give her father a kiss on the cheek. "You don't mind, Daddy, do you?"

"You kids go and have a good time," Neil responded.

As the children's voices faded, Delilah turned to address Dolores. "My granddaughter tells me that you and your son came from Alabama." Thanks to Vicky and Jenni's candidness, there was not one person at the table who was unaware of Dolores and Ethan's prior living situation. "I don't know much about that state," Delilah continued, "but I hear that there is a great deal of racial unrest there. Did you read about the four little girls killed by a bomb in the basement of the Baptist church?"

"Yes," Dolores responded, her hand on her heart. "I pray every day for those poor, sweet angels whose lives were taken. I also pray their families continue to stand up for what they believe."

"The black people are making their voices heard," Lieutenant John said. "And they have good reason. They want what is rightfully theirs: equality under the law, in education, in jobs, and in health care. Take Medgar Evers, for instance, the American black civil-rights activist who was shot in his own driveway in June. The man was virtually an unknown and now his name is almost as synonymous with black freedom as Martin Luther King, Jr.'s."

"I couldn't agree with you more. I, too, believe in their cause," Dolores proudly affirmed. She took a sip of her coffee and then continued. "Yes, Delilah, racial tensions keep surfacing; but it's not only in the South. Lately there has been discontent among black youths in East Los Angeles—less than twenty miles from here. And although I would hate to see anyone take extreme measures, equality is something every American deserves."

Delilah was taken aback that a white woman would be so supportive of another race. She had lived behind the gates of her estate for so long that she had no idea about lack of equality or that racial unrest was so close to where she lived. *Why didn't I know?* She asked herself. Delilah thought for a moment and realized that she did not have a single friend of color.

Dolores had barely spoken during the meal, but now she made up for her reticence. "I am proud to say that Ethan and I were fortunate enough to live with Ruthie Jackson. Ruthie helped me raise my son until the day she died. I consider her family. She was also a black woman. I thank the Lord for allowing me to share her life as He did."

Delilah, curious to know more, decided to press the issue. "It's not that I'm prejudiced, mind you. I support the Negroes just like our beloved late president. It's just that I can't imagine living in the South with Negroes."

Dolores touched two fingers to her lips and smiled. "I was given the chance to experience life with black people. My so-called community, the white people, wouldn't help me—not even when I feared for my life. But Ruthie was there for me and my children. The black people accepted us as folks like themselves; the whites shunned us and called us names. It taught me to embrace people on their own merits—not because they are black, white, brown, or yellow. If I could have one wish it would be that each white person could walk a mile in a black person's shoes, if only for one day. I assure you that the world would be a different place today."

Neil interjected, "Dolores acts on what she believes. She volunteers Saturday afternoons at a boys' club in East Los Angeles."

Dolores smiled at Neil and explained, "I was given the rare opportunity to experience life in a neighborhood other than my own. I learned how hard it is for blacks to live happy and contented lives with the hardships the whites forced on them." She added, "People speak of equality, but that word is meaningless unless one understands that it is meant for people of all colors. Every person deserves a fair chance in life. That's why I want to help the children before East Los Angeles becomes another Purvis, Alabama."

Agnes, who up until then had said little, chimed in. "So it is Negro boys you are helping?"

Dolores answered, "Not just blacks, Agnes, but Latinos, Japanese, and white youths, too. The program is designed to teach them to interact with one another."

"This seems to be a good cause, Dolores. I wouldn't mind giving up my Saturday afternoons for a good cause."

"Mom," Karen asked, "Does that mean you'll actually take a day off from the Bikini Hut?

Agnes's first sign of independence had been as a result of working at her daughter's bikini shops. "Yes, dear, I believe I could afford the time. Dolores, I would like to join you on Saturday, if you don't mind."

"We can always use another set of hands, Agnes. I would be happy to pick you up so that we could ride together."

"Wonderful," Agnes said.

Lieutenant John, proud of his wife for managing the Bikini Huts, chuckled. "What's next, Agnes? Are you going to run for office? Do we have a politician in the making?"

Flattered that the thought had actually crossed his mind, Agnes answered, "Well John, you never know!"

Dolores was grateful for the support she had received from the people around the table. She reflected how far she had come since she was Thom Drake's naive and abused wife. Ruthie Jackson had made her growth—her life—possible. Dolores could sit at the same table with more privileged and refined people and feel she was every bit as good as them. She raised her glass of water in a toast. "I am thankful to our hosts for this gathering and to Ruthie Jackson."

Neil cleared his throat, "Yes, it's Thanksgiving and we have something else to be thankful for. We have a major entertainer in our midst—Miss Sarah Robbins. She cut a record a few years back."

Sarah blushed, but through her sallow skin color, it was difficult to tell. "I almost forgot about 'Better Days Ahead.' That was the record I made for a friend, but it was never distributed."

Neil urged, "Would you sing it for us?"

"Oh, I don't know," Sarah stalled.

"Hey, Billy," Neil called out. "Help me talk your mom into singing for us."

Billy ran back up the corridor with the three other friends following closely behind, "Please, Mom, you haven't sung a note since Donahue's." He took a drink of water and bragged, "I was raised backstage at the club while my mom sang. People used to come from all over Ohio just to hear her!"

"We'd love to hear you," Delilah said.

Sarah really wasn't up to the task but conceded, in part, to their wishes. "You have given me such a wonderful holiday, it's the least I can do. However, I'd like to sing something other than 'Better Days Ahead.' That song still belongs to my dearest friend," she said referring to Sam Donahue.

"All right, then. Let's all go into the living room. Name your tune, Sarah, and I'll accompany you on the piano," David said.

"That's good because I'm not one for singing a capella."

Sarah leaned up against the baby grand. It felt good to have an audience again, even a small one. "Do you know 'Sentimental Journey'? F sharp, please."

David, who had played the piano since he was five, knew it well. It was an old favorite of his mom and dad's. He gave her an elaborate introduction and, like the professional she was, Sarah took it from there. At the song's conclusion Sarah was more than ready to call it a night. Just singing out loud required more energy than she had to spare. Although she never told anyone, she knew it was her swan song.

David continued playing while Sarah squeezed in between Neil and the end of the sofa. Neil said, "That was one heck of an audition, Sarah." He winked adding, "I'm sure you got the part."

While the guests were enjoying the impromptu entertainment, Rosa had answered the front door. Standing before her was a limousine driver wearing a peaked cap and double-breasted suit.

"I'm here to pick up a Stratton."

"No, sir! Mr. Stratton no call for a car." Rosa said, stumbling on her English.

Rosa seemed to irritate the man with the offensive body odor. He persisted, "Like I said, lady, I'm supposed to be here at seven and here I am. Someone in there needs a ride."

"No, I don't tink so. Mr. Stratton no tell me."

"Forget it, lady," he said, pushing her out of his way. "I'll see myself in."

"But sir, you no go in," she argued.

"Don't tell me what I can and can't do, you Mexican dimwit!"

"But sir," she wailed. But she was silenced when the man cocked his fist and struck her jaw. Rosa was knocked out cold; the intruder dragged her into the kitchen and out of his way.

David stopped playing the piano and said, "What the…?"

David and Sarah were the only two who had heard Rosa's exchange. Unlike David, Sarah immediately recognized the harsh, abrasive voice. She remembered Jack's comment about his relationship to Alfred Stratton. While David went to check things out, Sarah quietly excused herself.

"I need to use the powder room. Billy, walk with me."

"Okay, Mom." He turned to the other children and added, "You guys can't tell any more riddles till I get back."

With Billy at her side Sarah walked right past the restroom on the lower level. "Mom, here it is," he pointed.

"I want to use the one upstairs."

"Jeez, Mom. A bathroom is a bathroom."

Bypassing the front hallway, they found the second, smaller servant's staircase that was not as obvious as the grand spiral staircase that graced the main entrance. "Take my arm, son. Help me up the stairs."

Billy aided his mother and as they trudged up the stairs he said, "You look real pale, Mom. It must have been all that singing, but man, oh, man, were you good! I was proud of you."

"Thanks, Billy. Let's go in here," she said as she opened a guest bedroom door. "I'll use the bathroom in here."

"Mom, is it okay for us to be in here?"

"I don't think Karen would mind. I just need some privacy for a few minutes. Why don't you go out on the balcony and wait for me there? I'll only be a minute."

Assuming his mother would be a while, Billy opened the French doors and made himself comfortable. Looking down on the pool, he wondered why the floodlight wasn't lit. Usually glowing, it was a beacon in the darkness. However, on this Thanksgiving evening all that could be seen was an occasional twinkle from a distant passing ship.

Five minutes passed and the bathroom door remained closed. Billy figured his mother was vomiting, because of late that was what she did after every meal. This time Billy was wrong. Having carried the telephone into the restroom with her, Sarah was talking to the operator. "We need the police at 411 Ocean Boulevard."

"What seems to be the trouble, ma'am?"

Excitedly Sarah blurted out, "A wanted man by the name of Jack Stratton is on the premises. There's a warrant for his arrest in Cleveland, Ohio, for grand theft. Please send the local police and notify Sergeant Graham of the Cleveland Police Department. I'm sure they'll want to have him extradited."

Downstairs David walked up the corridor and faced the intruder. He recognized him as the limousine driver from BAI who had picked him up at the airport the month before. "Jay? What the hell are you doing here?"

"I thought I'd drop by and say 'Happy Thanksgiving' to the elite Stratton clan."

"I beg your pardon?"

The driver leaned to the side and shouted past David. "Alfred, Delilah, you might have squashed me once, but you won't do it again."

"Now see here," David said, attempting to contain the man. But the driver would not retreat. He pushed David aside and forced his way into the living room.

"Ah, ain't this a cozy little family gathering," he grunted.

David, fast behind him, cried out, "I don't know what you want, Jay, but you better get the hell off my property before I call the police."

"Shut it, Dave."

With dignity and defiance Alfred stood up and scolded, "Last I heard you were locked up in Cleveland State Penitentiary, Jack. I'm sorry that I wasn't notified of your recent whereabouts."

Shoving the elderly Brit back down, he warned, "Don't get up until I tell you, Uncle Alfred. I'm in no mood."

He spun around to face the others and in doing so a small handgun tucked inside the waistband of his uniform became exposed. It was easily accessible to him and an unspoken threat to them.

"Dad, his name is Jay, not Jack. He's the driver from BAI who picked me up three weeks ago," David said uncertainly.

"That's not correct, son. His name is Jack Stratton, your father's nephew," Delilah interjected.

Neil recognized the name and put two and two together. He knew exactly why Sarah had left the room with Billy. It all made sense to him.

"Jack Stratton, Dad?"

"He's my younger brother's son, and I don't consider him family."

Jenni, who was sitting across the room from her mother, cried out, "Mommy?"

"Hey, the little Stratton," Jack smirked. "You're Jenni Lynn, right?"

Jack leaned over Jenni's shoulder and mumbled, "Better watch your p's and q's little one because you never know what might happen."

"Come over here, Jenni," Karen beckoned. "Come sit by me."

"No, little miss. You stay right where you are," Jack ordered.

Jack walked over to Karen and stood in front of her. "Karen, I haven't had the pleasure, have I? Quite a catch you got here, Dave old boy," he said as he slid his hand down the side of her face.

With Jack's gun in clear view, David felt powerless to prevent the intruder from molesting his wife, but he yelled helplessly, "Get your filthy hands off her!"

"Don't get bent out of shape, coz," Jack retreated. "It's not your wife that I'm interested in." He laughed and then asked, "Hey, what did you think of those birthday cards I sent you when you were no bigger than a pip-squeak?"

"I don't know what you are talking about," David said, gritting his teeth.

"I guess you'll have to ask your mother about that." Jack looked at Delilah and laughed again. "I told you that time was on my side, Delilah."

"Rosa," David hollered. "Call the police."

Jack nodded his head and said, "Ah, yes, your immigrant housekeeper…well, she's taking an extended break. I figure she'll be indisposed for at least an hour or so."

"Jay, or Jack, whatever your name is, what the hell do you want with us?" David shouted.

"Tell your boy, Alfred. Tell him how you fucked me out of my share of the inheritance. Tell him that I'm here to collect my half."

"You got nothing because you deserved nothing," Alfred yelled. "Now get out of here."

"I'm not budging, Uncle Al. Not without a shitload of trinkets and whatever else your son has locked in his bedroom safe. I want the diamond jewelry and the stocks and bonds. Oh, and don't think for a moment that cashing the certificates will be a problem; I've been practicing my cousin's signature for years." He turned toward David and added, "You know, I haven't had a new car in I don't know how long, coz. I'd also like the keys to that little convertible parked out on the driveway."

Disregarding any threat, Alfred said, "What makes you think we'd give any of those things to you?"

Jack patted the front of his waistband. "Because, Uncle Al, you don't want anything to happen to the little heir, do you?"

"Mommy…" Jenni cried.

Ethan, who was holding Jenni's hand, whispered, "It'll be okay, Jenni. I'll protect you."

"What's that, boy? You'll do what?" Jack yelled.

Ethan stared back at him. "I'm not afraid of you!"

"Stand up," Jack screamed while pulling Ethan by the hair. "You've been disrespectful to me. I know a place with bars on the door and lights out at ten where they'd take care of runts like you."

"I'm still not afraid of you. I've been through worse."

"Oh, yeah? Well, see if this compares." Jack flung out his arm and slapped Ethan across the face; the force of the blow slammed Ethan up against the fireplace. "Now keep your trap shut and show me some respect."

"Ethan!" Dolores screamed.

"Ah, now that was too easy," Jack said sarcastically. "A mother can't help but stake claim to her litter."

Jack was quickly bored with Dolores and her son. They appeared penniless in their less-than-fashionable garb. He pointed to the Allens and sneered, "So you must be Karen's folks. You're the retired Lieutenant, hey? Payroll must be good for someone at your level. So, I'll just take your wallet and your wife's jewelry. You can place your offerings on the table."

"Coz, it's about time we took a trip upstairs. That is where you keep your safe, isn't it?"

Sarah had slipped out of the bathroom and was already downstairs. As she entered the living room, she said, "Well, well, well, Jack. What a coincidence meeting you here."

"Oh, now isn't this a pretty day? My fucking wife shows up out of the blue. How did you do it, Sarah? Did you go through the entire phone book? Did you call every Stratton in California?"

Delilah interrupted him and asked Sarah, "You're name is Sarah Stratton? I thought it was Robbins."

"Robbins is my maiden name and Stratton is my married name. However, after seeing you Jack, I've decided that I want to be called Sarah Robbins until the day I die."

"Yeah, well you look like you're dying," he laughed. "Man, oh, man, you sure look bad! Need another drink, Sarah?"

"I don't care what I look like. What did you do with the money, Jack? What did you do with Sam's entire life's savings?"

"Hell, I had the time of my life." Bending down to Jenni's eye level he whispered, "Money doesn't last forever. Does it, little miss?" He stared at her long and hard and then added, "She's going to be quite the looker in a couple years, coz. I'll have to stop by again and see for myself."

"You half-witted piece of garbage! Get away from her," Alfred yelled.

"What's the matter, old man? Can't stand not being in control? Well, you've had your day and now I'm going to have mine."

"I said, leave the child alone," Alfred demanded.

"Shut the fuck up, Alfred. Don't give me an excuse to use this," he said patting the butt of the gun. "Nothing would make me happier than giving you your just deserts."

Fearing for his family and friends, David said, "I'll take you to the safe."

"Wait just one minute, coz. Where the hell is Billy boy? I haven't had the pleasure of slapping him around in a long time."

"He's not here," Sarah insisted.

"Oh yeah? Then where?"

Determined to protect her child, Sarah lied readily. "He's in San Diego with friends."

"That's too bad. I always felt better when I beat the shit out of him, especially because I knew he'd never tell you. I sure do hate to miss out on a last-minute thrill."

David implored, "Let's go upstairs. I'll give you what you want if you'll just leave."

"Little miss, you come with your father and me," he said as he clenched David's arm. "I just need a little insurance, that's all."

"Mommy?"

"He said he'd give you what you want. Now leave the child be," Alfred commanded.

"Hey, Delilah, how'd you like to be made a widow? Your old man, and I do mean old, is really asking for it."

"Please don't hurt us," Delilah begged.

Alfred, who was stern and deliberate, would not stoop to groveling. He stood up and moved to within inches of Jack's face and then shouted, "I said, leave the child alone!"

"You arrogant SOB, get the fuck out of my way." Jack pulled the gun from his waistband and slammed it into the side of the senior Stratton's skull. Alfred fell onto the marble floor and lay still; his blood trickled a crimson path through the snow-white grout. Delilah muffled her cries as best she could, but she couldn't prevent a sob escaping as she looked helplessly at her husband of thirty-three years who was now nearly unconscious.

"Dad," David cried as the room filled with gasps and screams. He jerked away from Jack to help his father but stopped short when Jack put the gun to his head.

"Your old man got off easy, coz. Make one more move and I'll start firing. And it doesn't make much difference to me if you're the first or your little miss gets the honor."

Karen sobbed while Agnes buried her face in her husband's chest. But it was Sarah, like Alfred, who defied him. "Stop it this minute, Jack. Leave these good people alone and let us help Mr. Stratton. He's bleeding terribly."

Jack stared down at Alfred and saw the aged man withering. His eyes were barely open and his senses seemed numb from the impact. "So the bloody old coot is bleeding. Let him rot for all I care."

"You won't get away with this," said John Allen, who up until then had kept silent.

"Oh, I'll get away with it," Jack said confidently. "I'll be in Mexico long before you'll be able to call the police."

With the gun still pointed at the group, Jack backed up to the floor-to-ceiling draperies and yanked two intertwined cords. "These should do fine," he grinned pulling out a pocketknife. "Lieutenant John, cut these up into three-foot pieces. And don't get any funny ideas," he leered.

The Lieutenant lifted his wife's head from his chest and promised, "It will be all right, dear. Stay close to Karen."

For a fleeting moment, the knife in John's hand gave him courage. But the gun that was now positioned in the back of David's head gave him reason to follow orders. Lieutenant John cut the cords as he was asked.

"Good. A real soldier you are, Lieutenant John. You take your commands well. Now I'd like you to tie everyone up. Start with Delilah and don't take too long. My finger is starting to get stiff," he hinted about its placement on the trigger.

John's face flushed with shame as he bound each person. No one complained as he whispered, "I'm sorry if this is too tight."

"Jack, please. Enough already," Sarah pleaded. "Take what you must, but please leave!"

"Lieutenant, take the scarf wrapped around the bitch's neck and shove it in her mouth. I've heard just about enough from the judge's whore." He chuckled, adding, "Yeah, I married Kinslow's piece of snatch."

Stunned that he knew, Sarah could only say, "But, Jack…"

She was silenced when John carefully pushed the scarf into her mouth. "I'm sorry, Sarah. Maybe the less said, the better," he whispered.

"Okay, Jack, I'm finished. Everyone is tied up, just like you wanted," John said, indirectly apologizing to the victims.

"Not everyone, Lieutenant," Jack said as he shifted his head toward the table next to him. "Put the knife down slowly over here. Do it right and the little miss can stay down here. I won't need her for insurance."

Against his better judgment, John Allen surrendered the only weapon he would have had to fight him. Again, he obeyed the command.

"Smart man you are, Lieutenant. Now get in front of my coz and let him tie you up. And don't forget for a second what I'm holding. As to the rest of you people, shut-the-fuck-up. No more crying and that means you, Delilah. Otherwise, I'll be happy to shove a scarf down your trap."

Billy walked inside from the balcony upstairs to the bathroom that he thought his mother still occupied. "Mom, you've been in there a very long time," he said. "Are you all right? Do you want me to get something for you?"

Billy listened for her response but became alarmed when she didn't answer. "Mom, I'm coming in," he said as he slowly opened the door. "Mom?"

When Billy discovered that his mother was nowhere to be found, he shook his head and grinned. *How could Mom have forgotten about me?* Billy just shrugged it off as an honest mistake and headed back downstairs, retracing the route his mother and he had taken.

As he made his way up the corridor Billy noticed that it was very quiet compared to the laughter and chatter earlier. He knew that something was different and that something was wrong. Instinctively, he began to tiptoe toward the living room where his friends were gathered. The hairs on the back of his neck were raised, but he didn't know why until he heard a voice that made him cringe. It was the sound of the monster in his nightmares for the past eight years. It was the voice of Jack Stratton.

Terrified, Billy leaned up against the hallway wall. His breathing had accelerated into short rapid puffs. To silence himself, he used his hands to cover his mouth. He shivered, fearing it was only a matter of time before he would be discovered.

With his back against the wall he slowly inched his way toward the downstairs bathroom. It was a mere ten feet from the living room. When he reached the door, he quietly slipped inside the unlit safe haven. From there he had a vantage point. He could see through the crack in the doorjamb that Jack Stratton was holding a gun to Jenni's father's head. He prayed for guidance. *Please, Sam, if you can hear me, tell me what to do. Help me—help them.*

In the dark, windowless bathroom he blindly searched for a weapon. While he waved his hands in the air he came across an artificial floral arrangement in the corner on the floor. Billy fell to his knees and carefully slid his hands down the flowers to the heavy vase below; he sized the vase and discovered that the lower part was indented. Carefully, he removed the tall flowers and placed them on the floor. Billy lifted the heavy vase and stood quietly in the darkness. He heard Jack Stratton threaten Jenni Lynn's father. Jack had told him to start moving or else...

Billy knew they would have to pass him, so he slithered back behind the door and waited while clutching the vase to his chest. He peered again through the crack and saw Jenni's father exit the living room toward the corridor. Following close behind him, holding a gun to his head, was Jack Stratton.

The thirteen-year-old prayed again. *Give me your strength, Sam. If ever I needed your help, now is the time.* Billy bit his lip to keep from letting his presence known. He listened as their footsteps alerted him to their position. They were only a few feet away. He bit his lip harder, drawing blood; the taste gave him a sense of bloodlust. Deep in the shadows Billy kept still as Jenni's father passed by. Next he saw the gun and Jack's arm. And finally Jack was directly in view. He patiently counted backwards five, four, three, two…"ONE," he screamed, as he smashed the vase that shattered upon impact into the back of Jack's head. This single blow, delivered with all the hatred and force Billy could muster, brought Jack to his knees, just seconds before his body slumped over. He was out cold.

"Billy, thank God you were here," praised David.

"Did I kill him?"

"No, but he's gonna have one helluva headache when he wakes up," he said while he checked for a pulse.

"Sam was here, I swear it. He came down from heaven to help us."

"He might have been, Billy. We need to untie the others, but first get me some rope so we can tie him up."

"That won't be necessary, sir," a voice from down the hall yelled.

David looked up and saw an officer holding a pair of handcuffs and coming their way. "How did you know? Who called the police?"

The officer bent down and in one continuous motion, he cuffed both of Jack's hands together. "We got a call from Sarah Robbins. Looks like he never knew what hit him," the officer said.

"My father," David shouted. "We need an ambulance for my father. And somebody check on our housekeeper, Rosa!" David called out.

"There's an officer with her as we speak, sir. We found her unconscious in the kitchen. She's coherent now; we're going to send her to the hospital to get checked out. The ambulances are already on the way."

"Billy, come to me, Billy," Sarah cried out.

"Mom," he mumbled. He realized now why she had slipped out of the bedroom unannounced. She was protecting him.

Billy ran to the living room and Sarah where he saw two policemen attending to the other victims. On the floor sat Delilah, who was cupping her husband's head in her hands. His blood oozed onto the sleeve of her cashmere sweater. Anxiously, Delilah cried, "How long before the paramedics arrive?"

She had no sooner asked when sirens were heard blaring in the driveway. "He's going to make it, ma'am. They'll fix him up in no time," the officer soothed.

"But the blood…there's so much of it."

"Probably just broke the skin," he suggested.

"Nevertheless, I'm going with him to the hospital. He's my husband."

"Mom, I'll go, too," David insisted.

"It's not necessary. Like the officer said, he's going to be fine. You take care of things here. Karen and Jenni need your moral support."

David didn't argue with her. He knew that everyone was in some form of shock but found that each person was being comforted by a family member. The Allens held Karen and Jenni close. Dolores, who was no stranger to abuse, held an ice pack to Ethan's swollen cheek. Neil lifted a sobbing Vicky onto his lap. Finally, there was Sarah and Billy. After years of taking on the role of caregiver to his mother, the roles were reversed, as they should be. Billy rested in his mother's arms while she lovingly ran her fingers through his curly black hair.

The lead officer addressing Billy said, "You are quite the hero, young man."

"Hear, hear," Neil exclaimed. "Our hero—Billy Robbins."

"Yeah, Billy. If it weren't for you, we might have been shot and killed," Ethan said. The accolades for Billy came from all directions. It was a brief escape from the grief they were experiencing; but then they heard the wretched voice again.

"What the fuck!" Jack said, as he was awakened by a strong dose of smelling salts. His head ached terribly, but it wasn't his headache that bothered him. He couldn't understand why he was handcuffed and why his year-long plan against the Strattons had failed. The only thing he did know was that he wasn't going to Tijuana any time soon.

The officers lifted Jack to his feet and ushered him to the front entry. As they passed the living room, Billy raced up to him and without thinking shouted. "I got you good, Jack. I clobbered you in the back of the head. And you know what? Sam would be real proud of me!"

"What the hell are *you* doing here, runt?"

"You son of a bitch," Billy cursed and then quickly apologized for his choice of words. "'Scuse me, Mom. It's just that I hate Jack Stratton and what he has done to us."

"You can say whatever you want to him, son. I won't deny you the chance to say what is in your heart."

"You're a rotten, no-good scoundrel," Billy yelled. "I hope that wherever you go, they do to you the same as you did to me. I want them to burn your fingertips over a hot flame on a stove. I want them to dangle you over a bridge until you beg for your life. You remember that day at Rocky River? Cuz I do! And I hope that when someone needs a punching bag, it's you who gets slugged."

The more he remembered being tortured by Jack, the angrier he became. "You might have hurt my mom, and Sam and me, but you'll never hurt anyone of us again…you, you son of a bitch," he repeated.

"What's the matter, kid? A few black-and-blues never hurt anyone. Hey, it built you some character, didn't it?"

"I have nothing more to say to you, except good riddance to bad trash."

"I'll be back someday, kid, just ask my kin. I always come back," he laughed. "I've yet to find a prosecutor who can lock me up for good."

"Then I know what I have to be when I grow up. I'm going to be an attorney and spend my life putting people like you behind bars."

"Then I'm sure we'll meet again. One way or another…"

"I've said all I need to say to him, officers. Take him away," Billy said, with the words of an adult, although the child inside wished he could kick Jack in the shins first.

"Wait, please, sirs," Sarah beckoned. "Can I have a moment?"

"Just one, ma'am. We need to get going."

"Well, Jack, I was beginning to believe this day would never come. Unbeknownst to Billy, we moved out here so that I could seek restitution for Sam. I prayed that I would find you so that you could face charges in Ohio. Well, coupled with today's criminal charges, you might not get off as easy as you think. Isn't it funny how fate can intervene and ruin a scheme?"

"Fuck you, Sarah."

"The same to you, Jack," Sarah smiled.

After the ambulances departed with Alfred and Delilah, and Rosa, two officers hauled Jack away in a squad car. Then the last of the policemen made a final sanity check. "Is everyone all right?"

Between feelings of shock, fear, and finally elation, they nodded in the affirmative. We'll be fine, officer," David answered.

"Then I'll be on my way."

David closed the door behind the policeman and said, "Well, this is one Thanksgiving that I'll never forget. I could use a drink. Does anyone else want one? Neil?"

"I think I'll pass, David. Vicky and I are going to call it a night."

"David, you can make me a stiff one," Lieutenant John said. "And pour your mother-in-law a glass of sherry."

"Sarah, Dolores? Would you like a cola or ginger ale?"

"Thank you, no. Ethan and I need to go home."

"Nothing for me either," Sarah stated. "Like the rest, Billy and I need to be on our way."

After the formal good-byes Dolores, Sarah, and the boys headed outside. Following behind them were Neil and Vicky. "I'll see you to your cars." He opened the door to his own car and said, "Vicky, wait for me here. I'll be right back."

Neil rushed and caught up with Dolores and Ethan who were first to get in. Neil leaned inside the passenger window and said, "Ethan, I want you to know that you were just as brave a young man as Billy. It took guts to stand up to that man and you're going to have a shiner to prove it," he chuckled, showing off his wide smile.

"Shucks, it was nothing like Billy done. Billy saved us all. We could have been killed!"

"Yes, Billy did come through for us. Still, I'm no less proud of you."

After Neil's compliment, Ethan sat erect, ready to show the world his war wound. "Thanks, Neil. Hey, can you pick me up early for work tomorrow? Remember, Neil, there's no school."

"You don't want to sleep in on your day off?"

"No, sir! Billy and me got a lot of stuff to do."

"Then I'll be there at eight. Drive carefully, Dolores."

After Neil waved them off, he walked over to Sarah's station wagon. He overheard Billy talking with Sarah. "I can't believe it, Mom. I thought we came to California cuz you wanted him back. I'm glad you didn't want him back."

"No, I was done with Jack." Sarah rested back on the vinyl interior of the car. She added, "Isn't it amazing how things turn out? You met Neil on your way to the beach and he turns out to be a friend of the Strattons. It's a small world, isn't it?"

"Hey, you two," Neil interrupted. "What a night, huh?"

"You can say that again. The son of a bitch," Billy cursed again.

"Billy, that's enough of that, from now on you'll watch your language. Is it a deal?"

"Okay, Mom," he agreed, happy that he finally had a mom who acted like a mom.

"Sarah, in spite of everything that happened tonight, it was a pleasure hearing you sing," Neil praised.

"I told you my mom was good, Neil! Hey, Mom, maybe you can get a singing job when you're not sick anymore."

"Funny you should say that, Billy. I just told Neil this afternoon that is what I'm going to do…in the not-too-distant future."

"That's great. Neil, me and Ethan want to get a full day in tomorrow and finish the Coldson order."

"Ethan already gave me a heads-up, first thing tomorrow morning. Drive safely, Sarah."

As they drove off, Billy was still talking about what had happened. But Sarah quietly drifted into her own thoughts. Her life had come full circle. One by one she remembered the men who had shared her life. There was Henry, strong with a gavel in his hand, but weak when it came to personal decisions. It was also Henry who, albeit unknowingly, had fathered Billy. Her memories of him from when she was a child to an adult were bittersweet. Then Sarah thought back to the first time she laid eyes on Jack Stratton. She remembered being charmed by his English accent and rugged looks. So much so she married him at the first sign of a relationship. She knew now that it was all superficial, that her feelings never matured beyond infatuation.

She then thought about sweet, loving Sam. The man she should have married because he was the only constant in her life. Sam stood by her side in spite of all her flaws, but she never really appreciated him until it was too late.

Then it occurred to her how in each life a person is given a road with detours, yields, caution signs, and occasionally "smooth driving ahead." Although there were detours that were not her choosing, Sarah had to admit that she was responsible for choosing the one that had led to Jack, alcohol, and ultimately her fatal disease. That afternoon, as Neil pledged to adopt Billy, Sarah knew that she had finally returned to the road she had been given at birth. Sarah sighed contentedly. She knew that her body would not hold out long enough to see the lights of Christmas, although that no longer mattered. Her affairs were finally in order. She was at peace and could embrace the journey from this life to the next.

At the Strattons, Karen, David, and her parents were still shaken by the events of the day. When the phone rang the first time, Agnes gasped involuntarily. It was Rosa calling to say she had been treated and released. When the phone rang a second time, Agnes was less startled.

"Daddy," Jenni called out. "Grandma Stratton is on the telephone. She says it's important."

"Excuse me. Mom probably has an update on dad," he said optimistically.

"Hi, Mom, did they get Dad all bandaged up?"

"Honey, sit down," she stuttered.

"Mom, are you crying? What's wrong?"

"I don't know what happened, son. One minute they tell me he's fine…just a flesh wound." She paused an inordinate amount of time before replying; the delay petrified David.

"Mom, what are you trying to say? Explain to me about the flesh wound."

"Honey, your father had a major concussion. He died a few minutes ago."

David dropped the drink he was holding. "My God, it can't be," David yelled, his voice echoed down the corridor. "Dad…"

Hearing David caused Karen and her parents as well as Jenni to freeze with terror. It was obvious that this day of tragedy was not over.

Karen ran to him and pleaded. "What about your father? What happened?"

"Jack Stratton killed him," he said, forgetting to muffle the phone.

"Oh, dear Lord, no," Karen cried.

David suddenly remembered that his mother was still on the other end of the phone. "Oh, Mom, I'm so sorry. I'm coming to the hospital to pick you up. I want you to stay here with us."

"Son, I can't think beyond this very moment," she sobbed. Then she repeated David's words: "He killed him."

"Mom, stay there. I'll be right there."

"Don't come for me," she insisted. "I've already called for a cab to take me home. I want to be by myself tonight."

"But, Mom…"

"I'll talk with you tomorrow morning. I need you to help me make the arrangements," she said, attempting to keep her composure. "I'm going to hang up now, son."

"Mom?"

Delilah ignored him and placed the phone in the cradle. Her eyes were bright red and burned from salty tears. She extracted a pair of wide-rimmed sunglasses from her clutch purse. In the dark of the night, it was more dignified to hide behind the black-tinted lenses than to let people see her fall apart.

Delilah walked outside the ER entrance and waited for the cab. All alone she examined her life as it was…and how it was to be. At fifty-five years old she never imagined that she would be a widow. She never saw the possibility that her beloved Alfred, although ten years her senior, would be taken from her at such a young age. Her warm tears fogged the glasses. She couldn't see beyond them and yet she didn't want to

Alfred, where do I go from here? What do I do now? I thought I was stronger than this, but deep down inside I'm the lowly salesclerk I was when we first met. Without you, what do I have to live for? David doesn't need me anymore and neither does Karen. As for Jenni, she is too young to come to me for guidance. Perhaps someday she will, but not now.

I'm so lost, Alfred. That is why I need to leave California for a while. I'll come back when it's time, but for now I have to find my place in life.

Delilah removed a handkerchief from her pocket and blotted the tears that had fallen beneath the rim of the sunglasses. Taking a deep breath she stood up and put her shoulders back and straightened her spine. She removed the glasses and left them on the bench beside her and stepped into the cab that would take her home.

✧ ✧ ✧

Four weeks later David was sitting on the credenza in their bedroom suite and said, "First President Kennedy, then Dad, and now Sarah. I don't know if I could handle another funeral."

"The holidays will never be the same," Karen agreed.

"I know what you mean. I'm already dreading next year," he sighed.

"Well, in spite of everything, there is one ounce of good that came out of all of this. Neil will be adopting Billy."

"I know. He'll be a good father to him, and God knows Billy could use one," David said.

"Neil will have his hands full now that he will be raising two teenagers."

"I admire him for taking on the additional responsibility," David said while he untied the laces to his dress shoes. "Did you see Billy's face at the graveside? I don't know how he could have made it through the day without Neil at his side."

Karen's eyes welled up with tears as she said, "When Billy placed a white rose on her casket my heart melted. He asked her to say 'hi' to Sam for him and make sure that she tells him all about Neil."

"This was another emotional day for all of us. It's going to be tough for all of us during the holidays from now on." As he removed his trousers and put on a pair of shorts, he added, "I'm going to check on Mom this afternoon. Before she goes to Europe, she wants to discuss Dad's will with me. She indicated that I won't have to work another day in my life, if I so choose."

"No matter what is in the will, David, you're only in your thirties and far too young to think about retirement. I hope that you don't intend to surf every day for the rest of your life. I know that you thrive on business far more than the waves."

"I could never get tired of riding the waves, Karen."

"Okay, you'll know when the time is right to go back to work."

"I'll tell you what, honey. Come January 1965, thirteen months from now, I'll think about going back to work. Maybe I'll follow in my father's footsteps and open my own company. Who knows? Maybe I'll attend one of your breakfast meetings at the beach diner and give you and your mom some executive advice. Anything is possible."

"You attend a Bikini Hut meeting? That will be the day! But I'll support any decision you make."

"Still, we have to figure out a way to get through all our future holidays. If only I could think of some…" He stopped midsentence and just as if he had been given a shot of adrenaline, his eyes flew wide open. "Babes, I've got it! I know how we can get through Christmas next year."

"I'm listening."

"There's no room in life for being depressed during the holidays. Next year we are going to invite Neil, Dolores, and their kids on a trip to Hawaii, all-expenses paid. From now on we'll make the most of our holiday seasons. I promise. What do you say to that, babes?"

Before answering she briefly reflected on the incidents of the last three months: her husband's long-term affair with Jessica Heisen, his termination from BAI, the assassination of President Kennedy, the tragic death of her father-in-law, and finally the unexpected death of Sarah Robbins. She wanted to overlook all that had happened and simply say, "Aloha." Instead, she responded hopefully, "To better days ahead…"